Readers love
JAKE C. WALLACE

A Chance for Us

"Intense, fast paced, action driven and a bit of romance to boot
are all phrases that best describe this wonderful novel. I highly
recommend it to you."

—The Novel Approach

"This is a wonderful vampire series and I urge you to read this if you
love paranormals as much as I do."

—Alpha Book Club

Dare to Love Forever

"This author has a way with the smexy that should be considered
dangerous… There isn't much more you could ask for in this story
and if you couldn't tell already I loved it!"

—Diverse Reader

"I liked so much about this book obviously. The characters were
great and I found the entire story compelling… There's a lot more to
the story then the romance."

—It's About The Book

Soul Seekers

"I couldn't rip myself away from the pages and kept reading until
the wee hours of the morning. I was taken into a world of souls,
seekers, keepers, good and evil."

—Sinfully Gay Romance Book Reviews

By Jake C. Wallace

Jerricho's Freedom
Soul Seekers

NEW VAMPIRE JUSTICE
Dare to Love Forever
A Chance for Us

Published by Dreamspinner Press
www.dreamspinnerpress.com

JERRICHO'S
FREEDOM

JAKE C. WALLACE

DREAMSPINNER
PRESS

Published by
DREAMSPINNER PRESS

5032 Capital Circle SW, Suite 2, PMB# 279, Tallahassee, FL 32305-7886 USA
www.dreamspinnerpress.com

Jerricho's Freedom
© 2017 Jake C. Wallace.

Cover Art
© 2017 AngstyG.
www.angstyg.com
Cover content is for illustrative purposes only and any person depicted on the cover is a model.

ISBN: 978-1-63533-307-7
Digital ISBN: 978-1-63533-308-4
Library of Congress Control Number: 2016915180
Published February 2017
v. 2.0
First Edition published by Amber Quill Press/Amber Allure, 2015.

Printed in the United States of America

This paper meets the requirements of
ANSI/NISO Z39.48-1992 (Permanence of Paper).

When my LSBF (lil' sis best friend), Raine O'Tierney,
had to go into the hospital, I received this note:

Dear JC Wallace,

When I am in the hospital, will you write me a short story about a
man with tats having his first experience with another gentleman?

Sincerely, Sickly Raine

Raine also loves MPREG so I had to add that element
to this story as well. When I started writing this story,
it was supposed to be 12,000 words, but it grew…
and grew… and grew to over 100,000 words.
This book is dedicated to the now-healthy Raine
and her never-ending support of my characters and stories.

Also, a special thank you to my Speed Demon
for allowing me the time to finish this story.
With you, I've finally found the other half of my soul.
You are my everything.

CHAPTER 1

JERRY WAS in love and in a crapload of trouble. He yanked off his ball cap and growled under his breath, his frustration reaching an all-time high. He blamed his car for his current situation. If the useless hunk of fiberglass and steel hadn't cracked a head, he wouldn't have needed the weekend job at the construction site. Wouldn't have met the gorgeous foreman, Rex Callaghan. Wouldn't have learned Rex loved mythology, legend, and lore, Jerry's passions as well. Wouldn't have offered an all-access pass to the library archives where Jerry worked weekdays. He wouldn't have allowed those late-night sessions two nights a week poring over texts and manuscripts with the irresistible man. Pure torture.

Yeah, his car was to blame for revealing the existence of Rex, with his wide smile, sparkling green eyes, shorn auburn hair, and a personality so beautiful that Jerry couldn't stay away. He sighed. It didn't matter what or who had landed him in love. The death grip his heart had on Rex came from what Jerry's future held. No amount of wishing or hoping would change anything.

Fucking tradition.

"Man, what a fucking day. What's up with spring and the hot weather?" Keith chucked his tool belt into the trunk of his car. He frowned when he looked at Jerry. "Okay, Jerricho, what's twisted your pink panties into a knot now?"

Full name. Shit. Keith was annoyed. Jerry shrugged, knowing full well what had upset him. He didn't need Keith's lecture.

Keith huffed and crossed his arms. Dust and dirt covered his face and hair, but the olive color of his skin still shone through. "Shit, Jerry. I said what I said because you're pining over someone you can't have for a gazillion and one reasons. What kind of a friend would I be if I let you get the shit beat out of you? You're here to work. Not gawk at the hulk of a foreman who'll clean your clock for staring. I

1

don't care how many times you two have schmoozed at the library over magical history and shit. You've gotta stop it."

"It's mythology."

"Whatever. He's only interested in your books, not your booty. Outside of the library, he barely gives you the time of day except to teach you new ways to hurt yourself and destroy things on the site."

Jerry huffed.

"How much destruction did you wreak today? Know anyone who started a fire with the blowtorch?"

Jerry clenched his jaw. "Hey, I didn't know you weren't supposed to open the valve to the propane tank all the way when lighting it."

Keith pursed his lips and raised his brow. "Hmph. And you could have killed Steve by taking his ladder when he was on the roof and not telling him."

They looked at each other and broke into laughter.

"Okay, that wouldn't have been much of a loss, right?" Keith slammed the trunk shut and leaned his hip against his Subaru, no doubt waiting for something.

Jerry raised his brow. "What?"

Keith placed his hand on Jerry's shoulder, something he only did when trying to put Jerry back in his space. "Jer, we're on a construction site. Not many gay men hanging around here." Keith gestured around them with his other hand.

Jerry poked his finger into his own chest. "*I'm* a gay man hanging out at a construction site."

Keith shook his head sharply. "No. You're a gay man who's supposed to work at a construction site. If you don't watch what you're doing, we could both end up fired. I vouched for you, remember?"

He had, and might have even embellished Jerry's skills a tad. "I'm not going to get us fired, so quit your whining. Nearly burning up an entire pile of lumber didn't do it so…." It was something that nagged at him. Why did he still have a job?

Keith scowled deeply, and if Jerry kept arguing, Keith would soon tell him to piss off and that wouldn't be good. Keith was Jerry's main mode of transportation until he saved enough to overhaul his car's engine. A repair that would require more than duct tape and some string.

Swearing under his breath, Keith stalked off across the site. Probably forgot something. Jerry rubbed his chest, the continual heartache pulsing in time to the sorrowful beat of his heart. He shook his head. Pining wasn't going to change his situation. Right then he decided to officially enter post-relationship-recovery mode—even if that relationship hadn't moved past nights spent poring over books, laughing, sharing intimate moments (or so Jerry had thought), and talking about themselves until Jerry knew everything about Rex. But it had been over before it could start. Time to move on. Anything that ceased the constant thoughts of Rex would be a relief.

Jerry looked around the site. If Keith didn't hurry up, there was a high probability that Jerry would see Rex as he left the site. Jerry caught sight of Keith talking with Harry, and was about to shout for him to drag his ass, but stopped as Steve sauntered up to the car.

Steve was short and wide, with the arrogance of a guy who had wealthy parents. Why he had a job at the site, Jerry hadn't figured out yet. He was lazy and jacked off most of the day, making a fool of Jerry as often as possible. That appeared to be the extent of his talents.

"You still here, Book Boy? Thought you would've quit by now and run back to hide in your library." As Steve snarled the words, Jerry pictured the weasel's twisted and bloody body on the ground and grinned.

Steve snorted with anger. "Hey, I'm talking to you. Or has all that tattoo ink on your skin gone to your brain?"

"Steve, what do you want?" Keith stepped in front of Jerry.

Great.

Jerry placed his palm on Keith's shoulder. "Don't. Let's get out of here. He isn't worth it." Jerry rounded the car and opened the passenger door.

"I want Book Boy to answer me." Steve pushed past Keith, stopping mere inches from Jerry. To face Steve eye-to-eye, Jerry had to look down. Arrogant little prick.

Red-faced, Steve huffed as if that would back Jerry down. He glared back, not allowing the dipshit to intimidate him. If Steve only knew who

Jerry truly was—*what* he was—he'd back off quick enough. But Jerry couldn't share that part of his life with anyone outside of his clan.

"Is there a problem here?" The familiar deep voice buzzed through Jerry's body. He shuddered.

Rex stepped up close to Jerry's side, so close he got a whiff of Rex's scent, which had been kicked into high gear after a long day of work.

Steve quickly backed up a few feet with a nervous laugh. "Nope, it's all cool. See you guys later." His hasty retreat was anything but smooth.

Keith smirked. "It's all good, Rex. You know Steve. He's gotta give someone a hard time to compensate for his tiny dick."

Jerry would have laughed, but the gaze Rex had pinned on him had shorted out his brain. No doubt he waited for Jerry to corroborate Keith's story. Jerry struggled to keep his gaze on Rex's face, but damn, he was shirtless. His tan skin glistened, his large pecs and nipples right there. Jerry exhaled as visions of biting and pinching Rex's nipples, making him moan, messed with his equilibrium. If he tried to move, he'd end up sprawled on the ground. That would be smooth.

Not.

Jerry swallowed hard. "Yeah." So close to Rex. Too close. Jerry caught his hand from moving and finding out what the skin on Rex's chest felt like under his fingertips.

Rex narrowed his sparkling green eyes and tilted his head to the side. "Okay. But if he bothers you, I want to hear about it. He doesn't mess with my friends. The little brownnosing ass."

Keith chuckled.

Friends? Jerry's chest constricted. He didn't want to be Rex's friend. Want was a terrible thing. "Yeah." Jerry's voice cracked, and he cleared his throat. His forced smile had to look ridiculous. Too toothy. Too wide. Such a dork.

Rex hesitated for a moment, as if deciding what to say. He averted his eyes, and Jerry swore he looked nervous, which had to be Jerry's imagination. "A bunch of us are meeting at Jack's Tavern for some pool and beers at seven. If you're fr—I mean, if you guys, you and Keith, are free, stop by."

In all the time they'd spent together, Rex had never suggested meeting outside of the library. Jerry couldn't help but gawk. He couldn't have answered, even if his pants burst into flames.

You're in post-relationship-recovery mode. Say no! Say no!

Keith rolled his eyes and shot a glare at Jerry. Not answering was the easiest solution, so Jerry clamped his lips.

"Sure, Rex. Thanks for the invite. I'll be there," Keith said.

With that, Jerry figured Rex would leave, but he turned beseeching eyes on Jerry, who wasn't going to survive much longer. "How about you?"

How he wanted to say yes. Shout the word so everyone heard. He couldn't get "no" to form and fall from his mouth. The answer had to be no, so he went another route and… nodded. Why had he nodded? Balls, he couldn't have the man, so why torture himself by continuing to see him?

Kill me now.

Rex grinned wide. "See you later."

Jerry watched as he walked away, ass slim in his tight jeans…. He yelped when something hit the side of his head.

"Shit, Keith. What the hell?" Jerry rubbed his head. A sanding block lay on the ground near his feet.

"Get in, jackass." Keith was in the car before Jerry could ream him out. Not much point, though.

Grabbing his lunch cooler, Jerry climbed into the passenger seat. He'd barely clipped his seat belt before Keith shot out of the site and onto the road.

"What did I say about the staring?" Keith gripped the steering wheel. "And there you were again, eyes all lusty on the straight man."

Jerry frowned. "How do you know he's straight? Have you seen him with a woman?" Jerry should have just kept quiet, but he wasn't feeling agreeable.

A fire flared in Keith's eyes when he looked to Jerry. Quickly, though, it disappeared, and Keith sighed deeply, then turned his attention back to the road. "I don't think you should go to the bar tonight."

No, he shouldn't, but Keith telling Jerry not to pulled up his defenses. "Why not? I was invited too."

Keith snorted. "You and alcohol are a bad combination when you *aren't* drooling over a straight man."

Jerry crossed his arms over his chest. "Will you stop calling him a 'straight' man? You've beat that dog to death. Oh, and not once did I drool."

Keith ignored his comment. "Besides, even if he wasn't straight, you know your parents would never approve. He's not clan. And even if he *was* clan, you aren't allowed to date, Your Highness." Keith slammed the door on any hopes Jerry had falsely entertained since his encounter with Rex.

"Don't call me that." Jerry scowled. Gods, he hated that, and Keith knew it. "Fine. If you don't want me around, I'll go hang out with Annabelle."

Annabelle worked at the library with Jerry. She was mildly annoying, but could be fun.

Keith barked out a laugh. "Last time you hung out with her, she painted your toenails."

Jerry shrugged. They'd looked nice. The polish had been an oddly cool juxtaposition to the tattoos that covered his body. The tattoos his mother hated. Bonus.

Keith stopped in front of Jerry's apartment building and shifted into park. His eyes narrowed. "Listen, if you want to go, I'll pick you up. Just, ya gotta stop the staring, especially in the bar. The guys will be all over that quicker than a girl telling Steve to get lost."

Keith was right. Jerry was borderline obsessed.

He opened the door, then grabbed his cooler. "Okay, pick me up. I promise to behave myself."

Keith nodded reluctantly. "Six forty-five."

Jerry climbed out of the car and had barely slammed the door before Keith drove off. His promise to Keith was bogus. Why was he even going? Such a masochist.

He grabbed his mail from his box, and then hiked to his fourth-floor apartment. Truthfully, you couldn't seriously call it anything but a large room. There was a bed against one wall, a pseudo kitchen on another, and a separate bathroom the size of a postage stamp. The place was cramped, but it was his, the rent paid with money he made. He hadn't asked his parents for a dime, not even during the two weeks he ate nothing but ramen noodles. Supporting himself was too important for him to fail. Soon his freedom and independence would be taken away and his current life would be a memory.

His cell rang and he fished it from his pocket, sighing upon seeing who it was. Jeez, she was two minutes late. "Hey, Mom."

"Hi, honey. How're you doing?"

"Good. Just got home from work. I was about to jump in the shower." He sat on the edge of the bed and unlaced his work boots. Actually they were ones Keith had let him borrow for the temporary job.

"I don't know why you insist on performing manual labor. A person of your station in the clan shouldn't be doing menial jobs." She whispered the last sentence.

"Mom, don't be such a snob. Besides, you said the same thing about my job at the library." He kicked off the boots, pulled off his sweat-soaked socks, and then wiggled his toes. Standing, he groaned as he stretched his back. Damn, he was sore. A hot shower would hit the spot.

He smirked hearing his mother's long, drawn-out sigh. "You don't need to work, and you have less than one year before you take over your duties. You might as well—"

"How's Dad?" Anything to derail her line of questioning that, once started, was harder to halt than a runaway locomotive.

"Your father is more preoccupied than ever with all of those missing men."

Last Jerry had heard, a man from Alabama and another from New York were missing from other clans, but that had been months ago. "How many Anzuni are missing?"

"It's up to six."

Jerry gasped. "Six?"

"Yes, the last one was two days ago. They've all disappeared without a trace. It's as if the ground opened up and swallowed them. Of course, the madder theories say they've been abducted by the Braezelas. As if *they're* actually on Earth." She huffed. "Yes, our most feared enemy, who drove the Anzuni to the brink of extinction, enslaved our people, and whom our ancestors fled from, have hidden on Earth for a thousand years, biding their time, all so they can abduct young men now. Nonsense. Someone is taking those poor souls. They're all in their twenties, you know, which is why I worry about you, Jerricho. If you were at home, I would rest easier."

Everything came around to him moving home. His mother could make a tsunami in India into a valid reason for his return. In less than a year, she'd get her wish.

"Mom, I can't talk about this right now. Keith's picking me up soon. Gotta go, bye."

He hung up, guilty he'd cut her off, but he had to get ready and downstairs before six forty-five. Thinking he was doing his best friend a favor, Keith would coast by and leave when he didn't see Jerry.

I should let him, but I have to get used to being around Rex as only friends.

He sighed. A special kind of torture.

He stripped off his grungy clothes and took two steps to enter the bathroom. In the mirror, the dirt from a hard day's work covered his face. He focused on the eyes staring back. His mind had been through a shitload the past eight weeks. The future weighed heavy on his shoulders. There was only one thing to do. He was so getting drunk tonight.

CHAPTER 2

STEPPING INTO Jack's, Jerry made a beeline for the bar. Several guys from the jobsite already surrounded the pool tables, but Rex wasn't one of them. Iron-winged butterflies scraped Jerry's insides. That feeling intensified when the bartender stopped in front of him.

Shit. Why hadn't he stayed home?

"Prince Jerricho, Sire. What can I get you?"

Luckily, the man hadn't bowed.

"Shhhhh." Jerry looked around, but no one paid them any attention. "Tonight I'm Jerry, okay? Just another guy out for a drink like everyone else."

Keith sat on the stool beside Jerry and smiled. "Hey, man. What's up, Paul? Didn't know you were working here."

They easily slipped into grumbling about some baseball or football game, but Jerry couldn't have cared less about that.

"Hey, Paul, can I get a Corona?" Interrupting was rude, but he had been there first and needed a beer badly.

As if the king himself had made the request, the beer appeared in seconds. And didn't Paul go and bow slightly.

Jerry grabbed the cold beer. "Add no bowing to that list of things not to do."

He slapped a five on the bar and moved to a table in the far corner. No matter how hard he tried, his other life followed him around like a mangy stray. He chugged half of his beer as Keith pulled out a chair and sat down.

"What're you doing over here?" Keith asked, a Stella in hand.

"I don't think I'm going to be much fun tonight."

"It's because Paul called you Jerricho and bowed, isn't it?"

Jerry pushed his bottle back and forth across the table between his hands. "Some. My mother called and did the whole *you don't need to work and only have a year* speech." Wallowing wasn't Jerry's style, but he was knee-deep in the muck. He chugged the remainder of his beer and raised the empty bottle. That simple action would get him another.

"Wow, you are down." Keith leaned forward. "Listen, I know you hate the whole prince thing, but here, with these guys, you're the book nerd. Well, except with Paul, but that's it. Stop feeling sorry for yourself. For gods' sake, you're a prince. Next in line to be king. Shit, I'd trade places with you any day."

Jerry chuckled harshly. "So you want to be a twenty-four-year-old virgin who can't date who he wants because of some thousand-year-old tradition?"

Paul personally delivered another beer and set it on the table. "Anything else, Jerric—I mean, Jerry?"

"Thanks, but no. Put this on my tab, please."

Paul nodded—sans the bowing—and headed back to the bar.

Jerry guzzled half the beer and, after a loud burp, slammed the bottle onto the table.

"Yeah, you're a prince all right. And you're gonna want to slow down there." Keith sipped his beer.

"Why am I even bothering? I'm trying to be independent and support myself, but by this time next year, I'll be right back at the mansion, fulfilling mind-numbing bureaucratic duties and setting up house with someone I'll have to tolerate, maybe even hate. Why not give in?"

The table shifted violently to the left. Jerry grabbed his beer before it toppled over. "Did you kick the table?" Jerry gaped at Keith.

"Again, quit feeling sorry for yourself. Boohoo, I'm a prince, and my parents want to support me. Boohoo, I can't have Rex. Boohoo, I'm a virgin…." Keith's expression soured.

Jerry raised an eyebrow.

"Okay, so that last one, not so much, but the rest, yeah. And it could be worse. Your parents could have ignored you when you were sixteen and told them you preferred jacking off to your father's *Men's Health* magazine and not your mom's *Cosmo*."

"I never told them anything about 'jacking off.' And I think you're mistaking me for you."

Keith's brow raised freakishly high.

"I mean jacking off to my mother's *Cosmo*. Not *Men's Health*. You spent more time in my bathroom than I did. So don't get all defensive."

"I have a reputation to uphold with the ladies."

Jerry huffed, not going there.

Keith leaned forward. "You're going to get to marry someone with the right parts. Get over all of this shit for tonight and have some fun. Relax. You're about to split at the seams you're so wound up. Come on, let's play some pool." Keith stood and waved for Jerry to follow.

Jerry exhaled deeply, knowing his one-person pity party was a drag. Could have stayed home for that. Keith was right. He would get a husband chosen for him and not a wife. The Anzuni weren't as hung up on gender as humans. The rest of his life could be put on hold for one night.

He stood and followed Keith to the pool tables. The music and the voices were loud, pool balls clacked together, and darts smacked the boards. It was stress-free and could be good for improving his mood.

Keith laid two quarters on the closest pool table. Their coworkers, Harry and Nestor, trash-talked each other between their shots. Hearing Nestor call Harry a sloth-toed wonder nut brought a hearty laugh to Jerry.

He found the nearest empty table and sat to wait their turn. Keith stood nearby chatting with his other coworkers. He'd gone to work at the construction company fresh out of high school, so he knew everyone there. He tried to include Jerry in the conversations, but sports came up again, and Jerry tried to tune them out. If they wanted to talk about books, even the state of the economy, he'd be all in. Sports, boring.

"Next up." Harry set his cue on the table. His grin and Nestor's scowl left little doubt as to who won.

Jerry stood and grabbed his chair as he swayed. *Whoa, time to slow down.* He rarely drank alcohol. Drinking led to lowered inhibitions, and lowered inhibitions led to…. Well, nothing he could partake in, according to his role in the clan.

Jerry let Keith rack the balls and break. This was one game where Jerry excelled. The game room at the mansion had a table, but damn if his concentration wasn't focused on Rex showing up. His skin prickled, his heart raced, and those iron-winged butterflies continued to dig into his gut. Even distracted, Jerry managed to sink some balls, and some of them were even his. After two games, he loosened up, even striking up some shallow conversations with the guys. He was feeling good, until….

11

"Hey, Book Boy, what the fuck do you think you're doing here?" Steve.

Jerry ignored the parasite. Lining up his shot, he glanced around for Keith. He'd been pulled away to the side of the room and his attention wasn't on the game. Keith would have had better luck scaring Steve away than Jerry. Steve wanted a fight, but Jerry didn't partake in the manly ritual of fighting. Best to ignore him and hope he found another person to prove his manhood to. As Jerry took his shot, the end of his cue jolted. The cue ball rolled pathetically to the side.

Asshole.

"Awww, damn, you scratched, Book Boy." Steve's boisterous laugh clenched Jerry's jaw. His anger wanted to punch that attitude right out of Steve. But future kings didn't get involved in bar brawls—or any brawl at all.

Jerry calmly set the cue on the pool table, then made his way back to his seat. Of course, Steve followed. Jerry flopped down and Steve leaned over the table.

"What're you doing here, pansy? You don't belong here, and you don't belong on the jobsite. Who invited you, anyway?"

"I did."

Jerry looked up… and up… at Rex, who stood over him, mere inches from Jerry. Despite the overwhelming smell of stale beer and man sweat, Jerry inhaled the sweetest scent ever—kind of a woodsy, spicy fragrance. That smell had a direct connection to Jerry's cock.

Steve straightened and smiled nervously. "Hey, Rex. What's up?"

Rex scowled and motioned with his thumb over his shoulder. Steve took off. To Jerry's surprise, Rex pulled out a chair and sat.

"He's such a dickhead. I would've fired his ass months ago, but he's the nephew of the owner."

Jerry shifted in his seat to relieve the pressure against his hardening erection. Instant boner. So screwed. "I wondered who would employ someone like him. Now it makes perfect sense."

Wow, he'd spoken two full sentences to Rex outside of the library. At the jobsite, his nervousness never failed to get the best of him. But the library was a different story. That was his territory, and subjects that interested him were easy. But when the subject had turned to their personal lives, he said as little as possible. What he hadn't told Rex about himself could fill a book.

Rex grinned. "That's why he gets all of the shit jobs. When he does any work, that is." Rex rolled his beer between his palms and avoided eye contact with Jerry. Huh, that was different. Usually the man was so self-assured.

Jerry finished his beer, and before his bottle hit the table, Paul set another before him. Jerry cast him a wary glance.

"Um…. Thanks. Can you get Rex here another one too?" Might as well take advantage of the service.

Paul saluted and left. So much better than bowing.

"So, how are things at the library? Anything new I should rush over and take a look at?" Rex asked with a coy expression.

Jerry raised his brow. Rex would come running to the library when he heard what Jerry had for him. The excitement swirling in Jerry's gut was an omen he chose to ignore. "Well, I did get a loan from the University of Vermont. The book is about something like Greek mythology in modern tropes or something. I, um, could put it aside for you, if you're even interested in something like that." Rex didn't have to know Jerry had ordered that book specifically for him. Well, with the goal of guaranteeing Rex's company for a while longer. That had been before Jerry's decision to put Rex behind him. That had worked out well.

Rex huffed and grinned. "You know I want it." Rex gripped Jerry's shoulder, giving him a quick squeeze. "That would be great."

Jerry nearly melted in his chair. A shiver ran through his body, his heart raced, and his mouth dried from the touch. He hoped Rex didn't notice how flustered he'd become. Paul dropping off the beer took Rex's attention from Jerry for a moment.

"Thanks for the beer." Rex smiled warmly. "And thanks for hanging out with me so often at the library. I feel bad when I take you away from doing your job."

"No, problem. I get done at five anyway."

Oh shit.

The words had spilled out. Jerry closed his eyes and exhaled. How stupid could he be? Rex thought he worked in the evening, hence why he was always there at that time. Now Rex was going to question….

Rex leaned forward, eyes narrowed, darker and filled with confusion, his gears no doubt turning and processing. "You weren't working all of those times I came into the library?"

One sentence and Jerry had obliterated the reason he'd been at the library so late. Would he think Jerry was up to something? Had they even talked about Jerry being gay? Of course they hadn't. Would Rex throw a punch once he fully understood?

Act cool, Jerry.

"Um… y-yeah. I… I figured you knew that." He grabbed his beer and chugged half of it.

Rex stared, searching Jerry's eyes. His heart might explode. That was so like Rex, thinking before he acted. What he mulled over could erase Jerry from his life. Rex had befriended Jerry even after he'd nearly blown it. The first time Rex showed up at the library, he'd smiled wide upon seeing Jerry as if he'd come specifically to see him. Because of the possibility he'd swallowed his tongue, Jerry merely stared at Rex who raised his brow. Jerry had fallen into Rex's gaze, mesmerized. Damn the man was beautiful.

Rex cleared his throat, then told Jerry he thought being an Acquisition Coordinator was cool, and that he himself loved to read, Jerry's eyebrows had rose dramatically. Rex's resulting sullen expression had hit Jerry hard, especially when Rex walked away. Good thing Jerry's mouth had kicked in to find out the problem. A misunderstanding. Rex had taken Jerry's look of shock to mean he was surprised someone like Rex read anything. Truly no one had ever said Jerry's job was cool before. Once they sorted that out, they'd been good ever since.

Rex broke Jerry out of his memory as he leaned closer, as if to share a secret. "That's interesting. You and I have a lot in common. Well, except for the fact that you should never touch tools or work on a construction site again." Jerry chuckled, and some of the tension leached out of him. One corner of Rex's lips curled up. "I can't wait to spend time with you and have a look at that book. In case you didn't know, I *love* Greek mythology. I mean, a lot."

Rex pinned Jerry further with his gaze. His breath caught, blood rushed from his head, and the flutter in his chest unsettled him. Was he mistaken about the innuendo in Rex's words? Couldn't be. As Keith would say, Jerry heard what he wanted where Rex was concerned. Gods, Jerry wished Rex loved him like he loved Rex.

Jerry shook as he fought to keep himself from shying away from the intensity of Rex's stare. He surveyed Rex's face. Taken aback by the sincerity he found there, Jerry slipped further from his resolve not to stare. He could look at the man all day. Why Rex talked with Jerry when there were so many others perplexed him. Heck, a bunch of girls had infiltrated the bar, and the guys had instantly fawned all over them.

And there was Keith again in his head. "People don't fall in love from spending time in a library reading books and shit."

But he was wrong, because Jerry had fallen in love with Rex. He knew so much about Rex, like how he loved steak with honey barbecue sauce, how he thought riding his Harley was pure freedom, and how his idea of Sunday afternoon consisted of drinking beer in his backyard and barbecuing said steaks. The new *Spartacus* was his favorite TV show, and the original *Clash of the Titans* his favorite movie. He hated country and loved jazz. He lived alone in a small apartment that barely held his book collection. In short, Jerry knew Rex. But Rex had only told Jerry those things out of politeness since Jerry had asked. It wasn't as if they were even friends outside of the library. On the site, Rex only spoke when giving Jerry tasks to do or teaching him a new skill and how not to kill himself doing it.

"Yeah, mythology. I love it too." Jerry was unsure what else to say.

A few guys—Jerry wasn't sure of their names—came to the table to coax Rex into playing pool or meeting the girls, but Rex waved them off. Jerry needed more beer. So much more. He raised his bottle, and lo and behold, in less than thirty seconds, there were two fresh beers on the table.

Rex looked stunned by the service. "Is he a friend of yours?"

More like loyal subject. "Yeah."

Jerry picked up the beer, knowing the warm buzz he surfed on wasn't good. Still, he took a long drink.

Rex chuckled. "Rough day?"

Jerry would crawl across glass for that laugh. "Rough life," Jerry muttered.

Rex's expression took on a raw seriousness. "Want to talk about it?"

Jerry clamped his lips to stop from blurting out everything. Instead, he reminded Rex about the issues with his piece of shit car.

"You should get a bike. You'd look good on a Harley."

Rex leaned closer. Closer wasn't possible, but there was Rex, inches away. The leer as Rex spoke had to be more than wishful thinking. So many of Jerry's fantasies involved Rex on that behemoth, black motorcycle. And man, they were all dirty. But Rex on his Harley was akin to a god atop his powerful steed. Jerry pushed his palm covertly against his dick, which continually tried to break free of his jeans. A fine sheen of sweat broke out over his skin. He wanted, and needed, and, damn, could he say fuck his princely duties? Why couldn't he have sex? Maybe once he….

Jerry jumped up, knocking the table and nearly toppling their beers.

Rex's eyes widened. "You okay?"

"Yeah. Sorry about that. I'll be right back."

Jerry pushed through the crowd and made his way out onto the vacant back deck. Lights capping the posts of the surrounding railing threw soft light into the darkness. Jerry drew the crisp spring air into his lungs. What the fuck was he thinking? He hunkered against the wall a few feet from the open door. Rex was messing with his head, making Jerry think he could have things he couldn't. Grasping his hair, Jerry pulled the strands until the pain stopped him. Rex filled Jerry's head, along with warm fuzzy feelings and the need to be close to him, to touch him.

Ten months until he was twenty-five.

Nope. Jerry wasn't going to make it, especially with the perfection of Rex looming constantly in his mind. He had to quit the construction site, which meant he'd have to accept his parents' help. That was worse than almost anything… except—

A black figure stepping out onto the deck and turning toward Jerry caught his attention. His stomach climbed into his throat.

Rex.

CHAPTER 3

JERRY CLOSED his eyes, wanting to wail his frustration. What demon god insisted on testing him over and over again?

"Jerry, you okay?" Rex stepped closer and warmth blossomed in Jerry's chest. Rex was close. Too close to be casual.

Jerry swallowed hard and peered up into Rex's face. Shadows fell over his chiseled features and darkened his eyes. Jerry imagined, there in the night, they were lovers sharing an intimate moment. Thoughts like that would only break his heart.

"I need some air. There's a lot of people in there." It wasn't a lie. The bar had filled quickly, and Jerry wasn't used to crowds, being holed up with his books most of the day.

Rex nodded, then tilted his head to the side. His gaze focused on Jerry's neck, as visceral as a touch. Rex lightly caressed the sensitive skin of Jerry's neck with his finger. A shudder raced through Jerry like a shotgun blast. It was so unfair.

"The Raven," Rex said of one of the tattoos on the side of Jerry's neck. "The keeper of secrets."

Rex had mentioned Jerry's raven tattoo in passing at the library and its symbolism, his reason for getting the tattoo. Jerry had so many secrets in his life, he needed a keeper for the heavy burden.

"Ravens are linked to the void where universal secrets are kept," Rex whispered. More stroking of the raven. Jerry melted against the wall. No person, no man, had ever touched him so intimately. No one had ever been this close. The solid presence of skin and muscle, and musk carried on body heat comforted Jerry and a gut-wrenching need rose like an uncontrollable wildfire.

Rex leaned down, his lips mere inches from Jerry's mouth. His darkened eyes searched Jerry's. Gods, Jerry could fall into those eyes and live happily, forever. "Do you have secrets, Jerry?"

The whispered words fell in soft, heated gusts across Jerry's lips. His lungs seized, and his brain disconnected from his body, guiding him to lean forward. He connected with the moist, heated lips. Rex's tongue licked along the seam and pushed inside. For one perfect moment, time ceased to move, and Jerry's entire world focused on those tender lips.

Right then, he understood what he'd considered to be over-the-top reactions to being kissed in all of those romances he'd read, gay and het. Electric shocks coursed over his nerves, tingling and heightening a mere kiss into a toe-curling experience.

Rex moaned into his mouth, and Jerry's head spun. He gripped Rex's biceps hard, and damn, they were perfectly large. Being bold, Jerry pushed his hips toward Rex. In response, Rex rubbed his hard bulge against Jerry's stomach.

Oh. My. Gods.

Rex's strong fingers caressed Jerry's back, squeezed his ass…. He whimpered. Rex broke the kiss, grasping Jerry's hips and pulling him harder against him. Their raspy breaths filled the silence. Jerry couldn't help burying his nose into Rex's neck and deeply inhaling the sweetest, most intoxicating scent.

"Been coming into that library for months, sitting with you, talking, getting to know you, how smart and genuine you are. And watching you on the jobsite," Rex practically growled. "Your fucking tattoos are driving me crazy, your tight pants, your slim body. All I've thought about—" He ran his hot tongue over the raven on Jerry's neck, and Jerry sucked in a deep breath. "—is running my tongue over every one of your tattoos. I'm constantly hard on the jobsite when you're there. I had to stay away."

Jerry gasped as that magnificent tongue painted wet trails over his neck and collarbone. He fought for friction against Rex, anything to relieve the pressure building in his cock.

"Want you… too," Jerry said breathlessly.

Want you but can't have you.

Jerry's muscles tightened. What the fuck was he doing? No matter how much he craved Rex, desired the hulking foreman, he couldn't have him. And a one-night stand wasn't anything Jerry was interested in. Not with Rex. When Jerry looked at Rex, he saw a lifetime.

Fucking stupid fantasies.

Jerry broke away, despite his heart screaming for the opposite. The confused expression on Rex's face caused Jerry to fake a smile.

"Sorry, too much beer. Have to hit the head. Be right back."

Jerry stepped around Rex. Inside he snaked through the crowd, making it to the bathroom without encountering Keith or Steve. Luckily, only a few men stood at the urinals. Jerry found a stall and immediately unzipped his pants, freeing his erection. A shiver raced down his spine as he touched the sensitive skin, the grip mildly painful. If he didn't take care of it, he'd jump Rex right there in the bar.

Closing his eyes, Jerry envisioned the burly foreman naked, leaning back on that hog, body covered with reddish hair, legs spread wide, stroking his massive, hard shaft. Eyeing Jerry, he'd lick across his plump lower lip and pinch his own nipple to a hard peak. Those hooded emerald eyes would gaze at Jerry with a lust so intense....

Jerry's balls drew up and he bit his lip, cognizant that he wasn't alone. He jerked slowly to avoid the slapping sound of skin. He wasn't sure he could get off with the tempo until he envisioned being on his hands and knees and Rex pushing into him. He gasped. His stomach muscles contracted and his head fell forward. His mouth opened, and a small whimper escaped as ropes of creamy cum hit the water in the toilet. He continued rubbing the head of his cock, allowing his orgasm to push him high.

Another year? He wouldn't make it. He needed to have sex. He was a guy, for fuck's sake. Once puberty ended, his belief that his needs would rest at a level manageable by his left hand and porn had been erroneous.

Yeah, right.

He would have fucked a hole in the wall right about then, if he could've found one. Ripping off a piece of toilet paper, he wiped away the cum clinging to the end of his cock and hissed at the sensitivity. He tucked himself back into his pants and then wiped the wayward drops on the seat and flushed the toilet. When he left to wash his hands, he was grateful to find he was alone for the moment. He locked the bathroom door for added privacy.

He surveyed his face in the mirror. Dark circles rested under his eyes. The deep brown held a hint of defeat despite his recent orgasm.

Sex with his own hand couldn't compare to what had occurred with Rex. And that had only been a kiss. That brief encounter had surpassed every orgasm he'd ever had. Running his hand over his black hair, he sighed. He needed a trim soon, since the floppy part on top was too floppy, and the shaved sides had grown out.

There was a knock at the door.

"Just a minute!" He ran his finger over the black raven that had enamored Rex. More colorful tattoos crept up the other side of his neck and covered his chest, back, and arms. The ink was an amalgamation of images that, at first, had been rebellion against all the forced traditions. Soon enough, though, they'd become a form of self-expression. Most focused on how trapped he'd felt. The massive tiger with glowing yellow eyes hiding among bamboo leaves on his back represented what he imagined his unfettered self would embody. Strong, free, and hungry for life. Arching over his chest were the words *Set Me Free*. He'd failed to explain that one to his parents—who embraced their roles in the clan—about how trapped and stifled his life felt.

To please his parents, he had a tattoo of the crest of the Anzuni demon clan on his left bicep. The Anzuni were a lower-level race of demons who'd fled their dimensional world over a thousand years ago, ending millennia of persecution and enslavement by higher-level demons such as the Braezelas, a nasty race with oversized fangs who tended to drool a lot. The existence in that realm of demon races with more power than the Anzuni had ensured continuance of their enslavement. Jerry thanked the gods the Anzuni had escaped the Braezelas when a wizard named Jaevasez discovered that travel between dimensions was possible. The amount of despair and fear needed to make a demon willing to step out of one dimension and into an unknown world was nothing Jerry could fathom. But hope was hope. Once you got hold, you held on tight for dear life. When someone tried to steal that hope, you fought back as the Anzuni had when their plans were discovered. A war broke out. A war for freedom. Much like the fight Jerry had been engaged in since being old enough to understand he couldn't play freely like the other Anzuni children, and every important milestone of his life was manufactured to fit tradition.

Jerry choked out a laugh. Yeah, he'd won battles in his fight, which classified more as rebellion. No war would change anything for him. And even a war seemingly won could still be a loss. At the end of the Anzuni war, only three hundred of the nearly twenty thousand Anzuni escaped before the portal closed. A bittersweet victory to those who did escape, many having left family members to either die for their treason or continued enslavement by the Braezelas. A dimension away. Jerry's mother had been correct to laugh at the notion Braezelas were abducting Anzuni. Any of those nasty-looking demons who'd made it through the portal couldn't have hidden, lacking the ability to transform their appearance as the Anzuni could.

There was more pounding on the door. "Hold your horses!"

Jerry sighed and rubbed his hands roughly over his face. He forced himself to take a hard look at himself in the mirror. Whatever war he believed he'd been fighting hadn't been one at all. No matter his action, the time would come where he'd be forced to stand up and be the ruler his people needed. And he'd been running like a spoiled brat.

He caught sight of one of his first tattoos. An Anzuni babe. A symbol of his future, and the reason Jerry had to sneak out of the bar and avoid ever seeing Rex again. That realization smashed his already broken heart into thousands of pointed shards.

"Quit beating your meat and open the fucking door, asshole!" The door shook, as if the man were trying to rip it off the hinges.

Jerry paused by the door and desperately wished he could leave without Rex catching sight of him. Those green eyes would steal what little was left of Jerry's heart. A minute was all he needed to get out unseen.

The pounding stopped. Jerry exhaled and turned the lock. He yanked the door open, ready to give the ass on the other side a piece of his mind. Jerry's mouth gaped. Steve stood before him, fist raised, face twisted in rage, frozen like a literal statue. He poked Steve in the chest, but he didn't move—no breathing, not a flinch, not a twitch.

"Dammit!" Jerry rolled his eyes.

He moved past Steve and out into the bar. Everyone except Paul was frozen in place. Paul smiled as he dried a glass. Jerry might as well go with it and make his escape.

He'd never had control over his ability to freeze time. What had set his unreliable power off? Gods only knew. He stepped up to the bar next to a brunette woman, frozen, her head thrown back, mouth wide open in the middle of a braying laugh. Freezing time had given Jerry the chills since he was old enough to understand his power. Maybe his subconscious had taken his need to get out unseen and run with it. He could hear his mother now….

If you'd practiced your powers when you were young and hadn't rebelled against being a prince, you might have gained the ability to use them when you need them and not have them go all willy-nilly.

And he hadn't practiced much. Anzuni males in the royal line had, at one time, possessed great powers, such as freezing time, empathic abilities (his father's power, most likely why he excelled as a ruler), even telekinesis, all used in battling the Braezelas demons. Over the last thousand years, those with powers had dwindled in number, most likely due to the fact they were no longer needed for survival. Jerry was glad he hadn't cooperated as a child.

"I can tell by the look on your face it's been a while." Paul's pleasant affect was ever present. Did it remain even in sleep?

Jerry stuffed his hands into his jean pockets. "You can say that. My mother tried to make me practice, but I sort of avoided it. Anyway it's always been so… unpredictable. I guess when I was a baby, it ran rampant."

Paul chuckled. He set down the glass and picked up another to dry. "I heard some stories during that time. My brother was your pediatrician until you were five."

Heat flushed Jerry's face. The thing about Anzuni powers, they generally manifested in times of great distress. Time of distress like getting a shot. As a newborn, Jerry had been so "pissed" (his father's word) after getting a shot that he'd frozen time for a solid ten minutes, including the Anzuni doctor as well. From what Jerry had been told, that in and of itself had been amazing since Anzuni powers rarely had any effect on other Anzuni. Only his father had been unaffected from Jerry's time-stopping tantrum.

"Sorry for freezing your brother, I guess." Jerry frowned. Why was he apologizing for something he did as a baby?

"Not your fault."

Jerry nodded. "I'd like to settle my tab." *And get the hell out before time resumes.*

"Yes, *Your Highness*." Paul smirked as he placed the bill on the bar.

Jerry plopped down a fifty and pointed at Paul. "I'll give you that one."

Jerry scanned the bar but couldn't see Keith. Where was he? Being Anzuni, Keith wouldn't have frozen with the others. Maybe he'd left, which meant Jerry was going to rip him a new one because now he didn't have a ride.

When Paul caught his attention to take his change, Jerry waved him off. Another scan of the bar, and Jerry caught sight of Rex leaning against the wall, a pinched look on his face, his gaze turned toward the bathroom. *Shit.* Jerry's heart wanted him to run to Rex.

"Paul, could you call me a cab?" Jerry asked, knowing what he had to do.

Time to face the music.

CHAPTER 4

THE CAB dropped Jerry off outside the mansion where his family lived. The royal family. He paused on the stairs before having to face the frenzy of his mother and his father, not to mention all the drama. That reprieve lasted about three minutes before the door opened and Marco, the butler, stepped out.

"Prince Jerricho." He bowed deeply.

"Marco, my man. How's it hangin'?" Jerry ascended the stone steps.

Marco stepped back and allowed Jerry to enter. "It's hanging fine, Sire."

Jerry chuckled and entered the foyer. Even though he'd grown up in the enormous house, the ostentatious manor still overwhelmed him. Over-the-top was an understatement. Long sweeping staircases, ten-foot-high ceilings, everything gilded and ornately painted in old-world style. Not a piece of furniture was practical, or from this century, as if Queen Victoria herself had yakked all over the place.

"Marco, tell me my room is as I left it?" Jerry hadn't returned to his room in a couple of years. He wished he'd gone home to his tiny apartment where all his stuff was.

Marco had been like an uncle to him since Jerry was a babe. Marco smirked ever so slightly. "I made sure not one thing was changed, Sire."

Thankful for small miracles, Jerry headed for the stairs.

"Your parents are in the sitting room, awaiting your arrival," Marco called to him.

All Jerry wanted to do was slink to his room and lick his wounds for an extended period. Instead, he veered toward the set of french doors to the left. Before he could reach for the knob, the door opened, and his father—in his old-world, Hollywoodesque glory—stood before him. Well, old-world, Hollywood demon glory. He wore his customary velvet smoking jacket—this one in deep purple—with a gray cravat. A small horn sat on each side of his forehead, and his long tail brushed against the floor. Jerry could count on his hand the number of times his father had transformed while in the house, which merely meant losing the horns and the tail, which were composed of a soft exoskeleton of a reddish burgundy hue. Other than those features, their bodies resembled those of humans and were no different when transformed. It was the one power the Anzuni hadn't lost.

"Jerricho, son, so glad to see you." His father threw an arm over Jerry's shoulder.

His father was about the same height as Jerry, maybe an inch shorter. Not a thin man, he was larger in the shoulders and chest. He was strong and regal, and Jerry admired his integrity and mirth. They shared the same brown eyes, although his father's black hair had a blending of gray. Between his parents, Jerry had been closer to his father. He loved them both dearly, despite their insistence on ruining his life (not their fault... maybe).

On the couch, his mother furiously typed on her phone. As usual, she looked lovely, the picture of glamour and beauty, her reddish blonde hair coiffed in a french twist, dressed in a flowing flowered shirt and red skirt. The woman never stepped outside her bedroom looking anything less than perfect, which included makeup even on her horns to match her skin tone. Couldn't have those suckers all mottled and natural-looking. Drove his mother nuts how unkempt and untidy Jerry was about his appearance.

His father leaned closer and whispered, "Your mother's in the middle of planning an impromptu dinner party in your honor. If you love me at all, you will smile and accept."

The tension in his father's tone could only mean one thing—his mother had jumped on the "you let your son move out for the past four years" train again. With his father's blessing, which had overruled his mother's objections, Jerry had moved out when he was twenty, with an agreement that he'd return before his twenty-fifth birthday.

"Sure, Dad." After all, he'd come home to step up and do what was expected of him.

His father sighed with relief. "Riah?"

When she looked up, her blue eyes lightened and she smiled widely.

"Jerricho, honey. When we spoke today, you didn't mention you'd be coming by." She rose and practically glided to him, pecking him on the cheek.

"I thought I'd come by... maybe spend a few days."

She beamed, as if she hadn't known he'd be staying. Jerry had called and given Marco that information after leaving the bar. "Well, that makes my surprise easier to plan. I'm throwing a dinner party tomorrow night in your honor."

Jerry merely nodded, while his gut cramped painfully.

"You know, dear...." She took his hand and led him back to the ornately patterned sofa. In the expansive marble fireplace, a fire roared, even with the mild temperature outside. All about appearances with his mother. "Your twenty-fifth birthday is coming soon. Don't you think it's time to come home? There's so much to prepare for, plans to be made."

The same argument, the same reasoning. If in ten months, why not now? He swore his life had become his mother's hobby. He loved her, but why couldn't she take up painting or golf or play bingo like normal people?

When Jerry didn't answer, she continued. "You've had your independence, and now it's time to step up to your responsibilities. The clan is counting on you to produce an heir, and to eventually be their leader. It's tradition, Jerricho."

His bid to remain calm and cooperative quickly failed, and from the trepidation on his father's face, the man was aware of that fact. Jerry rose and walked to the fireplace to regain some measure of calm. His rebellious hackles rose, prepared for a counterattack. Leave it to his mother to steal his coming-home thunder. He wanted to do the opposite.

"Mom, I know all about tradition and the expectations of the clan." As if their culture and his role as a future leader hadn't been stuffed down his throat since he'd been old enough to comprehend. "How could I forget, since you remind me every time you call?" Keeping his tone even with the anger boiling in his veins was difficult, but hell, he was sick of hearing about it. He understood his role as prince of his clan and as a Baelso, a bearer of children. The small babe tattooed on the inside of his forearm was both a source of pride and a curse.

Being a prince in the royal line meant Jerry had the ability to bear children and was expected to have at least one child, as Jerry's father had borne Jerry. His mother had chosen not to give birth, so Jerry was an only child. As was true of his parents' mating, Jerry's mate would be an Anzuni chosen by his parents. So much for true love.

"Evin?" The exasperation in her sigh didn't help.

"Riah, it's late, and I'm sure Jerricho is tired. Let the boy go to bed."

She nodded reluctantly. Despite their butting of heads, they loved one another.

Jerry hugged his father and whispered his thanks. He bent and kissed his mother on the cheek. She wore her I'm-upset-but-trying-not-to-show-it face, and wasn't finished with Jerry.

With a final good night, he bolted from the room and took the stairs two at a time to the second floor. Only when he'd slammed and locked his bedroom door could he breathe again.

JERRY TOSSED and turned most of the night. He woke several times, having dreamt of Rex—taking Jerry over his hog, and in the bathroom at the bar, and on the dining room table during his mother's dinner party. That last dream had been disturbing and oddly arousing. After that, he sat up, trying to read, surf the net, play video games, anything to push that memory from his mind. His obsession with Rex was out of control. He had no choice but to give in to his parents.

Sometime around noon, after sulking in his room all morning, there was a knock on his door. No doubt his mother, with more details of her precious dinner party. He couldn't have cared less if they had three appetizers or four, and what the heck was a crudité? Nothing a twenty-four-year-old guy should know anything about.

Dread filled him as he opened the door.

"What the fuck, Jerry? What happened to you last night?" Keith pushed past Jerry into the room and turned, planting his hands on his hips.

Jerry closed the door and dropped onto his bed.

Keith raised his arms. "Well? I've been trying to call you all night, and you weren't at your apartment, and no one at the bar knew where you went."

Jerry narrowed his eyes. "How about I ask, where were *you* last night? I looked for you and couldn't find you, Keith." Really he hadn't looked, but Jerry had an idea about what Keith had been doing.

"I was there." Keith averted his eyes.

Jerry crossed his arms. "So you were there when I froze time?"

Keith's eyebrows jumped.

"Aha! Spill. And don't try to pull the 'I was temporarily abducted by a Braezelas and forced to clean its gigantic overbite,' because you already tried that one before."

"You froze time? You haven't done that in forever. You couldn't do it on purpose if your life depended on it."

"Quit stalling."

Keith rolled his head around dramatically. "Okay, okay. I… um… I may have been out in the car making out…." The rest of the sentence mumbled off into nothing.

What in the hell had Keith done? "Making out… and what's the rest?"

He heaved a sigh. "Making out with Nicola."

"You've got to be shitting me." Jerry jumped up from the bed. "That lying and cheating…. Ugh! What were you thinking?"

"Hey, we might be getting back together."

Oh no. He seriously wasn't defending the Anzuni woman who'd broken up with Keith by sending him a picture of her having sex with one of Keith's friends.

"You've lost your ever-loving mind!" Jerry shook his head. Unbelievable. Keith was heading for major heartache—again. And Jerry knew about heartache.

Keith narrowed his eyes and pursed his lips. "I could say the same about you, *Jerricho*."

"I have no clue what you're talking about." Because he didn't.

"You aren't good at playing dumb." Keith grinned. "Had a talk with Rex last night."

The name raced a shiver across Jerry's skin. "Y-yeah. So what?"

Keith cocked his head and his face softened. "What happened, Jerry? I mean you took off last night, and now you're here." He waved his hand around the room. "This is the last place you ever want to be."

28

Jerry dropped back onto the bed and raked his hand through his messy hair. "What did Rex tell you?"

Keith sat next to him. "Uh-uh. You first, lover boy."

Jerry rubbed his hands together. How much should he divulge? If he didn't get this off his chest, though, it would eventually eat him alive.

"Rex…. He…. We…." Why was it so damned hard? Keith remained quiet, giving Jerry time, but he decided to blurt it out. "Rex kissed me."

More silence. And then more. Jerry was afraid to look at his friend. "Excuse me?"

Jerry looked to Keith, whose mouth hung open.

"What did you think happened?"

Keith shook his head. "I mean, the way Rex was talking last night, I could tell he was into you. And you don't have to say I told you so. He asked me where you went. He seemed down when he realized you'd taken off. Now I know why."

"Ah, shit. I didn't mean to hurt his feelings." Jerry sucked at relationship crap. And this wasn't even a relationship.

Keith's hand landed on Jerry's shoulder. "So you ran here." His voice held no accusation. "Must have been bad."

Jerry snorted. "I'm so screwed, Keith. If I go near the guy again…. I *can't* go near Rex ever again. You don't know…."

Jerry rubbed at the knot of pain in his chest. Why did it feel as if an elephant sat on his rib cage? Why was he mourning the loss of Rex as if they'd been a couple? Even if he was in love with the guy, they'd only kissed once.

He swallowed the hard lump in his throat. "We've been seeing each other for months in the library and talking, and you know I more than like him, and now…." Jerry fisted his hair. "He kissed me, and I thought I was going to pass out and fly at the same time." The feeling had been so overwhelming, but Jerry would have gladly drowned in its wake.

Keith sat next to Jerry. "Oh shit."

"Yeah, oh shit," Jerry concurred.

"You think he feels the same about you?"

Jerry popped up from the bed and paced. "How would I know how he feels? I ran, took off and left him behind, because it doesn't matter, does it? Nothing I want matters so why wait? I'm here to move on. To face the inevitable black hole I've fought being pulled into. It's huge and dark, and it's going to swallow me whole. I might as well step right in its path. I'm tired of the dread and the fear. So what if my parents are going to choose my mate. So what if I'm going to have to live with this person for the rest of my life, without love, or passion, or anything I felt last night with Rex." He closed his eyes, shoving down the pain and heartache and panic, and took in several deep breaths. "I'm done. Tonight my mother's having a dinner party, I'm sure, to introduce whoever they've chosen for me, and then I can get on with my fucking sucky life."

Keith studied him for several minutes, then bit down on his bottom lip. "I guess it wasn't a good idea to give Rex your phone number, then."

Jerry dropped his head, wishing lightning would strike him dead.

CHAPTER 5

Jerry combed gel through his hair, trying to get his unruly locks to stay put. To say his mother had been upset over his lack of a haircut was an understatement. Her finger had hovered over the Call button on her phone, intending to book Jerry an emergency appointment with her own hairdresser. Mercifully, his father had intervened. This evening was nerve-racking enough without new haircut horrors. In less than thirty minutes, Jerry would come face-to-face with his future husband and father of his children. His heart skipped a beat and his stomach rolled over and back. If he didn't throw up before dinner, it would be a major feat.

He sighed at his hair. That was a lost cause, so he dressed in his ceremonial garb. Crisp, white button-up shirt and a blue tartan plaid *tilk*. It was similar to the traditional Scottish kilt, however there were several layers that wrapped around the waist. The end crossed over the chest and shoulder, and fastened at the waistband, in the back. The garment was a tactical nightmare that required Marco's assistance to put it on correctly. Once, in his teens, Jerry had accidentally tucked the bottom of the tilk up into one of the numerous layers. Which had caused Jerry to moon an entire room of people since underwear wasn't worn with a tilk. As if that hadn't been embarrassing at seventeen.

Once dressed, Jerry asked Marco for a moment alone. Before leaving, Marco paused. In a rare moment, he relaxed his stance and approached Jerry. "Jerricho, you've grown into a fine man. I understand this isn't the life you want, but know I'm proud of you."

Jerry swallowed against the lump in his throat. "Thanks, Marco, for being there."

"Always." Marco bowed slightly and left.

Once the door closed, Jerry picked up his phone. He'd turned it off after fleeing the bar the night before.

"I guess it wasn't a good idea to give Rex your phone number, then."

Jerry contemplated turning the phone on.

31

Don't be stupid, Jer. Rex didn't call you. He wanted to get into your pants last night, and when that didn't happen, he moved on.

After a moment's hesitation, Jerry powered up his phone. When he unlocked the screen, the phone icon showed three missed calls and there were three voice messages. The first two were from Keith, so he ignored those. The third was from an unknown number.

He pressed play. Rex's sultry, gravelly voice hit him hard. The visceral reaction was immediate. His heart pounded, his stomach clenched, and he was half-hard in seconds.

"Hi, Jerry. This is Rex. Um…. Keith said you had an emergency last night. I hope everything's okay. Anyway, I had a good time and wanted to see if you'd like to get together again…. I mean, if you want to. So call me. I want to see you soon."

Jerry threw the phone onto the bed with a frustrated grunt. Memories bombarded him—Rex leaning over him, touching him, kissing him. He shook his head, trying to clear them. Stepping in front of the mirror, he straightened the collar of his dress shirt and hardened his expression.

"Okay, Jerricho Alamande Trychovisca. Time to grow some and man up."

"JERRICHO, THIS is Tyranis Devintanzo. His family resides in the northern territory. I believe you boys met when you were children." The giddiness in his mother's voice nearly caused Jerry to roll his eyes. With pride, she introduced the gorgeous man slated to be Jerry's future husband. Tyranis was in his demon form, as was everyone else in the room. His horns were larger than most Anzuni, which meant greater fertility or something. Probably knock Jerry up with twins on the first shot.

Jerry didn't fall for all that pride-in-being-a-demon and had refused to transform, much to his mother's dismay. Her sour expression told Jerry they'd be speaking of his refusal later. What was she going to do? Ground him? Make him marry someone he didn't want to marry? Too late for that last one, and he was too old for the first.

"Please, call me Ty." His voice was rich and cultured. His hair was black as night, gelled into spikes in the front and cut tight on the sides. A

Roman face, cleft chin, and slim athletic body made up the man who was beyond handsome. His smile dazzled as he held out his hand.

Okay, maybe this could work.

Jerry took his hand, and Ty pulled it to his mouth and placed a kiss on the back. Jerry suppressed a frown. Did the man think he was a freakin' girl?

He coughed. "Call me Jerry."

Ty smiled and immediately turned and engaged Jerry's mother in conversation. Jerry stood by like a potted plant while his fiancé (*Oh, gods!*) spoke to Jerry's mother, then Jerry's father, and then practically every other guest. Jerry recognized several members of the Anzuni council and their partners. Other important Anzuni clan members were there, most influential leaders in their fields. Politics was the forte of the rich and privileged. Overprivileged and boring, if anyone asked Jerry. Soon he zoned out, his mind joyfully turned to thoughts of the books in the library, until a hand touched his shoulder.

Ty smiled and pointed to the table. "Dinner's being served." Ever the charming gentleman, Ty took Jerry by the arm, practically leading (or was it dragging) him toward the table. And shit if Ty didn't pull Jerry's chair out for him. All eyes were on the two of them, so Jerry sat without incident. When they were alone, however, he'd give Ty a piece of his mind for treating him as less than equal.

With dinner served, Ty continued his exchanges with everyone at the table, effortlessly moving from one topic to another—politics, economics, fucking traditions. A walking conversation. Just add people, and voilà! He continued his "vote garnering" speech as if he were running for office until Ty's uncle, Geraldon, a long-time member of the ruling council of the Anzuni people, spoke up.

"King Evin, I recently had a conversation with Senator Adams. We've entered a joint venture, and I have gained his trust and friendship, as I have with many influential politicians over the years. I believe the time has come to restart talks with the council about gaining recognition among the humans."

Silence reigned at the table, and Jerry ducked his head, peering sideways at his father. His neutrality was belied by the white-knuckle grip on the glass of wine in his hand. For years, Geraldon had spoken of the council's duty to approach the US government and reveal their existence. For years, Jerry's father had denied anything good could come from such a revelation.

"We're all aware of the chaos and devastation that revealing Anzuni existence could bring upon our people if that information was leaked, photographed, or even worse, videotaped. A proactive stance is the best measure." Geraldon never knew when to quit, and the fake grin wasn't helping.

Jerry's father sipped his wine and then set the glass down, his expression thoughtful. "While I agree, Geraldon, that unplanned exposure of the Anzuni race would not only be harmful to our people but immensely dangerous as well, we've taken great measures to assure we remain hidden among the humans. We educate our children on the dangers of such knowledge. We ensure that they understand the horrific subjugation and slavery that befell our people at the hands of the Braezelas."

Everyone nodded. The history lessons were designed to scare the crap out of all Anzuni children. Other lessons were to remind descendants of those who gave their lives escaping the tyranny of a race of demons so heartless, so cold-blooded, so ruthless, that revealing their existence on Earth assured the same fate.

"It will only take one slip, one careless act to reveal what we strive to hide," Geraldon insisted. "If we act first, we can orchestrate the revelation of an intelligent race on Earth other than humans. We can be in control."

Jerry's father leaned forward and narrowed his eyes. "And what makes you so sure that our actions won't have the direst of consequences? You speak as if you know the reactions of those in power. They could deceive us, betray us in ways that will once again enslave our people, even if only for experimentation."

Geraldon opened his mouth to speak again, but Jerry's father raised his hand to silence him. "This is a dinner party, not a council meeting, Geraldon. Let's drink and celebrate the joining of our two families."

"Here, here," Tanyon, the oldest member of the council, said, raising his glass of wine. "This is truly a celebration. There hasn't been a royal wedding in twenty-five years. To prince and future king, Jerricho, and his husband-to-be, Tyranis."

Everyone raised their glasses. Jerry smiled weakly as Ty beamed at the Anzuni around the table. Not once did he include Jerry as he continued in conversation with others. When Jerry glanced up, he found Geraldon scowling in his direction. He had never liked Jerry and his purported "indulged ignorance of Anzuni politics and tradition." Jerry smiled wide and Geraldon lifted the corner of his mouth in a pseudo smile. And to think Jerry got to marry his nephew. The rotten fruit couldn't fall far from the tree.

After the main course had been served, Ty touched Jerry's arm and quirked his mouth in a beguiling grin. Jerry smiled back despite himself. "I hear you work at the library."

Maybe Jerry had overreacted. Possibly Ty's actions had been the result of how he'd been raised. Now they could get to know each other.

"Yeah, I work in Acquisitions. I'm in charge of purchasing books, as well as managing the rare book collection."

Ty chuckled. "Books. How cute."

Jerry frowned. *Cute?* "So what do you do?"

Ty sipped his wine, his eyes everywhere but on Jerry. "I'm the vice president of a large and successful brokerage house. Complicated stuff. Nothing for you to worry about."

Seriously?

Jerry picked at his meal, silently brooding. Those around the table laughed and raved over Ty's stories and opinions, even though he said nothing of substance. Jerry recalled his conversations with Rex and how comfortable and important the man had made him feel every time they'd spoken.

"Jerricho, honey. Is something wrong with your meal?"

He looked up to see his mother's concerned—no, wait, impatient face.

Jerry plastered on his widest grin and shook his head. "Sorry, just thinking." He speared an asparagus and stuffed the entire stalk into his mouth. That was how he spent the rest of his meal.

After dinner, Jerry's father suggested he and Ty spend some time together… alone. The night kept rolling downhill, out of control. As

Jerry led Ty to the sitting room, he tried to keep an open mind. This unconventional meeting had to be as awkward a situation for Ty as it was for Jerry. Perhaps once they were alone, the tension would ease.

Jerry closed the french doors to the sitting room as Ty surveyed his surroundings.

"This place is amazing." Ty nodded in what seemed to be approval. "I'm definitely going to like living here."

Jerry winced. Permanently living back at the mansion. Man, he was going to miss his small apartment and freedom.

"Yeah, it's nice." The level of discomfort Ty caused Jerry in his own home threw him.

When Ty turned, all traces of his smile disappeared. "Everyone in the clan knows about you and your rebellious ways." His eyes hardened and appeared terribly unforgiving.

"Excuse me?" Jerry wasn't sure if he'd heard the words correctly.

Ty stepped closer, his disgusted scowl an expression Jerry had never imagined he'd see on the face of his future husband.

"Look at you." Ty surveyed Jerry's neck where his tattoos were clearly visible. "You've made a mockery of your position, marking your body with petty symbols. Even knowing you would someday represent our people. When I was chosen for you over three years ago, I warned your parents to rein you in and stop your rebellious nonsense. Everyone knows that you do not wish to be king, and that you deny your birthright."

Three years ago? His parents had kept Ty a secret for *three years*?

Jerry pulled back his shoulders in a show of opposition. "I have *not* denied my birthright. I'm here, aren't I? I've never denied who I am. I mean, I don't like the idea of my mate being chosen for me by my parents, but I have no choice in the matter. You're here by choice. You didn't have to accept. What would you know about what it's like to be in my position?"

Ty studied Jerry for a moment, and his face softened slightly. When he wasn't glaring, or being self-righteous, he was handsome.

Jerry tried not to tense as Ty circled behind him, pushing his chest and groin against Jerry. Ty's hands settled on his shoulders and then ran down each of his arms in a highly intimate motion.

"Despite the tattoos, you have a nice body, nice tight ass." Ty caressed Jerry's left ass cheek, and he held in a gasp. He imagined Rex touching and stroking and wanting him. Ty shattered the fantasy by speaking.

"Soon you will be the crown prince of the Anzuni clan, and, as your husband, that title shall be mine as well, and someday the title of king. You're mine, Baelso. On our wedding night, I will take your virginity, and soon after you will bear my children." Ty's hand smoothed over Jerry's chest. Despite detesting every word from Ty's mouth, the closeness of his hard body and Jerry's high libido rushed blood to his groin and filled his cock. "You will submit to me *in* bed and out. I won't accept anything less than your complete compliance and submission. I won't be made a fool of by your aberrant behavior." Ty reached around, cupping Jerry's growing erection.

An image of their wedding night screeched through Jerry's mind. Ty pushing him, holding him down, shoving painfully into him, uncaring of Jerry's pleasure. He'd be a conquest, a title, a position in society, and Ty was going to ride him all the way to being crowned king. An empty hollowness seeped into Jerry's heart, staining his insides with an inky darkness. With Ty, there would be no tenderness, caring, love, mutual respect, or pleasure. Just once, Jerry wanted pleasure. His first time should be special, with someone who respected him.

Someone who *liked* him.

Someone like Rex.

Jerry took a step forward and turned. He drew in a deep breath through his nose and willed the words to come out. "I understand."

Ty blinked as if he hadn't expected the answer. The delight that crossed his face sickened Jerry. "Well, perhaps you're smarter than I gave you credit for. Now, why don't you show me your gratitude and blow me before we head back to the party."

Jerry was seconds from hurling. "Um… sure, but I have to hit the head first. Be right back."

Jerry busted through the french doors, stopping to close them. Seemed as if he was using the bathroom excuse a lot lately. Not in a hundred million years would he give his virginity to that fuckhead. He might have to spend the next fifty agonizing years with the jerk, but there was no way the man was going to be his first.

Jerry veered off to the dining room and peered inside. Marco stood in his customary spot, directing the wait staff. Jerry cawed quietly, a signal they'd used since he was a child. Marco walked to Jerry and immediately grimaced.

"What's wrong, Sire?"

"Everything. I need to get out of here, now. Tell my father I'll call him tomorrow. Tell my mother…. Well, nothing you tell her will fix what I'm about to do, so never mind."

If he didn't get the hell out of there, he'd disintegrate where he stood.

Marco furrowed his brow. "He's a real ass, isn't he, Sire? Maybe if you spoke to your parents—"

Jerry shook his head. "You and I both know I've pushed too many boundaries and used up all my passes. Besides, after I bolt tonight, I'm sure my mother will have me under lock and key. I will come back, and I will marry the spawn of the Anzuni devil Dharita, but first I have something I need to do."

Despite trying to keep the uneasiness and fear from his voice, Marco understood and nodded.

"Call me and let me know when you'll return, Sire."

Jerry smiled wanly. "Thanks, Marco."

With a wave, Jerry ducked out the back door and headed toward the hole in the fence he'd used as a teen. If the guard at the gate saw him, Jerry wouldn't be able to leave. He pulled his phone from where he'd tucked it into his boot and called Keith.

"I would ask how the meeting with the future spouse goes, but since you're calling me, I'm guessing not too great."

"You guess right," Jerry groused, ducking through the fence. Shit, he hadn't done this since he was a teenager. It was a tight fit, but he made it through. "Pick me up at the end of the road?"

"I'll be there in ten."

Jerry pushed the phone back into his boot and chewed on his thumbnail. He needed a plan.

CHAPTER 6

KEITH DROVE Jerry to Annabelle's to pick up the keys to the library, and Jerry filled Keith in on his spectacularly awful evening. He wasn't going home. He could stay in his office at the library, lock himself in, and hide out until morning. Anyone looking for him would check at Keith's or Annabelle's house. He'd have time to formulate a plan. Already, his phone had rung numerous times, and he'd avoided looking at the screen, knowing it was his mother.

At the library, Keith followed Jerry into his tiny office. Jerry flicked on the light, heaving a sigh. Keith sat on the left side of the small couch stuffed in the corner. A mountain of books Jerry was in the midst of cataloging covered the other half. Keith cast a wary eye at the stacks, no doubt hoping they didn't topple onto him. Jerry sank into his office chair, bone-tired and wanting to forget the entire evening. Unfortunately, Keith required answers.

"So your future husband's a jackass." Keith did like to get right to the point.

Jerry nodded, unable to express how much of an asshole his intended was.

Keith leaned forward. The intensity of his gaze, the forthright expression, spoke of someone who had something serious to say. "You know what my Grammy Sarinsin used to say?"

Okay, not so serious. Jerry snorted. "Crazy Grammy Sarinsin?"

"Smart woman. Want Ty the tyrant to disappear? Dance naked in the waxing moonlight, on the first day of the harvest, and a Braezelas will do your bidding. Your future hubby will be dragged off as a slave of the creepy, drooling, bucktoothed lords of the *ick*." Keith added a visible shudder.

Jerry laughed. "Umm, I doubt Anzuni folklore will solve my jerk-off issue."

"Speaking of jerk-off issues, Rex called me again today."

Jerry's head popped up, but then he quelled his reaction and looked away.

"The look on your face…. You would've thought I'd told you about some rare book I found. And I'm thinking he likes you just as much."

Jerry tried not to smile. He kept his face down in case that joy escaped. His mood hit about an eleven on a scale of one to ten. "Why do you say that?"

Keith grunted loudly and Jerry had to look at him. "'Did he get my message? Do you think he'll call me?'" He'd lowered his voice to mimic Rex. "'Did you talk to him? I want to take him out on a date. What's he like to eat? Why won't he call me?'"

Each of those questions crashed hard into Jerry, plummeting his mood down to around a negative two.

"You know I can't go on a date with him. I just met my future husband for gods' sake." Asshole.

"Yeah, I know that, but what do *you* want? I've seen this prince crap tearing you apart for years. I can't see you living the rest of your life with a douche bag."

Jerry shrugged. Again, what he wanted didn't matter—except, maybe…. He sat up, a rush of adrenaline flooding his body.

"I want one night. One night that means something. I'm never going to feel anything for this guy unless he gets a personality transplant." Jerry needed something he could carry in his heart. "I want to know what it's like to be with someone who wants me back. Who…."

Jerry bowed his head.

"Who cares about you?"

Jerry wanted to say loves, but Rex didn't love him, so he agreed with Keith. "Yeah. But there's no one."

"Rex cares a fucking lot about you."

Jerry closed his eyes and swore at the burn of tears. He couldn't use Rex in that way, play with his emotions, and then leave him. Jerry wasn't that cold.

"I know, but I can't." Even if the idea of giving his virginity to Ty left him icy cold, Jerry didn't want to hurt Rex because…

Because I love him.

"So, maybe you have sex with someone else. You know, someone who isn't out to get something from you? Someone you can fuck… or who can fuck you?" Keith made a face, and Jerry chuckled. "I have no friggin' idea how that works."

Jerry huffed. "Uh, hello, virgin here. I'm pretty much clueless too." Although with the amount of gay porn he'd watched over the years, one would think he'd be an expert by now.

It was hopeless. Either way, his first time was going to be a huge disappointing disaster, like 99 percent of the world's population.

Keith stood and slapped his hands together with that I've-got-a-great-idea look. "I've got a great idea."

"Do I even want to hear it?"

"Yes. Yes, you do. It involves getting you something less girly to wear and hitting up the Blue Moon."

"Are you crazy? You want me to go to a gay bar? Why would you…. Oh no. I'm not having sex with some stranger." Jerry shook his head as Keith nodded.

"Yes, you are." Keith grabbed Jerry's arm and yanked him out of the chair. "And anyone you meet, well, you won't be strangers by the end of the night," Keith insisted. Once he got an idea into his head… well, it generally meant a whole lot of trouble for Jerry.

Keith pulled a reluctant Jerry toward the door. "It's a great idea. You get laid, and then you can go and marry the twat waffle."

Jerry planted his feet and yanked his arm away from Keith. "Wait."

Keith turned and raised his arms at his sides with a what-now expression on his face.

"I don't have any condoms." That was a good reason not to go along with Keith's idea.

Keith frowned. "But you're going to have sex with a human. There aren't any diseases you can pass to one another."

There were communicable diseases Anzuni could pass to one another, yet none that were shared between the Anzuni and another species.

Jerry rolled his eyes. "Duh! Prince? Pregnancy? Ring any bells?"

"I thought that couldn't happen until you were twenty-five?"

41

"*Around* twenty-five. It's not exact. It's tradition that places the mating exactly at that age. It's possible I'm capable of it now."

Despite that information, Keith snagged Jerry by the arm again. "So we get clothes *and* condoms. And then we go and get you laid."

When Keith cackled, a cold chill raced up Jerry's back. He should run.

HE SHOULD have run. The music in the Blue Moon was loud, and the bar was wall-to-wall men. Men of all ages and sizes and shapes, wearing leather and tight jeans and missing shirts and—holy shit— only a thong. Jerry was overwhelmed, and terrified, and he stuck to Keith's side as they walked up to the bar.

A shirtless bartender with pecs the size of a woman's breasts flashed them a smile. And damn, if he wasn't looking Keith up and down.

"Back off, gay boy." Keith held up his hands. "I'm straight. I'm here for my friend."

The bartender snorted. "Yeah. That's what they all say."

Keith narrowed his eyes. "What the hell does th—"

Jerry smacked Keith in the chest to shut him up. "Two Saranacs, please."

Another flash of a smile, and the bartender went off to fetch their beers.

Keith rubbed at his chest, scowling. "What the hell was that for?"

"You're in a gay bar. Of course guys are going to think you're gay." Jerry handed the bartender the money for the beers. The man's dark eyes were still all over Keith.

Keith ignored the leering and turned, looking out into the crowd. The place was massive, with a ton of people dancing beneath flashing lights. More men hung on the fringes doing more than just watching. Jerry had to admit it was a virtual smorgasbord of men.

"Okay," Keith yelled. "From what I can tell, your best chance of trying out some guys is to get out on the dance floor." Keith continued to peruse prospective lays as Jerry stared at his friend.

"What?" Keith asked.

A large bear of a man caught Jerry's attention as he passed slowly in front of them. A pelt of thick, dark hair covered his entire upper body. He wore leather pants and a studded leather belt-looking thing that wrapped around his torso. When his eyes landed on Jerry, the man swiped his tongue over his lower lip and nodded. Every cell in Jerry's body screamed in fear as Keith nodded back.

"What's up?" Keith smirked at the mountain of a man.

That earned Keith another smack to the chest.

"Cut that shit out." Keith scowled. "I'm trying to help you out here."

"Well, don't. That guy could break me like a toothpick." Jerry winced at the thought of that huge man pounding into him. Probably call Jerry his "bitch" or something.

"Pfft. Then what do you want?" Keith bounced on his toes to the music as he scanned the room, no doubt looking for someone else to throw Jerry at.

What did Jerry want? He wanted to go home to his tiny apartment and his books and not think about getting laid, or the stupid future. He wanted to hide. And think of Rex.

"Okay, dance, then. Get out there and get your funk on, or boogie, or whatever you gay guys do. Kind of looks like dirty dancing. So go Patrick Swayze someone."

Jerry shook his head and crossed his arms. "Uh-uh."

"No?" Keith raised an eyebrow.

"No." Jerry took a sip of his beer. Keith couldn't make him dance. Men were grinding, rubbing, and writhing against one another. The entire scene was like one huge orgy. Jerry could never do that and look his mother in the eye again. His face flushed red.

"Fuck. Are you blushing?" Keith's amusement was plastered all over his face.

Jerry ducked his head.

"Okay, okay." Keith placed his beer on a nearby table and then took Jerry's from him and did the same. "I don't know why I put up with all of this shit with you."

Before Jerry could speak, Keith grabbed his hand and yanked him through the throng of bodies. Jerry was tired of being pushed and pulled about. Smack-dab in the middle of the crowd, Keith stopped and turned.

"Dance," he commanded and then proceeded to do something that could have been mistaken for dancing.

Keith's jerky movements amused Jerry, and he laughed until a huge man approached Keith from behind. The guy was a brick shithouse, tons of hot, glorious gorgeousness and bald. He grabbed Keith's hips and jerked him back against his front. Keith flailed and sputtered as the man ground their hips together in an erotic motion.

Keith's mouth dropped open, and his eyes were comically wide. Jerry covered his mouth with his hand, suppressing a snort but unable to contain the laughter that roared out of him. The big man rubbed his hand over Keith's chest while his other hand held Keith tight around the waist. Shit, Keith wasn't going anywhere.

Jerry's amusement was cut short as hands grabbed him from behind. Soon, he was in the same predicament as Keith, and it wasn't so funny at first. However, the strong, sure hands on his hips and the rhythmic movements of their bodies lulled Jerry. The heat and sweat and beat of the music were hypnotic, and Jerry relaxed against the hard body. Beefy arms wrapped around Jerry's, and large hands caressed his chest and stomach. From beneath heavy lids, Jerry spotted Keith, and the blissed-out expression on his face was stunning. Damn, he was putty in that bear's hands, and Keith wasn't even gay.

Hot breath skated over Jerry's neck, and a moist tongue licked and sucked, and he'd never felt anything so erotic in his life except with Rex. He moaned his pleasure, lost in the hazy fog of the moment. His cock throbbed in his jeans, and his pulse thrummed through his veins. Flashbacks of the kiss with Rex assaulted him. Sweat broke out on his skin as he ground into a hard bulge at the base of his spine. Pseudo intercourse ensued. Maybe he could go through with Keith's plan. If he didn't look at the man, he could imagine….

"Missed you." The gravelly voice startled Jerry and he tried to turn, but the arms tightened around his chest. "I've done nothing but think about that kiss at the bar. Dance with me. Please?"

Rex held him.

Rex danced with him.

Rex had missed him.

How had Rex known he was at the Blue Moon?

Keith.

Later. Jerry would kill Keith later. Either that or thank him. For now, Jerry was in Rex's arms, and the sensual dance fired an ache for Rex's touch. In a bold move, Jerry guided one of Rex's hands down over his bulge. Rex gripped Jerry's shaft through his jeans, and he cried out.

"You're so hard," Rex whispered. "Feel how turned on you are. *Mmmm*. I'd love to put that cock in my mouth."

Jerry almost lost it right there. He turned his head, needing to taste him. When their lips met, Jerry opened. The demanding kiss was frantic and full of lust and desire. Jerry pushed his tongue into Rex's mouth, and Rex closed his lips around the muscle, sucking gently at first and then with harder pulls. Jerry groaned as if Rex sucked on his cock. Gods, he so wanted Rex on his knees before him.

Rex released Jerry's tongue, and his arms loosened. He spun Jerry around and Jerry attacked Rex's mouth, riding high on desire. He was ready for anything Rex dished out.

He looked up into Rex's lust-filled eyes. "Come home with me," Jerry whispered before realizing he'd spoken the words.

Rex gazed down at him, chewing on his lip, then finally nodded. Jerry didn't waste any time. Hand clasped tight in Rex's, Jerry pulled him through the crowd. He had to get Rex home before he changed his mind.

CHAPTER 7

AS THEY entered his apartment, Jerry reveled in Rex's hands as they roamed over his back. Once the door closed, they were all over each other. Hands yanked off clothes, and moans filled the air. Jerry batted away his doubts about sleeping with Rex as if they were annoying, buzzing gnats. Rex was there, and nothing was going to stop Jerry. Nothing. Not even his ringing phone. Jerry reluctantly stepped away from Rex. Grabbing the phone cord, he yanked it from the wall.

Rex raised an eyebrow, but then his eyes widened as Jerry pushed his own jeans down around his knees. In two steps, Rex had Jerry wrapped up in his arms, and they flopped back onto the bed. Jerry never knew kissing could be so erotic, and he fought to keep their lips together, but Rex pulled away.

"Said I wanted to suck your cock." Rex scooted down Jerry's body. Wet, moist heat engulfed Jerry's cock without pretense, and he gasped and groaned as Rex sucked and licked. Jerry grasped Rex's head as he assaulted his cock. The feeling of that mouth for the first time was beyond amazing. The sensation was too much.

"R-Rex…. Rex…. Oh, gods… gonna…." Jerry tried to pull him off, but Rex continued his rapid motion, and for one single, breathless moment, time seemed to stop. Time hadn't stopped, only felt as if it had as Jerry was suspended in a bliss-filled cloud of pleasure. His balls and shaft pulsed out a rhythm as his cum filled Rex's mouth. And, damn, he swallowed almost every drop.

Jerry gasped for air, his mouth open wide, his eyes focused on a spot on the ceiling. He was aware of Rex leaning over him but was unable to move or speak. There was the jingle of Rex's belt and the sound of fabric rustling, and then a naked body pushed against his side.

Rex's hand touched Jerry's cheek and gently turned his head, allowing Rex to once again plunder and own him. Jerry ran his hand down Rex's chest, over his stomach, and tentatively wrapped his fingers around Rex's hot length. Rex bucked and hummed his approval as Jerry stroked the shaft. The first cock in his hand other than his own, and the feeling was magnificent and glorious.

Breaking the kiss, Jerry pulled a bottle of lube from the bedside table drawer. He did a lot of jacking off. Rex sucked the skin on Jerry's chest and nipples. The relentless touches overloaded Jerry's system, and his cock hardened again. He flicked open the lube, and Rex held out his hand, allowing Jerry to liberally coat his fingers. Without hesitation, those fingers appeared at Jerry's opening, rubbing and seeking entrance.

Dropping the lube, Jerry opened his legs wide and pulled Rex on top of him. Jerry needed Rex inside of him, right then. Jerry had played with dildos in the past. Technically, he wasn't a virgin in that respect. Impatiently, Jerry reached between his legs and guided two of Rex's fingers to his hole. The burn was intense, but the pleasure was greater.

Rex's gaze pinpointed Jerry as he rode the large beefy fingers. The caring and lust in those heavy-lidded eyes was almost too much.

"You're fucking gorgeous." The growl in Rex's voice, the intensity of his gaze only added to Jerry's need.

"Please." Jerry grasped Rex's shoulder. So ready to give his first time to Rex.

He leaned down and kissed Jerry while adding a third finger. He pinched Jerry's nipple, assaulting the nub. Gods, Jerry ached, his cock rock hard again, as he writhed beneath this beautiful man.

"Fuck me," Jerry whispered when their lips parted. Rex gave him a crooked smile and produced a condom. He ripped open the package, rolled the condom over his shaft, and then quickly lubed his erection.

When Rex's cock nudged at his hole, Jerry was certain he was going to come again. With increased pressure, his muscle stretched and stretched as Rex's cock entered him. The burn intensified, and Jerry wasn't sure the pain would ever stop. He swallowed hard, clutching Rex's upper arms tightly as he fought to breathe. Rex stopped, allowing Jerry time to adjust, kissing Jerry's cheeks and forehead, his eyes and nose, rubbing his hands over Jerry's stomach. The gestures were loving and gentle, and Jerry relaxed. As he did, the pain eased, leaving him with the overwhelming pressure.

"You feel incredible. Fucking incredible." Rex withdrew his shaft and pushed back in. The pressure eased slightly, and more pleasure came to the forefront. As Rex continued to push in and pull out, he gazed into Jerry's eyes. Rex's green eyes shone brightly in the faint light of the room, and Jerry found himself falling into them. The pleasure spread from his ass into his groin. His sensitized skin heated as Rex explored Jerry's thighs, his stomach, his chest, his neck, finally resting his hands on Jerry's cheeks.

Rex furrowed his brow and bit his bottom lip and his thrusts increased, erratic and deep. Rex was close. Grasping Rex by the nape of his neck, Jerry pulled his lover down into a scorching kiss. Rex tensed and his breathing faltered, and Jerry wished for that moment to last forever. When he ended the kiss, time had ceased. Above him, Rex had frozen at the instant his orgasm hit. Bliss suffused his features, mixed with a myriad of emotions. For once, Jerry was grateful for the extra time. He lovingly ran his fingers over Rex's brow, along his cheekbones. He loved Rex. True, I-will-wither-and-die-without-you, love. But Jerry would never see Rex again, never hear his laugh or shiver under his touch again. A hot, wet tear rolled down Jerry's cheek.

Rex jerked and gasped, his cock once again pushing into Jerry. Rex hit that spot just right, and the tingling went straight to Jerry's balls. Ropes of cum shot from Jerry's dick without being touched. Rex lunged forward and latched onto Jerry's lips, wrapping his arms around Jerry's shoulders and rolling them onto their sides. Sated and floating on the cloud of two orgasms, Jerry sighed contentedly and drifted off to sleep, safe in Rex's arms.

JERRY TRIED to roll over, but a warm, heavy weight pinned him down. Rubbing his eyes, Jerry turned to look at Rex, who slept with his head on Jerry's shoulder. Closing his eyes, breathing deeply, Jerry tried to keep his emotions from taking over. He'd lost his virginity to Rex, and the act had been more than he'd ever hoped or dreamed it could be. Warmth had spread into the empty hollows of his chest, pure bliss and happiness, threatened by the icy coldness of what Jerry had to do.

Break Rex's heart.

What have I done? How could I hurt Rex like this?

Still Jerry couldn't regret what they'd done. Jerry worked his way out from beneath Rex. The man was a huge hairy blanket of warmth, and Jerry mourned the loss. He rushed to the bathroom and quickly cleaned up. His ass and legs were sticky with lube. Rex sure had been generous. His thoughtfulness was another way he was perfect for Jerry, unlike Tyranis Devintanzo. A cold shudder shook Jerry's body. He had to get out of there.

Once he'd washed up, he dressed, grabbed some clothes, a couple of books, and some things from his bathroom, and stuffed them into a duffel bag. He pulled his phone from his pants where he'd dropped them. His gaze kept going to Rex, sleeping in his bed. Jerry's heart ached, and tears burned his eyes again. Not able to resist, he pulled up the camera app on his phone and clicked a picture.

Closing his eyes, Jerry focused on calling his power to freeze time, wanting more, wanting that moment to never end, but nothing happened. Of course, it never would when he truly wanted it to occur. Leaning down, he placed one last gentle kiss on Rex's lips. He exhaled noisily and burrowed his head farther into the pillow.

Jerry smiled as his vision blurred, and he whispered softly, "I love you."

With that, he left his apartment and the one man who could make him truly happy.

IN THE cab, on the way to the mansion, Jerry crafted a good-bye text to Rex, reiterating over and over how sorry he was. That had been the hardest message he'd ever sent. He ignored the tears that ran down his cheeks as he left that life behind and returned to another. Stepping into the foyer at the mansion, he lost any hope that he could make a clean break to his room and mourn alone. It was eight a.m., and his parents sat in the sitting room, no doubt awaiting the return of their wayward son.

Merano, an aide to Jerry's father, wrote on a pad he carried. "I'll contact the police in that area and get what information I can. Fransziso Laranzina of the clan is aide to the mayor. I'm sure she can get us what we need."

"Good. The sooner we find these men, the better." His father looked tired. "I hope we find them alive."

Merano bowed, then nodded to Jerry as he exited the room, closing the doors behind them.

"Dad, is someone else missing?"

Jerry's father stared blankly at Jerry for a moment. Finally, he frowned and ran his hand over his hair. He sat down hard on the wingback chair. "Unfortunately, yes. A young Anzuni in California. This brings the total up to seven. Of course, no one saw anything."

Jerry nodded. He felt guilt over the grief he'd caused his father, who had so many other pressing issues to deal with. Jerry averted his eyes from his mother's death glare. She had every right to be pissed.

"Jerricho." Disappointment filled his mother's brief acknowledgment. Her displeasure dripped from everything in the room as she waited silently for him to speak.

"I'm sorry, Mom. I shouldn't have taken off without telling you."

Her eyes widened and her red lips pursed. "You shouldn't have left, period. Do you know how embarrassed I was when Ty informed us that you'd disappeared? I had to tell a room full of important Anzuni that my son left without a reason or an explanation. It was rude and immature. You assured me you were ready to fulfill your duties, and now people in the clan are questioning your dedication to your people." She sighed and ran her hand over her coiffed hair. "And what kind of impression do you think you made on your future husband? The man was devastated that you ran out on him."

Jerry suppressed a huge snort. He hadn't gotten his blowjob. That's why Ty had been upset.

"I'm sorry. I…."

"You're spoiled, Jerricho. Your father never should have allowed you to live on your own. I, for one, knew nothing good would come from allowing you to live away from home. You will apologize personally to every guest who was here, and to your future husband. Hopefully he won't call off the wedding."

His mother's words were harsh. How was wanting a life of his own, wanting true love, being spoiled? Customs and tradition had engulfed his parents' perspective and blinded them to what he needed, what he wanted. But then again, the focus had to be on what was good for the clan, not the individual members.

Jerry's father shifted in his chair but remained silent. Jerry nodded to his mother, whose expression softened slightly. He yearned to tell her about Rex, about the foreman who'd stolen his heart. He wanted to shout to the world that he'd found that one special person, but as with most everything else in his life, that would remain the secret of his raven.

He was tired and sad and lonely, and he wanted to be alone to fucking fall apart.

"Son?"

Jerry looked up at his father, who gazed at him with concern. "Is everything okay?"

Nothing was okay, but to say that would only cause more drama and lectures about responsibilities, when he was ready to shatter into a million pieces.

"It's all good, Dad. I need a shower."

His father nodded. His mother pulled out her phone, most likely texting an update on his return to the world. She offered him a small smile.

Jerry couldn't get to his room fast enough. In the bathroom, he cranked on the shower and ripped off his clothes. *Hold on a few more seconds.* The sharp pains in his chest had him convinced his ribs had shattered and poked into his heart and lungs. His head pounded a steady beat; a buzzing noise clouded his thoughts. His legs shook as if the floor beneath them were moving. When the water was tolerable, he jumped into the stall and shut the door. Dropping to his knees, he buried his face in his hands and sobbed until only harsh whimpers came from his throat. He relived the intimacy, the tenderness, the beauty of his first and last time with Rex. Jerry held no regrets about making love with Rex. Those memories would live forever in his heart, and carry him through a long and lonely life.

When he'd cried his heart empty, he had no choice but to move on. He only prayed Rex didn't hate him for what he'd done.

JERRY YAWNED as he listened to his mother ramble on about the rites and rituals of his future nuptials. The wedding was still a go, per his father. Jerry had yet to see Ty again. He had a feeling his future *husband* had refused to see him until he had to. Jerry was onboard with that idea. Show up on the wedding day, grit out their respective "I dos," and live miserably ever after.

Two days had passed since Jerry fled from his apartment and Rex. He'd refrained from moping in front of his parents and saved the maudlin shit for his room. He'd taken a few days off from the library to get himself together and straighten out the mess he'd made. In a show of truce to his mother, he'd personally apologized to each and every dinner guest he'd so rudely skipped out on. Then he'd shut his phone off and asked Marco to take messages from anyone who called the mansion. Of course, Keith had called, but not until yesterday. Why Keith hadn't called Jerry for two days after their trip to Blue Moon was strange. Jerry would call Keith back soon. Maybe tomorrow, when Jerry returned to work at the library. "Jerricho?"

Jerry looked to his mother, and she sighed. "Honey, you've been so distracted. You have dark circles under your eyes, and you're pale. Are you not feeling well?"

Only my heart dying in my chest.

Jerry shrugged, unsure what to say. He *was* exhausted, but he attributed his malaise to the depression that currently blanketed him. He needed time to get over Rex, time to mourn the loss.

Hard to do that when you're constantly staring at the picture of him sleeping after he took your sacred virginity destined for your future asshole husband.

Jerry had transferred the picture to his computer and stored the damning evidence in an encrypted file for safekeeping. He imagined his future spouse would be the controlling sort and spy on him.

His mother gently patted his arm, garnering his attention. "Why don't you take a nap? I'll have Marco bring you some tea."

Jerry gave her a wan smile and headed for the stairs. As he entered the foyer, Keith talked with Marco.

When Keith spotted Jerry, he bolted around the butler, determination covering his pinched expression. He grabbed Jerry's arm and yanked him toward the stairs. "I need to talk to you."

Jerry allowed Keith to lead him into his bedroom. Something was up with Keith. He collapsed into the desk chair, frantically rubbing his eyes.

Jerry shut the door. "You look like shit." Keith hadn't shaved in days, his curls stuck up in all directions, and his clothes…. Were those the same clothes from the bar? "What's going on with you?"

A cloud of emotions crossed Keith's face, and then he narrowed his eyes. "Oh no. I've been trying to call you, and you've been ignoring me. Rex has called me nonstop because you're not answering your phone."

Jerry's chest constricted, and it felt hard to breathe. "Wh-what does he want?"

"To talk to you, ya jackass. You fucked him, didn't you?"

Jerry chewed on his bottom lip. "More like the other way around."

Keith sat forward. "You say *I* look like shit. You should go look in the mirror." Keith sat back in the chair. He shook his head. "What're you going to do?"

Jerry furrowed his brow. "In ten months, I'm marrying Tyranis. I have no choice. You know that."

Keith huffed. "I meant about Rex."

Jerry knew what he meant but didn't want to say the words. "In a few days, I'll call him and explain somehow. He's going to hate me, but…."

"I don't envy you one bit," Keith said quietly, and then his attention wandered off.

Jerry eyed him critically. His normally vibrant eyes were dull and carried an edge of apprehension. Jerry rubbed his hands together, uncomfortable for the first time ever with Keith. Something had happened to him. He had a shell-shocked look about him.

"Anything you want to talk about?"

Keith grimaced. "Call Rex, and soon. I don't think I can take the boss man moping around the jobsite again tomorrow."

Jerry winced. Was Rex truly that upset? He'd used Jerry for the night and was supposed to move on. Jerry had been a one-night stand. Hurt like a bitch to think like that. Yet Keith's revelation negated Jerry's guilt-relieving excuse. Rex cared and Jerry had used him.

"I'll call. If not today, soon."

CHAPTER 8

THE NEXT day at work, Annabelle bombarded Jerry with a million and one questions about what had happened since she'd seen him last. Being a human, she wasn't privy to his demon status. Keeping secrets was his forte, and he spun a web of lies to placate her curiosity. What he didn't lie about was his broken heart, and, for his admission, he received a big hug and an offer to talk. He declined and ferreted himself away in his office to catch up on the work he'd missed.

The office had been his for over three years. Once he married, he'd have to leave the job. Couldn't be male and pregnant and not call attention to oneself. And he'd be pregnant soon after he was married. It was expected.

It was tradition.

He rubbed his hand over his stomach. Growing a life excited him. As a male, to be given the ability to procreate was a gift he'd learned to cherish as he'd come into his twenties. Forget customs and traditions, he wanted to carry a child and bring a life into the world. His hope had been the child would be created from love.

"Hey, Jerry?" Annabelle peeked around the door.

"What's up?"

"There's a guy here about a book."

Jerry threw down his pen and stood. A wave of dizziness hit him hard. He grabbed the back of the chair and the light-headedness passed quickly. Looking at his watch, he realized that it was almost 2:00 p.m. Damn, he'd forgotten to eat lunch. Again. He couldn't concentrate for shit. The guilt of using Rex had stolen his brain's resources.

Jerry froze when he stepped out from behind the circulation desk. His chest tightened, leaving little room for air. Rex stared back at him, his expression unreadable. Unsure of what to do, Jerry opened his mouth, but no words came out.

Rex stuffed his hands into the pockets of his leather bomber jacket and broke the stare. "Can I talk to you for a minute?"

Jerry almost said no as the heat of arousal smacked him, but he forced a nod. "Follow me."

A cold sweat broke out across the back of his neck, and his hands shook. How was he supposed to talk to Rex face-to-face? Fuck, why hadn't he called Rex? If he had, then Rex wouldn't be there.

In his office, Jerry stood by the desk, not offering Rex a chair. If he sat, Jerry might jump on him.

Rex rubbed his palms over his worn jeans. They were tight and molded around his large thighs. Jerry immediately shifted his gaze up.

"How are you?"

The question surprised Jerry. "Um... okay."

Rex nodded. "Listen, I know you said in your text that you couldn't see me anymore. I wanted to see you. Maybe we can talk about it. I... I like you, and I don't think of what we did as a one-night stand. It was so much more than that to me. I had hoped you felt the same. It was... special."

Seeing the hopeful glint in Rex's eyes, Jerry blinked rapidly. Rex's words thrummed Jerry's heart and brought hope he had no business feeling. He swallowed hard. Damn. "Nothing's changed, and I'm so sorry, Rex. I didn't want to hurt you. I promise, but...." He had to end this here. If Rex came back, if he kept calling, Jerry wouldn't be able to resist him. "I'm engaged to be married."

Rex's eyes widened, and his mouth fell open. The glint of hope in his eyes was replaced with a visible streak of pain that nearly undid Jerry. Nausea roiled in his stomach, and a humming sound filled his ears. Time to pound that final nail in the coffin.

"I'm sorry. I got cold feet and I... I slept with you, but...." His voice quavered. "It was a mistake. I hope you can forgive me."

A hard, unwelcoming mask clicked into place on Rex's face right before Jerry's eyes.

"Okay." Rex turned and left the office and Jerry alone with his misery.

A WEEK later, and there had been no further contact from Rex. Keith had texted a few times, but Jerry had yet to respond. He was back in his apartment and performing his pre-Ty routine of work and solitude. He'd argued with his mother that he needed to pack and refused her offer to hire someone to do it for him. He figured he could stretch the move out a couple more weeks. His mother had only agreed since an entire wing of the mansion was currently being redecorated for Jerry and his future husband. Jerry would hate every bit of what his mother chose, but what he wanted didn't matter.

One night as he sat in the silence of his apartment, still spending too much time thinking of Rex, a knock on the door startled him. That was nothing to the shock of seeing his father at the door. Jerry invited him in.

"I see you've done some packing." His father surveyed the room. He was in human form, sans his horns or tail. Jerry had seen him plenty of times without them, but still, the lack of his father's demon attributes was strange to see.

Jerry moved a box from a chair and offered his father a seat. In the four years he'd lived in the apartment, his father had shown up maybe twice. Each time, he'd been on a mission from his wife.

"Mom send you?"

His father shook his head. "No. I wanted to check up on you."

That only increased Jerry's nervousness. "I'm good." *Good as I can be without a heart.* He'd sloughed that painful sucker off weeks ago.

His father gave him a skeptical look. "Are you sure? Since the dinner party, you haven't been yourself. Are you sleeping?"

"Yeah, sleeping good." Better than good. After work yesterday, he'd crashed at seven and slept all night. Depression was wonderful that way.

His father shifted in his seat. "I understand the stress of what's happening. The fears and the uncertainty of having someone chosen for you." When he paused, Jerry remained silent. "Marriage is a huge step. And to marry someone you don't know, well, that can be… nauseating." Jerry cracked a smile, as did his father. "I threw up three times on my wedding day."

"Seriously?" Jerry chuckled.

His father's smile widened. "Yes, but once your mother and I were married, and we got to know each other, I found my parents had made a good choice for me. I'm hoping the same for you."

Jerry picked at a thread on his pants to avoid reacting negatively. He doubted his relationship with Ty would get any better.

"Did something happen when you were alone with Tyranis? Something that made you run?"

Jerry closed his eyes. Here was his chance to tell his father what a fake Ty was, the chance to try and get out of the arranged marriage. The chance to return to Rex. And he held that hope for all of fifteen seconds.

"Just freaked out, Dad. It's good now." Jerry hoped his forced smile would pass his father's scrutiny. He didn't want to disappoint him.

The charade worked. His father smiled and slapped his thigh. "Okay, then. I'm taking you out to dinner."

Jerry could have eaten a horse he was so hungry.

THE NEXT few weeks passed too quickly, and with the help of Keith and Marco, Jerry cleared out his apartment and moved back home. Keith was back to his old self (though strangely absent for long periods of time) and finally, at Jerry's insistence, he'd stopped talking about Rex. Despite that request, Jerry still yearned to know how his first lover was doing, to hear that he was okay. Jerry's missing heart still mysteriously broke at the thought of never seeing Rex again. Apparently, it wasn't missing, as Jerry had hoped.

The nausea that had started the day after he'd left Rex hung on. Thankfully, there were times when Jerry was hungry, so he wasn't losing weight. His mother finally stopped commenting about his mood and asking what bothered him because he'd denied anything was wrong every time. Each day he did the best he could, and that's all they could ask of him.

That night at the dinner table, the topic of conversation turned to Ty, and Jerry stuffed his mouth with linguine to suppress his negative comments. His parents spoke about Ty and his family, and their importance in the community where they lived. Ty had a successful business, and was competent, intelligent, levelheaded, and would make an excellent ruler. Throughout all their praise, Jerry gritted his teeth and bore every single word with self-restraint. He'd escape as soon as dessert was served.

As the dinner plates were cleared, Jerry tried to bow out, stating he didn't want dessert, but his mother shattered his plans into fine, inescapable dust.

"Tyranis will be here at seven tonight," his mother declared with an unconvincing show of innocence.

Oh hell.

Jerry's eyes could have popped out of his head. His father nodded, as if to punctuate the truth of her statement.

His mother sipped her coffee. "He wanted to talk to you, and possibly soothe some of your nerves. Now would be the time to apologize. He's making a great effort to come and see you after your behavior at the party."

Jerry heaved a dramatic sigh. "Why didn't you tell me this earlier?"

The are-you-kidding-me look his mother gave him was anything but subtle. "This way you don't have a chance to run."

Jerry lowered his head, the low blow hitting hard. "I would've agreed to meet with him. He *is* my future husband." Gods, he'd never get used to calling the asshole his husband.

"I'm glad to hear it," she said with a genuine smile. "You have enough time to change into something more presentable. He'll be here in twenty minutes."

Jerry continued to grind his teeth the entire time he changed his clothes, combed his hair, and brushed his teeth—which was hard to do when gritting them. The action continued as he waited in the sitting room for his future husband to show up. Gods, he hoped Ty didn't make a scene about their first meeting. He hoped the man would come, confirm Jerry would obey him, and then leave. Although, that would mean Ty had forgotten about the friggin' blowjob he'd been denied the last time. Not a chance.

The french doors opened, and Marco showed Ty into the sitting room. When the doors closed, Jerry was once again alone with Ty.

A scowl appeared on his fiancé's face. "If it isn't the runner." Ty clasped his hands behind his back.

Nope. Nothing about this was going to be easy. Jerry would pay for leaving.

"Listen," Jerry said, but Ty raised his hand and shushed Jerry.

Fucking *shushed* him. Jerry struggled to keep the disgust from his face.

"I'm not sure you know who you're dealing with here, but I will *not* tolerate the kind of behavior you've been allowed in the past." Ty stepped closer to Jerry. He appeared to grow larger as he neared. The menacing glare, the stiff posture, the tick in his jaw, raised alarm bells in Jerry's mind. He braced his legs to keep from stepping back and showing his submission, because that was what Ty wanted—his complete and total submission. "You *will* do whatever I tell you to do. You *will* follow directions. You *will* follow the rules I set. You *will* behave like the mature adult you should be. I haven't gotten this far to be made a fool of by some whiny little shit." Ty's large palm rested on the front of Jerry's neck, his thumb and fingers wrapping around the sides. Ty's grip was firm and tight, and came with an ominous warning. "And if making sure you stay in line requires a firm hand, I have no qualms about going there."

Jerry's body tensed as the air in his chest froze, stagnating in his lungs. His future husband had just told him that if he didn't obey, he was about to become a statistic. And Jerry had no doubt Ty would beat the shit out of him every time he said or did the wrong thing. If that were true, Jerry would be fucking bruised every single day of his life.

Ty released Jerry's throat and stepped back, opening the front of his pants. He smirked with the knowledge of the power he believed he now had over Jerry. "If I recall correctly, you still owe me a blowjob."

Jerry bit hard on the inside of his cheek, bringing tears to his eyes. His refusal would be painful, so he knelt, praying he didn't throw up all over the man's expensive leather shoes. The anger roiling in his gut rose, and he wanted nothing more than to bite down on the disgusting piece of meat once it entered his mouth. If only his mother or father would walk in and see what Jerry was being forced to do. No doubt Ty would smooth-talk himself out of any accusation Jerry made anyway. In the end, everything would be Jerry's fault.

Jerry closed his eyes to convince his mind he was going to suck Rex's cock, but the anger buzzed over his nerves and filled that emptiness in his chest, as if it was a living, breathing entity too large to be contained within his skin. He sucked in several deep breaths and raised his chin, glaring at Ty.

When his fiancé narrowed his eyes, Jerry didn't back down. He'd had enough. Fuck tradition and his responsibilities. He wasn't going to be anyone's punching bag. He had to do something now. Ty merely glared back with the smugness of someone who thought he ruled the world, but his rule over Jerry was ending. No way would he submit again to this douche bag.

"How's this for a rule?" Jerry snarled as he stood. "You will never, ever lay a hand on me again, because if you do, I will end you. I'm not going to be your fucking little bitch for the rest of my life. I don't give a shit *who* you think you are."

Ty took a menacing step forward, and Jerry threw his hands up into a boxing stance, ready to take on his future husband. If he didn't stand his ground now, he'd never get the respect he deserved.

Ty chuckled through a tight sneer. "Do you seriously think you can take me on? You're nothing but a fucking pansy." He growled and gave Jerry a disapproving once-over.

Jerry's anger caught hold of his brain, and he charged. Before he could swing, Ty snagged Jerry's shirt and shoved him hard in the chest. Jerry stumbled back, his shirt ripped open as Ty's hands held tight, the buttons flying into the air. Flailing to remain on balance, Jerry hit his leg on the wrought-iron coffee table and tumbled backward. He hit his back on the sharp corner of the table, sending a painful spasm up his spine and seizing his chest. He landed sprawled on his back, his shirt open, exposing his chest and stomach. Damn, he liked that shirt.

"Oh, my fucking gods!" Ty stalked toward Jerry, a fire of ten thousand angry demons in his eyes. "You're pregnant!"

CHAPTER 9

PREGNANT? JERRY shook his head at the allegation. The buzzing in his head sounded like thousands of wasps hovering in the air, waiting to attack. Ty pointed to Jerry's stomach, and when Jerry looked down, he gasped. *Holy shit.* A thin, dark red line ran from the bottom of his chest, down the middle of his stomach and under the waistband of his jeans. In an Anzuni, that line only meant one thing: he was pregnant. Had that telltale sign been there that morning? Jerry had overslept and rushed his shower to get to work on time. Even so, he would have remembered seeing something so shocking. So damning. Fuck.

Jerry's back ached and his head hurt, but he focused on being pregnant and only one person could be the father—Rex. The smile that spread across his face quickly faded. He was a demon, and Rex was human. A human who would freak when he learned what Jerry was, and that he was a pregnant male.

"You fucking whore!" Ty bent and grabbed Jerry by the flaps of his open shirt, no doubt ready to yank him off the ground and beat him.

Before he could succeed, the door to the sitting room crashed open, and Marco and Jerry's father ran in, followed by Jerry's terrified mother.

"I'm sorry! I'm sorry! I didn't mean for it to happen. I'm so sorry."

"Get your hands off my son." His father's voice filled the room as Marco grabbed Ty around the shoulders and forced the enraged man away from Jerry.

"What in the name of the gods is going on? Did he hit you, Jerry?" His father rarely ever showed his anger, and when he did, it was some scary shit.

Jerry could only stare at his father, unable to speak, terrified by what was happening. His mother raised her hand to her mouth. Oh yeah, she'd seen it.

Ty struggled against Marco. "Your whore of a son is pregnant!"

The shock and surprise in his father's face mirrored that of his mother.

The shaking started in Jerry's arms and quickly filled his body. He was about to fly into a million pieces.

Enraged past reason, Ty continued his rant. "I will not stand for this insubordination. You will abort that child immediately and remain in this house under lock and key until our wedding!" Ty practically foamed at the mouth, veins sticking out of his neck, his rage turning his face bright red.

His father's brow rose and he pursed his lips. "Last I checked, I'm the king of this clan, and I will be the one giving the orders. You will not disrespect me or my family in this house. Marco, put him in the dining room. I will be there shortly. Tyranis, you are to stay there until I come to speak with you."

Jerry's father wore his ruler face, and Ty seemed to understand his king meant business.

Ty's body relaxed visibly, but the scowling disgust remained. "Yes, Sire." He turned to leave, followed closely by Marco.

"Oh, and Marco, call the doctor to check on my son, please."

Marco bowed his head as he closed the doors.

Jerry curled in on himself. As the shock wore off, the pain in his back flared, and the buzzing in his head increased. He'd fucked up big-time. No one was going to be able to get him out of this mess.

His father's hand settled on his shoulder. "Are you hurt?" he asked softly.

"My back. I hit the corner of the coffee table when I fell." Jerry's voice shook, and he dragged in a deep breath, which only served to spike his pain.

"Did he push you?" His father's voice was a low growl.

Jerry wanted to say no because he'd charged Ty and the man had merely reacted, but he didn't want to get into everything that had happened. He nodded instead.

His father's jaw ticked. "Okay. First, let's get you off the floor and onto the sofa. Then you will tell me everything."

Jerry gazed up into his father's tense face. "I'm so sorry, Dad. I know I fucked up big-time. I'll do whatever you say to fix it. I promise."

His father's eyes clouded, and he gave Jerry a tight nod. It was more than Jerry had hoped for from the ruler. Slipping an arm under

Jerry's shoulder, his father gently lifted him to a sitting position. Jerry hissed as the pain ran into his lower back. That sound seemed to propel his mother into action. She rushed to set up pillows on the couch. Jerry stood with his father's help, and was lowered gently against the cushions, shifting until the pain receded into a dull ache. His mother laid a blanket over his legs and patted his arm.

His father sat on the coffee table across from Jerry and leaned forward with his elbows on his knees. The myriad of emotions racing over his face were intense. "Who's the father of your child, Jerricho?"

A shot of pain to rival that in his back hit Jerry square in the chest as he thought of Rex. He spilled everything to his parents—Rex, the night at the bar, his need to lose his virginity to someone who cared, and even his attack on Ty. When he was done, tears coursed down not only his cheeks, but his mother's as well.

She clutched at the pearls she wore around her neck. "This is our fault, Evin."

His father nodded sorrowfully.

Jerry frowned and looked between them. "No, it's not. I'm the one who screwed up. This is all on me."

His father shook his head. "We thought you needed someone who was strong and forthright, who could guide you, be your partner in ruling. Tyranis is self-confident, commanding. And—we thought—the perfect person to rule by your side. How could we have been so wrong?" His father rose. "I'm going to speak with him." With that, he left the room, and Jerry was alone with his mother.

"Oh, Jerricho." She sighed, but before she could continue, the doctor entered the room.

Dr. Likovitzka commenced examining Jerry. He asked forthright questions about Jerry's pain. He told Jerry his back was bruised, and he'd require a few days of rest. The doctor confirmed the pregnancy, leaving a questioning air, but didn't ask for details, except the approximate date of conception. That was an easy answer. When he informed the doctor that the father was human, his estimate for the due date wasn't set in stone. Anzuni gestational periods lasted around four months, but human DNA tended to lengthen the time.

"I've had female patients who've been impregnated by humans. Of course, you're the first male. Going by what I know of those pregnancies, I'd say your pregnancy will last closer to five months. Other than that, all were normal pregnancies. In about two weeks, you'll start to feel the baby move."

Jerry raised an eyebrow.

The doctor cocked his head impatiently. "Haven't you learned about Anzuni pregnancy yet?"

Jerry's mother pursed her lips, as if Jerry's lack of info was a direct reflection on her.

Jerry merely shook his head.

The doctor sighed. "As you may or may not know, Anzuni babies are carried in the upper abdomen, close to the belly button, which of course doesn't have the same origin as what humans have. In Anzuni, this is the *venanzis*, which is the Anzuni birthing spot."

That was something all Anzuni knew, even Jerry.

"Anzuni babies grow in a sac that's like an extra skin covering the baby in utero, kind of like a full body suit. The baby is close to major organs, and movements can be felt early in the pregnancy."

"Oh." Jerry hadn't known that part.

Jerry's mother looked concerned. "And the children who were part human? I mean, were they more human than Anzuni?" It was as if she believed keeping the child was a possibility. The thought of aborting Rex's child clawed his insides raw.

The doctor started to pack his satchel as he spoke. "Some have the Anzuni horns and tail, and some do not. There's no telling until the child is born. Of course, the mating of a royal male and a human has never occurred, so I have no information about how that will affect the passing of the powers in the royal line."

What does it matter? Can't control them anyway. He didn't give that thought voice. His mother would have something to say about that.

"I'll be sending over supplements for you to take daily. For the pain in your back, nothing more than an over-the-counter painkiller. Ice, as well, for twenty minutes every hour. I'll need to see you in two weeks to check on the pregnancy."

Jerry's mother rose with the doctor, following him as he left the room. "Thank you, Milnor, and as always your complete discretion will be deeply appreciated."

In other words, keep your mouth shut about our idiot son and his mistake. Jerry didn't want his child to be a mistake. He wanted the baby he'd made with Rex, and for them to be a family. A fairy tale for sure.

Jerry closed his eyes and rubbed his stomach, drifting off into a sleep, where he could momentarily escape the mess his life had become.

A NOISE next to Jerry forced him to open his eyes. He still lay on the couch in the sitting room. When he turned his head, he found Keith sitting on the coffee table. He should have been at work.

"Heard you got yourself knocked up." Keith appeared slightly amused.

Jerry groaned and rubbed his palms over his face, wincing as pain pulsed in his back. Nothing had changed. "What're you doing here?"

Keith turned his cell phone over in his hands. "Your father called me last night."

Damn, Jerry had slept on the couch all night. "Why?"

"Well, he knows I'm your best friend, and you might want to talk or something. I don't know, Jer. I mean, you've pretty much ignored me for weeks."

There was a hint of anger in Keith's voice, but mostly Jerry noticed strain in his words.

"I'm sorry." Hadn't he been saying that a lot lately. "I haven't been dealing with all of this very well."

Keith barked a laugh. "Obviously." He cocked his head. "Your father wanted to know how to contact Rex."

"You didn't tell him, did you?"

Keith shook his head. Thank the gods for his friend's loyalty.

Jerry groaned. "I got pregnant from a one-night stand."

"What're you going to do?" Keith chewed on his bottom lip. Keith would want him to do the impossible.

Jerry shrugged. "Don't know. I'm still waiting for that information. I fell asleep last night before my father could tell me."

Keith averted his eyes. Usually that meant he was going to say something to which Jerry would balk. "Fuck, Jerry. I don't know what happened between you two, but Rex is like a walking zombie. Except when he's ripping the heads off the guys on the job. He's miserable and cranky. I think you tore his heart out. I had no idea you two were so close. Whenever I try to talk to him, he shakes his head and walks away. He.... Why couldn't this work out for both of you? Damn, he's the father of your kid."

The word "father" flipped Jerry's stomach. "And what should I tell him, Keith? 'Oh, hey, Rex, I'm a demon prince, and by the way, you're going to be a father. Surprise!' He'd run screaming."

"Well, he's into all of that mythology crap. He might think it's cool. One good thing, though, you don't have to marry that asshole anymore." Keith's relief was apparent in his voice.

"What?" Had he heard correctly?

Keith's mouth formed an O. "Oops. Guess I let the cat out of the bag."

"What.... I don't understand." He didn't have to marry Ty?

"You won't be marrying Tyranis." His father came around the couch and gazed down at Jerry. His expression was tight. "Any man who raises their hand to my son, and uses threats and violence, is not worthy of you. Why didn't you tell me what was happening before this escalated?"

Jerry struggled not to avert his gaze. "I've screwed up so much. I didn't want to disappoint you with something that was so important to you and the clan."

His father let out a huge sigh and pushed Keith over to sit across from Jerry. "I don't care how important something is, Jerricho. If someone is hurting you or threatening to hurt you, I want you to tell me. Is that understood?"

Jerry nodded, still embarrassed by the shame he'd brought to his family.

"You're more important to us than all the tradition and customs we have. I admit, as a race, we tend to take them more seriously than we should, but out of necessity. We've assimilated into another culture, and it's easy to lose your own traditions under those circumstances."

And hadn't Jerry done that? Taken what had been traditions for millennia and shit all over them? "I'm sorry, Dad. Tell me what to do."

His father shook his head. "I've spoken with your mother, and as king, I have the right to tell you what to do, but as your father.... This is your mess, and you're going to have to decide how to clean it up."

No fucking way.

Jerry's panic rose. "I don't understand. What do you want *me* to do?" Jerry needed his father to make the decisions, because they were too important for Jerry to make. They involved not only himself, but his family, his entire race, and Rex, who he cared about too much to continue hurting him.

"Jerricho, listen to me. What you've done is going to cause a huge uproar in the clan. As we speak, I'm confident Tyranis will tell everyone how he was wronged by your becoming pregnant by another man when you were engaged to be married to him. While some people may understand, others will be angry and turn on you."

His father's words didn't help, and Jerry's stomach tied into a tighter knot as the ensuing panic threatened his ability to cope.

"But know this, son. No matter what mistakes you make, your mother and I love you. Yes, you have messed up in the past, but the result this time is a life inside of you. Every Anzuni life is precious. Whatever you decide to do concerning this child, we will support you as parents should... and as proud grandparents should, as well."

The happy glint in his father's eyes, and the gentle smile on his face, comforted Jerry. No matter what, his parents would accept his baby. That went a long way to calming Jerry's frazzled nerves.

His father's smile faded into a gentle nostalgia as he leaned closer to Jerry. "The happiest day of my life was giving birth to you. My greatest role hasn't been as king. It's been as your father. Now, you have to decide if you're going to deny the father of your child that experience."

"But he's human. If I told him, I'd be risking the secret of our existence." Jerry didn't want that responsibility on his head.

"Other Anzuni have taken human mates, and they've kept our secret once they learned we were demons," Keith pointed out.

"That's different. What if Rex…." He let out a deep breath.

"You're not concerned about the secrets of the Anzuni. You're worried that he'll reject you." Keith pointed his finger at Jerry. "That's a chance you're going to have to take. If you don't, well, you still won't have him, so there's nothing to lose by telling."

"Keith is right." Jerry's father snorted. "Never thought I'd say that."

Keith sat taller and smiled smugly. "Of course I'm right."

Jerry rolled his eyes.

"Whatever you decide, I will be here to help facilitate what Anzuni law dictates."

Jerry smiled gratefully at his father, who kissed his forehead and left the room.

"So, what're you going to do?" Leave it to Keith to push the point.

Rex would never understand. There was no way Jerry could tell him without negative consequences. He'd screwed up big-time.

CHAPTER 10

JERRY WAS stuck in the house for a week because of his back injury. During that time, he gave notice at work that he'd be leaving the job he loved. Annabelle could easily move into his position, so he only gave a week's notice. The thought of leaving the library and what he considered "his books" increased the nausea that had come and gone without notice. A nagging reminder of what he'd gained and lost. He tried to convince himself that having Rex's child was enough. In reality, Jerry was too chickenshit to tell the man who he was, and that he was having their baby. At least this way he didn't have to deal with rejection.

Once he was done with work for good, and when his mother wasn't harassing him about his future, Jerry spent most of his time in his room or in the sitting room. He needed the space, the time to think and decide what was best for him and his child. Meanwhile, the clan gossiped about his pregnancy, and the council pressured his father to know what Jerry would do now that the wedding had been called off. There were council talks about who would be the best choice to take Tyranis's place as Jerry's husband, despite him being an unfaithful mate. That comment had been kind compared to the others said without knowledge Jerry could hear. Most he ignored. One, though, pissed him off. Two council members had spoken outside of the sitting room, unaware Jerry listened. They extolled their good fortune that, despite the illegitimate child, any Anzuni would marry a whore if one day they'd become king. They were gone before Jerry had made it to the doors. If there had been an Anzuni gossip rag equivalent to the *Enquirer,* Jerry's face would have been plastered all over the cover weekly.

The highlights of his monotonous days were when Keith visited every few days after work. Those times almost felt as they had been pre-pregnancy. Watching movies, playing video games, eating tons of junk food. It would have been perfect had Keith not been so distracted

69

and fidgety. He couldn't sit still. Often when Jerry spoke, Keith wouldn't hear a word he'd said. Finally, Jerry had enough.

Jerry threw down the controller in the middle of a game. "Okay, spill."

Keith yelped as the mutant aliens Jerry's soldier had held off descended, and decapitated Keith's soldier. He scowled. "What the hell, Jerry? You can't desert a man when he's facing mutant aliens." His scowl turned into a pout. "It's not right. It violates the bro code—"

"What isn't right is the way you've been acting the past few weeks. You're jumpy and fidgety and don't even hear half of what I say."

"Do too." Keith avoided Jerry's gaze.

"You do not."

"I hear everything you say." Still no eye contact. When proving a point, even when he was wrong, Keith would get in the person's face.

Jerry gave Keith his smug look. "Oh yeah? What did I say I wanted to name this baby if it was a boy?"

Keith's brow rose and his gaze darted around.

"You don't know because you *weren't* listening!"

"So what! And nothing's wrong… with me." Keith's words had trailed off.

Jerry was right, and a horrible thought came to him. "You're back with Nicola, aren't you? Dammit, Keith. She's gonna—"

"No. Haven't seen her since that night at Jack's. She's called, but I haven't called her back. You're right. She's evil."

While Jerry should have been thrilled to hear that, Keith wasn't acting like himself. "You know you can tell me anything, right? I promise not to laugh or call you an idiot or anything."

Keith stared at Jerry, but he couldn't read Keith's thoughts.

Keith heaved out a breath. "Yeah, okay. Something's been *up* for weeks, but you've been too wrapped up in your shit to notice." Keith glared at Jerry.

Ouch.

Jerry rubbed his forehead. He'd been a shitty friend lately. "You're right. I'm sorry, but I'm here now."

Keith snorted. "I'm always right."

Jerry waited. He had little patience lately. Must be the pregnancy. Fuck, he was an unwed pregnant Anzuni prince. He needed to get a grip and focus on Keith. "So?"

Keith fiddled with his controller, and Jerry swore he saw panic cross his face. "I… um… I've been seeing someone." His words were weak. Maybe he hoped Jerry wouldn't hear.

Seeing someone? Wasn't that a good thing? "Who is she?"

Keith rolled his shoulders. What was the big deal? It wasn't Nicola, so—

"He."

Jerry's shock stunned him mute for a moment. "Wait. Did you say *he*?" Keith had never been with a guy. He'd always been a man slut around women.

Keith nodded sheepishly. "Yeah. Remember the guy from the club?"

Jerry frowned, and then his brain caught up. "That big bear from the club who grabbed you?"

Red crept up Keith's neck and into his cheeks.

Holy shit. It was. "Keith, you're not gay… are you?" It was a dumb question, but it had popped out.

He shrugged. "I went home with him… for two days straight."

Again, speechless.

"And we've been seeing each other a lot since the bar." A look of adoration came to Keith's face. The warm fuzzy smile that followed touched Jerry.

"So you're like, in a relationship?"

Keith was stolid for a moment, and nodded slightly.

"You waited over a month to tell me? This is huge, Keith, like me being pregnant huge. I mean… so does this mean you're gay?"

Keith ducked his head. "I don't know what it means." Keith's voice broke as he spoke.

For god's sake, Jerry, quit berating him.

"You really like this guy."

Keith huffed, shaking his head incredulously. "I do. It's different for me being with Gunn than with a girl. With girls, I was never

71

comfortable, wasn't able to connect. It all seemed so hard. This is just easier. It's like I finally found the secret to it, you know?"

Jerry didn't because he'd known he was gay since he was eleven. "Sounds gay to me." Jerry chuckled as Keith chucked a pillow at him.

"Son of a Braezelas."

"Hey, language. You know I'm happy for you." The fact that this thing lasted a month was amazing. Except for Nicola, Keith's relationships never lasted longer than a week.

Keith's smile brightened. "Yeah. And now I see why you like sucking cock."

Jerry cringed and made a gagging noise. "I can't believe you said that. TMI."

Keith let out an evil laugh. Back to his old self except for the being alone part. Even Keith had someone. Jerry didn't. But did he have to be alone? If he told Rex, he'd freak, maybe punch Jerry in the face. Maybe he'd go all Greek mythology and eviscerate Jerry or cut his head off. All of those would be kinder than hearing Rex say he wanted nothing to do with Jerry or his demon spawn.

Jerry felt nauseous again. Something jerked in his stomach. He frowned. Another jerk and a jump. Jerry gasped loudly. Was that…? No, that couldn't be what it felt like? He waited and nothing happened. The doctor had said it was possible, but he hadn't thought….

"You're white as a ghost. Are you okay?" Keith walked to the bed.

"No!" Jerry threw off his blanket and sat up despite the pain in his back. "Rex is going to hate me."

"Does that mean you're going to tell him?"

Jerry raked his hand through his hair. He looked at his stomach, resting his hand on it. He closed his eyes, picturing Rex smiling wide, his hand resting on Jerry's growing belly, laughing as the baby kicked. They'd created a life, a child who was a part of each of them. He grabbed his laptop and opened the lid, where Rex's picture was still up on the screen. Would their child have reddish hair and green sparkling eyes? Rex had told Jerry that his parents were his only family, and they were in their seventies. Rex deserved to know his child, even if he wanted nothing to do with Jerry.

"Jerry?" Keith hovered over him.

"Yeah, I'm going to tell him. It's his kid too."

Before he lost his nerve, he picked up his phone and called Rex. Keith watched him like a hawk. With each ring, Jerry's hopes fell. Rex's voice said to leave a message. The deep voice ran a bolt of electricity through Jerry. He closed his eyes and waited for the beep.

"Hi, Rex. It's Jerry. Could you call me back? I have something I need to tell you. It's important. Please, call me."

Jerry hung up, and Keith smiled, but the gesture didn't calm Jerry's racing heart.

"He'll call." Keith looked convinced.

Jerry wasn't so sure.

SEVEN DAYS. Seven days of sleepless nights and distracted days, and there had been no word from Rex. Keith tried to intervene, approaching Rex on site, but he refused to talk about anything concerning Jerry. Jerry had permanently alienated the man he loved. Still, he had to find a way to tell Rex about the baby, but the question was how. A letter was too impersonal, and there was no guarantee he'd read it. Jerry turned down his father's offer of sending guards to bring (more like force) Rex to the house. Not the way to start an important conversation, which was why Jerry waited by Rex's Harley for him to leave work.

He didn't have to wait long. Rex rounded the backhoe, his head down, approaching Jerry. Jerry's heart was close to exploding. Seeing Rex again warmed his chest, cleared all doubt in his mind that what he felt for the foreman was real. Rex was as beautiful as Jerry remembered. He clenched his hands together to stop the shaking. Panic shredded his stomach. When Rex looked up, Jerry held his breath.

Rex halted and stared at Jerry. His face slipped from surprise to stony nothingness in seconds. He continued walking. When he reached his hog, he nodded to Jerry without speaking.

"Hey, Rex." Jerry's voice cracked. *Dammit.*

Rex unhooked his helmet from the bike. "Hey."

That was it. Well, what did Jerry expect? A hug?

"I've been calling you. Left messages. Not sure if you got them."

"I got 'em." Rex's flat tone flayed away more pieces of Jerry's hope. This was a mission for their child, and Jerry had to accept he had no hope with Rex. The need to flee rose from the pit of Jerry's gut. He was good at running. He should run.

Before he could move, he felt the familiar jump in his stomach, as if the baby reminded him of his task. Their child deserved to know both of his fathers. Except, in the parking lot at the construction site wasn't the place to inform Rex of his impending parenthood.

"I… I know you don't want to talk to me. I hurt you and I'm sorry. Things got messed up. *I* got messed up."

Rex's body stiffened, but he appeared to listen.

Jerry rubbed his palm over his stomach, as if that would increase his courage. Where to start? Forced marriage seemed safe. "I was supposed to marry this guy my parents picked for me. It's a tradition with my people."

Rex cocked an eyebrow. "Your people?"

Shoot, not good. "I'll get to that in a minute." His hands sweated and his throat tightened. He needed to get the words out before Rex got sick of listening. "This guy my parents chose for me to marry. I met him the night we were at the Blue Moon, and I—"

"Wait. Your parents picked someone for you to marry, and you only met him a month ago and have to marry him because your parents say so?" Rex's disgust was a step up from indifference.

"Yeah. But I don't have to marry him anymore."

Rex's confused expression threatened to pull a laugh from Jerry, although it would have sounded like a high-pitched *hee-haw*.

"He was kind of an asshole. He threatened to hit me if I didn't do what he said. Instead, he, um… he ended up pushing me backward over a table when I refused to do what he wanted." Embarrassed, Jerry lowered his head.

A long silence filled with the noise of the traffic from the main road.

"Did he hurt you?" The guttural sound of Rex's voice made Jerry think his confession had angered Rex. Or it was more of a social justice type of thing Rex felt deeply about, like coercion through violence was bad or something?

"Did he hurt you?"

Jerry shifted uncomfortably. The large purple bruise had taken weeks to disappear. "Not bad. Bruised my back, but he's gone."

Rex studied Jerry's face, as if looking for something. Rex sighed heavily. "So you met this guy, and he was an ass to you, so you decided to get back at him by sleeping with me?"

Those words cut deep to the bone.

"What? No. I…." Jerry raked his hair back, pulling until a sharp pain stopped him. Should he tell Rex? Gods, it was as if his heart had spilled out onto the floor. He sighed. "I wanted my first time to be with someone that I cared for." He'd whispered the words, but from the stunned look on Rex's face, he'd heard every word.

"First time?" The darkness in Rex's eyes lightened.

Jerry laughed nervously. "Yeah. I was a twenty-four-year-old virgin, and you were my first time. I'd never had sex before you. Not even a blowjob. Never been touched by anyone else." He shrugged. "The whole tradition thing, you know."

Rex's mouth hung open, rendered speechless. Oh, he hadn't heard anything yet.

Rex set his helmet down on the seat of his hog and circled around the bike, stopping about half a foot from Jerry. He tilted his chin down and cocked his head to the side. Jerry swore the corner of Rex's lips twitched.

"That was damn good for your first time." The rough tone caught Jerry's breath. When Rex smirked, Jerry's body relaxed slightly, and he managed to smile… until he felt that familiar jump.

I'm getting there, kid.

He ran his palm over his stomach again, and Rex looked quizzically at the action.

"You keep rubbing at your stomach. You feeling okay?" Rex's tone showed concern.

I'm pregnant with your child.

"I'm okay. Nervous about coming here. I wanted you to know how sorry I am. I was wrong for using you like I did, and for running away without explaining…. I'm sorry for… everything. I understand if you can't forgive me, but I have something I need to tell you. It's important."

75

Rex nodded. "Go ahead."

Jerry scanned the empty parking lot, but still, they were at a construction site. "Can you come back to my place? Please? I know I don't have any right to ask you for anything, but I promise, once you listen to what I have to say, you can leave."

Rex looked out over the parking lot, appearing to battle with himself. After several stressful moments, he said, "I have to shower first, and then I'll be there." Rex picked up his helmet, and Jerry stopped him.

"I don't have my apartment anymore. I moved back in with my parents. It's part of the whole tradition thing."

Rex pulled out his phone. "Okay, give me the address."

Once he had the information, Rex pulled his helmet on and started up his hog. He looked to Jerry and had a partial smile on his face. Jerry dared to smile back and even wave as Rex fired up his bike. Jerry headed home to wait for Rex.

JERRY BURST through the front door and almost ran into Marco.

"Sire, what's wrong? Is it the baby?" Marco looked at Jerry's stomach with alarm.

Jerry raised his hands. "He's coming. I need everyone to clear out. No one can be here. He's coming, and you all have to leave." Jerry's words spilled out into a tangled pile at his feet.

Marco grasped Jerry's shoulder. "Who's coming, Sire?"

Jerry practically vibrated out of his skin.

"The baby daddy." Keith emerged from the kitchen hallway, carrying a huge sandwich on a plate. "So, did you tell him?"

Jerry shook his head. "I told him about the arranged marriage, and the asshole, and...." Gods, he'd been embarrassed so many times, what was one more? "And that he was my first time."

Keith grinned. "Smart move. I bet that's what got him to come over here. What guy doesn't want a virgin?"

Marco gave Keith a look of exasperation.

"Hey, I'm not a virgin anymore." Jerry remembered they had to leave. "You all need to go. I need to talk to Rex alone. This is going to freak him out enough without an audience. Where're my parents?"

"They're dining at the Howells'. They won't return for a couple of hours," Marco said, appearing uneasy with the entire situation. "Sire, have you spoken with your father about this?"

Jerry nodded impatiently. "He said I should tell Rex. Said he deserved to know."

"I was there." Keith spoke around what looked to be a large bite of ham sandwich in his mouth. "And I'm not going anywhere." Jerry narrowed his eyes, knowing Keith would be more of a hindrance than a help. "Well, I'm not. What if he gets pissed and tries to beat the crap out of you?"

"Rex wouldn't do that."

He hoped.

"Keith's right, Sire."

"As always."

Another scowl at Keith. Marco appeared to be two seconds away from flattening Jerry's friend. Instead, he huffed. "Sire, someone needs to be nearby." Marco squeezed Jerry's shoulder, and the imploring look on his face forced Jerry to nod in agreement.

"Okay. But you both have to stay in the game room." Far enough away that they couldn't hear and close enough that Jerry could reach them if he needed to.

"You don't need to ask me twice. Challenge you to a game of pool, Marco." Keith turned and headed for the hallway to the game room.

"Gladly," Marco called out. "What you're doing, Jerricho.... You're very brave."

Jerry shook his head. "Naw, I screwed up. Now I have to fix it."

Marco smiled warmly. "It's the bigger man who stands up and faces his mistakes and doesn't run away."

Jerry guffawed. "Oh, I've done plenty of running."

"It's what you're doing now that counts." With a final paternal pat on Jerry's arm, Marco left.

The silence caused Jerry to shiver as anxious energy zipped up and down his nerves. The baby took that moment to remind Jerry, once again, that he or she was there. Jerry smiled and patted his belly.

"I got this, little one. I'll make sure your daddy knows you're coming and that he's a part of your life. I may have screwed up my chances with him, but I'll make it right for you."

Another kick, and Jerry chuckled. The doorbell startled him. He sucked in a deep breath as he went to answer it. His stomach fluttered relentlessly. So nervous, yet he could barely repress his smile, caught up in the bliss of his pregnancy, sharing his joy with Rex.

Opening the door, he blinked.

Ty.

CHAPTER 11

"TY, WHAT do you—"

Ty's fist smashed into Jerry's cheek, snapping his head violently to the side. Stunned, his thoughts jumbled as the room spun. He flailed and stumbled back, barely managing to stay on his feet. As he regained his footing, Ty clutched his shirt, yanking him to him. Jerry yelled, but Ty cut him off with his hand over Jerry's mouth.

"You've made me the laughing stock of the entire clan. And I lost everything because of you. He... he took the only... the p-pers—" Ty appeared to give up speaking. He cocked his arm back, and Jerry threw up his hands, but Ty's fist connected with Jerry's jaw. With Ty's hand fisted in Jerry's shirt, he stayed in place for another punch to the side of the head. "It's all because of you!"

Jerry staggered when Ty released him, and crossed his arms over his belly. Through the haze of the beating, Jerry tried to protect Rex's baby. Why had he sent Keith and Marco into another part of the house? Pain filled his skull, and his vision grayed around the edges. He needed to get to the intercom by the front door. Lifting his knee sharply, he connected with Ty's groin.

"Fuck!" Ty bent over, groaning.

Jerry stepped back on wobbly legs as the entire room tilted. His vision doubled, causing him to walk a crooked line to the front door. Before he reached the intercom, Ty tackled him from behind. Jerry's stomach slammed into the tile floor. The sharp pain stole his breath.

Ty pummeled Jerry's back, each blow fueled by his rage and hatred. "It's your fault! I've lost everything that ever mattered to me!"

Jerry cried out. Ty wouldn't stop until his rage depleted. Both Jerry and his baby could be dead long before then. The man was past reason—beyond sanity. With each blow, the pain morphed, expanded, and then lessened. Jerry felt as if he floated. Anything was better than the bone-crunching, searing pain.

Ty continued to rant, but the intensity of his blows lessened. The weight disappeared from his back. Jerry laid his palms on the floor and pushed to get up. His arms gave out and he landed back on his stomach. Static crackled in his head, and his entire body throbbed like an exposed nerve. One more herculean effort and he was on his knees. He shuffled the remaining two feet to the door. With his last bit of strength, he slapped the red emergency button.

An alarm filled the house, and a voice came out of the speaker. "What's the emergency?"

"Help." Jerry fell forward onto his hands. As his arms quaked, he lowered himself to sit and lean against the wall.

"Security has been alerted," the voice said.

Jerry tried to focus on the movement in the room. His vision cleared enough to see Rex fighting with Ty.

"Rex," he whispered. Waves of agony shot through his gut, and terror he'd lose the baby seized his heart.

"What the fuck?" Keith slid into the room and ran to Jerry, kneeling beside him. "Oh, fuck, Jerry. Your face, you're bleeding everywhere. That son of a bitch." Keith went to get up, no doubt to kill Ty, but Jerry grabbed his arm. Hot tears stung his face as they fell. "The baby."

"Marco, I need help here!"

The gate guard ran through the open door, followed by two other guards. Marco had entered the foyer and directed them to where Ty and Rex fought, but Rex didn't need their help. His fist plowed into Ty's face once more, and the man went down like a rag doll and didn't move.

Rex rushed to Jerry and fell to his knees, eyes wide with fear. Marco yelled into the phone to someone, possibly the doctor.

Jerry grasped Rex's arm.

"Oh, god, Jerry." Rex raised his hand to touch Jerry's face, but hesitated. "Fuck, baby, what did he do?"

Another pain stabbed Jerry's gut. Something was terribly wrong. "The baby. I'm sorry I didn't tell you." Jerry squeezed Rex's hand as Keith wiped the blood on Jerry's chin.

"What baby? I don't understand." Rex took Jerry's hand. The gesture comforted him as his face throbbed with each heartbeat and the skin tightened as it swelled.

"Your baby, Rex. He's pregnant, and you're the father," Keith said without preamble.

Idiot.

Rex frowned deeply. "This isn't the time to joke around, Keith!"

Keith's expression said he was dead serious. "I'm not fucking joking, Rex! Jerry's the prince of the Anzuni demon clan, and that fuckhead who beat the crap out of him is pissed because Jerry got pregnant with another guy's kid, taking away his chance to be king one day. Now accept the fact you're going to be a daddy and help me lay him down."

Stunned, Rex didn't move. Jerry wasn't even sure he breathed. He touched Rex's cheek. "I'm so sorry."

Either the touch or Jerry's words snapped Rex out of it. He helped Jerry lie flat. Rex took the pillow Marco offered and placed it beneath Jerry's head. Marco remained nearby, cell phone to his ear, and Jerry's father's voice boomed through the phone.

Rex leaned over, his green eyes shiny. "Why didn't you tell me you're Anzuni?"

Jerry blinked.

"You know about Anzuni?" Keith stopped wiping Jerry's face.

Pain pounded incessantly in Jerry's head and dimmed his vision, threatening to pull him under, but he fought to keep his eyes open. It might have been wishful thinking, but the pain in his stomach seemed to subside.

"I've read about your race. You know how I like demon lore, but I had no idea that what I read was real, that they—you—existed." Rex ran his hand through Jerry's hair. "If you're pregnant, that means you're royalty."

Jerry nodded as Rex grasped his hand and lifted it to his mouth, placing gentle kisses on the knuckles. Jerry almost forgot the steady pulse of pain. All he cared about was keeping the life growing inside of him.

"It's your baby." Jerry tried to smile, but the swelling made it nearly impossible.

Rex rested his hand on Jerry's stomach. "Our baby." He smiled as wide as Jerry had imagined he would.

Keith disappeared, and Dr. Likovitzka knelt beside Jerry. He hadn't known he'd arrive. "Let me take a look, Your Highness. Are you feeling any tightening in your abdomen?"

"No. Just hurts. I landed on my stomach," Jerry said in a shaky voice. With two hundred pounds of fuckhead on his back.

The doctor placed the ends of his stethoscope into his ears and raised Jerry's shirt. Jerry flinched when the cold metal touched his stomach, but it warmed as the doctor listened to different parts of Jerry's stomach. When he finished listening, Dr. Likovitzka poked and pushed on Jerry's stomach, all the while frowning in silence. Jerry squeezed Rex's hand as his doctor hummed and continued his examination. Jerry's focus pinpointed on his doctor's face, waiting for any indication that the baby was okay or....

Don't think of the alternative.

The doctor sat back on his heels. "The baby's heart rate is strong and I can't feel any contractions, but that doesn't mean early labor couldn't start. We'll keep an eye on that. Most likely you've bruised your stomach, but I don't believe any harm has come to the baby."

Tears blurred Jerry's vision, and he looked up at Rex, and damned if he wasn't teary-eyed as well. Rex smiled and leaned down, pressing a gentle kiss on Jerry's lips. Jerry savored the feel, lifting his hand and setting it on the back of Rex's neck.

When Rex pulled back, he used his thumb to wipe at the tears on Jerry's face.

"I take it you're the baby's father?" the doctor asked.

Rex's breath visibly caught as he swallowed hard. A nod was all he managed. Fear made an appearance on his face, but then Rex grinned, and Jerry relaxed slightly.

The doctor rose. "I want to get Prince Jerricho into bed where I can give him a complete exam and monitor him for the next few hours. I can call the office and have a stretcher brought over."

"I've got him." Rex leaned down. "Tell me if I hurt you," he whispered.

Jerry raised his arms. Rex gently placed an arm behind his shoulders and another behind his knees, lifting Jerry from the floor. Jerry suppressed the whimper of pain as he laid his head on Rex's shoulder.

A bellow filled the entry, and Rex froze. Jerry's parents rushed to them, gasping at the sight of Jerry's bruised and swollen face.

His mother, in tears, touched his arm. "Oh, my baby." His mother might've been steeped in tradition and appearances, but when it mattered, she took on her mothering role.

"I'm okay. The baby is too." Jerry looked to Rex. "Mom and Dad, this is Rex. The father of your grandchild. Rex, this is King Evin and Queen Riah Trychovisca."

His mother and father both looked between Rex and Jerry, dumbfounded.

"Nice to meet you both... um... Your... Highnesses." There was a nervous twitch in Rex's voice.

"You told Rex about...." His father raised his eyebrows.

"About the baby, yes. And he knows we're Anzuni."

Jerry's father visibly flinched followed by a resigned sounding sigh.

"Your Highness, I must insist on getting Prince Jerricho somewhere I can examine him." Dr. Likovitzka's tone showed his impatience.

Jerry's father waved them on. "I'll be along shortly—after I deal with Tyranis."

Rex carried Jerry up the stairs and down the hall toward his bedroom. In Rex's arms, he'd never felt so safe and content, even with his face and entire skull throbbing incessantly.

"Damn, Jerry. Your face." Rex hugged him tighter.

Jerry gave a tight chuckle. "Hurts like a fucker."

Rex swallowed hard, and his jaw clenched. Rage flared in his eyes. "That asshole's lucky I didn't kill him."

It was Jerry's turn to swallow hard. "Thank you."

Rex nodded curtly. Jerry got the feeling Rex's anger over what Ty had done wouldn't fade anytime soon, judging by his expression.

"If I see him again, he won't be so lucky."

Not so good for Ty, although Jerry figured Ty's luck had already run out when he'd chosen to beat up a pregnant royal.

When they reached Jerry's room, Rex placed him on the bed. He sat next to him and pushed the hair from Jerry's forehead. "So. I'm going to be a daddy?"

"Yes."

Rex shook his head. "I can't believe any of this. It's so…."

Jerry held his breath. At first Rex had appeared happy with the news, but once the idea of a pregnant man with a demon baby sunk in, he might run.

"Awesome."

Jerry's grin tried to break out, but his swollen cheeks hindered the action. Dr. Likovitzka rushed into the room, followed by Jerry's mother and Marco, who carried a basin of water and several towels. Jerry stopped the doctor as he tried to get Rex to move. Jerry needed to know where he stood with the father of his child.

"I know I screwed up and you don't want to be with me, but I want you to be a part of our child's life. I want that if you can."

Rex took Jerry's hand and rubbed the back against his cheek. "This is a huge surprise. I mean, if you'd asked me yesterday what I thought the strangest thing that could happen to me…. Well, that wouldn't have even come close to what you've told me today. Yeah, I'm shocked, but I've wanted you since the first day I saw you on the work site. Why do you think I spent all those hours at the library?"

Jerry's mouth opened, then closed as he frowned.

"Because I wanted to get to know you, be close to you. Along the way, I fell hard for you. I wanted to tell you so many times."

Jerry touched Rex's arm. "Why didn't you say something?"

Rex shrugged. "I didn't think you'd be interested in someone like me. I'm only a foreman, and you're… well. Back then I thought you were a librarian. Now you're actual royalty. We couldn't be more different." His uncertainty and humble opinion of himself was endearing.

"You're not 'just a foreman.' You're so much more than that." Jerry winced as the pain in his face increased.

"I don't know about that. I've always strived to make myself better. I'm proud of my job and the work I do. I want kids, but I thought I'd have to adopt. We'll make our relationship work, no matter what."

With that promise, Rex placed his palm on Jerry's stomach. "And he or she will be the best kid ever."

Rex wanted their relationship to work, but what that truly meant for Jerry, time would tell.

JERRY OPENED his eyes. The left one wasn't swollen too badly, but the vision was still blurry. The vision in his right was clear. The moon shone through his window from high in the sky. Pain continually pulled him from sleep. Rex had molded to Jerry's back, his hand protectively over Jerry's belly, so he didn't mind too much. No bones were broken, and his doctor had assured Jerry, again, that the baby was okay. After the beating, how could he not worry? But he'd dodged a bullet—a fuckload of bullets. Ty's temper would have brought that first beating soon enough after their marriage—possibly sooner. And Jerry would have taken the punishments he would get for his defiance and become a battered husband. And he wouldn't have told anyone. Macho pride or not, he would've taken it all. He shivered.

Rex groaned in his sleep. His grip tightened around Jerry's stomach, and he rubbed his nose on the back of Jerry's neck. The heat, the closeness of Rex's hard body hadn't gone unnoticed by Jerry's cock. The thing had a mind of its own and had gotten Jerry into a world of trouble.

Or so he'd thought.

Stopping to think of getting what he wanted—except for the beating, of course—Jerry couldn't help but feel foreboding. When had he ever been able to choose his life's path without suffering negative consequences? Jerry finally drifted off, knowing he had to wait for morning to get answers.

CHAPTER 12

DURING THE night, Rex had whispered to Jerry about his happiness at having a baby, his joy at having Jerry back in his life, and so many more promises. Now, in the cold light of day, would Rex still feel that way? Jerry had saddled him not only with a child, but Jerry himself, and a demon clan with strict rules over Anzuni mating with humans. Rex's life was no longer his own, and would change in ways he never could have imagined.

The thoughts crashing around Jerry's head caused a barely containable anxiety. He wanted to shake Rex awake and pour everything onto the table, lay it all out and hope he'd stay. It was the fear of losing Rex, of not having him in his child's life, that kept Jerry from doing that.

Deep, steady breaths.

One step at a time, or he'd lose everything he'd appeared to gain. Once they were up and out of bed, the world would encroach on them and demand their attention. Here, in the sanctity of Jerry's room, they were sheltered, at least for a little while.

Jerry rolled carefully in Rex's arms and faced him. He couldn't have chosen a better man to father his child. Rex was loyal and trustworthy and full of life. He laughed hard and smiled wide, and when he had a job to do, that task was done right. Jerry had come to admire Rex in the months he'd known him. His respect for the man was immense. The Anzuni couldn't have asked for a better mate for their prince. Except Rex was human. Jerry closed his eyes. Chaos would ensue once the Anzuni learned that in addition to the future heir being an unwed father, the father of his child was human.

Oh fuck, Jerry, what have you done?

When Jerry opened his eyes, Rex watched him, a playful smirk pulling up the corner of his lips. Even in the dim glow of morning light, his green eyes were bright. Rex trailed his fingers down Jerry's cheek, and he sighed.

"Good morning, baby." He leaned in and placed a kiss upon Jerry's lips. *Not so fast.*

Gently, Rex placed his hand on Jerry's hip as he pulled back from the gentle kiss. Still, he grinned wide. He looked....

Happy?

Excited?

Thrilled?

Endorphins rushed in and dulled the aching pain of Jerry's face, back, and stomach.

"Good morning." Jerry tried to grin back. He imagined the grin was more of a lopsided, palsy-like smile. Reminded of how bruised and swollen his face was, Jerry tried to turn away from Rex.

Rex stopped Jerry from rolling away. Rex raised himself up on his elbow. His grin faded, but his gaze was soft and welcoming. "What's wrong?"

Jerry frowned. "I look awful!"

Rex barked out a laugh, and Jerry couldn't imagine what was so entertaining. Rex ran his fingertip over Jerry's bottom lip. "You're as handsome as ever, and what I care about isn't here." His fingertip continued over Jerry's cheek. "It's here...." Rex rested his palm on Jerry's chest. "And here...." Rex moved his palm to rest over Jerry's abdomen, below his belly button.

Jerry moved Rex's hand higher on his stomach. "This is where Anzuni babies grow."

The connection Jerry felt between them ran deep. Was it one-sided? Jerry bit down on his lip, deciding what to say. He could let Rex off the hook—and tear his heart out in the process. But hey, what he had instead of Ty was so much better.

"Listen. I know this was all thrown onto you. Heck, I was shocked, and I knew I would eventually be pregnant. You weren't prepared for this."

Rex looked down at Jerry but remained silent.

"Anyway, this isn't something you signed on for... at all." Jerry let out a nervous chuckle. "If this is all too much for you, I'd understand. I get it."

Rex raised his brow, as if questioning what Jerry said.

He could raise this child alone. Maybe his parents could even find someone who would rule with him despite—

"Jerry?" Rex's hand stiffened on Jerry's stomach. "Have you changed your mind?" Rex's tone steady and measured.

"Changed *my* mind?" What did that even mean?

Rex narrowed his eyes as he did whenever someone at the work site was being an idiot. Mainly Steve. Great. Now he was in the same category as Steve.

Rex continued to stare. Whatever tension and suspicion he held disappeared. His face softened. "I could say this wasn't freaking out at least some part of me, but that would be a lie."

Now it was Jerry's turn to tense. Rex rubbed soothing circles over Jerry's stomach while he struggled to corral his speeding thoughts and emotions. As Rex continued to stare, Jerry agonized every second, not knowing what Rex would say. Was this it? The end? Not that Jerry would blame Rex for darting out of the mansion and never looking back.

"All of a sudden, there are men who can get pregnant, and a demon clan I thought was a myth is real, not to mention you're a prince." Rex's head fell back and he huffed. "I really know how to do it right."

Jerry couldn't help smirking. "Oh, you know how to *do* it right." He focused on the expanse of Rex's neck stretched tight. Rex swallowed, and Jerry watched his Adam's apple move with the action. The man was irresistible. When Rex lowered his head, dark green lust-filled eyes struck Jerry hard. His breath caught, and he clenched his fists to keep from grabbing and mauling Rex.

The corner of Rex's mouth quirked. "Are you playing up my ego, Prince Jerricho?" The throaty whisper wrapped tight around Jerry, a comforting balm to his worries and fears. "And no, Jer, while you may have changed your mind, I haven't."

Jerry had no clue what that meant, and almost blurted out as much, but Rex kissed him. That shut Jerry up. The pain in his jaw and lips was second to the beauty of their mouths joining, spiking Jerry's pleasure. Unfortunately, with the sorry state of his body, they couldn't do much.

When the kiss broke, Jerry panted, needing to reassure Rex. "I haven't changed my mind about anything. I want you to be part of this child's life. And if you can ever find a way to forgive me, I want to see where this can go with us. I know I have to earn your trust, but when I'm with you, this feels…." Gods, he was gonna get sappy, but he couldn't help it. "It feels right."

"Yeah, it feels right to me too. I've spent months getting close to you. And can I tell you that you're a tough person to read?"

"Seems like we were both hiding something. And we almost lost—"

Rex pressed a kiss to Jerry's lips, then pulled back. "But we're here now. And you're a guy who's pregnant, and…. Man, it's gonna take some time to wrap my head around that one." He puzzled and then gasped. "How… I mean… you're a guy… how does…." The color drained from his face, and he appeared close to throwing up.

"Whoa, big guy, take a couple of deep breaths." Jerry rubbed Rex's arm.

"How does the baby get out?" Rex whispered, seemingly terrorized by the thought.

Jerry winced as he laughed out loud. Damn, he felt that in every bruised cell in his body. He pointed to his navel. "Here. Only Anzuni males in the royal line have what looks like the human belly button. Other Anzuni don't have this. What is a puckered scar from the umbilical cord in humans, is the birth canal for us. The opening will enlarge and allow for the baby to come out."

Rex swayed, a sickly shade of gray. Jerry pushed him back onto the pillow. "Well, I can see you won't be hanging around at the time of the birth." Jerry chuckled.

Rex shook his head. "No, it's… a baby comes through *that*?"

Jerry gave him a reassuring smile. "Anzuni males of the royal line have been having babies for thousands of years, just as my father birthed me, so did his father, and so on."

Rex nodded dazedly, and then seemed to sober. "Wait, your father's married to your mother. Don't you need sperm to get pregnant? How in the heck does that work?"

"In Anzuni, all males and females carry eggs and sperm. For some reason, only the royal line of males can be impregnated. I've never asked why. Anyway, in Anzuni, the sperm is released by both males and females during intercourse, and only needs to infect the other person. It enters the bloodstream and fertilizes the egg."

"You mean like a virus?"

"I guess." Jerry shrugged. See, he did know something about pregnancy in Anzuni. "So I'm guessing, despite using a condom, your sperm got free and—"

Rex placed his finger on Jerry's lips with a smirk. "I think I get the picture." Rex raised Jerry's T-shirt, bunched the material up near his throat, and placed a gentle kiss on his collarbone.

He eyed the pendant resting against Jerry's breastbone. The intricate gold design of interlocking branches around a medallion with ancient Anzuni symbols in the center was something Jerry rarely took off.

Rex picked up the pendant and studied the design. "It looks old. What is it?"

"A family heirloom. It has some connection to Anzuni history, but I'm not sure exactly what. It belonged to my Uncle Rainyard, my father's older brother. He was king before he died in a plane crash along with his wife and their two kids. Their chartered plane went down over the mountains in Colorado. I was around two years old. When I was a baby, I used to love playing with the pendant whenever my uncle held me. My parents gave it to me when I was older. It means a lot to me." Jerry pulled the chain over his head and slid it over Rex's head.

"Why did you do that?" Rex looked down at the gold medallion, which rested over his heart.

"I want you to wear it, please."

"It's beautiful." Rex bent and kissed Jerry's chest. He trailed his tongue over Jerry's skin, raising goose bumps. "But not as beautiful as you." He sucked Jerry's nipple, rolling the nub around his tongue. Jerry arched his chest and reached for Rex, but he blocked Jerry's hand.

"You don't need to do anything. This is for you." He kissed across each letter of the word *free* tattooed across the top of Jerry's chest. The *F*. The *R*. Each *E*, as if he understood the symbolism that represented Jerry's rebellion. As Rex kissed and licked down his body, a thought formed.

Could he live the life he chose, love who he wanted, marry Rex, and raise their child? Was it all possible?

When Rex bit onto one of Jerry's nipples, Jerry's mind emptied, and he grasped Rex's head, encouraging his ministrations. *Fuck the pain.* Goose bumps covered his arms. His cock was so hard, and he was desperate for Rex's mouth on him.

"Mmmmmm." Rex continued to lick and bite and suck.

As he moved lower, Jerry gasped and whimpered, eliciting a low chuckle from Rex.

"Damn, Jer, the noises you make drive me crazy." Rex continued kissing down Jerry's stomach, moving closer to his cock. Not fast enough for Jerry.

"You...." Jerry sucked in a deep breath as Rex licked the head of his cock, sending stabs of pleasure through Jerry. "Ohhhh... oh my gods.... You're the r-reason." Jerry exhaled and immediately pulled in another breath, despite the pain pulsing in his ribs.

"I like that." Rex sucked the head of Jerry's cock into his mouth. Heat flooded Jerry's body, covering him like a warm blanket. A flush raced across his chest, and blood pulsed in his cheeks. He'd never get used to having Rex's hot mouth on his cock. He wasn't sure how long he'd last, and was proven right as Rex pushed his entire shaft to the back of his throat. The sharp sensation of pleasure rushed blood from his brain. Lost in the confines of his bliss, Jerry grunted and emptied his balls into Rex's mouth.

"Ah, fuck." Pulse after pulse of the orgasm left his body boneless and depleted.

Rex rose and, with great care, pushed his tongue into Jerry's mouth. His own bitter saltiness coated his tongue. Rex moaned, furiously stroking his own cock. Unable to resist, Jerry grabbed the head of Rex's dick, alongside his hand, and squeezed. Rex bucked forward, and within seconds, ribbons of warm semen decorated Jerry's chest. Their kiss continued as Rex shuddered and whimpered above Jerry. When Rex pulled back, Jerry caught sight of his swollen red lips, the red sweaty flush to his skin, the hooded, sated eyes... so hot. Without breaking their gaze, Rex rubbed his palm over Jerry's chest and stomach, spreading his seed, marking Jerry. Claiming him.

CHAPTER 13

JERRY WOKE to an empty bed. Running his palm over Rex's side, he found the sheet was cold. The clock said 5:00 p.m. Damn, he'd slept all day, and his body still ached like a bitch. The doctor had warned him he'd feel worse before he felt better. He hit that nail square on its shiny, flat head.

Sitting on the edge of the bed, Jerry groaned and immediately reached for the ibuprofen and water. Maybe a warm bath would help with the pain? Maybe after he found Rex. Jerry shooed away the niggling fear that Rex had left. When he looked around the room, he couldn't locate any of Rex's clothes or his shoes.

"Of course, he got dressed to leave the room." Would he ever stop fearing Rex's devotion to him had to do with the baby only? Was he going to be one of those whiny partners constantly seeking reassurance? He had to trust Rex. Trust a man he'd known for only a little over two months.

Ugh, stop it!

Time to get out of his room and face whatever lay in wait. He would handle whatever was thrown at him, and he'd do so because he didn't have a choice. Besides, he didn't have to marry Tyranis—he should be dancing a jig.

In the bathroom, he surveyed the damage to his face. He looked as if he'd gone ten rounds with a boxer. While his left eye was no longer swollen shut, the bruising on the left side of his face was bright red tinged with purple, meaning Ty was right-handed. No bruising had appeared on his stomach, but his abdomen still ached. Gods, he looked like hell.

He jumped into the shower because, frankly, he smelled like sex and cum. His room must've smelled as bad. Once dressed, he stripped the bed and stuffed the dirty sheets into the hamper. He opened a window to air out the room. All he needed was Helena, the maid who cleaned his room, smelling the evidence. Although she'd no doubt discovered proof on his sheets of his nighttime emissions as a teen. That thought reddened his face.

Jerry made his way down the stairs. His parents weren't in the sitting room. Five was too early for dinner, but he checked the dining room anyway. Empty. His next stop was the kitchen. Magda, their cook, furiously chopped veggies with a huge-ass knife. She'd worked for his family for around ten years, and was a nice lady when you weren't messing up her kitchen or interrupting her preparations.

Jerry backed out of the kitchen, but not before Magda spotted him. The smile that split her wrinkled face was unexpected. "Prince Jerricho! Come, come. Let me see you!" Her excitement startled Jerry, causing him to freeze in the doorway. Magda pointed the knife in his direction and waved the blade. "Come, child."

With skittish steps, Jerry walked toward her, keeping an eye on the blade.

"Hey, Magda. What's cookin'?"

Her expression changed. Man, she looked pissed. Her lips formed a thin line, and her violet eyes narrowed as she surveyed his face. She shook her head violently and muttered something under her breath. Finally, she dropped the knife onto the counter and grasped his face, placing her palms on his cheeks. Her smile returned, and her eyes twinkled once again.

"My dear child, I hear you're cooking a bambino." She placed her hand over his stomach. "Such happy news!"

Jerry refrained from pushing her hand away. He imagined more than one person would be invading his personal space in the future to touch his belly. Despite his discomfort, her excitement surprised him. Stepping back, she cocked her head and furrowed her brow.

"You don't wish to be having a baby?" She wiped her hands on her apron, but her gaze never faltered from Jerry.

He stuffed his hands into the pockets of his sweats. Happy? He was thrilled, but there were many who wouldn't share in the good news.

"Yes, I'm happy about it, but…."

She waved her hand dismissively. "Like I told your young man earlier, love is what matters, not a stupid tradition that dates back thousands of years. And I can tell he loves you, Prince Jerricho."

Jerry forced himself to ignore the comment about Rex's love for him. "You've seen Rex? Is he still here?" The mention of Rex's name was enough to kick-start Jerry's pulse.

Magda smiled knowingly. "Ah, I see the love flows two ways. He's here. I believe in the Congressional Room."

What the hell?

Magda patted Jerry's arm. Picking up her knife, she continued chopping, ignoring how her news had stunned Jerry.

He headed for the Congressional Room, which was limited to formal meetings for clan business. That sinking foreboding rose and he ran, ignoring every jarring pain and hoping what he thought was happening wasn't without his knowledge. *Fuck!*

Skidding around the corner in his sock feet, he barely managed to avoid smacking into a wall. Two guards stood outside the thick wood double doors. Their presence only meant one thing. The council was inside. Both men watched as Jerry barreled toward them. He recognized Lanzo, but the other guard was new. He was a large man, wide in the shoulders, with a full black beard trimmed neatly, hair pulled back into a long braid that hung over his shoulder, and ice-blue eyes. Since Jerry had rarely come home in the past four years, maybe the guard wasn't so new. Also, they were part of the large cadre of the king's guard, many of who were assigned to council members when they weren't in the mansion.

"Prince Jerricho, is something wrong?" Lanzo asked.

As Jerry neared the door, he gasped for breath. Damn, the short run had taken a lot out of him.

A murky cloud passed over Lanzo's eyes. "Is this what Tyranis did to you?" He gritted the words through clenched teeth.

The other guard scowled as well.

"Umm… yeah, but there were extenuating circumstances, and…." He was defending Ty, but only because Jerry had screwed up too.

Lanzo huffed. "If he touches you again, Sire, I will end him."

The solemn promise glinted like steel in Lanzo's eyes. Jerry had always liked Lanzo.

"Thanks, but I think my father has dealt with him. What's going on? Is Rex in there?"

Lanzo frowned. "Rex? There's an emergency meeting of the clan council about…. Oh, Rex. Your…."

Jerry rolled his eyes. "The father of my child." Hopefully, his future husband. He had to wait to confirm that one.

Lanzo raised his eyebrows, seeming surprised by Jerry's bluntness. "Yes, he's in there. The meeting started about fifteen minutes ago."

"Fuck!" Jerry was ready to bust inside when a voice caught his attention. The door was slightly ajar. Jerry wasn't sure who spoke, since there were ten council members representing ten different regions around the world. Anzuni clusters existed all over the planet. Delegates lived near the royal mansion and spoke for their cluster's interests, kind of like ambassadors. The entire system was democratic, in a way.

The man inside continued speaking. "His mate was chosen years ago, sanctioned by this council, and now you're telling us this union will no longer happen?" Annoyance dripped from every word. Geraldon.

"I have already explained the circumstances under which this occurred."

Jerry snorted, hearing his father's impatience. Geraldon had a way of exasperating everyone.

"Yes, Your Highness, you have explained how the prince has managed to get himself impregnated by this… human." Jerry could hear the sneer in Geraldon's voice. He'd never cared for the narcissistic man who constantly spouted about the sanctity of traditions and laws, while he'd bent or ignored many to suit himself. "Any man would have been enraged to find out his fiancé had been unfaithful and whored himself out to a human."

Jerry flinched from the slanderous words. The silence that followed was weighted. When his father finally spoke, Jerry could hear the restraint in his voice.

"I will remind you that you are speaking of my son, Geraldon, the future crown prince of the Anzuni, and I will not tolerate your tone. Your disappointment is highly noted, since Tyranis is your nephew. However, he tried to harm my son and his unborn child." Geraldon tried to speak, but Jerry's father summarily cut him off. "The man beat my son, and would have continued to do so if Rex had not arrived to stop him."

"Surely the entire matter has been exaggerated, as can happen with such delicate matters." Geraldon's tone remained respectful, despite having called his king a liar.

Jerry clenched his fists as his father assured Geraldon the matter was anything but an exaggeration. Time to step up and defend not only his father, but the father of his child as well.

As Jerry pushed the door open, the baby gave him a few kicks. "I'm on it, little one."

Raising his chin, Jerry walked into the room and slammed the door behind him to garner the attention he desired. Every eye immediately focused on him, and the chorus of gasps from the council caused Jerry to bite his lip to keep from smiling. Adding to the drama of his bruised face, he shuffled forward, exaggerating the pain he felt. Eyes narrowed around the table where the council sat, his father at the head. Rex, who stood before the table, rushed to assist Jerry.

"Are you okay?" Rex placed a protective arm across Jerry's back.

Jerry kept a neutral face. Out of the corner of his mouth, he whispered. "I'm fine. I'll deal with you later."

Amused by the height Rex's eyebrows rose, Jerry forced his attention to the council, especially Geraldon. That quashed his need to laugh. Seriously, Tyranis could have killed him.

"Prince Jerricho." Syrana, a delegate from Japan, bowed her head slightly. Her black hair pulled into a tight bun gave her a perpetually surprised expression. "Are you okay?" The shock on her face, on many of their faces, drove home how awful he looked.

Jerry sighed heavily. "I'm as well as can be expected given my injuries."

Geraldon glared daggers at Jerry until they made eye contact. Geraldon quickly looked askance.

"Surely you're doing well, since you walked here under your own power." Geraldon scowled. "And your father has assured us your illegitimate child is unharmed."

Whispers filled the air as many members conferred among themselves. Jerry held the neutral expression, waiting for one of the council members to speak. Next to him, Rex tensed, and Jerry felt the anger waft from him. His father wore the same impartial political expression as Jerry, since it had been his father who'd taught Jerry neutrality in the face of opposition. One of the tools of an effective ruler, he'd told Jerry, who would have rather left the ruling to someone else. Damn his single child status. He couldn't even pawn the job off on a sibling.

"Is the child you carry truly unharmed?" Nicholaus, the delegate for several of the southern states, leaned forward and clasped his hands on the table. Youngest on the council, possibly in his late thirties, as opposed to most of the council members who were in their fifties and older.

In a dramatic fashion, Jerry placed his hand over his stomach and gazed down, crowding as much worry and concern as he could onto his face. "The doctor examined me and said the heartbeat was strong. I only pray there's no hidden damage." Truthfully, he was terrified by the possibility. What if the beating from Ty had hurt the baby physically and the damage was undetectable?

"As we all do, Prince Jerricho," Syrana said in a gentle tone. "All Anzuni life is precious."

Jerry nodded, hoping the council understood the seriousness of the attack. Next, he had to find out why the council had called Rex. Jerry hated politics with a passion.

At the center of the table, Tanyon smiled warmly. He was the oldest member of the council and represented clan members in the western US. "Jerricho, so good to see you again, despite the circumstances. How far along are you, my boy?"

The question caught Jerry off guard. "Umm… little over a month."

Tanyon grinned wide, and he looked… happy? He nodded but said nothing. Again, whispers rose among the council members. Jerry caught his father's eye. With a gentle smile, his father nodded and cleared his throat, the noise echoing off the stone walls of the room.

"As you can see, my son was brutally attacked in our home by the man who'd been chosen to be his future husband. The attack was vicious and done with intent to harm. Without intervention, Tyranis could have killed not only my son, but my grandchild as well."

Warmth blossomed in Jerry's chest at hearing his father take on the grandfather role. The bond between Jerry and his father was strong. Jerry admired his gentle and caring nature, and his fierce passion for the Anzuni people. If you messed with any of them, his father's niceness faded and he became as fierce as a lion.

"I ask the council to render punishment to the full extent of Anzuni law against Tyranis Devintanzo." His father held the gaze of all the members, his voice sure and filled with conviction.

A volley of voices from the council members filled the air. Geraldon's voice rose above the melee. "Certainly, there are extenuating circumstances at play here. What man would not be enraged to learn his intended fiancé has been impregnated by another man? For three years, Tyranis was led to believe he would marry the prince, and would rule the clan by his side. Yet with one selfish act, everything he'd been promised was ripped away by a wayward mate. I believe proper compensation is due to Tyranis for breach of contract."

Jerry's eyes widened. Ty had nearly beaten him to death and compensation should be provided to him for his troubles? What the hell?

CHAPTER 14

GERALDON SNEERED at the other council members, who were as astonished as Jerry at Geraldon's claim. "That's Anzuni law."

Geraldon's angry tone polluted the room, and Jerry shrank back, realizing he had indeed broken a deal brokered by his father for the good of the clan. A hand settled on Jerry's shoulder. Rex gazed down upon him with a smile of encouragement. Jerry forced a wan smile in return. Jerry had fucked up, and not everyone was going to see what Jerry saw in Rex. What they were going to see was a human.

Jerry's father raised his hand, and the room quieted. "As far as I'm concerned, Tyranis lost all claim to compensation when he took revenge on my son. I agree Jerricho made a mistake in seeking companionship outside of the prearranged relationship. He's admitted his fault in this matter. Compensation would have been made if, and I stress *if*, Tyranis hadn't taken matters into his own hands."

Geraldon leaned forward, bracing his hands on the edge of the table. His teeth gnashed together, the lines on his face hardened, his skin flushed red, and Jerry expected to see steam pour from his ears. Maybe he'd self-destruct? Geraldon had lost out big with Ty's failure to marry into the royal family. But what exactly had he lost?

Geraldon's gaze fixed on Jerry, who had to blink when the man's demeanor changed. The anger fled, his face softened, and he looked as if... as if he'd made a decision he hadn't been sure about. He wore satisfied resolve.

"This is not the only matter before the council. There is an unwed Anzuni prince, and the father is human." Geraldon had practically spat the words from his lips. "A human has never ruled the Anzuni clan. This goes against every tradition carried into the free world by those who fled the oppression of another race."

Baltheus, the delegate from South America, nodded in agreement. "Yes. We have never had anyone outside of the Anzuni race rule the clan, but... Anzuni are mating with humans, and that number increases each year."

"Anzuni have assimilated into human culture, and to have the human perspective, from a ruling standpoint, would be invaluable," Tanyon stated. His opinion reflected progressive thinking Jerry hadn't expected from the elder. "However, the human must prove his loyalty to the clan before the mating can be complete. I believe this is in the best interest of the clan. This is written in the *Daenose*, which makes this fact irrefutable."

"I'm glad to hear your agreement with following the Daenose." Geraldon's wide, self-satisfied grin splitting his face sent a chill through Jerry.

Geraldon rose from his seat and Jerry tracked him as he crossed the room and opened the large ornate cabinet filled with texts of Anzuni history and law. Something akin to victory covered Geraldon's face.

Jerry's gut told him he'd be on the losing end of whatever Geraldon was up to.

Council members spoke among themselves as Geraldon pulled out a large red book. The Anzuni coat of arms graced the cover. Geraldon cradled the book in one arm. After opening the book, he perused the pages with a steely determination and an outright giddiness. Rex leaned down, his lips hovering next to Jerry's ear. Rex's proximity jolted across Jerry's already frazzled nerves.

"What's he doing?" Rex asked in a hushed tone.

Jerry shook his head. "No clue." He'd expected Geraldon would demand harsher testing requirements for Rex to join the Anzuni clan and marry a prince, which made sense. The ruling family required the trust of the people to rule, and qualifications that were more stringent would assuage most fears. If that had been his intention, why had Geraldon pulled out an Anzuni book of law?

Turning on his heel, Geraldon returned to the table, ignoring his seat. Placing the book on the table, he clasped his hands before him. His face took on a fake neutrality. Tension tied Jerry's muscles into tight knots, and he rubbed his palms together as an ominous feeling crept over his skin.

His father's jaw ticked as he eyed Geraldon. It was never a good sign.

"Geraldon," Jerry's father said in an abrupt tone. The council members turned their eyes to the slimy man. Snake oil salesman came to Jerry's mind.

With a theatrical gesture that would garner top acting awards, Geraldon sighed heavily. His expression morphed into one of trepidation and woe. "As Anzuni, we're proud of our heritage, of the strife and struggles of a people who suffered under the tyrannical rule of another race. We were a race of slaves until our ancestors escaped. In this world, they found freedom among the humans. To ensure that freedom continued, they created a set of laws and traditions to ensure the Anzuni would never forget their ancestor's plight or allow another race to control us."

Geraldon paused and sent Jerry and Rex a brief, cutting glance. Rex shifted uncomfortably under the scrutiny. Jerry grasped Rex's hand.

Jerry's father looked apprehensive with his lips thinned and posture ramrod straight. Jerry's heart faltered. Did his father know what Geraldon was about to say?

Geraldon had captivated the room, his influence as the second-longest member of the council well known. Most of the council members even respected the man. Even so, Jerry had never trusted the fake sincerity he'd encountered over the years.

"In the interest of the Anzuni, our forefathers wrote into our foundation of laws a stipulation, which we have followed since inhabiting the human world. In matters of mating, this includes proving allegiance to the Anzuni. All who are non-Anzuni *must* participate in the *Klaestrom*. The trials of initiation are something we continue to this day."

Jerry's father leaned back in his chair, crossing his arms over his chest, while an undeniable annoyance crossed his face. "Is there a point to your reiteration of Anzuni tradition, Geraldon?"

Geraldon gave a courteous bow of his head. "Yes, Your Highness. Just now, as we were speaking, I recalled reading something in the Daenose."

Eyebrows raised, and Jerry sat forward in his chair. *What the fuck?*

Rex crouched down and whispered, "What's the Daenose?"

"The basis of all Anzuni law. A doctrine. Kind of like your American Constitution. It covers the rights of all Anzuni, and protection against violations by another race. And, like the Constitution, every conflict and resolution is weighted against those rights."

Jerry had studied the contents of the Daenose years ago. The five-hundred-page declaration was a monster to read, much less understand. The subjective interpretation of exactly what had been intended by those who'd originally laid down the words had been—and still was—cause for great debate.

Jerry frowned. No one aside from Anzuni scholars who'd spent years dissecting the ancient text could recollect a single passage. Geraldon had come primed for this meeting with a clear agenda, and fuck if Jerry could even guess what that was.

He squeezed Rex's hand harder as his pulse kicked into overdrive. Fearing the council would bar Rex from his life and force Jerry to live a life of servitude in a loveless marriage was merely a glimpse of a massive rock buried in the soil. Jerry now envisaged something much graver.

"Rex will endure the same trials as every other human who has joined our clan." His father smiled smugly.

"Yes." Rex's voice was sure and honest. "I agree to whatever is required to join the Anzuni clan. I would be proud and honored to participate." His deep voice resounded through the hall.

Several members of the council, including Jerry's father, nodded in approval, while a few wore trepidation and refused to look at Jerry and Rex. Their collective reaction puzzled him, since the trials to join the Anzuni clan weren't deadly. While some required bravery, and others trust and loyalty, many were downright boring, requiring the participant to learn Anzuni history and customs. Snoozeville.

Geraldon cleared his throat and continued. "Another stipulation, which was designed to maintain the sanctity of the Anzuni clan, states only full-blooded Anzuni will rule."

Jerry inhaled sharply and laid his palm on his stomach. His child couldn't succeed the throne? Then his father's line of ruling the Anzuni would end with his stupidity. He sank back in his chair and peered at his father, who would comprehend the implication. Jerry wanted to fall to his knees and beg his father's forgiveness for his impulsiveness.

"I am well aware of the law as written. And I can assure the council that Rex will refrain from making decisions on any matters pertaining to ruling the Anzuni. He will be *claxton* to the prince, and remain so when Jerricho is crowned king."

Before Rex could inquire, Jerry said, "Claxton means mate or spouse." Gazing up, Jerry found Rex beaming. Warmth filled the cold ache in Jerry's chest but did little to relax the knotted muscles in his gut.

His father continued. "Secondly, since the heir to the throne will be half human, allowing that child to take the throne would violate the Daenose, which, in my opinion, is an outdated document, written when circumstances were different for the Anzuni."

Geraldon raised a sardonic eyebrow. "Surely you aren't dismissing a document forged by our ancestors after enduring years of suffering and torture at the hands of another demon race?"

Council members shifted uncomfortably in their chairs. Jerry fought to remain still and neutral. "Save your grandstanding for another time, Geraldon. My point, before being taken out of context, is that in the future many of the ideas in this document should be reexamined, and possibly brought up-to-date for the current times. And yes, we are all aware changes to the Daenose must be brought before the entire clan and gain the majority of the vote before changing the laws."

His father sounded intent on changing the law stating only full-blooded Anzuni could rule the clan. Maybe there was a way to salvage their reign as the royal family after all.

"Now, I believe we've cleared up the concerns brought to the council by Geraldon. We can move on to preparations for welcoming a new heir to the throne." Jerry's father's expression morphed from tense and worried to one of joy.

Could it be so easy?

"Begging your pardon, Your Highness," Geraldon said. Every nerve in Jerry's body fired. "There is one other matter that needs to be addressed by the council."

So much for wondering. Jerry's father looked as if he'd suppressed an eye roll. Geraldon pushed on the king's last nerve. Not a smart move. Yet Geraldon stood tall and confident, as if he held all the aces.

"What haven't we covered here, Geraldon?" His father's neutrality cracked with a sneer.

Geraldon looked at Jerry with dark gray eyes, sending a shudder through Jerry's frame. "The punishable act of treason committed by the prince of the Anzuni clan, Jerricho Alamande Trychovisca."

CHAPTER 15

JERRY'S STOMACH flipped, and cold sweat broke across the back of his neck. Treason? Because he was an unwed pregnant prince? How did that translate into treason? Unless…. Did the Daenose label his behavior as treasonous? Shit, he'd more than screwed up.

"Do you care to explain your claim of treason?" Jerry's father's voice filled the room.

Jerry cringed, as did many of the members around the table. His father, when he was pissed, was cower-worthy. Rex moved behind Jerry and placed his hands firmly on Jerry's shoulders. Jerry was more than grateful to have Rex with him.

Geraldon glanced around the table and raised his chin with a steely repose. "The gravest of offenses outlined by the Daenose is revealing the existence of the Anzuni to humans without permission of the council. As a demon clan living in the human world, knowledge of the Anzuni given without the full vetting of this council could be detrimental to every life in the clan."

Ice water pulsed through Jerry's veins as his heart raced. He wiped his clammy hands on his pants. Had to be in reaction to Jerry's increased heart rate, the baby kicked hard, and might have even rolled. Whatever the reason, his nausea increased tenfold.

Jerry turned a hopeless eye to his father, whose scowl was more the face of a contemptuous man than the compassionate king he was. Despite the threatening glare, Geraldon continued.

"Perhaps my claim has been made in haste," Geraldon said with feigned acquiescence. "Since the future prince-mate knows of the Anzuni, I may be mistaken in believing Prince Jerricho was the one to reveal the information. Is there another circumstance, Prince Jerricho, that you wish to share with the members of the council for your behavior?"

If having dozens of eyes pinned on a person could melt them, Jerry would have liquefied right there in his chair. He opened and closed his mouth, unable to respond. He hadn't told Rex. Keith had, but the situation had been dire and the revelation unavoidable. Well, probably unavoidable. Would the council consider the compulsory nature of the disclosure? Before Ty had shown up, Jerry had planned to do the same. He recalled what his father had said the day they'd learned of Jerry's pregnancy. *"I will be here to help facilitate what Anzuni law dictates."*

He'd glossed over his father's direction in his rush to tell Rex about the baby. He couldn't rat on Keith. He wasn't the one who'd fucked with his family's honor and the secrecy of Anzuni existence. Why hadn't Jerry accepted who he was, taken pride in his people and the importance of the clan? No, he'd rebelled, gotten tattoos, lived on his own, worked at the library... gotten pregnant. This was *his* punishment to take. What did they do to traitors? He shuddered.

Rising from his chair, Jerry winced and hissed as his muscles and back protested after sitting for so long. Rex grasped his elbow and assisted him to stand. Jerry had milked his injuries for all they were worth and he'd get no further sympathy.

"I did tell Rex that I'm Anzuni." He could lie and blame the moment, but now was the time to show his maturity, his commitment to his people. "I asked him to come to the mansion because I wanted to tell him he was going to be a father. I was mistaken in foregoing Anzuni law. I take full responsibility."

Geraldon grinned maliciously. "It seems Prince Jerricho has created a pattern of ignoring Anzuni law. Perhaps a symptom of a graver issue, one calling into question the ability of the current monarchy to reign."

"This has nothing to do with my father! I'm the one who made the wrong choice. Despite your views of me, I wouldn't shirk my rule, or deny my heritage. With the exception of my father, you've all been allowed to marry someone who loves you for you and not the status they would obtain by marrying you." Jerricho gave Geraldon a pointed glare. "I know that's not a valid reason for what I've done, and, as I said, I take full responsibility for my actions. This isn't anything my father condoned."

Jerricho wouldn't let any of them see his hands shake, his jaw quiver, or the tears pricking his eyes fall. No, he stood tall and proud and ready to take whatever they dished out. When he glanced at his father, the mix of pride and trepidation in his expression was a double-edged sword.

Tanyon raised his hand. "This is a serious charge of treason cast upon a member of the royal family. Yet, I'm not sure this charge is valid."

"There hasn't been a charge of treason brought before the Anzuni council in hundreds of years." Janines, the delegate from Canada, had been quiet up until then. She tended to speak only when she believed strongly in something.

"He has admitted to the crime!" Geraldon screeched, the echo volleying about the stone room. "Prince Jerricho has revealed Anzuni existence to a human."

"Rex knew of Anzuni existence before he even met me."

Geraldon sneered. "He told us of his knowledge of mythology. Knowing of a myth and knowing that the myth is a truth are two different things."

Before Jerry could respond, Tanyon rose from his seat. His neatly tailored gray suit complemented his white hair. He walked with the grace of an elder, the poise of a leader. Jerry admired him for his diplomacy and his fairness.

Approaching Geraldon, Tanyon said, "I too am quite familiar with Anzuni law. As a lad, my Great Uncle Sylvanius thought studying the old traditions was a form of entertainment for children. I can tell you it wasn't," he added, as if trying for some levity amid the seriousness. "And if I recall, treason must meet several specific standards to be termed as such."

Crowding out Geraldon, Tanyon stood before the book of Anzuni laws. He pulled a pair of glasses from his breast pocket, perched them on his nose, and leaned over the book, humming and nodding as he read.

Jerry turned to find Rex appearing overwhelmed by the entire situation, his expression nearing panic. Shit. If anything was going to make him break camp and flee, this would be it.

Jerry stepped before Rex, and he blinked as if Jerry had magically appeared. Jerry cupped Rex's cheeks, bringing his focus only on him. "You okay?"

Rex nodded. "What're they going to do to you, Jer? Treason sounds…. It's serious, and that guy, Geraldon, has it out for you." His normally vibrant voice cracked and barely reached Jerry, despite their proximity.

"Whatever happens, we'll get through it, yeah?" He hoped to the gods they could get through it. More to the point, he hoped Rex didn't see this as a huge hassle. Their relationship was so new and fragile, and if the wind blew too hard, it might shatter.

"I… I just got you back. What if—"

"Here's what we need." Tanyon grinned despite the seriousness of the moment. "The tenants of the law state treason must meet three requirements, which are, and I am paraphrasing: knowingly brings harm to the Anzuni people with the intent of malice, or knowingly and with malice deems to undermine the ruling authority of the Anzuni through acts of murder, willful neglect, or misrepresentation, or reveals the location of the Anzuni people to those whose tyrannical rule they have escaped."

Jerry held his breath. While he was confident most of those didn't apply to this situation, the law was a mouthful of words, and subject to interpretation.

Geraldon crossed his arms as Tanyon removed his glasses and stepped away from the book. That damn buzzing started again in Jerry's head, and he looked helplessly to his father. It was the curve at the corner of his father's lips that said Geraldon hadn't succeeded with his claim.

"Unless I'm to believe Prince Jerricho revealed the existence of the Anzuni for reasons of malice, the claim of treason isn't valid according to the law. If anyone on this council feels differently, they can indicate it with their vote." Tanyon turned on his heel and returned to his seat.

The vote was fast, with the majority agreeing the charge of treason was unfounded.

If Jerry thought he was home free, he was mistaken. Geraldon glowered at him from his seat.

Tanyon, who'd staunchly defended Jerricho, frowned as he surveyed his fellow council members. "Despite the charge of treason being dropped, Prince Jerricho did willfully ignore the traditions and laws of the Anzuni. This behavior is unsettling given he's next in line for the throne."

This garnered Geraldon's attention, and he sat forward. Something big was coming.

Jerry looked to his father, who appeared to agree with Tanyon's assessment of Jerry's actions. Hearing what he'd done spelled out in detail highlighted his selfishness.

"The council must address how to move forward and I move the council meet in *senzanis regaliso,* due to the conflict of interest." Tanyon turned to Jerry's father, who nodded in understanding.

"What's happening?" Rex asked as Jerry's father excused himself from the table.

"I'm not sure." His father crossed the room to them. "Dad?"

His dour expression seized Jerry's heart. "Both of you join me in my study."

His father left the room, no doubt expecting Jerry and Rex to follow. Rex took Jerry's hand, and silently they left the Congressional Room and proceeded down the corridor where they entered his father's study. Jerry watched his father sink into the leather chair behind his large wooden desk. Colorful Anzuni tapestries depicting historical scenes of the clan covered the wall behind him. Jerry had spent hours during his childhood staring at the fascinating scenes hand-stitched into the fabric. Now they'd lost all the vibrancy and magic he'd believed in as a child.

"What does *senzanis regaliso* mean?" Jerry sat in a chair before his father's desk.

"In absence of the king. The decision will be made without my input, because my judgment would be clouded."

Ten people were deciding Jerry's fate, without the mediating neutrality of his father.

"But you're anything but biased. You would do what is best for the clan, right? Even if it involves me."

He was a fair king. Rex squeezed Jerry's hand once, but he was past the point of comfort and verging on full-on panic.

"Don't let them decide without you. Geraldon would like nothing more than to get rid of us and jump in as ruler. Did you hear him in there? He counted on Tyranis becoming ruler, has influence over him. What if they try to make me marry him anyway? What if they take Rex away from me? What if they take my baby away? What if they throw me in prison?"

Jerry tried to draw in a deep breath, but his throat closed. They were going to destroy what happiness he'd found. Nothing would change. What if they wanted him to marry someone worse than Tyranis? What if they voted his father out as king? How could Jerry live with being the cause?

"Jerricho."

Rex knelt before his chair. He laid his hand on the back of Jerry's neck, and he stroked Jerry's skin lightly. Rex's eyes focused intently on Jerry's. "Breathe, Jer. It's going to be okay. Whatever happens, we'll deal with it. No matter what, I am not going to lose you. We're a family, and they can't take that away from us, okay?" The gentle tone and confident demeanor pushed past the panic, calming Jerry. He normally wasn't so reactive. Had to be the pregnancy hormones.

He nodded and wrapped his arms around Rex. Over Rex's shoulder, he caught sight of his father, who nodded as well. Jerry wanted to believe the council wasn't planning something hideous, but the odds weren't in his favor. Maybe he could abdicate as future ruler, live a quiet life as a loyal Anzuni subject. His father's disappointment would be great, but Jerry wasn't giving up Rex. They were having a child. Certainly, that would have some bearing on any decision made by the council.

"Why don't you rest on my couch, Jerricho? Their deliberations could take a while, and you look exhausted." His father nodded to the large gray sofa across the room. His office was the one place in the mansion that his wife allowed comfortable, functional furniture.

"Good idea." Rex took Jerry's hands and pulled him to stand. He led him across the room.

Jerry agreed only to avoid an argument, but his nerves jumped beneath his skin. Rex sat and placed a pillow on his lap. As he laid down, Jerry put his head on the pillow. He stretched his aching limbs across the couch. Rex rhythmically ran his fingers over Jerry's temple and scalp, convincing Jerry's body to calm, pulling him into a peaceful, relaxed state. Jerry slipped into a restless sleep until Rex roused him.

"Jer. Hey, wake up. The council has reached a decision."

Panic shoved Jerry out of sleep. Reality crept back in, and he considered Rex's loving gaze. Panic wouldn't help either of them at this point.

"You awake?" Jerry reached for Rex, who seized his hand. Warm lips pressed against his fingers, the touch stirring Jerry's desire. If he wasn't in such a shitload of trouble, he'd drag Rex upstairs and let the man fuck him until he was unconscious again.

Jerry smiled tenuously and stood, a tad wobbly as sleep filtered out of his brain. "Where's my father?"

"He had to speak to someone about something. He's busier than the president."

Didn't Jerry know it. "He's like a president. There aren't as many Anzuni as there are Americans, but he does rule an entire race located around the world."

And he did a damn good job. And what had Jerry gone and done? Tarnished his family's reputation with his willfulness and stupidity. He hoped whatever the council decided, he would be able to accept the ruling without freaking out.

Rex pulled them together. Jerry reveled in the heat and solid presence of his man. In Rex's eyes he saw something akin to adoration and desire wrapped together. Jerry lifted his chin, a silent request for a kiss. Rex smirked, tentatively bringing their lips together, rubbing and teasing. His tongue traced Jerry's lips, and a low groan filled Rex's throat. Jerry's lips tingled, and heat flushed his skin. The kiss was perfect. His man was perfect. He'd fallen for Rex, and nothing could break the spell Jerry was under.

Nothing.

He was in love, even if saying those words scared him. What if everything happening with the council led Rex to eventually hate Jerry?

His tension ramped up. Rex broke the kiss. His tender gaze drove Jerry's fears back. He'd be the happiest person alive if Rex looked at him like that for the rest of his life.

"I'm nervous about what the council will say."

"Everything will be fine, as long as we're together." Rex smiled gently. Jerry couldn't help but smile back.

Reluctantly, they separated and returned to the Congressional Room. Rex stopped Jerry before they reached the door. Two different guards stood on either side of the open entryway. Jerry knew both of them. Lorac was tall and thin, with a baby face and large green eyes, and while looking harmless, he was fast and deadly. The other guard, Fillian, was shaved bald with near black eyes, and reminded Jerry of a bulldog, with large jowls and a permanently pissed-off look. When the two guards averted their gaze, Jerry's gut flipped.

Rex faced Jerry, the tension in his jaw evident, yet he still smiled. "I want you to remember." He clasped both of Jerry's hands. "Whatever happens in there, you're mine and I'm yours. No matter what. Okay?"

Jerry nodded. What he'd dreamed of for months was right in front of him and could be lost in one fatal moment. They walked into the room where their future would be decided.

Ten pairs of eyes turned to them. Two chairs had been placed in the center of the room. Tanyon motioned for them to sit.

"Thank you for joining us, and for waiting patiently as we deliberated." The cadence of Tanyon's tone was light and practically joyful, restoring Jerry's hope for a favorable ruling. Yet, when he spotted the grin on Geraldon's face, he swallowed hard as bile surged into his throat. A gleeful Geraldon could only mean the decision had gone in his favor.

Oh fuck.

CHAPTER 16

JERRY'S FATHER leaned forward with his elbows on the table, his expression neutral, but his leg bounced, revealing his nervousness. Before returning to the room, his father said he had little control over whatever the council decided, but added he trusted them to hand down a fair decision. What they considered fair and what Jerry wanted were no doubt miles apart.

Tanyon didn't waste any time. "The council has examined the facts and deliberated on the best course of action. The future safety of the Anzuni race depends on the ability of the royal family to rule, which has always been central to the Anzuni culture. Anzuni rest easy knowing that major issues and the development of their clan lies with those placing the clan before their own agendas and personal desires."

Damn, if they all weren't looking at Jerry, who in all fairness had done just that. He raised his chin to show he understood his selfishness had cast doubt on his father as a ruler, and on Jerry as the future king. Perhaps they would ask him to remove himself as the heir.

"Prince Jerricho, you and your claxton, please stand."

Jerry turned a shocked expression to Rex, who looked confused for a moment but quickly schooled his features. Jerry's father gazed at them, his eyes showing his confusion as well.

"It is the ruling of this council that Prince Jerricho Alamande Trychovisca is guilty of disregarding Anzuni customs and laws set forth in the Daenose. First, he violated the marriage contract entered by his father, and second, revealed the existence of the Anzuni to a human without gaining council approval. Prince Jerricho has trained since birth to assume the role of crown prince and king when the time came. He cannot feign ignorance, and is summarily found guilty on both counts."

Tanyon's expression morphed from that of kindly patriarch to one of stern disapproval. The breath was knocked from Jerry's lungs as the words sank in. What did he mean by "guilty"?

Jerry forced himself to breathe as he searched his father's face for any idea of what would happen, but his father's eyes gave nothing away.

"As such, I will now render the sentences, which are to commence at the close of these proceedings. Prince Jerricho Alamande Trychovisca, since you have failed to obtain the proper training and knowledge required to assume the role of crown prince on your twenty-fifth birthday, you are hereby sentenced to an intensive training course supervised by myself. You will be schooled daily on the contents of the Daenose and customs of the Anzuni clan."

Jerry scanned the other council members, who had remained silent. Many scowled as Tanyon spoke, but many others appeared to be sympathetic to what occurred.

"Michael Rexford Callaghan."

Jerry raised a questioning brow hearing Rex's full name, but Rex's attention was on Tanyon.

"You will complete the Klaestrom required of all humans. However, since you will be the claxton to the future Anzuni king, you too will be required to study extensively in the Daenose and customs of our people. While you have no guilt in what has occurred, and have suffered from the deceit of Jerricho, you will be an Anzuni citizen and are bound by the ruling of this council."

Okay. This wasn't so bad. He and Rex could study together. But that meant Rex would have to leave his job. He'd summarily lose his freedom and his ability to live a normal life. Was their child—was Jerry—worth that to him?

"You must agree to this sentence to continue as part of the Anzuni clan, and to gain the council's permission to take your place as the claxton to the future crown prince. This means life as you know it will be forever altered. Your dedication, your service, your life belongs to the Anzuni clan and your future mate. Do you understand this?"

Rex shifted nervously as Jerry glanced sideways at him. When Jerry looked to Geraldon, his gleeful expression disturbed Jerry. He believed Rex wouldn't agree to their stipulations. He didn't have to and it might be best if he didn't.

"Rex, you don—"

"I understand your stipulations, and I agree to them," Rex said, his tone clear and confident.

Geraldon scowled. How long before Rex regretted those words? Tanyon rose and picked up the Daenose from the table. He held the massive book before Rex, and Jerry frowned, as did his father.

"Do you, Michael Rexford Callaghan, swear to uphold the laws and accept your position in the Anzuni clan?"

This was the induction that occurred only after a human had completed the Klaestrom. But Rex was being sworn in *before* he'd completed the training. Something wasn't right.

"Do you swear to recognize the king of the Anzuni people, the ruling family, and this council as your leaders, without question, and with full allegiance? Swear this now by placing your hand on the Daenose and saying 'I swear.'"

Rex placed his hand on the book, and Jerry looked helplessly to his father, who glanced nervously at the council.

"I swear."

"Rex, claxton to the prince, you are now bound by Anzuni law, which supersede your human laws. As such, you are now a member of the Anzuni clan."

Rex beamed as he glanced at Jerry. Rex's smile faded, no doubt seeing Jerry's confusion. He tilted his head to the side. "Jer? What's wrong?"

Something, but Jerry didn't know what. He looked to Geraldon. The satisfied expression on his face nearly tore Jerry's heart from his chest.

Tanyon looked past Jerry and Rex, toward the entrance to the room. Jerry looked over his shoulder to see who was there. The guards waited as they kept their attention on Tanyon.

"Take them into custody. You're not to let them out of your sight until we leave," Tanyon instructed.

"Wait, no!" Jerry scrambled back as the guards approached.

Custody. Were they under arrest? But he hadn't committed treason. He was pregnant, and they wanted to throw him into jail?

"Is this necessary, Tanyon?" His father stood, his eyes flaring with anger and fear. "Jerricho and Rex will abide by the council's ruling without resistance. Why is this necessary?"

"They will be under guard until they have completed the requirements of this council," Geraldon snarled.

"But why're you throwing us into jail?" Jerry's heart nearly stopped as the two guards approached. "Rex, you don't have to do this. You can say no. You're—"

"He's an Anzuni citizen now, bound by our laws. If he refuses, he will face an even stiffer penalty." Geraldon smirked.

Jerry gaped, surveying the council members, immediately knowing who had agreed and who'd had no choice.

"The sentencing guidelines handed down do not require they be taken into custody." Evidence of his father's disapproval laced his voice. "They will complete the conditions you have set forth without incident."

"Despite the leniency of the sentence," Baltheus stated, "all Anzuni must understand our customs and laws are to be taken seriously." He glared at Jerricho. "Even a *prince* can't escape punishment and retribution."

Damn, who shit in his Wheaties? From his tone and expression, one would have believed Jerry had personally wronged Baltheus.

Jerry's father glared. "We're fully aware of the seriousness of these charges—"

"Please, everyone." Janines interrupted the chatter. "I believe the word *custody* is harsh and doesn't truly reflect the nature of the ruling by this council, or its intent. No one is going to jail."

She circled the table, her slim form graceful, her tail coming to an inch from the floor. Anzuni women had shorter horns and tails than males. Her wide eyes were a lovely shade of blue.

She smiled as she moved past Tanyon. "You may be a wise elder, but at times, your educated brain gets in the way of your ability to empathize and deliver information with compassion."

Tanyon smirked, and his gaze on her filled with mirth. "Is that so, Janines?"

"That is so, Tanyon," she stated emphatically. "Jerricho and Rex. Please, let me be the first on the council to congratulate you on the future birth of your child. While not under the best of circumstances, I can see the love you share in the tenderness of your expressions for one another. Love is the greatest gift life can give us. Don't you agree, Geraldon?" she asked over her shoulder.

The resulting snort filled the room.

"Anyway. You will be required to complete your training, but you will be together. However," she said, eyeing them both, "that training will be completed with Tanyon in California, where you will learn from the top Anzuni scholars."

Jerry's brow rose. "How long?"

"Until this council is satisfied you have fulfilled your sentence." Geraldon had barely gritted out the words between his clenched teeth.

Janines rolled her eyes dramatically and cleared her throat.

Geraldon sighed heavily. "Fine. *Recommendations*."

Jerry looked to his father, his expression showing the same dismay as Jerry over the idea. He'd be over a thousand miles away for an undetermined amount of time. While Jerry had spent most of his short adult life fighting for freedom, he'd done so no more than a few miles from his parents.

His father, most likely seeing the forlorn look on his face, left the table and approached Jerry and placed his hands on his shoulders. "You'll be in safe hands. And Rex will be with you. Before you know it, you'll be home and taking your rightful place as crown prince of the Anzuni. Despite everything, know that your mother and I are proud of you, son, and love you very much."

Jerry clasped his father's forearm. "I'm sorry for the trouble I've caused you. I will make you proud. I promise."

"Of that, I have no doubt."

"I have already made travel arrangements. We leave first thing in the morning." Tanyon's announcement jerked Jerry's gut. So soon.

CHAPTER 17

"YOU'RE LEAVING? Today?" Keith looked stunned.

Jerry merely nodded as he packed his clothes. He stopped and threw his hands up. "What am I supposed to do?"

Keith shrugged. "Aren't you still healing? You look like you were hit in the face by a line drive and then the bat. Should you even be traveling?"

"I hurt a little, but not too bad thanks to some painkillers."

"Did you threaten to run?"

Jerry frowned at Keith's change of topic. "What?"

"The guard outside your room, and the one following Rex as if he's gonna bolt at any second."

Jerry rolled his eyes in an unprincely manner. "The council wants all Anzuni to know how serious they take the crap I pulled. You know, paying for my *crime* and all."

Keith snorted. "You committing a crime? That's about as likely as me following the rules."

Jerry huffed. "Geraldon wanted to throw me in jail for treason, so I should be grateful I only have to be babysat by a guard. I wouldn't do well in jail." Jerry shuddered.

Keith slapped him on the back. "Yeah, you'd be crying after the first hour."

"Fuck you." Jerry swiped at Keith, who danced away, laughing.

Damn, Jerry was going to miss him.

Jerry threw more clothes into his bag, scrutinized them, and pulled them back out. He replaced them with others from his drawers. He had no clue how long he'd be gone, no clue when the council would allow him to return. His stomach would expand and nothing would fit anyway.

"I don't want to go, especially not when I'm pregnant, but we have to do what the council says." He looked about the room. "Where the heck are my gray sweats?"

He wished Rex would return. He had gone downstairs under Fillian's watch to call his parents and his boss, essentially ending his life as he knew it.

Keith stood and pulled the sweats off the chair where he'd sat. He handed them over. "It's going to be okay." Keith always picked up on Jerry's impending meltdowns.

"I'm sure you're right."

"Jeez, of course I am. And you two can smooch over those smelly old books and hold hands under the table. Just like high school. Maybe you could even have a prom."

Jerry narrowed his eyes.

Keith raised his hands. "What?"

Jerry sat on the bed, wishing their time in California would be so simple. "I can't believe the mess I've caused, but…."

"You wouldn't change any of it."

Jerry grinned. "No, I wouldn't." If not for the entire mess, he'd be destined to a life of spousal servitude with Tyranis. He sighed. "Damn, I'm going to miss you."

Keith ducked his head. "Yeah. It's going to be boring as hell not having to keep your ass out of trouble. You need to call me every day so I can harass you."

Jerry grunted. "Right. *You* keep my ass out of trouble? As if. Are things still going hot and heavy with Paul Bunyan?"

Keith flushed bright red in the face, and he fidgeted. "None of your fucking business, *Your Highness*."

Keith grabbed the bag Jerry had filled earlier and bolted from the room with it.

"You can run, but you can't hide!"

"I'd never hide from you, *Your Highness*." Rex walked into the room. And Jerry smiled wide seeing him. Fillian closed the door, giving them some much-needed privacy.

Rex stopped next to the bed. He never failed to take Jerry's breath away. The urge to apologize hit Jerry hard. What kind of apology did one give for yanking someone from their life and condemning them to a lifetime as an Anzuni? Rex met Jerry's gaze. He surveyed Jerry's face, and his expression, which had been tentative, closed, seemed to open.

119

"I spoke with my folks. Told them I'd be away for a while." He didn't move forward, didn't seem as if he wanted to.

"That's good." Jerry rubbed the back of his neck. "I'm so sorry about all of this."

When Rex snorted loudly, Jerry's head snapped up.

"I am! Please believe me. I never meant to drag you into this."

Rex stepped forward. It took everything Jerry had to stand his ground.

"You should be sorry."

"I am. Believe me." Jerry would apologize until Rex told him to shut up.

"Are you sorry I'm here?"

The question confused Jerry.

Before he could speak, Rex said, "Are you sorry you dragged me kicking and screaming into your world?"

Jerry shifted nervously. Gods, this felt like a trap.

"I... I... um...."

Rex took another step and lowered his voice. "Are you sorry that you hooked me with those beautiful brown eyes, made me ache for that hard ass, tempted my tongue with those tattoos, made my fingers itch to touch you?" Another step and he was inches from Jerry. Rex's proximity flushed Jerry's skin, or was it his words? "Are you sorry for capturing my heart with your kindness, making me a slave to your laugh, addicting me to your smell so that every time I left the library after being with you I had to jerk off more than once to calm myself down?" Rex caressed Jerry's cheek and he shivered. "Are you really sorry, Jer? Because I'm not."

Mesmerized by the darkening green in Rex's eyes, Jerry barely managed to shake his head. He'd never be sorry for falling in love with Rex, but he couldn't make his mouth form the words. Rejection was still his greatest fear.

"Good," Rex whispered across his lips. "Now don't forget that."

"I-I won't."

Rex growled, kissing Jerry, who ignored the pain in his face. When the kiss ended, Jerry buried his nose in Rex's neck and inhaled deeply.

Just his scent hardened Jerry's cock. Rex ran his large hands over Jerry's back and he relaxed. Maybe they had time for one last romp in the sheets.

"I see you've packed your hard-on." Rex pushed his thigh between Jerry's leg, and he groaned from the pressure.

"Get hard every time I see you. It's an affliction that I'll have to live with for the rest of my life."

"You'd better fucking believe it," Rex whispered, and attacked Jerry's lips.

Jerry sucked on Rex's warm tongue, riding his muscular thigh, pushing harder and higher, seeking release, his balls drawing up tight as heat radiated into his gut.

Rex broke the kiss, and his lips skated over Jerry's jaw. "Fucking want you, Prince Jerricho."

"The guards are outside." Jerry moaned as Rex nipped and sucked on his neck. He bucked his hips harder, faster, needing to come. Who gave a shit what the guards heard? "Please."

In one fluid movement, Rex had Jerry on his back on the soft mattress. Rex yanked Jerry's pants off and then his underwear. Rex attacked Jerry's cock. No teasing. No taking it slow. Jerry grasped Rex's head as he sucked Jerry's balls deeply into his mouth, stretching the skin until each ball popped from his mouth. Rex skated his large hands over Jerry's thighs, his stomach and chest. When Rex sucked on the head of his cock, Jerry's hips bucked involuntarily.

"Lie still," Rex commanded, and the sound was enough to push more precum from Jerry's cock. "Or I *will* have to punish you."

Oh, hell! The warning had Jerry's hips moving again. He yelped as Rex flipped him onto his stomach and yanked him onto his knees.

"I warned you." Rex grasped Jerry's shoulder hard. Without warning, a stinging slap landed on Jerry's ass.

"Fuck!" Jerry bucked forward, but Rex held him in place. Before he could utter a word of protest, Jerry's other cheek was slapped. Jerry bellowed as the sting ran over every nerve in his ass. He gasped and tried to squirm away, but Rex held him tight.

"You will take all that I give you."

Another slap, this one over the crack of Jerry's ass. He groaned as slaps rained over his ass and the backs of his thighs—even his balls. He pushed into the slaps, his cock tight to his belly, painfully hard and drooling precum.

"Oh…. Oh Gods…. R-Rex!"

The stinging morphed, dancing and twisting into a ball of pain and pleasure, leaving Jerry practically hyperventilating, his hands twisting and pulling at the sheets. His mind clouded with the rush, and his vision whited out until he floated as his orgasm screamed through him.

When his senses returned, he was on his back, Rex on top of him, placing gentle kisses on his cheeks, his forehead, and his lips as his cock rocked slowly in and out of Jerry's body. He groaned as Rex changed his angle, hitting his overstimulated prostate.

Jerry sighed deeply, boneless, enjoying the rhythmic movements, the slide against his muscles.

"You are fucking amazing," Rex whispered in his ear. Jerry tried to lift his arms, but they were heavy and uncooperative.

"Best orgasm ever." Jerry moaned as Rex hit that spot again. "Right there."

Rex pulled Jerry tighter to his body, pushing deeper, and Jerry bit into his shoulder, producing a mark.

"Oh yeah," Rex groaned as Jerry's teeth dug into his flesh. "Bite me harder."

Jerry applied more pressure, his teeth pinching the skin.

"Harder!"

Jerry complied, his cock hardening with the friction. Rex plowed into him. Jerry released and bit down again without hesitation, causing Rex to fuck him so hard that he was pushed up the bed, with Rex following. His reaction to the bite pushed Jerry closer. He released the skin, clamped down again on Rex's shoulder, and reached between them, pinching Rex's nipple as hard as he could. Rex screamed through gritted teeth. With one last thrust, he emptied into Jerry's ass. The spasm of his cock in Jerry's hole brought on his second orgasm, not as brilliant as the first, but perfect.

Rex collapsed at Jerry's side, wrapping himself around Jerry's body, his head on Jerry's chest. Every cell in Jerry's body vibrated, and his heart beat furiously against his ribs. Rex's chest rose and fell rapidly, sweat glistening on his skin. Jerry ran his hands through Rex's hair, continuing to ride the high of their lovemaking.

When Rex didn't speak or move for several minutes, Jerry asked if he was okay.

Rex sighed, his hot breath skating across Jerry's skin, causing him to shudder. Rex lifted his head and gazed down on Jerry, appearing to be searching for something. Jerry refrained from squirming under the scrutiny.

"I never thought I'd feel this way about anyone. Connected. I'm not sure how to describe it." Rex averted his gaze. "It's kind of like finding something I didn't know was missing."

Jerry caught Rex's embarrassment on his face. He cupped Rex's cheek and prompted him to turn his head.

"I know it sounds corny. Guys usually don't say things like that to each other…. Well, I've never heard any of my friends say anything like that before, but…." Gods, Jerry loved Rex. "When I first met you, I was attracted to you, and when I got to know you, well, something felt right. I'm generally restless and stumble along." Jerry gazed at Rex's lips as he slid his thumb across the lower one. "But with you I don't feel so lost. More centered than ever. Maybe we were meant to be."

Rex smiled gently and clasped hands with Jerry, gently kissing his fingers. "Sounds good to me."

They laughed at their mutually sappy declarations of love, but Jerry was also happy finally feeling he'd been allowed something he wanted. What more could he want?

JERRY GROANED as the plane rocked. The relentless turbulence caused his stomach to lurch every time the plane did. Rex rubbed the back of his neck as Jerry leaned over, his head between his knees. The flight attendant had offered him Dramamine and frowned when he'd declined. He gave a lame excuse about being on another med and shouldn't mix them. She'd never believe the real reason he'd declined. If he could make it through another hour, they'd be in Southern California. He'd flown several times before, but never while pregnant.

"How are you doing, Jer?" Rex was being so attentive and calming.

"I'm in the seventh level of hell, but I'm pretty sure I'll survive." The plane bounced again, and his stomach pushed up into his throat. "Oh gods, make it stop."

Rex continued rubbing Jerry's neck. "Are you going to throw up?"

That would be the climax of his humiliation. Maybe he should head to the bathroom, just in case, but he feared any movement would trigger his puke reflex. Plus, his face throbbed, and his back was sore as hell. Keith was right. He should be home in bed healing, not crossing the country.

"Is he okay?" Merano asked. His father's assistant had accompanied them to assure Jerry's needs were met while carrying out the council's requirements. Jerry imagined he wasn't too happy about the assignment. Who knew how long they'd be gone? At least they were free of guards for now. Tanyon had taken an earlier flight to prepare for their arrival and would bring his own to the airport. As if they would try to escape.

"He's holding on. I wish we could call the doctor and see if there's anything we can give him." Rex's distress was apparent in his voice.

He patted Rex's leg. "I'm okay. Once we got off this flying tin can, I'm sure it'll pass quickly." He hadn't told Rex the nausea had appeared after eating lunch, and not on the plane.

Rex massaged Jerry's back, sweeping in large circles, which took Jerry's mind off the churning of his gut. With pure willpower—and Rex's distraction—Jerry managed to avoid tossing his breakfast before they landed. Once they were off the plane, Rex wrapped his arm around Jerry's waist to steady him as they walked.

Shit, what was wrong with him? Maybe he was sick. Maybe he had the Anzuni flu. The virus tended to attack the nervous system and caused trouble walking. He needed to see a doctor, and told Rex as much.

Rex agreed, and when they met Tanyon at the entrance to the airport, Merano let him know what Jerricho needed.

"I'm sorry you aren't feeling well, Your Highness. I will call ahead and request the physician see you as soon as we arrive."

"Thanks." Jerry leaned heavily against Rex. He had to admit, even off the plane, he still felt like crap.

"Come on. Let's get you into the car."

Rex led him to the curb. The car turned out to be a limo. Two guards in suits opened the doors when their group approached. Damn, they were larger than Rex.

Tanyon motioned to the limo. "Come, gentlemen. We have about a half-hour ride."

Tanyon and Merano climbed in, sharing the seat facing backward, to Jerry's relief. He wouldn't escape puking if he had to ride sitting backward. Rex helped Jerry in and settled beside him. The car rocked as the oversized guards settled into the front. The closed glass partition blocked out their sounds.

"Will you be okay, Prince Jerricho?" Tanyon asked, concern lining his forehead.

Jerry leaned into Rex, who wrapped an arm around him. "I don't know what's wrong with me. I feel worse since we got off the plane." Gods, he sounded so whiny.

Rex squeezed him, and Jerry nuzzled into his chest as his head spun. He wished he were home. They headed off into the unknown, at the council's mercy, and what they deemed restitution for his crime. Being sick on top of that wasn't going to make it any easier. He'd gladly serve his sentence, but he wished he'd been able to do so at home.

"Would you like some water?" Tanyon asked as he held out a bottle.

Rex took the water from Tanyon and opened the bottle. Keeping his head on Rex's chest, he took a sip. "Thanks."

Tanyon smiled approvingly. His grandfatherly air appealed to Jerry. While a majority of the council members had ignored Jerry since starting his freedom sabbatical, Tanyon took time to speak with him when they'd crossed paths. If Jerry had to choose from the lot, he'd go with Tanyon.

Jerry listened as the men talked, drifting away. The vibrations in Rex's chest when he spoke lulled Jerry further into himself and a deep sleep.

Jerry jerked awake. A heavy weight lay across his back, pinning him to his own legs. He panicked, struggling to move.

"What're you doing?" Tanyon sounded pissed.

The heavy weight on Jerry was Rex, and he wasn't moving. "Rex!"

CHAPTER 18

JERRY GRUNTED beneath the dead weight pressing on him. He managed to wriggle free and sat up. With the glass partition lowered, the guard in the passenger seat aimed a gun at them.

Merano slumped over in his seat. Tanyon shouted and lunged forward. Before reaching the man, Tanyon stiffened and his hands went his side of his neck. Jerry pushed back against the seat, waiting for the gush of blood, but none came. Tanyon's eyes fluttered, and his body fell limply across Merano.

Jerry wished the seat would swallow him as the sneering man turned his attention on him. That gun disappeared. Another appeared, pointing directly at Rex. "Don't worry, princey, that was only a dart gun. This one here"—he waved the weapon—"is the real deal. Orders are we can't tranquilize you, so if you try anything, I'll shoot your human in the head. Do you understand?"

The malicious glint in the man's eye told Jerry he'd enjoy doing it too. Jerry nodded. "Why? What do you want?"

The man smirked. "You'll see soon enough. Now shut it, or I'll be the next one to fuck up your face."

Jerry turned his attention to Rex. His chest rose and fell evenly, but no amount of prodding woke him. Jerry's phone was in his pocket, and to get it, he'd have to move Rex. If he tried Mr. Trigger Happy would shoot Rex. Jerry had to play along with his kidnappers until he had a chance to get them help. What the hell else could he do?

JERRY PACED the small room where he'd been dumped hours ago. Screaming and ranting, he'd demanded to be taken to Rex. The nausea that had plagued him the entire trip had passed, a plus since, besides a cot, there was only a dirty bucket in the room. If he puked in that, he'd be stuck with the foul smell. The boxlike room had no windows, and the door wouldn't budge despite the handle turning. Had to be bolted on the outside. A single caged bulb in the ceiling provided the only light.

Two people had come in earlier, and Jerry had to laugh seeing the woman and man, who guarded the door, wearing green-and-purple-feathered Mardi Gras masks covering the upper parts of their faces. His amusement quickly turned to anger as they both ignored Jerry's demands to see Rex and know what their captors wanted. With great efficiency, the woman took what had to be a pint of blood from Jerry's arm. Every scenario Jerry imagined of overpowering them ended with fresh bruises, possibly broken bones, or death. Nothing came to him before they left.

Frustrated beyond words, Jerry had kicked the door as it closed and locked. He rammed the solid wood with his shoulder, but it wouldn't budge, so he'd given up and paced for hours, too revved up to sit still.

The painkillers he'd taken on the plane had worn off, and his entire body was one exposed nerve. The baby kicked hard, and had been moving nonstop, ever since he'd been deposited in this closet. No doubt the adrenaline running through his body affected his child.

Why had they been taken?

Ransom was his first thought. His parents' greatest fears when he was a child had been kidnapping and the one fear that had pissed Jerry off the most. Sheltered, protected, not allowed to go anywhere without a guard, his friends' families vetted for something as innocuous as a playdate. He'd been unable to do half of the activities his friends had partaken in. Since he'd become an adult, his parents' fear had waned, but now Jerry understood their concern.

Revenge could be another reason. Who would want revenge on him? Tyranis for sure. He'd essentially stolen the future rule of king from the psycho man. Cheated on him, humiliated him, and because he'd attacked Jerry, he was on his way to what amounted to Anzuni prison. But he was in custody, so it wasn't him. Geraldon hated Jerry for taking the throne from his nephew and probably a million other reasons. He'd been so smug at the sentencing, so adamant about their incarceration. Gods, what if he'd kidnapped them? What in the hell would he do to them? If he showed his face, he could never let them go. Which meant....

Jerry rammed the door again, not losing hope it would pop open if he hit it hard enough. Although he wasn't sure what he'd do if he were free. Find Rex, but he didn't have a weapon and any guards, regardless of their size, would be able to take him down in seconds. The building could be miles from anywhere, or if they were lucky enough, smack-dab in the middle of a city. He scrubbed his face with his hands and flopped onto the cot. He prayed Rex was okay, that he was unharmed, and trying to get to Jerry as well. Knowing his protective streak, he'd fight his captors and endure any torture to protect Jerry and their child. That scared Jerry most.

More hours had passed when the *click* of the lock startled Jerry. He jumped to his feet. The door opened slightly, and a covered tray slid across the floor. Before Jerry reached the door, it was slammed shut and locked again.

Jerry pounded his fists against the wood. "Come back here! Open this fucking door!"

When nothing happened, he kicked it, the impact shooting pain through his boot and up into his leg. "Fucking bastards!"

He eyed the tray and squatted, lifting the cover. A sandwich and chips, apple juice, and green Jell-O. Jerry slammed the lid on the food, refusing to eat their crap. He held out as long as he could, his stomach persistently growling its demand for food. With the pregnancy, he'd been eating about six times a day. Refusing to eat would harm not only him but the baby.

Reluctantly, he pulled the tray into his lap and devoured every bit of the food. He placed the tray on the floor and rolled onto his side, staring at the wall. He seethed with anger at Geraldon. If he was responsible for their capture, Jerry would make him pay, if it was the last thing he did. Eventually, he drifted off to sleep on a tide of anger and sorrow.

NAUSEA RIPPED Jerry from sleep. His mouth watered, and he sat on the edge of the cot, leaning over as his stomach clenched. He wouldn't escape throwing up this time. He swallowed repeatedly, willing his stomach to cease its protest. He wrapped his hand around his middle as his skin flashed hot and cold. He heaved, barely making it to the bucket as chunks of food exited his body. The heaving spasms were relentless as his stomach emptied but finally stopped, leaving him a sweating drooling mess.

He plopped onto the floor and slouched against the wall. He repeatedly spit into the bucket, unable to rid his mouth of the foul taste. The room spun, his vision blurred, and he wiped cold sweat from his brow. He barely moved as the door opened. A large blurry figure entered, grabbed the bucket, and dropped another in its place. A bottle of water was shoved into Jerry's hand. Without a word, the person exited.

Jerry lay on the cool tile floor. He'd gotten sick after he'd eaten. Same as earlier. Was something wrong with him? Was something wrong with the baby? Morning sickness had passed a few weeks ago. He pushed himself up to sit and cracked open the water, sucking down the cold liquid. Still nauseous, but his stomach had settled a bit. He dragged himself to the cot and lay down, wishing the room would stop spinning.

JERRY JERKED out of sleep, momentarily disoriented by his surroundings. As he came around, he recognized the bland walls of his cell. Something had woken him, but the room was silent. Perhaps they'd delivered another tray. He looked to the floor, but nothing was there. He had to piss like crazy, and couldn't ignore using the bucket any longer. As he relieved himself, a loud roar startled him. Jerry's body went on high alert. The noise had come from the other side of the wall. He tucked his cock back into his pants and zipped up. Placing his ear against the cool wall, he listened for any sounds.

Another muffled scream and then a roar. "You fucking bastards!" Rex screamed in agony, cursing whoever tortured him.

"Rex! I'm here!" Jerry pounded on the wall frantically as there were more screams. "Stop! Stop hurting him! Please!"

Jerry slammed into the door over and over as Rex's howls and pleas filtered through the wall. They went on and on, as Jerry screamed until he was hoarse and his voice broken. He'd bruised his shoulder and bloodied his fists from pounding. The helpless way Rex screamed panicked Jerry. Rex's shout cut off. Jerry sobbed, fearful they'd killed him.

"Rex." Jerry sobbed. He slid down the wall and curled up on the floor, holding his stomach. What did they want from them?

CHAPTER 19

THE NEXT time the door opened, a body flew across the room and landed on the floor. Jerry bolted upright. A man in a black mask with a long narrow beak stood scowling in front of the open door. Next to the cot, Tanyon struggled to get up. Damn, they shouldn't be throwing an old man like him around.

"Tanyon." Jerry was never so happy to see someone. "Are you okay?"

Jerry helped him to his feet, and Tanyon glowered at the guard. A large bruise covered Tanyon's left cheek. "I can walk, you know!"

The guard remained silent.

Jerry grasped Tanyon's arm. "Have you seen Rex? He was screaming and they wouldn't stop hurting him. Then there was silence." Jerry's panic spilled over, but he didn't care.

Tanyon's crestfallen expression scared Jerry.

No, please no.

"I haven't seen him, but they want something, Jerricho. They said Rex had it, but he refused to give it up." He swallowed hard and placed his hand on Jerry's shoulder. "They tortured him for hours, but he didn't tell them where it was. If they don't get it, they'll kill him." Tanyon's aged face paled.

"What is it? Whatever they want, they can have it!" He'd give anything to spare Rex's life.

"They want your pendant. The one that belonged to your uncle. They believe Rex had it, but I told them he couldn't because you rarely ever took it off. I'm not sure why they thought he would have it."

His pendant? Maybe it was more valuable than Jerry had believed. And he'd given it to Rex. Why hadn't he handed it—

Jerry wiped his shaking hand over his mouth. Before they'd left for the airport, Rex had handed the necklace to Jerry, asking him to

130

put it in a safe place so he wouldn't have to take it off going through security. He feared being responsible for the sentimental pendant. Someone knew Rex had been wearing it. Someone in the mansion, because anyone who'd seen Rex had seen the pendant around his neck. Geraldon was one of them.

"He wore it before the council yesterday. Do you remember?"

Tanyon shook his head.

"He was wearing it, but he gave it back to me before we left the mansion. Why do they want it?"

"As proof they have you."

So they wanted something from his family. "I have it."

Tanyon's eyes narrowed, then lightened. "Thank gods, Jerricho. You've saved Rex's life."

"It's in my suitcase, the blue one."

Tanyon narrowed his eyes. "They said they looked through all of your luggage."

"It's in a compartment on the left-hand side. You have to push on the panel, and it'll pop open. It's there, I promise." Jerry turned to Birdman. "Please, you can have it. Just let us go."

Birdman didn't say a word.

Jerry leaned in and whispered into Tanyon's ear. "Do you think Geraldon is behind this? Maybe he's going to make my father pay for what I did to Tyranis."

Tanyon's eyes widened, as if he hadn't put two and two together. He gasped quietly. "He's the one who insisted your sentence be carried out away from the mansion. That's what took so long to deliberate. He wouldn't budge. But why would he want the pendant?"

Jerry had suspected Geraldon was the one behind that stipulation.

"Let's go." Birdman grabbed Tanyon by the arm and pulled him toward the door. Jerry held Tanyon's sleeve, desperate to keep him there.

"Let him stay with me, please?" When they got what they wanted, what would they do to Tanyon? To Rex?

"Do what they say and everything will be okay. Please." Tanyon was yanked from the room, and the door was slammed and locked.

JERRY WASN'T sure how long he'd been in that room. After two more meals where he'd become violently ill, he quit eating the prepared food, opting instead to drink the sealed juice. Still he got sick. Even the juice had been tampered with, so he stopped drinking as well. He'd surpassed hunger, even dreaming about food. He'd have killed for a cracker, anything. He was weak and light-headed. When a large black bird entered his room, he knew he had to be hallucinating. As the form came closer, he realized it was Birdman.

"Since you won't eat, we're going to have to do this the hard way."

Birdman flipped Jerry onto his back as more masked people entered the room. That brought Jerry hope, because if they hadn't planned on eventually releasing them, they wouldn't have bothered with masks, right?

One man wore a white lab coat and a feathered mask like he'd seen on others, but some of them were scarier, darker, medieval. Two of the men tied Jerry's arms to the metal frame of the cot with leather straps.

"What're you doing? Please, my father will pay you. Let me call him."

If Geraldon was responsible, perhaps his minions could be bought, but no one answered him. He kicked his legs out, but was too weak to raise them high enough. He must not have eaten for days. How long had he been here?

The man in the lab coat leaned over him, and he realized that *he* was a *she*.

"Please," he whispered, but she didn't answer.

He flinched as she pushed a needle into the back of his hand. Another masked man pulled an IV pole with a bag of clear liquid into the room. The tube from the bag was attached to the port in his arm.

"Hand me the syringe with the antiemetic. Next time he's puking his guts out from a violent reaction or anything like that, tell me immediately." The terse tone punctuated her annoyance.

A large man with the full-face silver metal mask shrugged. "Sorry, Doc."

"You know he can't be harmed. If he dies, then this is all for nothing. All of it. I need at least another twenty-four hours before I can do what he wants."

He? Geraldon?

"What does he want? Why's he doing this?"

She ceased moving, opening her mouth as if to speak, but pursed her lips and continued with her task. When she finished taping the site, she left the room and her entourage followed, slamming the door on Jerry's screams and pleas to tell him Rex was okay. He needed Rex.

MASKED PEOPLE came in and out of his room to change the IV bag, which he believed was chock-full of calories, since he was no longer starving. What plagued him with fear was the substance they'd been injecting into his IV. What if it harmed the baby? The doctor had told her lackeys he couldn't be harmed. Did they even know he was pregnant? If they knew he was Anzuni, they had to know about the pregnancy. Every Anzuni had to know their prince was pregnant with an illegitimate heir.

The worst of the visits were those where his pants had been yanked down and a bedpan shoved beneath him. He had to use it with Birdman watching. Topping off the nightmare of his embarrassment had come when Birdman had wiped his ass. Fucking embarrassing.

No matter how much Jerry pushed each person who entered the room for information, the most he received was a command to shut up. He wasn't sure if he should be comforted that he hadn't heard Rex's screams again. The silence could mean they'd tortured him to death. If Geraldon wanted revenge on Jerry, killing Rex would destroy him. Without Rex, he wanted to curl up and fade away. His body ached for his gentle touch and kisses, the closeness they had come to share in such a short amount of time.

Jerry tried to be optimistic. He envisioned Rex alive to bide his time until they were rescued. Despite his resolve, as time slipped by, Jerry drew deeper into his sorrow, mourning his partner, his best friend, his lover, and the father of his child. He vacillated between states of hope and despair as he lay on that hard cot, his world crashing at his feet. The only comfort was the continued movement of the baby in his stomach, which had grown noticeably since their capture. Knowing whatever they'd been shooting into his IV hadn't killed the baby comforted him. Each movement of Rex's child helped Jerry to feel less alone.

SOMETHING RATTLED as it rolled down the hallway outside his door. The sound grew louder. Except for Rex's screams and the clicks of locks, there were rarely any noises outside his room.

No one had come into his room for what seemed like days. Lying in the same position for so long, Jerry was stiff and sore. Except for a mortifying experience where his clothes had been stripped off his body and he'd been given a sponge bath, Jerry had been immobile.

The rolling sound stopped. A key was inserted into the lock and the door opened. Several of the masked men entered, including Birdman, whom Jerry had come to hate. His narrow, heartless eyes, how he carelessly yanked Jerry around instead of asking him to move, his delight in Jerry's pain.

Birdman removed Jerry's restraints. Without warning, the cot skidded across the concrete, and away from the wall. Jerry tried to lift his head, but the stiffness in his neck wouldn't allow it. Hands grabbed his shoulders and his feet, and lifted him from the bed. He groaned as pain shot through his rigid muscles and joints. The men dumped him onto a gurney in the hall and once again strapped him down. This time even his feet were bound.

"Where are you taking me?" Jerry's voice had weakened after days of not speaking much.

Again, no one responded. Once he was secured and his IV bag tucked at his side, the gurney moved along a hallway lined with dozens of closed doors. Industrial tiles and long tubes of fluorescent lights lined the ceiling. Nothing on the walls gave any indication as to where they were holding him. At the end of the hall, the gurney pushed open two swinging doors and they entered what looked to be a large operating room lined with medical equipment. Jerry couldn't see much from his prone position. When the gurney stopped, Jerry sucked in a breath.

"Rex!" Jerry's weakened voice didn't carry far. He yanked on his restraints and struggled to get up.

Strapped into what resembled a dental chair, Rex was upright. His glassy eyes fixed on a location in front of him, no expression, nothing to indicate he was cognizant of his surroundings. He was naked from the waist up, and Jerry's brow rose seeing his pendant around Rex's neck. What the fuck? That had been proof they had Jerry. Why did they have it on Rex?

"Rex. It's Jerry. Look at me."

Rex didn't twitch, didn't even blink. Except for looking pale and drugged, he appeared unharmed. Jerry's stomach roiled. How had they tortured him without leaving a mark?

"*Rex!*" No recognition appeared, no movement from his lover. He was catatonic.

The masked doctor who'd cared for Jerry stepped up beside him.

"What did you do to him?"

She held a syringe and searched his arm, no doubt for a vein. He hissed as the needle punctured his skin. When the vial had filled with blood, she removed the needle and walked away. One of the masked men stepped up and placed a Band-Aid on the site.

"Jeez, thanks, Sasquatch." The man growled, and Jerry waited for him to retaliate. When he stepped away, Jerry focused back on Rex.

A few feet away, the doctor worked with the blood she'd drawn, but Jerry couldn't see much of what she was doing. She turned to Rex, holding a larger syringe filled with red liquid. Was that Jerry's blood? What was she going to do with it?

"Stop this, please. Geraldon wants me. Don't hurt Rex. He didn't do anything!"

The moment of hesitation as she held the needle above Rex's arm didn't last long.

"Get on with it."

Jerry couldn't see who'd given the command. The doctor stabbed the needle into Rex's arm and pushed the plunger.

"Get ready with the crash cart." She stepped away from Rex.

She expected his heart to stop? "What? No! What did you do? Rex!" Jerry yanked on the restraints, uncaring of the pain he caused himself. Was the plan to kill Rex right in front of him? Was that his punishment?

Within seconds, Rex's eyes widened and he gasped. Jerry held his breath. Rex's eyes focused, and he blinked several times, taking in his surroundings. When he looked to Jerry, his eyes widened even farther and showed recognition. Rex opened his mouth to speak, but instead of words an earsplitting scream came from the depths of his chest. He writhed and bucked against the restraints. His howls of agony were deafening. Jerry called out to him, but he couldn't compete with Rex's sounds of agony.

"Help him!"

No one reacted as they stood back watching pain tearing apart the person Jerry loved. Rex was dying. Jerry's heart clenched, fighting to beat as he watched his entire world being ripped away.

Abruptly, the screams stopped. Rex's entire body seized, shaking the chair with his spasms. A guttural gurgling came from Rex's open mouth as his eyes rolled back into his head. Gods, it looked as if his face were changing. Jerry blinked several times at the grotesque sight before him. He yelped as Rex's canines grew past his bottom lip.

"Fuck me. It's working." The doctor stepped back, her face paling, fear taking the place of astonishment.

What were they turning Rex into? Jerry was helpless as Rex's face widened and his nose flattened slightly. When short corkscrew horns grew from his forehead, everyone in the room gasped. Some even swore. Rex's eyes flamed, burning an amber hue. Jerry could do nothing but stare until his memory kicked up an image. Jerry had seen something like the monster Rex turned into.

What had taken less than a minute seemed more like hours. Rex's head fell back against the chair, his chest heaving, sweat trickling down his changed features.

136

The doctor turned to the large mirror on the wall. "The transformation has been successful." Her flat tone hinted at defeat and not victory. But of what?

"Excellent," the disembodied voice said again. Jerry didn't look to see if he could catch a glimpse of the person. His eyes were locked on what had once been Rex. Though shocked, Jerry worked through sifting for more memories, and when he placed the image, his hands clenched, and his chest seized a beat. He had to breathe through the fear.

Rex had become a Braezelas.

CHAPTER 20

JERRY HUDDLED on the cot as a cool breeze filtered through the bars of the cage he now occupied. His head swam, and the fogginess in his brain had yet to lift. After realizing what they'd turned Rex into, Jerry had screamed, unable to stop. Even threats from Birdman had been unsuccessful in stopping Jerry. He'd accused them of turning Rex into a monster. Screamed that he'd see them all dead, making sure they did so slowly and painfully. One of the masked men told Jerry they had merely forced Rex to reveal his true form, that of a Braezelas. Jerry ended up hyperventilating until his limbs were numb and his vision cloudy. They sedated him, and for once he'd been glad to fall unconscious.

He woke back in his room, sequestered there for an eternity and heavily drugged. Time meant nothing in his semiconscious state. When the man with the metal mask had entered the room, he mentioned five days had been long enough. After that, Jerry woke in the cage, where he continued to lose his mind and any hope. Even now, he believed he was in some alternate universe—one he couldn't escape, one where Rex had transformed into the feared enemy of his people.

Oh gods. Rex—a Braezelas?

It wasn't true. It couldn't be. First off, Braezelas were ugly, drooling creatures with sharp claws. Yes, they had the corkscrew horns and the enlarged teeth. But Rex hadn't truly resembled the drawings in so many of the Anzuni fairy tales. He hadn't been hideous. Besides Braezelas were trapped in an alternate universe, forever separated from the Anzuni they'd enslaved. This hadn't been a simple kidnapping. This was something more sinister, more evil than Jerry could have imagined.

Now he was in a cage surrounded by a thick and vast darkness. Around him were the noises of others, breathing and groaning and shifting. Maybe there were more Braezelas ready to enslave Jerry and other Anzuni. Maybe the Braezelas had found their way onto Earth, planning to overtake the Anzuni, but their plot had been foiled when Jerry's captors forced them to reveal themselves. If so, why had Jerry been taken as well? He wasn't one of them.

But his blood had been injected into Rex. Had that been responsible for forcing the change? Rex as a Braezelas had been forever burned into his mind. His lover, the other half of his soul. His mind couldn't fathom that reality. Had Rex targeted Jerry with a purpose, tricked him into falling in love to infiltrate the monarchy from the inside? *Was* he a spy? Jerry's stomach roiled. Everything Rex had said, his promises, his confession of love, had they all been lies? Tears burned Jerry's eyes, his world crumbling around him, his heart dying once again. He choked on his grief, as sharp as if Rex had indeed died.

Hadn't he?

His Rex, or who he'd believed Rex to be, was gone forever, leaving Jerry pregnant with his baby. A child who would be half-Braezelas. Jerry shook his head. Would his child be a monster, an aggressive, domineering spawn? His child, whom he already loved, a half-breed, an enemy?

No. A baby was born innocent. Those who raised the child were responsible for that child's moral development. His next thought nearly stopped what was left of his pathetic heart. What if they took his baby at birth? He couldn't let that happen. He had to escape for his child's future.

A door slammed, the boom echoing throughout the room. Light filled the room around his cage and pierced Jerry's eyes. He covered his face. When he removed his hands, he blinked to adjust to the light, ignoring the pain shooting into his eyeballs. More cages surrounded him, at least a dozen, each with a cot. Some were occupied, but he couldn't tell if they were Anzuni, Braezelas, or human. Jerry sat up, leaning back against the cold bars. He gazed around the warehouse-like room. The few windows he saw were close to the ceiling, and dark. He couldn't tell if it was night or if they'd been blacked out.

To the left of Jerry's cage, about ten feet away, a person lay motionless on a cot. In the cage to the right, a man lay facing Jerry. Large brown eyes blinked, appearing to stare off into nothing. Jerry climbed off his cot, the cage tall enough to allow him to stand upright. He grasped the bars, peering at the man's slim, pale face. Awareness hit Jerry. He was one of the men who'd gone missing. His face had been on the news, his picture presented to Jerry's father, his fate unknown. This was more than revenge or ransom. What was Geraldon doing with these men? Gods, the man was deranged.

"Hello?" Jerry whispered.

A blink, and then the man's eyes focused on Jerry.

"You're new," the man whispered back. "I'm sorry." Remorse filled his face, as if he were personally responsible for Jerry being there. The man's eyes widened and he sat up and looked at Jerry's stomach. His surprise morphed into confusion, and then recognition.

"Prince Jerricho?"

Jerry nodded.

"But what are you doing here? How…."

"I was brought here along with my mate, Rex, my father's assistant, and a member of the council."

"You mated? But the ceremony…. You aren't of age yet."

Most Anzuni knew he was coming of age and would soon marry and produce an heir. The event only happened once every twenty-five years or so and tended to be big news.

"No." Jerry sighed. "It's a long story. You're Eli Snow, aren't you?"

Eli nodded.

"You were reported missing. How did you get here?" Jerry looked to see if anyone listened. No one had entered the room, but there could be cameras with microphones.

"I was walking home from class one night, and someone grabbed me and shoved a needle into my arm. When I woke up, I was in this cage." He looked to his lap, then back at Jerry. "I don't know how long I've been here. Do you know what the date is?"

Eli's beseeching gaze showed his innocence. He was only eighteen.

"We were taken on May fourteenth. I'm not sure how long we've been here. I think it's been a couple of weeks."

Couldn't be longer than that, although what did Jerry know?

The distress on Eli's face tugged at Jerry's heart. Shit, was he going to cry? "May? My parents must be freaking out. I want to go home."

Jerry gripped the bars of the cage, enraged by the person responsible for stealing this man-child from his life. Most likely the other missing men were there as well. But there were only seven reported missing. Who occupied the other cages?

"Do you know why we're here? What're they doing?"

Eli shook his head. "They keep shooting us up with something, then take our blood. It was all routine until a couple of weeks ago. They started operating on some of the others and...." Eli visibly swallowed and his eyes widened. "Some of the guys, they've... changed."

"Changed?"

"Their faces, and they called them Braezelas, but that's impossible, right?" His eyes pleaded with Jerry to agree.

"I don't know. They resemble the illustrations I've seen, but they aren't as scary. You said they're giving you injections. Anything else?"

"They poked around my stomach and did an ultrasound, but besides drawing my blood all of the time, they didn't do anything else that I know of. They don't talk to us. They treat us as if we're nothing. And when we try to get them to notice us, to tell us anything, they beat us." He drew in a shaky breath. "It's best not to provoke them, or refuse what they want. They'll beat your ass. And...." He averted his gaze. "They've done things to some of the guys who haven't changed. The ones who've been here the longest, they were the ones they operated on. After a few days, they placed them in with the ones who changed."

Eli drew his knees to his chest.

"What happened? Did they tear them apart?"

"They give the changed guys something, and it drives them crazy. They become aggressive... and h-hard and they.... Well, you know. So no, they don't tear them apart in a sense."

141

Jerry closed his eyes. Those poor men, raped by the Braezelas. But why? What was the point?

The person in the other cage stirred. Eli's eyes widened, his gaze shooting over Jerry's shoulder.

"They've been shooting that one up with something a few times a day. He hasn't been here that long, but he's getting more aggressive and pissed-off by the day. They sedate him before they go anywhere near him. He's different from the others, older, and they keep shooting him with darts. I don't understand what they're doing to him."

Jerry looked over his shoulder. The man stood with his back to Jerry. His long, muscular back was bare, as were his feet. The red sweatpants he wore were tattered and ripped in some places. His shoulders rose and fell with his rapid breaths. His hands gripped the bars before him. He grunted, maybe even growled a few times. Jerry assumed he hadn't bathed in a while since his black hair appeared matted and greasy. When the man howled and banged against the bars, Jerry jumped back. When the man turned, the familiar blue eyes were wild and filled with rage.

"No fucking way."

Recognition came fast to those eyes. Jerry backed away even more as he watched a crazed Tyranis ram the bars, his arms outstretched, as if he wanted to tear Jerry apart. If Tyranis were free, he'd rip out Jerry's throat. What was strange, Ty didn't appear to be looking directly at Jerry. His feral gaze reached over Jerry's shoulder in a far-off stare.

"Get back, you fucking animal." Birdman approached the cage with a metal rod. When he touched the end to Tyranis's arm, he howled in pain and backed away, cradling his arm to his chest. "Keep it down, or I'll fry your balls."

Tyranis whimpered and crawled onto his cot, as far as he could get from Birdman. Must happen often given Ty's immediate retreat. Birdman wandered away, and Jerry looked around at the other cages. The noise had pulled the others from their cots. There were three other young men like Eli. Huddled in the cage across from Jerry was a man with shaggy blond hair and blue eyes. He looked gaunt and pale, and appeared utterly defeated. He too only wore sweatpants, his torso bare. Across the top of his stomach was a long red scar.

Jerry pointed to the man and looked to Eli. "What happened to him?"

"That's Stephanos. He was one of the ones they operated on. He had stitches for a while. Not too long ago, they took him away. At the same time, they took wild man over there for something as well. When they brought Stephanos back, he was bruised and... I think they put him in with a Braezelas, like the others."

Which meant he'd been forced to have sex. Jerry shuddered.

"He doesn't talk much anymore," Eli whispered mournfully.

In the farthest cages, near the door, were the ones Eli referred to as "changed." They resembled Rex after his transformation. Their cheeks more pronounced, their eyes a fiery amber color. Corkscrew horns and elongated canines. The works. Despite their physical changes, they weren't ugly, and the closest one to Jerry was handsome for a vicious demon.

Shit, had he thought a Braezelas was handsome?

He observed them for a while. None of them seemed aggressive or threatening. They lay on their cots, looking as forlorn and lost as the Anzuni. But they were Braezelas, and if what the guard had told Jerry was true, they'd been hiding their true form from the Anzuni, waiting to enslave them again—although Jerry had added that fact to the mix. He needed to get out of there. The only question was how.

JERRY DOZED off, the boredom mind-numbing. There was nothing to do but watch the others, who sat in silence as well. Masked men wandered about, guarding the zoo of men and supposed Braezelas. He dreamed in fits and starts—images of home, the library, his parents, Keith, and Rex all entwined into scenes that made no sense. Finally, his pregnancy became the focus of his dream. He was in labor, the pain harrowing as he panted through the contractions. He was alone in a white room. Where were the doctor and nurses, and where was Rex? Painful pressure pushed screams from him. Gods, it was as if he was being torn apart—and then the pain ceased. A nurse appeared out of thin air, holding a swaddled babe. Desperate to see his child, Jerry reached out, and the nurse laid the newborn in his arms.

Jerry cried out, and his head reared back when he saw the Braezelas features.

"He's beautiful." Rex appeared next to Jerry in demon form. When Jerry looked back at their baby, he'd lost the demon attributes.

Confused, Jerry looked to Rex, and before him was the man he'd fallen in love with, his demon form gone as well.

"Everything will be okay. We love you." Rex then reverted to demon form, as did the babe in his arms.

Jerry woke with a start, the dream fresh in his mind. Time to ponder the meaning was cut short when someone opened his cage door. Rex—or what used to be Rex—was pushed inside and the door slammed shut. Rex, wide-eyed, rushed to Jerry, but halted as Jerry scrambled back on the cot until his back hit the bars. Sorrow filled Rex's now-amber eyes. Striking, yet Jerry couldn't stop to think that. He was trapped with a Braezelas, one who'd tricked him, lied to him.

"Jerry?" Rex's voice was huskier than usual, but still sounded like Rex.

"Stay away." Jerry raised his hand as fear and anger knotted his gut.

Rex wore a white tank top and red sweatpants. On the inside of his elbow, tape covered a piece of gauze. They'd drawn his blood recently. Rex clenched his fists at his sides, and Jerry took that as anger.

"Foiled your plan, did they?"

"Jer, please, I need you. I don't know—" What looked to be panic and confusion etched into Rex's face, but Jerry wasn't buying it.

"No! I don't need any more of your lies. You tricked me, used me, and thank the gods someone stopped you before you could take over and enslave us all."

Jerry cowered farther against the bars, less from fear and more from wanting what he could no longer have. Rex's touch as a Braezelas would, for sure, sear his skin and kill his hope permanently.

Rex stepped forward, clearly wanting to go to Jerry. "What? I don't know what you're talking about. They turned me—"

"Stop!"

With his shout, others around them stirred restlessly. Eli stared pointedly at Jerry, panicky fear all over his face. Then he recalled what Eli had said about the changed ones being placed in the cages with the Anzuni. His heart raced, and his mind numbed with terror.

"Please don't touch me." He barely managed to utter the words through the tightness in his throat. He couldn't believe he had to tell the love of his life to stay away.

CHAPTER 21

REX'S HEAD lowered. He fell back against the bars as if his legs wouldn't hold him. When he sank to the ground, he pulled his knees to his chest and lowered his head into his hands. Jerry relaxed minutely. Why wasn't he attacking, forcing Jerry to do as he said? Braezelas were ruthless and demanding, and when they didn't get what they wanted, they tortured those who disobeyed. But Rex.... He acted like a kicked puppy, far from a terrifying beast. Braezelas were also known to be intelligent and cunning. Well, Jerry wasn't falling for Rex's tricks again.

"Leave me alone." Jerry turned away.

In the cage next to him, Eli clutched his thin blanket, and Jerry saw his concern. Jerry should've shared that apprehension. Even with a Braezelas so close, he wasn't afraid of being harmed. Shouldn't he be terrified, given all the tales of the ruthless Braezelas and their reign of terror over the Anzuni?

He peered at Rex, who remained huddled in the corner, curled in on himself. Jerry then looked to the others who'd been changed. Except for alterations in their appearances, their scared, pitiful, and desolate expressions weren't those of powerful, domineering demons.

They'd been forced to transform, given what the guard had said. Curiosity tempted Jerry to ask Rex if he was a Braezelas, when Birdman stepped up to the cage. In his hand, he held something black. Behind him, more men surrounded a gurney. When the door opened, Rex jumped up and placed himself between Jerry and Birdman.

"Stay away from him!"

Birdman advanced into the cage, and Rex backed up until his calves hit the cot.

"I'll fucking do whatever I want. Step aside, demon."

Rex growled low. "Stay behind me," he said over his shoulder to Jerry. "Back off, fuckhead!"

146

Ty howled and banged on the bars. His normally wild and unfocused eyes were riveted on the guard in Jerry's cage. Veins bulged in his neck and forehead, his rage reddening his face. Was he pissed off the man was coming for Jerry? If he was, it wasn't because of potential harm to Jerry, since he was here because Jerry had been responsible for Ty failing his uncle.

"You're going to be in a world of hurt if you don't get out of my way." Birdman waved what he held, grinning.

Rex and Birdman were evenly matched in size, but Birdman had weapons that could kill. Jerry crawled across the cot and touched Rex's shoulder.

He flinched but didn't turn away from the guard. "Stay back, Jer!"

He called him Jer and was protecting Jerry without caring about what happened to him. So much like Rex.

His Rex.

The doctor had said they couldn't hurt Jerry. He could step in front of Rex and Birdman would back off. Before Jerry could act, Rex lunged at Birdman and grabbed him by the neck with a rage Jerry had never seen from his gentle mate.

"Rex! Stop! Don't! He won't hurt me!"

Rex snarled and slammed Birdman repeatedly into the bars. The guard raised his hand and smashed the black thing he held into Rex's ribs. Rex's entire body stiffened and convulsed, then collapsed into a heap on the floor.

Rex lay motionless.

"What the fuck did you do to him?" Jerry feared going near the guard to get to Rex.

The Birdman smiled maniacally. "Just a jolt of electricity from my trusty Taser. Fucking stupid demon." He kicked Rex in the stomach and spat on him.

"Don't!" Jerry jumped off the bed. When the guard lifted the Taser, Jerry halted.

"I imagine that demon spawn in your gut would fry pretty quickly with a jolt from this."

Jerry seethed, wishing he had something with which to beat Birdman to death.

Birdman grabbed Jerry's arm, yanking him over Rex's body. Jerry stumbled as he tried to look back and see if Rex breathed. Jerry felt a minute amount of relief when he caught the rise and fall of Rex's chest, but feared there could be permanent damage.

Jerry protected his stomach as the guard pushed him into the gurney.

"Take it easy!" The man with a mask like the Phantom of the Opera pointed at Birdman. "If you do anything to fuck up that pregnancy, he'll put a bullet between your eyes." He looked to Jerry. "Get on the gurney."

Jerry climbed on and lay down, knowing any argument would get him zapped. Straps were pulled across his chest and thighs, then tightened, leaving him immobile. He reminded himself they weren't going to hurt him. He kept his eye on Rex for as long as he could, but he still hadn't moved. Eli watched Jerry as he left the room, his expression saying he didn't expect Jerry to return. He would—and then apologize to Rex until he forgave him.

Down the hall, they entered an exam room. The doctor and another man in a similar mask were huddled around a large machine with a screen. The guard parked the gurney next to it.

"Pull up his shirt." The man pushed Jerry's shirt up to the strap on his chest. Jerry's round stomach was on display.

"What, no foreplay?"

The man's mouth thinned in disgust while the corner of the doctor's mouth twitched and her eyes lightened. She felt around his swollen stomach. "Given his size, the growth hormone is working." Again the doctor sounded resigned.

"What do you mean, growth hormone?" He wasn't sure if he'd been imagining growing quickly. "Is that what you were giving me? Why I was so sick?"

The man stabbed his finger at Jerry. "Shut up, or I'll tape your mouth."

Fuck them.

The doctor squeezed cold liquid on Jerry's stomach, and he gasped as goose bumps covered his skin. Pushing buttons and turning dials, she placed the flat end of a wand in the gel and spread the goop over his belly. Narrowing her eyes, she moved the wand over his skin, her eyes glued to the screen. The man in the mask peered over her shoulder.

"How is the fetus progressing?"

Something niggled at Jerry's brain—that voice was familiar. He tried to see who he was, but the mask covered his entire face.

She huffed with impatience. "Could you give me a minute to get some measurements?"

Were they looking at his baby? Was he okay?

"Are you looking at my baby? Please let me see."

The doctor continued her movements over his stomach, working the machine. Fuck, they weren't going to ignore him!

He didn't care about the threat of getting his mouth taped. "Tell me! Let me see! Is the baby okay? I need to know."

Nothing. They continued to talk about measurements and size. Jerry squirmed, but the straps held tight. If they took them off, he could see what they were looking at. Where would he go with them standing right there?

He had an idea. He moaned and thrashed his head. The doctor lifted the wand from his stomach.

"What's wrong?"

Jerry moaned again and made a gagging noise. "Think I'm going to be sick." He heaved and turned his head to the side.

"Unbuckle the restraint on his chest. I'll get a bucket." The doctor moved away.

The man released the clasp on the strap, and Jerry sat up. The screen was in full. An image of his baby, maybe a side profile, filled the screen. An eyelid, small nose, and lips were visible. Horns and tail were absent, since those developed after birth. A hand with tiny fingers. A leg pushed up against the baby's chest. A foot with five toes. His baby looked fully developed, which was impossible.

The doctor plopped a bucket on Jerry's lap and frowned as she surveyed his face.

"I feel better since I sat up."

He swore she smiled, then took the bucket back and shoved it at the man.

"Lie down." She palmed her wand again.

Jerry complied, elation ballooning in his chest. His baby with Rex. The memory of Rex in a heap on the floor ramped up his fear.

Someone ran into the room. "Hey! Number four's seizing. We need you out here!" The doctor dropped the wand. She grabbed a cart near the door and pushed it into the hallway, followed by the guard, who said, "Watch him!"

The man raised his hands and dropped them in frustration. "Can't anything be easy around here?" He walked over to the opened door and leaned against the doorjamb. Pulling out a cell phone, he tapped on the screen, oblivious to Jerry.

If Jerry could get that phone, he could call his father, but what would he tell him? He had no clue where they were except that Geraldon was most likely responsible. That might be enough to lead the Anzuni security force to them.

Reaching down, Jerry grasped the clasp of the ratchet strap across his thighs and, holding his breath, slowly lifted the latch. If his heart beat any faster, it would shatter his sternum. The man continued to tap on the screen of his phone, ignorant of Jerry's movements. Was he an idiot?

When the latch released, Jerry loosened the strap enough to pull his legs out from beneath it. He had to move fast, fearful the doctor would come back. Counting to ten, he waited to see if the man would turn around. When he didn't, Jerry pulled his legs from under the strap, moving at a snail's pace, fearful the slightest noise would alert his foe.

Once off the gurney, he grasped an IV pole. He lifted the pole as he took four steps and slammed the metal base against the man's head as he looked to Jerry. The phone popped out of his hand, he stumbled into the hallway, and his head slammed against the opposite wall. Jerry charged the stunned man and hit him in the head again, dislodging the mask.

"What the hell?" Jerry's jaw dropped when he saw Merano sprawled unconscious, half seated on the floor. "Son of a bitch!"

Wasting no time, Jerry grabbed the phone and sprinted down the hall in the opposite direction the doctor had gone. His heart beat wildly in his ears, muffling his hearing, and his hands shook. He had no clue where he was going, but he needed time. Luckily, the phone was still on the home screen and hadn't locked. He stopped at the corner of the hall. He found his father's personal contact information and started the call. Placing the phone to his ear, he peered around the corner, hoping no one was in sight. Seeing the hallway empty, he sprinted as the phone beeped in his ear.

"Come on, Dad. Pick up?"

"Merano, how's my boy doing?"

Jerry had never been so relieved to hear his father's voice. "D-Dad, I—"

"Jerricho, I'm so happy to hear from you. Merano told me you were deep in study last I called. I was hoping to hear—"

"Dad, listen, we've been kidnapped, and Merano is in on it. I hit him and took his phone. The missing Anzuni men are here, and I think there are humans as well. And Rex...." He choked on the name.

"Jerricho, slow down! What're you talking about?"

"We were kidnapped and taken somewhere. They're experimenting on people, and they turned some into Braezelas. I think Braezelas are on Earth, but it doesn't add up. Rex... they gave him my blood, and he changed. I don't know if he *was* a Braezelas, or if they changed him into one."

"What are you talking about? Braezelas? I don't.... Are you okay? Did they hurt you? Do you know where you are?" His father's panicked roar filled the hallway. "Can you get out?"

Men shouting came closer, and Jerry ducked down a darkened hallway. *Shit.*

"I'm okay, Dad. But I don't know where we are." He found an alcove and slipped in, crouching on the floor. His father hadn't even known he was missing. "I don't think I can get out, but it's Geraldon, Dad. I haven't seen him, but Tyranis is in the cage next to me, and he's crazy. Fucking feral."

"Tyranis? He's supposed to be in jail. What—hold on, son." Jerry's father spoke rapidly with someone. When he came back on, he asked, "Did you land in California? Did Tanyon meet you?"

"Yes, they've taken Tanyon too. I've only seen him once since we've been here. But we were in the limo for what felt like hours, and I couldn't see where they were taking us." Jerry verged on tears, so happy to speak with his father finally. He had to hold it together so he could give him the information he needed.

"That slimy son of a bitch. Merano has been calling me daily to keep me up to date on your health, and…."

"And what?" Jerry whispered.

"Geraldon was here after you left. He helped contact other clans about the missing men."

Jerry clutched the phone. "How long have we been here?"

There was a pause, as his father gave more directions. "Three weeks. Dammit, Jerricho, I didn't know you were in trouble. I've been going about my business as if everything was fine."

Jerry's chest ached, hearing the distress in his father's voice. "You didn't know. But you have to find us fast. They're doing things to those people, changing them into—" Voices down the hallway froze Jerry. "Hold on. I think someone's coming." Jerry clasped the phone to his chest and shrank back into the corner. Two men spoke to each other, coming closer to him.

"I need that information as soon as possible."

Jerry recognized that loud, booming voice.

Geraldon.

CHAPTER 22

HE WAS going to find Jerry. Maybe he could spring a sneak attack when his kidnapper passed. But Geraldon wasn't alone, and Jerry was *very* pregnant. Before they reached the spot where he hid, a door opened. The voices became muffled, but the door hadn't been closed. Peering around the corner. The door was slightly ajar.

Jerry closed his eyes and fought to control his breathing. He lifted the phone to his ear. "Dad, are you still there?"

"Jerricho, what happened? Are you okay?"

"Yeah. I heard Geraldon. He went into a room down the hall, and the door's open. If I get close enough, I might be able to hear something. I'm going to put the phone down and get closer."

"Jerricho, don't! Stay where you are. Don't put yourself in danger."

Too late for that. Any moment someone would find him. He wasn't hidden from sight. If he could get a clue about where they were….

"They're going to find me any minute now. I'll leave the phone on. Maybe you can trace the call or something." He hesitated, clutching the phone, not wanting to hang up. "I love you, Dad, and Mom… please tell her. I'm sorry I messed everything up. I'm so lucky you're my father." Jerry hiccupped, his throat tightening, eyes burning.

"Son, I love you too. Please, be careful. I'm coming for you." His father's confident tone gave Jerry renewed hope.

Jerry set the phone in the darkened corner, leaning against the wall to block the light from the screen. Crawling on his hands and knees, he stopped before the door. What were the chances he could learn exactly where they were? *Slim to none, Jer.* He might, however, overhear something to clue him in to what Geraldon had planned. He'd caged his own nephew, and appeared to have experimented on him as well. He was ruthless, maniacal, and certifiable.

He was going down. Jerry hoped that happened before they were all dead. He placed his ear near the crack of the door, unable to see anything but a gray wall. From the sound of Geraldon's voice, he was closer to the door. An overhead blower pushing cold air masked his ability to hear the second voice clearly. Jerry leaned in closer. Gods, he hoped no one came around the corner.

"I know what we're doing isn't ideal, but how else were we to deal with the situation? You agreed to the stipulations. Drastic measures had to be taken." Geraldon sounded angry.

Jerry huffed quietly. Drastic all right. Fucking kidnapping and experimentation.

"I know, I know," a muffled voice responded. Definitely male.

"Is the prince cooperating, or is he being the insolent little shit he's always been?"

Fucking dickhead. Who was he to talk?

Jerry couldn't hear the other man's reply, but the anger in Geraldon grew. "You listen. I have a lot riding on the outcome of what you're doing here. I stand to lose more money than you've ever seen if this doesn't work out."

"Calm down, Geraldon. You've doubted my plan since the beginning, and I've proven you wrong every step. You know everything's going according to plan." Had someone else who'd shown allegiance to Jerry's father been stabbing him in the back as well? Nothing they said gave Jerry the information he needed. He leaned even closer, annoyed with the blower, wishing the noisy fan would shut off.

A phone rang in the room. "Hello?" Pause. "What's the emergency?" Pause. "I'll be right there."

Shit! Jerry was the emergency, and they were going to find him.

"Can you excuse me for a moment?" the second man said.

Jerry crab-walked backward, trying to stand.

The man stepped out of the room. Jerry's gaze climbed the tailored gray suit, the sapphire blue tie, until he came to the familiar face. Tanyon stood over Jerry, as shocked to see Jerry on the floor as Jerry was to see him exit the office.

"T-Tanyon? What the fuck…. They kidnapped you. What're you doing with Geraldon?" Tanyon had been taken like Jerry and Rex… beaten and…. *Crap.*

Footsteps pounded down the hall. Birdman came around the corner and stopped upon seeing them.

"There you are, you pain in the ass." He advanced on Jerry, who shoved himself against the opposite wall to keep everyone in view. He wasn't getting out of this, and he hadn't learned anything helpful. "I think Merano would like to have a word with you."

"Shut up, you imbecile," Tanyon whispered. He reached for the doorknob, but Geraldon exited before he had a chance to close the door.

Geraldon's eyes widened seeing Jerry, and then narrowed when he noticed Birdman.

"Prince Jerricho? Why are you on the floor? Are you okay? Did this man harm you?" Geraldon's caring tone was as fake as his loyalty to his king.

Tanyon crossed his arms. "Oh, give up the act, Geraldon. You don't give a rat's ass about Prince Jerricho. You're such an idiot."

Geraldon glared at Tanyon. "How dare you speak to me like that? And what's going on here, Tanyon? Why is Prince Jerricho in this hallway? You assured me that he was properly sequestered with the tutors you provided. I demand his sentence be completed by the terms laid out by the council. I won't stand for—"

Tanyon pulled something from his jacket pocket and punched Geraldon in the side. He jolted, much as Rex had when Birdman shocked him. Tanyon tossed the Taser to Birdman. "Get the *prince* back into his cage."

"What should I do with *him*?" Birdman scowled down on Geraldon.

"Lock him up. Soon his nephew is going to take revenge on the uncle he believes turned his back on him."

Tanyon snagged Jerry by the shirt and pulled Jerry to his feet. His sneer was unlike anything he'd ever seen on the elder's face. "If you fuck this up for me, former *Prince* Jerricho, I swear you'll never see your child born. I'll kill you and let the little bastard suffocate inside of you." The venomous words clutched Jerry's chest. Tanyon shoved Jerry back, and he slammed into Birdman's chest.

155

Wrapping a beefy arm around Jerry's chest, Birdman half pushed, half dragged Jerry back to the room of cages. Once inside, Jerry's relief swelled upon seeing Rex pacing inside of his. The guy with the metal mask, whom Jerry had named Metal Head, opened the cage door, a cattle prod pointed toward Rex. Jerry rushed to enter the cage when a ruthless shove caused him to fall onto his hands and knees. Pain radiated through the bones of his knees and wrists.

"Leave him the fuck alone!" Rex slammed against the door, but the lock had already been engaged.

Birdman chuckled as he walked away with Metal Head.

Rex knelt next to Jerry. "Are you okay?"

Jerry pushed himself up onto his knees and threw himself into Rex's arms, burying his face in his lover's neck.

Rex held Jerry close. "Hey, it's okay. I've got you. You don't know how scared I was when I woke up and you were gone."

Being in Rex's arms again was like coming home. He didn't care if he was a true Braezelas. Rex loved him.

"It's Tanyon. He's behind this… whatever this is. And Merano's helping him. I hit him in the head and called my father. He didn't even know we were missing. And Tanyon shocked Geraldon, and he's going to have Tyranis kill him and make it look like revenge, and… and he threatened to kill me and the baby." He gulped in air. The world spun out of control, and Jerry couldn't make it stop.

Rex tensed, then shushed him, running his palm over Jerry's back in soothing circles. As he did, a low humming sound came from Rex's chest. The soothing rhythm calmed Jerry. He relaxed against Rex and barely noticed as he rose, taking Jerry with him, and lowered them both to lie on the cot.

"I'm sorry for how I reacted earlier," Jerry whispered.

"I understand, Jer. I know I look horrible. I haven't seen myself, but… I felt my face, and I'd be scared too."

Jerry gazed into Rex's amber eyes. "You don't know what you look like?"

Rex shook his head. "What did they do to me, Jer?" Rex's beseeching gaze said he was scared.

156

"The guard said they'd forced you to reveal your true form. That you're a Braezelas."

Rex flinched and then shook his head. "I'm not a Braezelas demon. I've read about the Braezelas and I'm not one of them. They don't exist in this world."

"But… look at you." Jerry's voice rose.

Rex placed his finger against Jerry's lips. "Shhh. I don't want them to hear us."

Jerry nodded. "Sorry." Was Rex in denial about what he was? Maybe he truly didn't know what he'd been. "Maybe you're a Braezelas, but you've never transformed?"

"I was born human, Jer. I'm not a demon in disguise. My parents weren't demons."

"But then what are you?" Jerry wasn't sure what to believe.

Rex shook his head. "I'm not sure what they did, but this demon wasn't hidden inside of me. Do you remember me telling you about my Aunt Renee being the reason I got interested in mythology?"

"You mentioned her once."

"She was a scholar, a researcher of ancient myths and legends, including the Anzuni demon clan. She had manuscripts, old ones about Anzuni history. She found conflicting views about the history of the Anzuni and their appearance on Earth. It was a long time ago, but I remember something about the Braezelas and a conspiracy about their origin. I always wondered how a myth could have a conspiracy theory." He shrugged. "I never read what the conspiracy was believed to be, but I did read that the Braezelas were a gentle race, subservient and submissive. Nothing like they're portrayed in Anzuni history."

"What're you talking about? Those demons were horrible, awful creatures that enslaved my people. Every Anzuni knows that. We all learned about the Great War, and how only three hundred Anzuni escaped the Braezelas's torment."

Rex blew out a breath. "I'm not saying what she said was true. I can only tell you what she told me. When she died, all of her papers and research and books were donated to the university."

Jerry wasn't sure he could be more confused, overwhelmed, and exhausted. Deciding what was real and what wasn't scrambled his mind, and his head hurt. For now, he had Rex back. Jerry ran his palm over his shoulder, his strong arms. Despite his facial transformations, what Jerry could see of his body was unchanged.

"I saw our baby," Jerry whispered.

Rex's brow rose with a hopeful gaze. "You did?"

"They did an ultrasound, and I saw the baby—perfect, and whole, and growing so big."

"I noticed you've grown fast. Are you sure the baby's okay?"

"I don't know if there's anything wrong. I mean, I feel like everything's okay. But the doctor said they've been giving me a growth hormone. The baby is growing faster than normal, but they wouldn't tell me why." Tears burned his eyes, but he forced them to stop. The baby would be fine, he assured himself.

Rex exhaled. "We have to get out of here before the baby's born."

His unspoken words hung in the air. What if Tanyon took their child, or harmed him or her in some way? What if they wanted to experiment on the baby? Jerry shuddered, and Rex pulled him closer. Rex hadn't deceived him, hadn't used him. Jerry recognized his lover behind the demon. Closing his eyes, he imagined Rex, the green eyes, strong jaw, and leaned in to kiss him.

"Wait." Rex touched his cheek gently.

Jerry opened his eyes, and the raw pain etched on Rex's face clawed at Jerry's gut. "If you're going to kiss me, I want you to keep your eyes open." His lip trembled slightly. "I might be like this forever. Can you kiss me when I look like this?"

Without hesitation, Jerry sealed his lips over Rex's. He squeezed him tighter, eyes trained on Rex's. This was right, this was Rex, and he loved him dearly. Rex's eyes closed, and he slumped against Jerry, but then lifted his head. Jerry drew in a sharp breath and ran his fingers over Rex's face, unsure if he'd lost his mind.

Rex frowned. "What happened? I think I blacked out for a second. I feel kind of strange."

"You look like you again. The horns are gone." Jerry caressed Rex's cheek and forehead.

"What?" Rex sat up and ran his hands over his face frantically, dumbfounded for a moment, and then his expression filled with hope. "Do you think maybe the change wasn't permanent?"

"I don't know. I can change between forms whenever I want."

Rex's brow lowered. "How do you do it?"

Jerry shrugged. "I think about my demon form and it happens. We learn to shift when we're small. Try thinking about the Braezelas form."

Rex closed his eyes and appeared to be concentrating hard. He opened his eyes. "Anything?" He ran his hand over his forehead where his horns should have been.

"No. Maybe what they did was short-term." Jerry hoped that was true, and that the mission these psychos were on wouldn't stick. The doctor had seemed surprised the transformation even happened. So if it wasn't permanent, if they weren't useful anymore, what would happen to them? Jerry didn't want to contemplate that further.

Jerry wrapped his arms around Rex's neck and gazed up into his emerald eyes. He meant everything to Jerry. "I love you," he whispered against his lips.

Rex's lips quivered as they lifted at the corner. Jerry lay back, holding out his arms. Rex stretched out next to Jerry and rested his head on his shoulder, his hand on Jerry's stomach. Everything would be okay once they escaped the hell they'd been dragged into.

"I love you too," Rex whispered, and they held each other, drifting off to sleep.

CHAPTER 23

JERRY KEPT track of the days based on the delivery of the meals, which were less than appetizing. Breakfast was either oatmeal or runny scrambled eggs. Cold, of course. Lunch was sandwiches. Dinner generally consisted of some dry piece of mystery meat and soggy vegetables. Four days of nothing but blood draws and ultrasounds, where Jerry learned nothing. Merano hadn't returned. Maybe he'd seriously hurt the man. He hadn't seen Tanyon or Geraldon either, and Ty grew more agitated and feral by the day.

They'd moved Rex into a cage across the room, and Jerry mourned his loss. Their interactions were limited to expressions of encouragement, understanding, and mouthing their love to one another. Jerry ached to have his Rex close. If Jerry stayed in his cage one more day, he'd go insane. Sleep was the only escape, and he found himself sleeping more as depression settled in.

He lay on the cot, utterly bored, his gaze fixed on Rex, who appeared to watch over him, his protector. Jerry smiled and snuggled into the thin blanket, drifting off into a fitful doze. When he found himself wrapped in Rex's arms again, he burrowed into his heat, as he floated on the veil between sleeping and waking. Why had he been in such distress when the moment felt like heaven? Hands grabbed him, tore him from Rex's arms, and shattered that peace.

"Wha—hey!" The room tilted, disorienting Jerry until his senses caught up.

He looked for Rex on the cot, but he wasn't there. He'd dreamed it. Birdman and Metal Head carried Jerry by his shoulders and feet and set him down outside the cage. Eli wore an expression of fright as he was pulled from his cage as well. He didn't struggle, which was smart. Birdman held a Taser at Jerry's side while Rex was also released from his prison.

"Don't try anything."

Rex nodded, and a guard told him to move. Jerry pushed to follow. A choking sound caught Jerry's attention. In his cage, Stephanos threw up into his bucket as a guard watched over him. He looked like hell. Jerry gagged and looked away as Birdman kept the Taser trained on him. They passed more cages, and Jerry noticed many of the Braezelas were missing. Glancing back, Eli followed, his expression having morphed from fear to terror. Jerry couldn't blame him on that one.

After walking down several hallways, they entered a large room filled with comfy sofas and chairs. About half-a-dozen well-dressed men and women—or make that barely well-dressed men and women—lounged on the seats. The missing Braezelas were there between the legs of the men and women, sucking and licking. It looked like a brothel, and smelled like he imagined one would. The air was hot, heavy, and musky. In the corner, a man fucked one of the changed men over a stool. The Braezelas's eyes were glazed over, his gaze far-off, his face covered in pleasure. His cock was hard and dripping precum. Was he enjoying it?

Jerry looked away.

"Ahh, our guests have arrived." Tanyon patted the head of the Braezelas sucking his cock, who continued without faltering.

Guests?

Jerry's stomach turned. Something about Tanyon seemed off. His eyes had that stoned, glazed look about them. That's when Jerry noticed the trays of needles, some filled with red liquid and others empty, scattered on the tables. The men and women using the Braezelas turned their attention to Jerry and Rex. Eli remained hidden behind them. The man in the corner continued pounding into the whimpering demon, the look of ecstasy on his face disturbing. All the demons continued their ministrations, seemingly unaware of what happened around them.

"Beautiful, aren't they?" Tanyon grabbed the hair of the demon sucking him and pushed him away. He stood, tucked his cock into his pants, and zipped up. The demon scurried to the next woman, her pussy being devoured by another Braezelas. She pulled the other demon to her breast, and he latched on as she groaned. "They're the best little sex slaves, and I have you to thank, Prince Jerricho."

Jerry's jaw dropped. The men and women around the room nodded and laughed in agreement. One man shifted the Braezelas in his lap to the side and laid him on the couch. The Braezelas's hard cock looked painfully engorged. The man straddled the Braezelas's upper chest and stuffed his cock into the demon's open mouth. The woman next to him, whose open shirt exposed her round, pert breasts, climbed onto the demon's erect cock and rode his shaft, her head thrown back with pleasure. The Braezelas emitted a muffled groan around the cock stuffed down his throat.

"I had nothing to do with any of this! Let them go!"

With a swift move, Tanyon smacked Jerry hard across the cheek, and he stumbled backward. Rex lunged for Tanyon, but the Taser brought to Jerry's throat stopped him.

"Insolent little shit! You've always been a spoiled brat. Now we'll see how you like being told what to do."

To the right, the man with his cock down the Braezelas's throat howled as he pulled out and came all over the demon's face. Tanyon grinned and the man, his chest heaving, smiled and nodded his satisfaction.

Tanyon studied Rex. "Still in human form, I see. I'd hoped putting you back with your mate would trigger a change, and I was right. None of the other Braezelas have reverted to their human form, no matter what I've tried. I need them to blend into the human world. Makes them easier to transport."

"Change me back into a human, now." Rex's jaw ticked.

Tanyon looked down his nose at Rex, as if he were nothing. Jerry touched Rex on the arm, trying to calm him. If Tanyon didn't have his guards and Tasers, Rex wouldn't have been standing back.

"Nothing will change what you've become."

Jerry scowled. "Do these men have demon in their ancestry, or is the demon part suppressed and you forced their shift?"

Tanyon laughed. "None of these men have Braezelas in their ancestry, nor are their demon sides suppressed. I made them, same as our Anzuni ancestors created the first Braezelas, with the blood of a pregnant Anzuni male and the talisman your uncle left you."

That wasn't true. The Braezelas were from another dimension and had terrorized the Anzuni for thousands of years. "I don't believe you."

"You've seen it yourself with your claxton. You can't deny what he became right before your eyes. And my investors who've partaken in the magnificent submission of these demons are waiting to see how a Braezelas is born. Strap him down." Tanyon nodded to Metal Head.

Jerry balked as Metal Head forced Eli into a chair. He struggled when a strap was secured around his chest. His arms and legs were also secured to the chair.

Tanyon picked up a syringe from a table and handed it to the doctor. "Prince Jerricho, if you'd be so kind." Tanyon motioned, and the doctor approached Jerry. She'd stuck Jerry more times than a blood-hungry mosquito. The Taser still poised at Jerry's neck meant he didn't have much of a choice.

Rex watched, his panic and frustration evident, as she drew a vial of Jerry's blood. Being a guinea pig for their vampirism was growing old.

The doctor then prepared another syringe, adding Jerry's blood and other liquids he didn't recognize. Jerry cringed when she took the syringe to Eli and swabbed his arm. Tears filled the young man's eyes, his body nearly frozen except for his shallow breaths. The investors watched wide-eyed, almost giddy at the show before them.

Sick bastards.

Tanyon slipped Jerry's pendant around Eli's neck. The needle plunged into his arm and the contents emptied. Eli squawked, then panted heavily. As with Rex, he howled in pain, struggling against the restraints. Jerry closed his eyes, unable to watch. In less than a minute, the struggle ended. Jerry had to look. A dazed Eli—now a Braezelas, horns and all—slumped in the chair.

Gasps and polite clapping filled the room, however most hadn't ceased having sex with their Braezelas. Gods, how Jerry hated them all.

"I never tire of seeing the change. As you see, the blood of a prince in the last month of pregnancy, along with the pendant, have created what long ago was taken from the Anzuni." Tanyon grinned maliciously.

"The last month? But I'm in my—" The growth hormone. What had Tanyon done to his baby?

"I have what I need from your blood to create not only Braezelas, but to ensure that I never run out of that blood. Once again, the Braezelas will serve us." Tanyon patted Eli on the shoulder.

"The Anzuni weren't the ones who were enslaved." Tanyon huffed. "The history books were doctored by those who believed using the Braezelas was immoral and wrong. The truth is, Braezelas were created for pleasure, to serve the Anzuni. They're such subservient creatures, so willing to please." Eli scowled at Tanyon.

Rex laughed. "He looks submissive. He does."

"Not so submissive yet. Only needs a little help."

Tanyon grabbed another syringe and passed it to the doctor, who advanced on Rex. He stepped back, narrowed eyes focused on the needle. The man holding the Taser waved it before Jerry as a reminder to behave. Rex halted and turned his head as the doctor drew blood from his arm. She handed off the syringe and drew another vial. Rex's anger pulsed from him as his entire body tensed.

"Braezelas blood holds wonderful properties. In their own kind, it's an addictive aphrodisiac, with a few additions." Tanyon spoke nonchalantly.

The doctor again went to her cart. Minutes later, a new syringe was emptied into Eli's arm. The scared-stiff demon relaxed in his restraints, his head lolling slightly, his eyes hooded and glazed over. His sweats tented, his hardened cock trying to escape. The lustful gaze on his face was stunning—and scary as shit.

Tanyon gestured to a large, gray-haired man. "Renaldo, I believe you've paid for the honor of this Braezelas. Didn't I tell you he was magnificent?"

Renaldo stepped forward and held out his arm. The doctor injected the man with the same concoction as Eli. Renaldo sighed, his pupils immediately narrowing to pinpoints. He chuckled and threw his head back with a deep sigh of satisfaction.

The guards released Eli. Immediately, Renaldo shoved his pants down and grasped his cock, moaning. "Suck it."

Eli fell to his knees and took the head of Renaldo's cock into his mouth, sucking as if it were a source of nourishment. Guilt and fear commingled on Rex's face as he clenched his jaw, the muscles bulging. Their blood had changed these men. Some had been Anzuni, and some had once been human, as Eli had feared earlier.

"He's lovely. And not a hair on his body, as you requested. He will serve you well."

"You can't do this!" Rex leaned forward, fists clenched at his side.

"I can, and I have. Look at him. He already loves serving. It will be his new purpose in life, to serve his master and pleasure him. He will be taken care of, and never need to do anything but give pleasure. I gave this to him."

"You *forced* him to do this! You didn't give him a choice! You can't do that!"

Tanyon rounded on Jerry, eyes burning with fire. "You have no power here, *Your Highness*. Your small-mindedness, like that of Geraldon, will do nothing but get you killed. After your stunt in the hallway, I tried to reason with Geraldon, get him to see what I was doing was for the greater Anzuni good, and to join me. But he kept spouting that Daenose bullshit. It's all made up!" Tanyon snorted. "To get where I am today, I had to wait years for the next Anzuni male pregnancy. Pregnant Anzuni females didn't work, only pregnant Anzuni males, as the records I found indicated. Luckily, you wore that pendant of your uncle's in full view for me."

"Wait. Eli said he's been here a couple of months. And some of the men were missing longer. You didn't know I would get pregnant that long ago." Tanyon was full of shit.

"The entire Anzuni clan knew you would be pregnant not long after your twenty-fifth birthday when you wed. This entire place was set up just for you. You would have been here sooner or later, even if you hadn't turned into a tramp and screwed around on poor Tyranis. I'd like to thank you, though, for speeding up the entire process by getting pregnant with your little bastard." He chuckled and ran his hand through Eli's hair as the drugged demon sucked Renaldo. The man had some awesome staying power.

Jerry wasn't going to take the blame. "Geraldon had nothing to do with any of this?"

"Oh, Geraldon wasn't above seeking revenge for how you'd wronged him, all right. He insisted you go to jail, and he bought many of the council members' votes so the majority would rule his way. That would've ruined my plans, which he was unaware of at the time. So I shared them with him, and promised him your demon child after birth to sell to the highest bidder. When Tyranis wasn't going to be the future king, he practically salivated over the offer, and agreed willingly. Couldn't trust me though and had to come here to make sure you were behaving and the cash cow you were growing remained unharmed. Ignorant fool."

"He was going to sell my baby?" Jerry wrapped his arms around his swollen belly and took a step back. No one was getting his child! Rex reached for Jerry's arm, but the guard knocked his hand away.

Tanyon ignored the question. "I'd get my blood from a pregnant Anzuni male, and Geraldon would keep his mouth shut and not question how I would benefit from the deal. He thought he'd gotten the better deal, not realizing what will become a billion-dollar industry. Clients with too much money will pay for their demon sex slaves as well as the addictive aphrodisiac to control them. In humans, that same serum creates an effect akin to heroin but without the addiction. Do you have any idea what humans will pay for a drug like that?"

Tanyon's sick, twisted plot turned more macabre by the minute. Selling drugs, trafficking innocent men? Endless victims, Anzuni and humans, turned into sex slaves. But to do all of that, Tanyon needed blood from a pregnant Anzuni prince. What he had could only go so far.

"I won't be pregnant much longer, since you've sped up the growth of my child, so your supply of blood from a pregnant royal will dry up."

Jerry wanted nothing more than to smash Tanyon in the face as he smirked.

"I've been busy, Jerricho, finding all of the variables for this venture, which do seem infinite. But when you have a vision and a mission, you're only limited by the drive to reach your goals. Your goal, which will keep you alive longer, is to shut up and keep pushing out Anzuni." He waved his hand at them. "I have guests to attend to. Be assured, Jerricho, I have access to an endless supply of pregnant Anzuni male blood. I never said the blood had to be from a royal." He looked to Birdman. "Take them back to their cages."

Tanyon returned to his demented party of investors who chatted excitedly. As the guards herded Rex and Jerry from the room, Tanyon announced, "If you're unable to find something to your liking among this merchandise, a fresh batch of Anzuni arrived last week and are being prepped as we speak. I'm confident you'll find what you want among them. And once the money is transferred, we'll sort out the shipping details."

More Anzuni had been captured to be changed and sent off to gods knew where on the planet. Once those men left the building, they'd never be found. How could Jerry stop that from happening?

CHAPTER 24

WHAT TANYON hadn't revealed was the fate of Jerry and his baby, who Geraldon wouldn't get to sell. From what Tanyon had said, Geraldon was dead. And Rex. Braezelas were made for one reason: to serve their masters. Would Tanyon turn Rex into a submissive slave? How much time before someone bought Rex and shot him up with that concoction so he'd—

Jerry stumbled, envisioning Rex on his knees, sucking another man's cock. Birdman chuckled as he let Jerry back into his cage. He ignored Birdman, instead squeezing his eyes shut, unwilling to let his imagination construct images in his head. But what Eli had done willfully.... He'd become a slave to the drug they pumped into him and whatever person had been demented enough to buy another human being.

Jerry glanced sideways at Rex, his face awash with determination, confusion, anger, and sadness. Tanyon was a raving lunatic followed by a bunch of crazies. What was Tanyon saying? Anzuni history had been changed to point fingers at the Braezelas and hide the truth. The Anzuni had created the demons for their own hedonistic pleasures and fornication. Then where had the Braezelas created in the past gone?

Jerry, once honored to be Anzuni, proud of their struggles and victory, felt dirty and disgraced. His forefathers were whoremasters, enslaving a race they'd created for their own immoral purposes. The Great War touted as a fight for freedom from the Braezelas most likely had been waged against the Anzuni to free the race they'd created. Possibly that was what had wiped the Braezelas out.

When they passed the cage where Rex had been earlier, Jerry dared to hope they'd be together again. Not so. Rex nearly took Birdman out as he forced Rex into Eli's cage. Touched with the prod, Rex howled and stumbled inside. The cage door was slammed and locked.

Ty banged on his cage, startling Jerry. The once poised and charming man wore a mask of insanity. Jerry swore hell itself burned in his eyes as he glared. Under his breath, he chanted something Jerry couldn't make out. The guard warned Ty to get back and shut up, but Ty banged harder, shouting garbled words that sounded like, "Mine! Mine!" He chanted over and over, his gaze far off, unfocused. Jerry was certain Ty wanted to rip him apart, and the only thing keeping that from happening was the iron bars between them. Whatever they'd done to Tyranis had made him a hundred times more dangerous.

Jerry turned his back on his ex-fiancé and faced Rex. Jerry grasped the bars, rocking his head against the cold metal. Rex modeled Jerry's stance. They gazed at each other until there was only Rex and no one else.

"I love you," Rex whispered and placed his hand over his heart.

Jerry choked, half laugh, half sob. He'd either laugh away what remained of his sanity or cry until he drowned. "Love you too."

A guard wandered by and sneered. "Don't get too comfortable, lovers. They've got plans for both of you."

He laughed as he walked on, banging his prod against the bars of each cage.

"Don't listen to him."

Jerry nodded, but he was fresh out of hope that anything good could come from their situation. "Lie down and rest, Jer."

Jerry obeyed, flopping onto the cot, seriously exhausted. Rex sat on his cot and kept watch over Jerry, creating enough safety that allowed Jerry to drift into something resembling sleep. He continually opened his eyes to assure himself Rex was okay. The baby somersaulted in his gut. If only the little guy or girl would sleep, maybe Jerry could as well. The relentless kicking to his liver, kidneys, and spleen was getting old. Shifting on the cot, he tried to get comfortable, and Rex gave him a sympathetic look.

"I'd rub your back if I could," he whispered.

Jerry smiled gently, wishing they were together, even if it was inside of a cage. The boredom only intensified, and with too much time to think, Jerry's mind spun to make sense of what he'd learned.

Tanyon didn't need Jerry's blood any longer, didn't need the blood of a royal pregnant male. He could get it from any male who—

Jerry lifted his head and looked at Stephanos, stretched out on his cot, asleep. The operation. Forced to be with a drugged horny Braezelas. Throwing up. Jerry frowned when the truth hit him.

"Oh my gods."

He reeled back and covered his hand with his mouth.

"Jerry, what's wrong?" Rex asked.

"Stephanos."

Rex frowned and looked at the sleeping man, then back to Jerry. *He couldn't have. It isn't possible.*

"Jerry?"

Jerry couldn't take his eyes off the scar on Stephanos's stomach. "Tanyon said he found a way to get blood from any pregnant Anzuni males. He didn't need mine. They operated on Stephanos, and Eli said they'd taken him away and... Eli was sure they'd put him in with one of the drugged Braezelas. Earlier, he was throwing up."

Rex looked at Stephanos, appearing to process Jerry's theory. Reality dawned across his face. "You think he's pregnant? That was serious."

"It makes sense—well, nothing here *makes* sense. If he's pulled it off, he'll have unlimited blood from pregnant Anzuni males. This is a manufacturing plant of blood to make Braezelas sex slaves, and drugs for humans." Jerry shook his head and wrapped his arms around his stomach, pure fear pounding his heart. "Rex, what will they do with the babies?"

Rex's mouth dropped open, and his stunned expression said he understood the magnitude of what Tanyon had created. He swiped his hand over his mouth. "I don't know, but I have a feeling he'll find a market for them as well."

Fear unlike Jerry had ever known tried to suffocate him when he thought their baby would be sold. Tanyon couldn't get away with this, right? His father had to find them. He had to, because right then, he was their only hope. But... Jerry felt as if he'd been slammed in the chest by a two-by-four. He had to be responsible for everything Tanyon had dreamed up and made a reality. He didn't want to believe that.

"Jer, what's wrong? You look pale. Are you sick?" Rex's tone implored Jerry to answer.

"Do you think the blood they took from me…? Do you think I'm the reason this is happening?" Gods, why was he even asking? He already knew, but had to ask, as he became light-headed. "I'm the only Anzuni male besides my father who can get pregnant and now, if Stephanos *is* pregnant…." He shook his head and gripped the bars, feeling as if he were spinning out of control.

"You don't know if he is." Jerry might have agreed if Rex's tone had been more convincing. Then Rex asked something Jerry had wondered about. "Your father can get pregnant. Why not take him and knock him up? Why wait?"

"I don't know. I mean, he is the king and people would notice him missing. And if Tanyon was caught with my dad, there wouldn't be a trial. It's an automatic death sentence." Jerry smiled.

"What?"

"I can't believe I forgot this. Do you remember how I told you there's sperm present in both males and females? In females, it's released in their… parts." Jerry waved his hand at his crotch. "Sperm is absorbed like a virus and infects both partners. It doesn't matter if one of them is human. Same thing happens. The sperm activates the immune system, causing it to create antibodies that will attack any future sperm that didn't cause the antibodies. The more of that person's sperm absorbed, the stronger the antibodies. And if the Anzuni gets pregnant, those antibodies are a hundred times more effective in killing off future invaders."

"That seems backwards from human evolution. I mean, guys are hardwired to procreate from the moment puberty sets in and would if not for societal norms. Why lessen the gene pool?"

"You got me. No one knows. But if someone wants to have a baby with someone else, it's much harder to become pregnant, especially if they've had a baby. Not that it can't happen. It's just that the body doesn't see the initial person's sperm as something to get rid of. And the antibodies do decrease over time if no additional sperm is introduced."

"So, my swimmers are using your immune system to protect their territory." Rex's poignant stare hit Jerry hard.

"Yeah," Jerry whispered.

"That means you're mine. Not just your heart but your body too."

Gods. Jerry managed to whisper, "Yes."

"I like that."

Jerry loved it.

THE DAY stretched on. In between the guards wandering by, Jerry tried to get Stephanos's attention, but even awake he wouldn't answer. He'd been traumatized, violated by both surgery and a Braezelas, and more than likely had a fetus growing inside him.

Jerry gave up after a few hours of Stephanos ignoring him. His attention had turned to the newest arrivals mentioned by Tanyon. A few had been placed into the empty cages. More trickled in sporadically. The first ones to arrive had already gone through the change and were as docile as the others who'd previously occupied their cages. The Braezelas were obedient, almost too compliant, except for Rex, who was far from the submissive type. Perhaps those men had been chosen for their submissive natures and their obedient personalities.

Other unchanged Anzuni were wheeled into their cages, where they were shifted onto cots. Their movements were guarded, careful, as if in pain. They donned hospital gowns, and IVs hung above their cots. And Jerry would bet his next crappy meal they'd been operated on to allow for conceiving and carrying a child. More young men, all taken and violated, lost to the outside world, all to benefit one man. Jerry wanted to tear Tanyon apart, eviscerate him, and burn his remains. But death was too good for him.

For now, Jerry couldn't help anyone, which frustrated the future ruler in him. Rex distracted Jerry as time passed between new arrivals. They whispered across the space separating them, sharing thoughts and dreams about their baby. They spoke of everything from diapers, to sleepless nights, to his or her first steps. They talked of family vacations to the beach and walks in the sand, teaching their child to swim. Realizing they hadn't chosen any names for their offspring, they lost themselves in a game of the most outrageous names they could think of. Talking of their lives as if being kidnapped was temporary blocked out their desolate fates.

After Jerry ate his lunch—something highly unrecognizable—he glanced around at the new faces populating the cages. His confidence had been high that his father would find them, but he'd also told his father that Geraldon had taken them. If tracing the cell signal had failed, then places Geraldon owned or was known to visit would be the focus. That search could be extensive and drag on for a long time.

The main doors opened, pulling Jerry from his thoughts. Another gurney was wheeled in and stopped across from Jerry. The patient wore a hospital gown, meaning he'd most likely endured the surgery and hadn't been changed. His face wasn't visible as he lay on the gurney. He had no clue what they'd done to him or what he'd suffer when he healed. A Braezelas impregnating him by force. A pregnancy to provide Tanyon with his blood and Braezelas to stuff his coffers until they overflowed. Jerry hated every evil, sick thing about it all. Maybe this man and Stephanos could comfort each other, having shared similar experiences.

As they lifted the man from the gurney, the large Braezelas in the cage to the left beat against the bars. His face contorted with rage, and his muscles bulged. He wasn't small or submissive like the other men who'd been forced into this hell. He resembled Rex in height, but bulkier, with wide shoulders and a thick neck. His cage groaned as he shook the bars, and might collapse if he continued. His fiery gaze never left the man laid on the cot. The man lifted his head and looked to the Braezelas.

"It's okay, Gunn."

Shocked, too fucking stunned to even breathe, Jerry cursed out loud, knowing that voice. Large brown eyes turned toward him, and terror washed cold through Jerry, not a molecule spared until he shook.

He barely managed to whisper, "Keith. Fuck no, Keith."

"Dammit!" Rex slammed his palm against the bars, rattling his cage.

Jerry looked to the Braezelas Keith had called Gunn. His shouts increased, his cage rattled as he stared at Keith. Was that the man he'd met at the Blue Moon?

The guards turned their attention to Gunn.

Keith tried to get up, but he winced and sucked in his breath, no doubt in pain. "Jerry? Rex?" He gritted his teeth, then let out a breath. "What the fuck? You're both supposed to be serving your sentence with Tanyon! What the hell?"

Keith was there.

Keith.

That information took time to sift through Jerry's shock. Why? Because he knew Jerry?

The guards threatened to Taser Keith if Gunn kept his tirade going. He growled and then paced his cage.

Jerry looked to Rex who furrowed his brow, his expression one of apology. But it wasn't Rex's fault for what had happened.

The guards locked Keith's cage and wheeled the gurney toward the exit. Birdman followed and waved his prod in warning as he passed Gunn.

When the doors shut, Jerry said, "We were all captured, and have been here since we landed in California. Tanyon is the one behind all of this."

"And exactly what is *this*?" Gunn asked, white-knuckling the bars, his huge biceps flexing. Shit, Jerry wouldn't be surprised if he bent the thick pieces of steel with his bare hands.

Tears burned his eyes. They'd captured his best friend, operated on him, turned his human boyfriend—if that's what he had been—into a Braezelas. How did he tell them what Tanyon planned? He couldn't. Not yet.

"Keith, how did you get here? What happened?"

Keith made a sour face, pursing his lips. "Fucking assholes grabbed us outside of the Blue Moon. One second we're walking, and then some guys shot us with something. Next thing I know, we're in cages… somewhere. And then…." He choked. "They cut me open and turned Gunn into that." He pointed at his boyfriend. "I heard someone call him a Braezelas."

What a nightmare. Keith now had the ability to get pregnant. Why bring Gunn, though? He wasn't subservient, and he was anything but small as the others had been. Jerry scrubbed his face.

"It's true. They changed me too," Rex said. "Along with a bunch of other guys. Some of the others they operated on so—"

"Wait." Jerry watched as a guard entered the room with another Braezelas. Once the demon was secured, the guard left.

Ty banged around his cage, growling and slamming into the bars, his attention once again past Jerry.

That drew Keith's attention. His eyes widened. "Is that Tyranis?"

"Yeah, that's him."

Ty paced, growling under his breath, eyes wild and barely Anzuni any longer.

"Did they do that to him?" Keith asked.

"Yes."

"Good. I see they brought his inner beauty out. What are they doing with him?"

"No fucking clue." Jerry paused and tightened his lips, not wanting to say his next words. "Keith, I have to tell you something about the operation you had."

"Did they put something in me?" He visibly shuddered. "Shit, tell me it's not some evil demon parasite."

"Not yet," Rex muttered.

Jerry didn't want to tell him. Keith and Gunn both stared at him with trepidation.

"I think they made it so you can get pregnant."

Keith's eyes practically popped out of his head. "Excuse me?"

Nodding, Jerry pointed to Stephanos, who still lay on his cot, staring at the ceiling as usual. His stomach protruded. "He's Anzuni. They operated on him. I'm pretty sure he's pregnant."

Keith and Gunn both turned their attention to Stephanos, who, except for breathing and the occasional blink, didn't move a muscle.

"He's one of the missing Anzuni men." Rex's jaw clenched and cords popped on his neck.

"What's wrong with him?" Gunn asked.

"We think they gave one of the Braezelas a drug that made them insanely horny and that he... um... forced himself on Stephanos."

Keith gasped, and Gunn banged on the bars, yelling to be released.

"Gunn, calm down! They'll hurt you." Keith reached his arm through the bars, hand outstretched to Gunn, but he'd lost his ability to listen, to rationalize. Guards flooded the room and jammed their prods into Gunn's chest and stomach. He continued to attack the bars, howling with each shock.

Rex begged Gunn to drop to the floor, but nothing got through. After minutes of being assaulted, his beleaguered body went down and he was out.

"Gunn! No, nononono...." Keith curled onto his side, his pain creasing his forehead, his gaze set on Gunn.

"He's okay. I can see him breathing. He's just out," Rex said.

Keith nodded but remained silent, his body shaking. Gunn was much more than a fling to Keith. His actions said he cared deeply for the man, and from Gunn's reaction, he felt the same about Keith.

"I'm sorry," Jerry whispered, desolate of hope. The scowl on Rex's face told Jerry his determination to escape hadn't diminished. Jerry hoped they all survived.

Sometime before lights out, the guards came in and shot Ty with a dart and carried him away. At least Jerry could relax without the threat of death from his former fiancé.

CHAPTER 25

KEITH HAD given in to sleep after Gunn woke and assured him that he wasn't injured. Hard to believe after the repeated shocks. The man was strong. Jerry kept a close eye on Keith. After lights out, Keith called out to Jerry.

"What's wrong? Are you okay?" Jerry stumbled to the door of his cage.

"Yeah. Why're we all here besides the obvious craziness? Does anyone know where we are?" The hope in Keith's voice was disheartening. Jerry sighed and told Keith what he'd learned about the altered history, how the Braezelas were an Anzuni creation, about the drugs and Geraldon, and the Anzuni men like himself, now able to carry a baby. He mentioned Stephanos and called out to him again, but only silence reigned. He hadn't expected him to answer. In the end, Jerry had left out the need for royal blood and the pendant. He was to blame for the changes even being possible, and admitting so was too hard.

"You're pregnant?" Gunn asked. "But you're a guy. Wait. What am I saying? I'm a fucking demon, and I'm in love with one too."

"You okay, babe?" Keith asked, his tone filled with his concern.

That confirmed Jerry's suspicions. Keith with a guy, not experimentally. Go figure.

There was a moment of silence. "Taking it all in, love."

Rex chuckled morosely. "Takes a while to wrap your head around any of this, for sure."

Gunn only grunted in response.

"I'm pregnant." The meek voice cut through the darkness.

"Stephanos?" Jerry was surprised to hear him speak. "How're you doing? I mean…."

Before he could add anything else, Stephanos barked out a hideously dire laugh. "Fuck if I know. I've been altered, fucked, and now

177

I'm pregnant, and in a cell, and my… m-my….” He sighed. “Doesn't matter because he's gone now. Shit couldn't be crazier.”

Jerry wanted to ask who was gone, but the cracking in Stephanos's voice stopped him.

“Rex, you're a Braezelas now too?” Keith asked.

Rex grunted. “Yeah, I am.”

“But you still look like you. Your face doesn't look like Gunn's.”

In that blackness, others shifted about their cages, awake and listening.

“He did look like Gunn, but when they put Rex into my cage with me”—*his fucking cage*—“he eventually reverted back to his human form. Tanyon said he couldn't make it happen with the other Braezelas he'd created, but, for some reason, he came up with the idea that a true mate could trigger the change.”

“Are you mates?” someone to Jerry's left asked.

Jerry turned his head toward the voice. “Yes, we are. What's your name?”

“Sal. My mate, Tomasa, and I were taken together. They operated on him. He's sleeping, but I think he's okay. I was changed too. I heard one of the masked men mention mates.”

“Jerricho and his mate Rex were taken as well,” Keith said, and that brought a gasp from Sal. Keith never tired of reminding Jerry of his royal status.

“Jerricho? Prince Jerricho?” His disbelief was apparent in his voice.

“The one and only.”

“Your Highness, please accept my apologies for not addressing you properly,” Sal said.

Keith snorted loudly. “Never get tired of that.”

Jerry sighed. “Here it doesn't matter who I am. We're all prisoners of a psycho.”

“What's a mate?” Gunn asked.

“It's what we Anzuni call the person we want to spend our lives with, the person we believe connects with our soul.” Keith's words cut a tentative path through the darkness.

Silence. And then Gunn asked, “Are we mates?”

Several breaths passed. "To me, yes."

"You're definitely my mate, love."

Jerry swore he heard a beaming grin in Gunn's voice.

"I-I'm David and I'm human," a deep voice called out. "My mate, Tenyris, is Anzuni. They changed me and operated on him."

"Hi," a timid voice said, no doubt Tenyris.

"I'm Paul and my mate, Henri, is here too."

"Why're they doing this to us?" a wavering voice asked. He sounded terrified.

"It'll be okay, Henri." There was a growl underlying Paul's voice. "I won't let them hurt you, honey."

"Jerry." Rex's whisper barely reached him. "They're all mates."

They were, and that made their kidnappings much more heinous. Being forced to watch their soul mate suffer, as Jerry and Rex had, was the harshest torture they could experience.

"Jerry. Did you hear me? They are all mates."

Understanding crawled over Jerry like an icy hand running across his skin. Eli hadn't said anything about mates when talking of those who'd first occupied the cages. Neither had he mentioned having a mate taken.

"How many mated pairs are in here?"

More responded, and when totaled, including Rex and Jerry, there were six couples. A few of the Anzuni men who answered had been there when Jerry and Rex had arrived. They were unmated, and the operation had turned them into baby carriers. Two of them were no doubt pregnant, since being fucked by a drugged Braezelas.

"So the mates are part of the new shipment Tanyon was talking about," Rex said.

Jerry snorted his disgust.

"Why mates?" Keith asked.

Rex shifted restlessly in his cage, and Jerry pictured him pacing. "Because for some reason it makes their mates transform back. I did after being placed in Jerry's cage. Braezelas that look like humans are easier to transport."

Silence allowed the information to sink in.

"What does that mean?" Keith asked. "Are they sending us somewhere else?"

There was no getting around the truth. "The Braezelas are made to be sex slaves. When drugged with Braezelas blood mixed with something, I don't know what—" He paused and drew in a deep breath. "—they become submissive, and willing to service whoever demands it. They crave it."

A chorus of shouts erupted, and in less than a minute, light flooded the room. Jerry blinked rapidly as the doors busted open. Silence reigned as the guards entered with threats of electric shocks if the prisoners didn't keep quiet. Jerry climbed onto the cot, exhausted. He focused on Rex, and thousands of unsaid words passed between them. If their rescue wasn't soon, they'd spend the rest of their lives at the whim of someone else and more than likely separated from their mates.

THE LIGHT filtering through Jerry's eyelids woke him. The sun shone through the windows. Jerry got a good look at the men he'd spoken with the night before. These Braezelas didn't appear to be as submissive as the ones who'd initially been changed. They were larger and lacked the subdued personalities of the prior men. If that first group of men had been chosen for their submissive qualities, then taking mated couples wouldn't allow Tanyon to be so choosy.

Ty's cage was still empty. Who knew where he was, but Jerry wasn't upset that he hadn't returned.

Jerry curled up on his side, the baby kicking like crazy. Rex slept in the cage next to him. His restlessness had woken Jerry several times during the night, and Jerry was exhausted. There was a steady pain in Jerry's back. He rubbed his hard stomach. His last month of pregnancy. How much longer did he have? Weeks? Days? Having his baby in captivity terrified him. Once he was no longer pregnant, Tanyon had said he'd be knocked up again until his usefulness ended, unless they truly needed the Braezelas's mates to instigate the change. Was it possible he and Rex would be sold together?

As for their child, well Jerry didn't even want to think about that. He hated not knowing what the future held, not knowing if he or Rex would see their unborn child, get to hold him or her. He hugged his stomach as tears burned his eyes.

"Come on, Dad. *Please* find us."

MIDMORNING, HE was led from his cage and met Keith's worried glance.

"Going for a checkup, that's all."

Keith nodded. He sat upright and didn't appear to be in as much pain as the day before. The lines on his forehead and those around his eyes had smoothed, but he was still pale.

Back in the exam room, the doctor drew more blood. Another ultrasound, where Jerry learned nothing. He returned to his cage. Rex was next. He smiled reassuringly as he passed Jerry's cage. He gripped the bars, his gut twisting into knots. Each time Rex disappeared through those doors terrified Jerry. Visions of him being drugged and forced into submission by some sick fuck had him shaking. So far Rex had only been forced to donate blood. Each time he returned significantly weaker and slept for hours. At least he'd returned unharmed. Jerry prayed this time would be the same.

He sank back onto the cot and surveyed the other cages. Another day filled with boredom where he'd crawl out of his skin was before him. Jerry looked to Keith who smiled slightly as their gazes connected. Jerry returned the smile, but when the guilt became too great, he lay on his back and stared at the ceiling.

Birdman and Metal Head dragged a weakened Rex into the room and then dumped him back into his cage. He mouthed "I love you" to Jerry before falling asleep. The lights went out, and Jerry lay awake in the dark for hours, thinking too much, until he drifted off.

Someone roared and Jerry jumped from his cot, disoriented. Gunn growled at the collection of guards near his cage. Keith begged Gunn to calm down. A guard opened Keith's cage and entered with a Taser. They loved those fucking things. With the threat to his mate, Gunn backed down.

"Get down on your stomach." Birdman pointed to the floor. Gunn grudgingly obeyed, his gaze never wavering from Keith. A zip tie secured his arms behind his back. The doctor entered the cage and stuffed a needle into Gunn's arm. When she exited, two guards hoisted Gunn from the floor and dragged him to the door of Keith's cage. Gunn's chest heaved and his head hung low as his hands were cut free. Opening the door, Metal Head shoved Gunn at Keith. Gunn plastered his back to the bars as if Keith were a dangerous animal.

Keith frowned. "Gunn?"

Gunn grunted, and Jerry saw the tent in his sweatpants. They'd planned for Gunn to fuck Keith.

"Keith, stay back!" But Keith didn't appear to hear him. Birdman turned and growled at Jerry, but he didn't back down. "Gunn won't be able to control himself."

"Gunn, fight it!" Rex shook his cage door. Keith, wide-eyed with fear, crouched and pushed himself into the corner of the cage. "Gunn? Are you all right, babe?"

Gunn took two steps toward Keith and then stopped. He gripped his head in his palms, grunted, and then shook his head. More grunts as Gunn's breath came rapidly. "No." He pushed back against the bars again.

"Fight it, babe. Try to fight it."

Metal Head stepped up to the side of the cage where Keith crouched. He pushed a tube through the bars, and it bounced on the cot. "I'd get myself lubed up before he lets loose on your ass."

Keith didn't move, his focus entirely on Gunn, who snarled and dropped his hands. He stalked toward the bed again, this time not stopping.

"Gunn, no!" Rex slammed against the door to his cage.

"Gunn, don't hurt him!" Jerry had never felt so fucking helpless.

Birdman stalked to Jerry's cage, lifting the prod. Through gritted teeth, he said, "Shut it, or I fry you!"

"Back off!" Rex pointed at Birdman. He went to Rex's cage and shoved the prod through the bars but missed Rex.

Gunn visibly warred with himself, and Jerry prayed he fought to keep from violently fucking Keith.

Keith looked to Jerry with wide, glassy eyes. "Maybe I should let him. He's so hard. It has to be painful."

Gunn would tear him up. "Don't."

"Gunn, it's okay. I know you can't stop." Keith crawled to the end of the cot.

Gunn howled, then ducked his head and rammed into the bars.

"What the hell's he doing?" Metal Head asked as Gunn rammed his head into the bars, over and over.

Tears ran down Keith's face. "Gunn! Stop!"

"Tranquilize him before he kills himself!" The guards didn't move.

Gunn didn't cease ramming the bars until his head was covered in blood and he sat dazed on the floor.

Keith jumped off the cot and dropped to his knees next to Gunn. "Babe? Oh shit. He's bleeding. Help him!"

Tanyon strode through the doors, a glint of determination in his eyes. He scowled, looking down on Keith and Gunn.

The doctor's eyes flared with anger upon seeing him. "I told you mates were a bad idea. His need to protect his mate is so strong, that instead of risking him harm, the Braezelas nearly beat himself unconscious."

Keith ran his palm over Gunn's cheek. Gunn gazed up at Keith, grasped his hand, and brought it to his mouth. The love that passed between them stole Jerry's breath and brought on a hot rage.

"Tanyon, you motherfucker! Look what you're doing! Look! I'm going to kill you when I get my hands on you!" Jerry should shut up, but Tanyon had ruined lives, stolen freedom, all for profit. "You're a fucking psycho, and one day soon, you're going to get what's coming to you!"

Tanyon pursed his lips and furrowed his brow. Straightening his suit coat, he approached Jerry's cage. Looking down his nose, he surveyed Jerry as one would an annoying gnat. "Is that what you think, *Prince* Jerricho? *You* are the reason I was able to create the Braezelas and the drug to turn them into lustful slaves, and"—Tanyon grinned—"the reason other Anzuni males are able to get pregnant. Your blood allowed everything to happen."

Jerry didn't take his bait and dropped his guilt. "My father will figure out that you're behind this, and you'll pay for all of the nasty, vicious things you've done. I hope you suffer."

A dry chuckle escaped Tanyon. "Your father believes I'm dead. Didn't you know we all perished in a fire? You, Rex, Merano, Geraldon, Tyranis, and myself. The highly bribable coroner confirmed that we have all met a most gruesome fate in an explosion at one of Geraldon's properties. There were victims, but only three. Geraldon, Tyranis, and Merano were the only ones who truly perished."

Stephanos wailed in his cage, and Jerry was unsure what upset him.

He faked an expression of sorrow. "The Anzuni are mourning the loss of their prince and his child. Evidence planted points all fingers at Geraldon, as well as"—he turned to Rex—"your claxton."

Jerry shook his head. "That's not true."

"I'm going to fucking kill you!" Rex would or die trying.

"I highly doubt that. Now, I have guests arriving, and they're looking forward to sampling the merchandise. I was saving the best for later, but since you ran your mouth, I think now's a good time. I have a buyer willing to pay millions for a tall, muscular Braezelas. Guards, bring the former prince and his claxton to the lounge. Let's see how Jerricho likes watching his mate service another man. You can kill him if he resists. I couldn't care less if this Braezelas can revert back to human form. I'm sure we can box him up and ship him wherever he needs to go."

As Tanyon left the room, Birdman opened Jerry's cage and yanked Rex out by his arm. "You know, the boss often lets us work off steam with the Braezelas once the investors are done using them. I'd like a go at your boyfriend."

Jerry shoved his knee into Birdman's groin. The guard bent over, roaring in pain, but quickly recovered and backhanded Jerry. He fell back onto the bed, bounced, and then rolled onto the floor. His vision grayed, and then he was yanked off the ground.

Rex tried to break free, but the guards held on to him tightly.

"Maybe I'll fuck your claxton right here." Hellfire lit Birdman's eyes.

Jerry shuddered, believing Birdman would go at Rex while Jerry watched.

Metal Head pointed at Birdman. "You heard Tanyon. Get these pieces of meat to the lounge." Birdman complied, being none too gentle as he led Jerry through the doors.

Jerry looked over his shoulder and mouthed, "I'm sorry."

Rex shook his head and looked away. Damned if that wasn't a stake to the heart.

CHAPTER 26

ONCE AGAIN the lounge was populated with men and women. Braezelas were present sucking, licking, and being fucked. Jerry searched for Eli, but he wasn't in the room. He could have been anywhere on Earth by then.

Birdman strapped Rex to a chair. Jerry's heart rate kicked up and his gut tightened as he gazed helplessly at Rex. He wrapped his arms around his stomach, wishing he had any kind of a plan.

Tanyon entered from a door to the right, followed by a tall man in an expensive blue suit and a red tie. He was clean-shaven, and his black hair slicked down. On his left hand was a large gold ring. On his right wrist was what looked to be a Rolex. Had to be the man with millions to throw around buying slaves. He appeared familiar, which meant he had to be another Anzuni turncoat. As his gaze passed over Jerry, something flickered in the man's eyes. His leer settled on Rex and hit Jerry hard in the chest.

The doctor entered the room and waited to one side.

"Fine specimen, isn't he?" Tanyon asked the man.

"He's everything you promised and more." His dark, cold eyes never wavered from Rex.

"I assume you'd like to sample the merchandise." Tanyon waved to the doctor.

"Stop." Everyone in the room ceased what they were doing on the man's command.

Tanyon raised his brow. "Mr. Stoddard?"

"Clear the room of everyone, including the doctor. I *will not* be on display for the likes of these people. One guard, and the prince can stay as well."

Tanyon frowned minutely, then smiled graciously. "We have another room that is most comfortable, where you can—"

Mr. Stoddard narrowed his eyes. "Here."

"The doctor is needed to deliver the injection."

Impatience covered the man's chiseled face. "*You* can give the injection. Unless it's too much for you to handle. I thought you could deliver what I want. If that isn't possible, then I'll leave."

Tanyon continued to smile, although the muscles in his jaw bulged. "Ladies and gentlemen, we have another room set up where you can sample our other merchandise. Bernard, will you lead these fine people and tend to their needs?" He held his hand out to the doctor. She handed him the syringe and left.

Only Jerry and Rex, Mr. Stoddard, Tanyon, and Birdman remained.

"There. Alone as requested," Tanyon said, approaching Rex with the syringe.

Jerry tensed. He couldn't allow this to happen. Couldn't sit back and watch Rex change before his eyes and then desire to pleasure another man.

"Let me do it." Mr. Stoddard held out his hand, grinning maliciously at Jerry. A cold shudder wracked his body. "I'll take great joy in changing the claxton of the prince of the Anzuni into my sex slave."

Tanyon complied. Apparently, money overrode his need to be in control.

"Don't." Jerry stood near Rex ready to bat the needle away when it came near him. "Don't do this! We don't want this!"

If there was ever a moment for his ability to freeze time to show its cowardly face, it was now. His childhood rebellion was going to cost them everything.

Rex scowled, and Jerry flinched. Was Rex so angry with him that he'd choose to be a slave?

Mr. Stoddard ignored him, plunging the needle into Rex's arm. He gritted his teeth. When he screamed, Jerry jumped. His head thrashed and his muscles tensed. His nose flattened, his cheekbones became more pronounced, followed by the eruption of horns from his forehead. When the transformation was complete, Rex slumped in the chair, chest heaving, his muscles quivering. His head lolled, eyes heavy lidded, mouth slack. And his cock hard in his sweats.

187

Tanyon removed the restraints and then pushed Rex forward. He fell to his knees before Mr. Stoddard, as if worshipping the bastard. Jerry begged Rex to fight the drug and stop what would happen right before him. The guard gripped Jerry tighter. But Jerry couldn't stop. In a haze of pain from the fingers digging into his arms, he didn't stop trying to free himself and didn't care if Birdman killed him.

"He's a feisty one, isn't he?" Mr. Stoddard eyed Jerry. "Maybe I'll buy them both." He unbuckled his belt and opened his pants.

"The prince is not for sale," Tanyon stated emphatically.

Mr. Stoddard smirked as he lowered his zipper. "Everything's for sale. You just have to be willing to pay for it." He gazed down at Rex, grasped his chin, and lifted his head. Surveying his face, he appeared to be searching for something.

Jerry closed his eyes, unwilling to watch Rex suck someone else without a fight.

"What the fuck?"

Jerry opened his eyes in time to see Mr. Stoddard backhand Rex, snapping his head to the side. He hit the floor hard, curling in on himself. "He's fucking soft! What the hell am I supposed to do with a slave whose dick doesn't get hard? He should be dripping and begging me with his eyes to suck my cock!"

Tanyon's jaw dropped as he looked frantically from Rex to the buyer. "I-I…. He should be. The formula has worked flawlessly on every other Braezelas. You saw them when you came in earlier. Maybe it was a bad batch. Let me get another dose, and—"

Mr. Stoddard's face contorted in rage and Jerry cringed. All that was missing were flames shooting from his eyes. Tanyon shrank into himself.

"My time is valuable, and your failure is unacceptable. I didn't make the trip here to be an audience for your incompetence." Mr. Stoddard gazed at his watch. "I have a conference call." He turned on his heel and headed for the door.

Tanyon practically tripped over his own feet to catch up. "Mr. Stoddard, please wait."

Mr. Stoddard huffed and turned.

"Please forgive me. I'm sure we can do something to make your trip here worthwhile."

Mr. Stoddard crossed his arms over his large chest. Jerry had a fleeting feeling of déjà vu. He'd crossed paths with Mr. Stoddard before. Gods, he might have even shared a meal with Jerry and his parents, sat right at their table. Jerry scowled at the traitorous dick.

"What could you possibly have that will make up for wasting my time?" Mr. Stoddard curled his fingers and studied his nails, the epitome of privileged boredom.

Panic ruled Tanyon for a minute, and then he appeared calmer. "Once the child is born, you can have the former prince as well. The child will go to the highest bidder, and Jerricho is one pain in the ass I don't need."

"No! You can't take my baby!" Jerry looked to Rex for his reaction, but he hadn't moved.

No one paid Jerry any attention, and it pissed him off.

"You expect me to wait for what, another couple of months? Not interested."

Tanyon grinned. "The gestational period for the fetus has been sped up just a bit."

That got Mr. Stoddard's attention. "What do you mean *sped up*?"

"A growth hormone developed by the doctor you met earlier. Administered in the first month of pregnancy, it can decrease the gestational period by months. The latest tests, place the fetus at full-term."

Jerry had believed he had more time, that they'd be rescued before the baby was born. If they sold his baby, he'd never see him or her again.

"You can have my baby over my cold dead body!" Jerry kicked his legs as he tried to break free of Birdman.

Tanyon ignored his outburst. "We can induce labor at any time, and then you can take them both. Seriously, this one has been nothing but a pain in my ass for years. I'm sure you'll see to it that he lives in a manner to which he *isn't* accustomed. I've heard you're... rough with your toys."

Tanyon hated Jerry for no reason he could fathom.

"And this"—Mr. Stoddard sneered at Rex unaware on the floor—"will be ready as well?"

Tanyon glared lasciviously at Rex. "I will personally assure he's working properly."

Tanyon squawked as Mr. Stoddard grabbed his arm, and Jerry secretly cheered the manhandling. What he wouldn't give to go a round with Tanyon.

"You will not touch him. No one is to touch him. Not a finger. Any merchandise I purchase will be unharmed, not a single bruise. No one fucks him or gets their cocks sucked unless I say so. From this moment, he's my property. Do you understand?"

Those commands should have relieved Jerry, but it just pointed to the reality of their dismal fates. Even if sold together, Rex would be Stoddard's sex slave. And Jerry could be headed for even worse.

Fear fled from Tanyon, and he straightened. "He's yours, once the wire transfer is complete."

Stoddard released Tanyon with a slight shove, then smoothed the front of his own suit coat. "We'll discuss the terms of the sale after my conference call. I assume you plan to induce labor soon?"

"Tomorrow."

Jerry wanted to scream, but his fight had fled. Mr. Stoddard stepped before Jerry and gave him a quizzical look. "Where's the fight you were so full of just minutes ago?"

Jerry averted his eyes, squirming under the man's scrutiny. When Jerry failed to answer, Mr. Stoddard didn't force a reply from him.

"While I like a man who's submissive and thrives on serving me, I'm also thrilled by the fight, by the one who doesn't succumb so quickly, isn't easily broken."

Jerry shuddered. Stoddard liked to fuck the unwilling? If he tried to stick his dick near Jerry without drugging him, he'd get a fight.

"Seems he needs a reminder of exactly what he's fighting for." He returned to Tanyon. "Put them together for the night. Let Prince Jerricho remember just what he's losing."

Stoddard left the room, sealing Jerry and Rex's fate with a slam of the door. One day left with his baby. One day left with the man he loved. One day left free of pleasuring a sadistic bastard who would break them both.

JERRY PULLED Rex closer on the cot they shared. Tanyon complied with Mr. Stoddard's demand they be placed together, which shocked Jerry. Rex slept, the effects of the shot still present. Jerry snuggled closer, but with his large stomach, it was like having a beach ball shoved between them. Despite the difficulty, Jerry clung to Rex for dear life, their child cradled between them.

Tomorrow they'd force his baby from his body, take him or her away, sell the helpless half Anzuni, no doubt to a coldhearted deviant, as nothing more than an exotic pet. Or possibly someone who yearned for a child to love would be the buyer. Not beyond the realm of possibilities, and hope was the only thing left to grasp onto.

Rex lifted his head, blinking several times. Recognition slowly seeped back into Rex's eyes. He scanned the area around them. "Jer, what... what am I doing in your cage?"

Jerry closed his eyes, opening them when Rex's fingers trailed over his cheeks.

"Jer, talk to me?"

Jerry avoided Rex's questioning gaze. "Mr. Stoddard requested we be put together."

Rex frowned. Then, his face frozen in a mask of panic, he pulled away. "Jer... I-I'm so sorry. Oh... gods," he whispered, wiping his mouth with the back of his hand.

Jerry had to roll to get off the cot. When he stood, he reached for Rex, who cringed.

"Hey, it's okay."

"How can you say *that*?" He gripped his head with his hands. "I can't remember anything, but you had to watch."

"You didn't have a choice. You were helpless on that drug, even if you wanted to stop. But you di—"

Rex stumbled off the cot and fell to his knees, his back to Jerry. His rib cage expanded and contracted rapidly. "I should've been able to fight it."

Jerry tried unsuccessfully to suppress his bark of laughter. He climbed off the cot and knelt beside Rex, taking his hands. "I'm sorry. I laughed because maybe you did fight it." Jerry smiled, seeing Rex's confusion. "Nothing happened. You didn't get hard. You didn't do anything to Stoddard."

Rex glanced down at his groin and then back at Jerry. "But I know they gave me the shot. My arm hurts like hell." He rubbed his cheek. "My face too."

"Stoddard smacked you when you failed to perform. He wasn't impressed when you weren't dripping hard for him."

Rex's imploring expression was priceless. "I didn't do anything with him?"

Jerry shook his head, and Rex fell into his arms, shuddering. "Thank gods. If I did, I'd never forgive myself."

Jerry sighed. "I wish the news got better, but...."

Looking over Rex's shoulder, Jerry locked eyes with Keith, his gaze beseeching Jerry for any information. Jerry shook his head and Keith frowned. Jerry mouthed, "Later."

"But what?" Rex asked, forcing Jerry's eyes to his.

"Mr. Stoddard wants the drug to work. He's coming back tomorrow and... he's buying both of us."

CHAPTER 27

"BOTH? BUT they need you for blood. And what about our baby?" Rex grasped Jerry's biceps.

Keith moved closer to the bars. A guard lounged in a chair near the door, but appeared to be snoozing. Gunn watched Keith from his cage like a hawk.

"Tanyon's inducing labor tomorrow. He said the baby's full-term." Jerry swallowed hard around the lump in his throat. "He's going to auction off the baby. He won't need me after that. He has other pregnant males now."

"Shit, Jerry. We have to stop this. It's not right," Keith said in a weak voice.

Jerry refused to let Tanyon take his time with Rex. Tomorrow they'd rip his baby from his body. Today was for them. Possibly the last moments they'd be themselves, free, even though they weren't.

Rex clutched him tightly. "It's okay. They won't get our baby. No matter what, I'm going to get us out of here."

Jerry rested his chin on Rex's shoulder. When the time came, Jerry would be right by Rex's side, fighting for freedom. But there was nothing to be done then. "Right now, let's not think about what could happen, please?"

"Sure. I love you, no matter what happens." Rex cupped Jerry's face in his hands. Sure emerald green eyes gazed at him. "Whatever happens, you belong to me, Jerricho Alamande Trychovisca. You." Kiss. "Are." Kiss. "Mine." Kiss.

Jerry smiled. "And you're mine."

Keith gagged but then looked longingly at Gunn. Jerry and his best friend had both found love only for greed to snatch their happiness away.

Jerry and Rex spent their time curled around one another, talking, but this time they stayed away from the future. They'd abandoned the weirdest baby name contest, in something akin to a silent realization that all their planning might not matter. They stuck to talking of the past. Despite the lack of privacy, there was still intimacy. For the most part, they were left alone. Well, except for Keith making snarky comments such as "get a room," but Jerry was grateful for the normalcy.

"I love you, you know that, right?" Rex asked in a hushed tone, the tenderness pulling Jerry from his thoughts.

Meeting Rex's gaze, the sincerity, the raw emotion, Jerry brushed his knuckles over Rex's cheek. He ran his fingertips over his brow, his forehead, his nose, his lips, his scruffy jaw. He couldn't remember a time without Rex, couldn't recall what his life had been like before he'd fallen for the steadfast foreman.

"I know," Jerry whispered. "I'm so lucky." The irony of that statement, given their current situation, wasn't lost on Jerry, but the words were true enough.

Jerry startled when a cage door slammed. He peered up to see Stephanos being led out by the guards. Like Jerry, he was subjected to daily ultrasounds and, given the size of his stomach, most likely given the hormone to speed the growth of the fetus. Stephanos nodded weakly as he passed, and Jerry nodded back. He tried not to think of what might become of the man after the birth. Would he be impregnated again, over and over, until his body gave out and his usefulness ended? Jerry shuddered, and Rex hugged him tighter.

"Okay, demon. Get on the ground. Time to earn your keep."

Jerry lifted his head as Birdman growled and entered Gunn's cage. "No fighting, and we'll let you visit your boyfriend for some fun."

Gunn lay on the ground willingly. The other captives watched with trepidation, except for Henri, who huddled on his cot, his head buried under his arms. He had the right idea.

Not again.

"Leave him alone!" Keith watched as Birdman cinched Gunn's wrists with a zip tie again. Metal Head yanked Gunn from the floor, and he hissed in pain. They led him to Keith's cage. Birdman freed Gunn's wrist and then forcefully shoved Gunn inside, slamming the door behind him. They didn't give him the shot.

Birdman tapped his prod on the bars. "This is your only chance. You'd better fuck like bunnies, or we'll shoot you up to make sure the job gets done."

Keith's eyes widened, and then he frowned. "Can't we even get a room for some privacy?"

"Get to it! You've got the lube. Make sure you shoot your load in him, demon." Birdman crossed the room and stood, his eyes on them.

Keith and Gunn stared at each other, neither moving. Jerry wanted to say something, but what?

"Let's give them some privacy." Rex climbed onto his cot and lay down. Everyone blinked out of their stares and turned their backs on Keith and Gunn. "Come on, Jer. Lay down with me."

Being forced to have sex in a room full of people would mortify Keith. Even if no one watched, they could hear everything.

Jerry nodded to Keith, who jerked his chin in acknowledgment and turned away. Jerry heard Keith whisper, "I don't think I can do this."

"We'll go slow. I promise I won't hurt you. Hey, we do this all the time."

Keith snorted. "Yeah, well, it was me sticking my dick in you."

Jerry's eyes widened. Keith had never…. Shit, could there be a crappier place to lose his virginity, not to mention get pregnant as well? Jerry couldn't stand this anymore, couldn't take the injustice, the god-awful inhumane treatment, as if they were animals. He dropped onto the cot, unresponsive to Rex's pleas to talk to him. He quickly spiraled deeper into depression.

He tried to block out the sounds of kissing, low moans, the cot squeaking.

"Jer?" Rex ran his hand over Jerry's stomach. He rolled into Rex's embrace, snuggling into his heat. Just knowing what Keith and Gunn were doing, Jerry was half-hard. Rex's hands running over his back didn't help.

"It's not fair. We should be home, getting ready to have our baby—on the due date—planning our futures together. I so wanted to spend my life with you."

"Shh. I don't know how yet, but I promise you I'll get us out of here before they can take our baby." Rex tensed, a steely determination in his tone. "We *will* have that life. We *will* live happily ever after."

Jerry refrained from disagreeing and allowed Rex to believe he could free them. In their bubble, nothing could touch them, and they remained cocooned in their own private world. Jerry didn't rise when Gunn protested leaving Keith, or when Keith swore up a storm because they used the cattle prod on Gunn. The lights went out, and Jerry fought to stay awake, without success.

Rising through layers of sleep, pleasure heated his groin and ran up his spine. Instinctively, he pushed into the tight grip around his cock. The pressure was perfect as the rhythm picked up. He groaned. Rex ran his large hand over Jerry's side, his hip, and his thigh as he continued to fist Jerry's cock. Rex growled, and his tongue trailed up Jerry's neck. He shuddered and pushed into Rex's hand.

"Fuck." He panted.

"That's it, Jer. Love the noises you make." His lips trailed over Jerry's jaw, and then licked across Jerry's lips.

"Faster." Jerry chased his orgasm, his balls pulling up tight.

Rex complied, twisting his fist over the head of Jerry's cock, drawing whimpers from him.

"I want you to fuck me so bad." Jerry bit and then sucked on Rex's lower lip.

"Oh, I'm going to fuck you right here."

"W-we don't have anything." Jerry pouted as Rex continued long strokes over Jerry's cock, and he realized how easily his cock slid through Rex's hand. "Nice."

Rex chuckled. "Keith was nice enough to share." Jerry grasped Rex's dick through his sweats. He groaned, "Oh… yeah."

"Knew I was friends with him for a reason."

Rex released Jerry and pulled down his sweatpants. His finger probed Jerry's hole. Jerry almost came and panted to hold off.

"Missed you so much, Jer," Rex whispered, nipping at Jerry's neck.

He pushed his finger past the tight ring of muscle. Jerry gasped and muffled his groan against Rex's shoulder. His heart swelled, loving the intimacy he and Rex hadn't shared in weeks. Another finger joined the first, stretching and filling him. Jerry freed Rex's cock and licked his palm, and then stroked slowly from root to head.

"Oh, gods." Rex bucked into his hand.

Precum coated Jerry's palm as he rubbed over the head. He returned to the base and pulled long strokes, picking up speed as Rex pushed his fingers farther into Jerry, stretching him so wide. The love he felt for Rex almost pushed him to orgasm, but he held on, needing to come while Rex was inside of him.

"Now."

Rex removed his fingers. Jerry rolled onto his back. Rex's hands ran over his stomach, so large and round, the skin stretched tight. Jerry chuckled. How would they do this?

"Why're you laughing?"

"Give me your hand." Jerry guided Rex's hand to his huge stomach. "I'm so big. How can we even do this?"

"Lay on your side."

Rex removed his sweatpants. Jerry rolled like a large whale rotating in the ocean and settled onto his side. If he wasn't so horny, he might be too disgusted with his body to fuck. Didn't matter. He needed Rex, now.

Rex lay behind Jerry. He leaned back and draped his leg over Rex's thigh, opening himself up. Rex's cock touched his hole, and Jerry shuddered hard. The head met the resistance of Jerry's tight hole, maintaining pressure until it popped in, pain tightening Jerry's muscles.

"We'll lay here until you're ready," Rex whispered. His breath tickled Jerry's ear.

"I'm good."

"Yeah?"

"Yeah."

Rex wrapped his arm around the bottom of Jerry's stomach, pulling him back as his dick opened Jerry, filled him. The burn was intense.

Rex's hot breath skated over Jerry's ear and cheek. "You're wrapped so tight around me," Rex whispered. "Can't ever get enough of you."

A quick thrust and Jerry whimpered as Rex's balls rested against Jerry's ass. "Fuck, you're big."

"You still okay?"

Jerry moved his hips experimentally, and groaned as a jolt of pleasure raced to his groin.

"Oh, fuck." Rex moaned. "Tell me you're ready."

Jerry reached back and grasped Rex's hip. "Fuck me."

Rex drew back with excruciating slowness. He bucked his hips, again burying his cock balls deep. Gasping, Jerry dug his fingers into Rex's arm.

"More." Jerry's head fell back on Rex's shoulder as Rex relentlessly thrust. He lifted the leg Jerry had over his, going deeper, varying the speed and angle until Jerry practically sobbed. It was as if he were a large nerve being stroked over and over in amazing, mind-numbing pleasure. Rex's breaths increased, and his sweat-slicked chest rubbed against Jerry's back.

Jerry's cock throbbed, pushing against the bottom of his stomach. He reached for his cock, needing to come. Rex slapped his hand away and grasped Jerry's sensitive shaft, jacking Jerry off to the rhythm of his thrusts. Jerry thrashed his head, bucked his hips into the fist and then back onto the cock. His impending orgasm blossomed from his balls, expanding and vibrating his muscles. He shook, needing to come, needing something to cause him to tumble into the warm abyss.

"B-bite my shoulder. I need…." Jerry's head spun as he practically hyperventilated.

Rex mumbled something incoherent under his ragged breaths. Rex must not have heard him, maybe too lost in his own head. Instead, Rex clamped his large hand over Jerry's mouth. Before he could protest, the sharp bite on his shoulder forced a sharp intake of air through Jerry's nose. He emitted a high-pitched wail into Rex's palm as hot sperm shot all over his stomach. The tight clench of his ass around Rex's hard shaft incited more spasms in his balls.

"Oh fuck." Rex snapped his hips faster, filling the air with the sounds of slapping skin. Jerry didn't care if the others heard. Nothing mattered but the bliss they shared. Rex thrust once, then twice, and rammed his dick into Jerry's gut, groaning as his cock throbbed in Jerry's ass. Rex's choppy breaths fanned Jerry's neck as he buried his face. Jerry rested his hand on Rex's arm, which wrapped around Jerry's enlarged belly. Gods, he wanted to crawl right inside the man.

"Damn, I haven't come that hard in a long time." Rex's chest heaved against Jerry's back. Jerry had to agree. They were meant to be together, and he didn't know what he'd do without Rex.

"I love you, baby," Jerry whispered.

"Love you too, Jer."

They remained wrapped around each other during the night, their desperation to squeeze all of the love they could in those final hours increasing as the dawn approached. Jerry dozed lightly until the doors to the room opened and thudded closed. Jerry refused to look up when someone unlocked his cage.

CHAPTER 28

"RISE AND shine, maggots. The big day has arrived."

Jerry shuddered, and Rex hugged him tighter. "It's going to be okay. Do what they say. Our child may be born in this hell, but keep hope."

Jerry nodded into Rex's shoulder. A hand grabbed Jerry's arm, and he was yanked away. He lost his balance and rolled off the edge where he landed on his hands and knees.

"Get the hell up!" Birdman growled. "Stay!" He pointed his weapon at Rex, who no doubt was rising to attack him.

Jerry scowled. "Give me a minute. I'm fucking pregnant, asshole."

Birdman could've laid him out flat, but Jerry didn't care. If they were going to force him to do something he didn't want to do, he'd take his time. Birdman backed off and waited, surprising Jerry.

Jerry bit back the sob working up from his throat. He held his hand out, and Rex grasped it tight. When Rex stood, he enveloped Jerry, kissing his forehead as Jerry held on for dear life.

"Remember, you concentrate on you, not me. No matter what happens, you hear?"

Jerry nodded, and Rex laid a gentle kiss on his lips. His eyes were glassy and his smile fleeting as they left the cage, Rex's hand around Jerry's like a vise. Jerry caught sight of Keith on his cot, his knees to his chest and his arms wrapped around his legs. Keith wouldn't be able to sit like that anymore once his stomach grew larger.

"See you soon," Jerry said.

"Yeah, soon," Keith responded. His expression wasn't only one of fear but of good-bye.

"The only thing you'll be seeing soon is your new owner. Move it." Birdman pushed Jerry, causing him to nearly lose his grip on Rex's hand, but Jerry held on tight. Watching Rex get zapped wasn't anything he wanted to see on the day of their child's birth so he kept his mouth shut.

Each of the prisoners nodded to Rex and Jerry as they passed their cages, knowing their time would come soon.

Jerry kept his eyes on the floor as they walked into the exam room. New equipment and machines had been brought in. The gurney was gone, replaced with a hospital bed. Across the room there was an incubator for the baby. At least they were serious about keeping their child alive.

The doctor typed something on the computer across the room and ignored their entrance. A woman in blue scrubs and a bright blue, feathered mask approached Jerry. There must have been a Mardi Gras clearance sale.

"Hello, I'm Karen, and I'll be your nurse. Please take off all your clothes, put this on, and then lie on the gurney." She handed him a gown and smiled.

Warily, Jerry took the gown. Rex shielded him from the others as he disrobed, and Jerry had to chuckle.

Rex arched an eyebrow. "What? This is all mine, and no one gets to ogle you but me."

"Ditto, baby."

The ball of pain pushing on Jerry's heart doubled in size. Rex tied the back of Jerry's gown and patted his bare ass as he helped Jerry onto the gurney. He then covered Jerry's legs with a sheet.

"Thank you." Jerry ran his palm over Rex's cheek. Rex smiled, but the glassiness in his eyes didn't give the smile credence.

Voices across the room caught Jerry's attention. Karen and the doctor appeared to be disagreeing over something. The doctor pointed to Jerry. The nurse glanced toward the door warily. The doctor grabbed a bag of liquid and handed it to Karen.

"Set up IV now. We don't have a choice."

The nurse took the bag and approached the bed. Her blonde ponytail flapping behind her appeared too peppy for the moment. She put down the bag on the tray table.

"I need to get an IV started, so relax."

Jerry nodded and lay back against the raised head of the bed. Rex stroked his arm, the touch reassuring. The nurse glanced out of the corner of her eye, and Jerry swore she smiled briefly, but then it faded.

She searched Jerry's arm for a suitable vein, tapping in a few places and rolling her thumb over his skin. Appearing satisfied she wiped the area with an alcohol pad and picked up the needle.

"Okay, a quick pinch, and…." She pushed the needle into his skin, and Jerry barely felt a thing.

"You're good." He should know after the amount of blood they'd siphoned from him.

"Lots of practice." She hooked the tube to the IV port and then covered the site with white tape.

Jerry furrowed his brow as he surveyed her. Her cheerful demeanor and her kindness made Jerry want to ask her to help them. She couldn't be one of them. Perhaps she didn't know these people were truly pure evil.

"Thanks for being such a cooperative patient."

She continued smiling as she hung a smaller bag on the IV pole. She connected that tube to an IV port and fiddled with the flow. "This will get those contractions started."

She patted his hand and moved away with her supplies. The cold liquid infiltrating his vein caused him to shudder. Rex sat on the edge of the bed and ran his thumb over the back of Jerry's hand. They remained silent, Jerry grateful Rex was with him. Was it for the entire labor? Again, that seemed more humane than anyone there was capable of.

The nurse returned, holding a long elastic belt, about six inches wide, with a large plastic disk attached. A cord ran from the disc and was plugged into a monitor beside the bed. "Sit up, hon, and let me strap this around your belly."

Jerry complied, and she lifted his gown. He was naked underneath and flashed the room. Rex was quick to cover Jerry's exposed dick with the sheet. The nurse wrapped the band around his back and then cinched it tight in the front. She fiddled with the disk, moving it around his belly.

"This will monitor the baby's heart rate, and your contractions." She flicked a switch on the monitor. As she moved the disk around again, the monitor emitted loud crackling noises, like someone hitting the end of a live microphone. Moving the disk increased the crackling, but also brought forth a faint beeping noise. Moving the disc an inch to the left flooded the room with the rapid thumping sound.

"Is that the baby?" Rex squeezed Jerry's hand. This was Rex's first time hearing the heartbeat. Jerry's chin quivered. She nodded, and Rex appeared even more distressed. "Isn't it too fast?"

She gazed at him softly. "That's normal for a baby in utero." She pointed to the monitor. "Around one hundred and sixty beats per minute. Perfect."

Rex visibly relaxed as the nurse left them alone. The corner of his lip rose. "That's our baby."

Jerry nodded, knowing if he spoke he'd end up blubbering. Rex rested his palm on Jerry's taut stomach.

"Oh look. You're having a contraction." She pointed to the printout from the machine where a small arch stretched across the paper. "Can you feel it?"

"Just feels crampy."

"That's it. Soon you feel your stomach tightening with each one." She turned her attention to the IV.

With the sound of their baby's heartbeat filling the room, Jerry tried to picture this moment with normalcy. Rex supporting him through his labor—soon he'd be in labor!—anxiously awaiting their child to be born. Jerry's parents and Keith in the waiting room. Jerry's mother would exude confidence despite her nervousness. His father, quiet and calm, his mask of indifference nowhere near expressing the pride and joy of his grandchild coming into the world. His only break in that calm would be his annoyance with Keith's pacing, impatience, and snarky remarks.

Jerry's stomach continued to feel crampy as they waited. It wasn't long before each single contraction was noticeable. At first, the muscles tightened gently. As time passed, the pressure increased with each one and they lasted longer. They were about three minutes apart when Tanyon and Mr. Stoddard entered the room. Gods, he hoped they weren't going to hang out and watch.

Mr. Stoddard—dressed in a gray suit and, this time, a blue silk tie—scowled. "You've started already? I believe I said I wanted to be here before you induced labor."

Tanyon's brow rose. "He's only just been given the inducing drug. You're here in time."

Mr. Stoddard growled and turned on Tanyon. His height was impressive. "Again, Tanyon, you seem to think I'm someone you can discount. Do it again and our transaction will end here and now."

"Of course." Tanyon looked angry enough to slug someone.

Mr. Stoddard came to the bed and stood next to the IV pole. Jerry kept his head down, holding Rex's hand firmly.

"What's this Braezelas doing here?"

No. No. No. Jerry tensed as another contraction hit. They couldn't kick Rex out. Jerry couldn't do this without him. His stomach tightened again and continued, reaching just this side of unpleasant. Sweat broke out on his forehead, and he blew out the breath he'd been holding.

"Anzuni labors are easier with the mate present. Their bond will help the Anzuni remain calm, hence speeding up the delivery. I imagine this spoiled one would throw a tantrum if his mate wasn't near." Tanyon sneered at Jerry, who sneered right back.

Stoddard pointed to Rex. "Come here." Shit, Rex was going to kill the man, given the fire flaming in his eyes along with an overt challenge. He didn't move.

A powerful contraction hit Jerry and knocked the breath from his lungs. Jerry's stomach tightened, and it kept on for several seconds, this one accompanied by pain around his upper stomach.

Fuuuuuuck!

He drew in deep breaths through his nose and exhaled through his mouth as the contraction climbed higher and higher, finally peaking and then subsiding. Weren't they supposed to gradually get more painful?

Rex held his ground, in a stare-off with Mr. Stoddard. Birdman stepped up and yanked Rex's arm behind his back. Rex hissed, but he didn't fight as he was shoved around the bed. Stoddard placed his hand on Rex's shoulder.

"Kneel." The deadly fire in Rex's eyes remained, but he knelt beside Stoddard. "You may hold his hand. Anything to speed up this process so we can get out of here."

The nurse approached the bed warily. "I need a blood pressure." Her eyes flicked to Mr. Stoddard as she took the cuff from the basket on the wall and wrapped it around Jerry's upper arm. Her sideways glances continued as she squeezed the bulb, the cuff squeezing his bicep harder. A contraction chose that moment to hit, and he sucked in a breath.

"Breathe, Jer. Come on. One… two… three." Jerry focused on Rex, exhaling and inhaling, trusting Rex to guide him through what everyone had promised would be a long, painful, god-awful birth.

"Blood pressure is good." She unwrapped the cuff and put it away. "You're doing great. I'll get you some ice chips to suck on." Karen patted his leg and then exited the room.

Jerry lay back again. Rex's hand was like a lifeline between them. Jerry wanted to beg Mr. Stoddard to buy his baby too, but he knew the man wouldn't agree. Hope was hard to hold on to as Jerry's contractions came closer together and intensified. A glint of something shiny turned Jerry's attention on Mr. Stoddard. The silver pocketknife in his hand. Jerry looked to Birdman, who stared at something on the wall. The doctor remained at the computer. Tanyon glared at his phone, tapping away furiously.

Jerry cringed as he eyed the knife. When he looked up, Mr. Stoddard shook his head minutely. Another contraction squeezed Jerry's stomach, and any chance to protect himself fled. He pulled air through his nose. What if he stabbed Rex? But that would be absurd given that Mr. Stoddard had paid for them. Add in the way Tanyon gave into his buyer's every whim, and the price had to be high.

Mr. Stoddard covertly took hold of the tube from the IV bag feeding Jerry the inducing medicine. With the knife, he sliced through the tube and dropped the end he held. Jerry slowly exhaled as the contraction peaked, higher than the last. He looked up at his owner—

how could one person own another?—eyes wide. Mr. Stoddard met his gaze. He lifted the right side of his suit jacket, revealing a gun in a holster under his arm. Why had he shown Jerry? And cutting the IV tube would probably stop Jerry's labor. Hadn't Mr. Stoddard insisted that Jerry have the baby before he took them to wherever? Was he trying to kill his baby?

Jerry's heart rate accelerated, which in turn pushed the baby's higher. The doctor looked up at the machine recording the contractions and frowned. She slid off her stool and approached the bed.

"Don't move," Mr. Stoddard mumbled to Jerry.

Mr. Stoddard reached into his coat.

"Wait." Tanyon held up his hand as he squinted at the screen of his phone. He looked to his client and then back to the phone. "You. You're not Stoddard!"

Like a western gunslinger, Stoddard ripped the gun from the holster under his arm and, in quick succession, shot the doctor and then Tanyon. Instead of blood, red darts stuck out of their chests, and they both went down. Movement pulled Jerry's attention to the left as Birdman tried to draw his gun. Rex growled and dived over the bed, smashing into the man before he could shoot. The gun skidded across the floor. Rex slammed his fist into Birdman's face, the mask breaking and falling away. Birdman was an ugly man, with a crooked nose and a flat face. Gods, Jerry would wear a mask too if he looked like that.

Blood spurted from the guard's nose, yet he still managed to buck Rex off his back. They clashed again, wrestling, jabbing, punching. Stoddard tried to get off a shot, but with the two bouncing around the room, chances were high that the dart would hit Rex. Birdman clocked Rex in the jaw, and he stumbled back, shaking his head, stunned.

"Rex!" Jerry rolled awkwardly to get off the bed. He hissed as the IV was ripped from his arm.

"Stop!" Mr. Stoddard, or whoever he was, tried to grab Jerry.

Rex looked to Jerry, then snarled as he threw another punch that connected with Birdman's jaw. Another punch and then another. The feral look on Rex's face shocked Jerry. One last punch and Birdman crumpled onto the floor. Stoddard shot him with a dart. Rex spun around on Stoddard but noticed Jerry. He scooped Jerry up in his arms. Jerry latched onto Rex.

"Who are you?" Rex stepped back until he hit the wall next to the door.

Mr. Stoddard holstered his gun. "I'm Jackos. Member of the king's guard."

"What?" Jerry surveyed the man's face, then glared warily. "No, you're not. I've never seen you before."

The supposed Jackos peeled off his suit coat. Red suspenders ran over the crisp white fabric of his dress shirt. The holster straps ran over his shoulders. He tossed the jacket haphazardly onto the bed. "I was outside of the Congressional Room the day you went before the council. I was on guard with Lanzo."

Jerry narrowed his eyes, then shook his head.

"You came skidding around the corner. Your face was bruised from Tyranis. Lanzo wanted to find the man and kill him with his bare hands. I had the same thought."

Rex scowled at Jerry. "Why didn't you tell me you knew him?"

"I don't, I mean, yes I do, but you've met him too."

Rex looked at Jackos. "Nope, don't remember ever seeing him."

"That day at the mansion when the council was deliberating our punishment, he was one of the guards outside of the Congressional Room."

"Picture a full beard, long braid, and blue eyes." Jackos's hair had been cut in an expensive pompadour and his face clean-shaven.

Rex crossed his arms. "Your eyes are green."

"Colored contacts."

"I didn't pay you any attention, so really you could be anyone."

"Fair enough." Jackos reached behind him and produced another gun. He strode over to Birdman and searched him, finding a small gun in a holster velcroed to the guard's ankle. Jackos also removed the Taser from his belt. "But decide now if you're going to trust me so we can get out of here. If not, you can stay here and live the rest of your life as someone else's bitch." Jackos sent Rex a pointed glare. "But know this. I cut off fifteen inches of my hair to go undercover to save your asses. Scissors haven't touched my hair since I was thirteen. I might get cranky if I did that for nothing."

Rex worked his jaw. "Give it a chance. You might like looking preppie."

"Excuse me, ginger? Preppie?"

"Whoa. What the fuck, Rex? Jackos risked his life to rescue us, and we're getting out of here before the baby is born and you're calling him names?" Jerry wasn't sure he could take one more thing going wrong.

The door opened, and everyone jumped. Karen entered. She was going to ruin everything.

CHAPTER 29

REX STARTED for her, but Jackos grabbed him.

"She's with me."

"Oh. Well, that's good." Rex stepped back.

"Karen's a doctor I brought in under the guise of a nurse as part of my deal with Tanyon in case either of you need medical treatment."

"Prince Jerricho. Claxton Rex." She bowed to both of them and Rex's brow rose dramatically. Jerry shrugged. He'd never get used to the bowing. "Are you still having contractions?"

Jerry paused, as everyone watched. His stomach tightened slightly, but nothing like the pressure from before.

"Small ones. They're getting weaker."

Rex sighed and pulled Jerry closer.

"We have to get out of here before a guard checks in. Karen, help Prince Jerricho to get dressed." She nodded and retrieved his T-shirt and sweats. He quickly pulled on the sweatpants. Karen helped him from the gown. T-shirt on, he was ready to roll.

"Wait." Rex held up his hands. "Is there anyone else with you? Tell me there's an army outside of this door."

Jackos pursed his lips. "Right now, it's just me and Karen. This place is like Fort Knox. Your call to your father gave us an area to search, not the exact location. When we finally pinpointed your location, there was no way to breach the property, even though your father wanted us to go in with guns blazing. Tanyon has this place fortified with metal fences, trip wires, surveillance, and booby traps. This building sits in the middle of three hundred acres of rocky wilderness. Tanyon would have known the guards were coming. He might have killed you before we even reached the building."

"If you had a location, then what took you so fucking long?" Rex narrowed his eyes.

209

"The fire at Geraldon's summer home stopped our search efforts in this area. We assumed that you'd been moved there because...." Jackos shifted uneasily, glancing from Rex then back to Jerry. "The coroner fraudulently identified the bodies of you and Rex, as well as Geraldon, Tanyon, Tyranis, and Merano. There were a few others who weren't identified. We believed you'd all perished in the fire."

"Oh shit. My parents." Why hadn't he thought about them when Tanyon had mentioned the fake deaths? His parents thought he'd died.

Jackos nodded in understanding. "The king.... I've never seen a man so brokenhearted, so defeated, and so determined to bring those who murdered you to justice. The king has another coroner working to identify the bodies found in the fire. There were eight in all. A preliminary examination didn't find the remains of a pregnant man, so we knew to keep looking."

"Well, Tanyon said Geraldon, Merano, and Tyranis died in the fire. But who were the others?" Rex asked. Jackos shook his head. "No idea. Hopefully when we get Tanyon into custody, he will tell us. Whether it truly is Geraldon, Merano, and Tyranis, we'll have to wait for confirmation from dental records."

"Well, Geraldon was here and so was Ty so it's highly likely."

Jackos looked surprised by that revelation. Jerry quickly filled Jackos in on the incidents with the two men.

"We can sort the details later. Right now, we have to get both of you to safety before the others get suspicious." Jackos moved until Rex spoke.

"Wait." Rex looked as if he wasn't going to budge.

"Rex, what're you doing? We have to get out of here now."

Rex's expression softened as he looked to Jerry. "I'm trying to keep you safe, Jer."

Jerry bit his lip and nodded, letting Rex continue. He trusted Rex more than anyone. "Tell me why you didn't break us out of here last night. Why wait until today?" Rex's face was a stony mask of determination. Jerry hadn't even thought of that. Maybe he should be more suspicious.

Jackos appeared to struggle, reining in a need to slug Rex. His hands went to his hips, and his brow furrowed. "Listen, we had no clue Tanyon was involved until we found this location. And again, Fort Knox. The only way we were even able to gain entry was by intercepting the real Mr. Stoddard—who is Anzuni—and with some… persuasion, he gave us a rundown of the twisted shit Tanyon has going on here. He postponed his appointment with Tanyon until I could take his place."

"That doesn't explain—"

Jackos raised his hand, cutting Rex off. "Tanyon is very careful. When a buyer comes onto the property, that person doesn't leave until he's purchased what he came for or decides not to buy and loses a 20 percent fee. The money for the purchase plus 50 percent for incidentals are secured in an account held by a third party so Tanyon can be assured that the buyer isn't a fraud or someone who will reveal his operation. We'd hoped by getting inside I could locate the prince. I almost crapped my pants when Tanyon presented me with both of you. I'd planned on using Stoddard's money and walking out of here with both of you but hadn't counted on you being even close to delivering. Tanyon inducing moved up my plans. I figured you didn't want to have your child here."

Jerry shook his head as did Rex, and then he cocked his head. "How much were you paying for us? Just for shits and giggles?"

"Twenty million."

"Dollars?" Rex turned his shocked expression on Jerry, who couldn't argue with the amount.

"You're worth every dollar," Jerry said.

Jackos moved to the door. "Now let's blow this place."

"And how're we going to do that?"

"Through the front door."

"What?" Rex asked incredulously. "You can't be serious? You're going to get us all killed."

"Oh, I'm serious."

Rex grunted. "Give me a gun and then we'll talk."

Without hesitation, Jackos pulled out a gun and handed it to Rex. "Don't accidentally shoot me with that." He smirked, then bent over and scooped up Tanyon, throwing him over his shoulder.

"Why are you taking him?" Jerry pointed to Tanyon, limp as a dishrag over Jackos's shoulder.

"Like I'm going to let him get away. Also, we need him to get out."

Jackos had his hand on the doorknob. "What about the others? My friend Keith and his mate are here and others, Anzuni and human. They're selling them, and they're going to disappear. What if we leave and can't get back in?"

Jackos nodded. "I know your friend is here as well as the others, but—"

Rex scowled. "How did you know that?" His tone was once again accusatory.

Jackos rolled his eyes dramatically. "Because he's missing, as are other pairs of mated Anzuni. We assume they're here since, Jerry, you told your father you'd seen the other kidnapped men. You just confirmed our suspicions." Jackos shifted his burden and placed his hand on Jerry's shoulder. "Can we get out of here now? Your father and mother are waiting anxiously in the next town over. If we're late, I'm sure the king won't be happy."

Jerry's heart leaped hearing they were so close. "Yes."

He reached for Rex, who hesitated and then conceded. Jerry could only pray Keith and the others would be safe until help could return. With Tanyon as their captive, they had leverage.

Jackos opened the door, peered into the hallway. He signaled for them to follow. Jerry looked to Karen, whose calm demeanor had slipped. Jerry smiled and she tried to smile. She probably hadn't counted on having to escape a fortress. Jerry followed Jackos into the hallway and held his breath. Rex trailed behind him with a protective hand on his back. The quiet was unnerving, but Jerry did his best to calm his speeding heart.

They turned down the hallway where Jerry had discovered Tanyon was behind all the madness. He glared at the back of Tanyon's head as he swung limply over Jackos's shoulder. The traitor would get what was coming to him—what he deserved—soon enough, and Jerry and Rex were going to be free to raise their child together.

Halfway down the hall, a man with a brush cut, wearing a polo shirt and jeans, casually rounded the corner at the end of the hall. Jerry gasped and Karen yelped at the same time. Rex shoved Jerry and Karen behind him and raised his gun, as did Jackos.

"Put your hands on your head."

The man's eyes widened as he looked to each of them. He looked confused. "Der—"

"Shut up!" Jackos advanced on him, gun at the ready. "Hands on your head!"

The man raised his arms and placed his palms on the top of his head.

"Turn toward the wall!"

Still frowning, the man complied. Jackos put his hand into his pants pocket, pulled out a bundle of zip ties, and held them up. "Rex, tie him up."

Rex snatched up the ties and yanked the man's hands behind his back. Jackos then commanded his captive to lie down.

Rex bent and secured the man's legs. Jackos pulled a handkerchief from his pocket, shoved it into the man's mouth, and then patted him on the cheek. "Hold on to that for me, will ya?"

The man sneered, then lowered his head to the floor.

Jackos motioned them forward. They moved through the corridors, blindly following Jackos, hoping he could get them out of there. Jerry's back throbbed and his stomach burned. He cradled the bottom of his belly. His weeks of captivity had weakened him. His breaths came in short pants, but he focused on freedom.

"What's the plan?" Rex whispered as they rounded another corner. The hallways were all the same, plain white walls and closed wooden doors. It was like a fucking rat maze.

Jackos continued to move warily, gun still drawn. "Get to the front door and get the hell out of here. My car's down the road, about five miles outside the gates. I was brought here by Tanyon in a helicopter."

"Jerry *can't* walk five miles!"

Jackos shushed Rex. "I didn't plan on it. That's why I have Tanyon. He has the keys to get out of here as well as access to the garage and his vehicle."

Jerry raised his brow. "You couldn't have taken the keys and left him behind?"

"It's not that kind of key. I need his eye for the retinal scan. But I could rip it out," Jackos said—with too much enthusiasm.

"Hell no." Jerry shuddered. "Proceed."

Another hallway and a turn, and they came to a large gray metal door. Beside that was a keypad beneath a small screen. Jackos dropped Tanyon to the floor with a thud. The man moaned but didn't wake. Jackos hit a button, and a green light flashed. He lifted Tanyon, positioning his drooping head in front of the screen.

"Rex, lift his head and hold his eye open for the scanner."

Without hesitation, Rex yanked up Tanyon's head, not too gently, and pried open his eye. A green light scanned Tanyon's eyeball. There was a metal *click*. Jackos grinned, then hefted Tanyon over his shoulder.

Pushing his shoulder against the large metal door, he said, "This way to freedom, lady and gentlemen."

Jerry stepped forward and flinched at a pull in his side. Rex touched his shoulder. "You okay?"

Jerry wasn't going to let anything stop him. "Yeah, let's get out of this godsforsaken hellhole."

Rex searched his eyes for a few seconds. "Gladly."

Exiting, Jerry winced as the bright sunlight blinded him. He tried to look to Rex, but the pain wouldn't allow his lids to stay open. He rubbed his eyes as he stumbled forward.

"Fuck, that's bright." Rex grasped Jerry's arm.

Jerry slammed into the back of Jackos, who'd stopped abruptly. He wobbled, and Rex yanked him close.

Rex gasped. "Fuck me."

Jerry squinted and then blinked rapidly until the group of people in the driveway came into focus. "No."

Geraldon, very much alive, with that sick sadistic smile was all he could see.

"Prince Jerricho. How nice to see you again, and so"—his gaze fell to Jerry's stomach—"ready."

214

Two men flanked Geraldon. Jerry recognized them as the ones who'd picked them up from the airport. What were they doing with Geraldon?

"You're dead," Jerry blurted out.

Geraldon smirked. "News to me, although I'm sure Tanyon believes I'm dead. What he didn't understand is I've been in control from the beginning. He was a useful pawn, but he underestimated me, figured me for a fool. Well, who's the fool now? You've already met my associates"—Geraldon waved at the men flanking him—"and there are several more inside Tanyon believes work for him. He sent me off to my death with my own men."

The man's ego was massive. Jerry couldn't believe he was alive. He tried to gauge when Jackos would react. He unloaded a still-unconscious Tanyon onto the pavement. Three against four.... Well, three, because Jerry was in no shape to fight and Karen looked as if she was going to pass out.

Jerry struggled to stay upright. He trusted Jackos to get them away. The king's guards were marksmen, trained killers, if needed. Jackos equaled three men. And Rex had the gun from Jackos. Geraldon wasn't too smart after all.

Rex maneuvered Jerry behind him and shielded him from Geraldon. Jerry had to suppress the urge to jump in front of Rex to protect him. He had to think about the baby, who flipped around, making him nauseous. From the corner of his eye, Jerry watched Jackos, waiting for the fight to ensue, terrified they would all be shot.

So close to freedom, only to die.

Jackos didn't raise his gun as Jerry expected. Instead, he tucked his weapon away. Geraldon nodded in what seemed to be approval.

"You did well, son. You're proving yourself to be a trustworthy asset."

Son?

"What the fuck?" Rex corralled Jerry behind him and raised his weapon.

Son? As in....

Geraldon patted Jackos on the shoulder. "Derian is my son. I have many children, most who are less than adequate as Anzuni.

Derian has joined me and is proving his worth. Although I'm not sure why he dragged two of our most important experiments out here with him."

Anger and shame showed on Derian's face. "They were in the room at the only time I had access to Tanyon without his guards surrounding him. Of course, none of the guards who are loyal to you were around. I couldn't shoot the pregnant one with a dart, and if I had shot this one"—he motioned to Rex—"the prince would have freaked out on me. I told them I was there to rescue them. It worked. By the way, Rex, that gun isn't loaded."

Rex frowned and opened the magazine. Empty. He'd been right to be suspicious, and now they weren't any better off than before.

Geraldon surveyed his son's face with a pinched expression. He had a feeling Jackos—Derian—had screwed up, and it wasn't the first time.

Jerry glared at Jackos—*Derian*. Fuck, just how many traitors were there among the Anzuni? His anger quickly turned to Jackos. "You're a member of the king's guard! How can you do this?"

"He's a member of the king's guard because I wanted him there. I needed him to have inside access to the Anzuni government, and he had to prove his loyalty to me and not his king," Geraldon stated matter-of-factly.

"My father trusted you, Geraldon. Even if you are a self-righteous asshole."

Geraldon's face flushed red. "The king doesn't deserve to rule. Your family has allowed the Anzuni to live as second-class citizens in this world for far too long, hidden away as if we're beneath humans. Gods, it's disgusting. What we need to do is populate the world with Anzuni, increase our numbers, until we're a force to be reckoned with."

Rex snorted. "There're billions of humans, and what? A couple of million Anzuni? Before those numbers come anywhere near enough to even attempt to control of anyone, we'll all be dead."

Geraldon glared. Then his face twisted into a disgusted grin. "You humans are so confident that you're unconquerable. Truthfully, you're shortsighted and self-centered, dividing off into countries and factions, groups of people out for what they believe is right. It's easy to divide humans with causes and injustices. People will fight for almost anything if you convince them they care about it enough. Give them a little *help,* and they'll do whatever you want, despite what they truly believe. Even the king believed what he was told to be the truth—that his only son, the future heir he carried, and his claxton, were killed in a fire."

Jerry tried to lunge for Derian, but Rex held him back. "You said my father knows I'm alive and he's here. You were pretending to be a buyer to get us out... you... you...."

Jerry fell back into Rex's arms, knowing the fake Jackos had lied, but Jerry wanted what he'd promised to be true. Derian merely shrugged and bared his teeth in a feral grin.

"I now run this operation. I'm taking over what I started in the first place." Geraldon turned to Derian. "Check Tanyon for a key fob, which will override the need for the retinal scanners at front gate."

Derian checked the pockets of Tanyon's coat and removed the fob, tucking it into his own pocket.

Geraldon pointed to Tanyon. "Clean this up," he said to the two guards. "Put him inside and secure him away from everyone. I need him alive. He has the passwords to encrypted information. Get those, and then we'll dispose of him."

"Yes, sir."

"Tanyon thought someone hacked his computer systems and he was right. He feared someone would discover the identity of his largest backer. Little did he know; *I* am his largest backer."

CHAPTER 30

"YOU BACKED this whole operation?" Rex growled. "Then why the fuck did Tanyon want to kill you?"

Geraldon sneered. "Not important. You're both a means to an end. The prince's blood provided what was needed to allow Anzuni males to get pregnant, thus creating the ability to increase the population quickly. Tanyon was kind enough to fall for a scheme that a doctor brought to him about the Braezelas and drugs. Tanyon did the hard work for me. But don't fret. He'll get the credit he deserves. I'm dead to the world now. This building will be destroyed, along with Tanyon. No one will look further."

"We still have the matter of your nephew," one of the guards said as he lifted Tanyon from the ground.

Geraldon snorted derisively. "Don't worry. He couldn't have gotten far. Most likely eaten by a mountain lion or some other wild animal by now."

Ty had escaped? Jerry shuddered, glancing toward the edge of the thick woods that surrounded the compound. Given Ty's state of mind, he'd kill Jerry on sight.

"He's a mere thorn in my side. I have bigger issues to deal with. And even if he does manage to make it back to the king, the evidence I've planted against him will assure his execution. There's nothing like a pissed-off king to dispense some true justice. And he won't be king for long anyway."

"Leave my father alone! Haven't you done enough damage?"

Geraldon ignored his outburst. "Get them back inside. The prince has a child to deliver. And Derian, any of Tanyon's people who don't swear allegiance to me will make excellent test subjects. Lock 'em up." Geraldon headed for the door and paused. "Oh, and get those stupid masks off everyone. Tanyon had some kind of love affair with drama and theatrics." Geraldon disappeared into the building.

Jerry clutched Rex. He'd never see his parents again. And whatever Geraldon had planned for them was going to be worse than being sold to someone as a sex slave.

REX AND Jerry weren't returned to their cages, but to a small room with a cot much like the one Jerry had occupied when he'd first arrived. Somewhere in the middle of fucking nowhere, without a chance in hell of getting out. The enemy was inside as well as out, with Ty possibly creeping around in the woods.

Jerry sat on the cot in front of Rex, who rubbed Jerry's back. He moaned with gratitude. He was in the early stages of labor, but said nothing. His gut tightened sporadically. Earlier he'd covertly lifted his shirt and found his birth canal had only opened a fraction of an inch. He wasn't leaking the telltale fluid that came before the birth yet. The slippery liquid to ease the baby through the canal came closer to the end of labor. He wouldn't deliver soon if left alone.

Rex dug his fingers hard into Jerry's muscles.

Jerry lowered his head as Rex massaged the back of his neck. "Damn, I love you."

"How far apart are the contractions?"

"How did you know I was having contractions?"

Rex ran his hands over Jerry's arms. "I know you, Jer. I can feel your back muscles tensing with each one. Does it hurt?"

"No. Just feels like muscle contractions right now. It's my back that hurts most."

"I need you to tell me what's going on, okay? I know you don't want me to worry, but I can't help you if you don't tell me. I feel so helpless. I should be doing something to get us out of here."

Jerry twisted to face Rex and took his hand. "I have a feeling no one could escape from here, even if they managed to get outside." He swallowed hard. "Do you think Ty made it anywhere?"

Rex sighed heavily. "I don't know. He was pretty far gone. I don't think he was sane enough to survive. Three hundred acres of mountains is a lot of land to get lost on."

They gazed at each other for a few minutes. There wouldn't be any more moments such as this between them.

"When I first saw you at the jobsite with those tattoos…." Rex smiled gently. "I fell hard. I didn't know if you were gay or not. My brain and my crotch didn't care. When I wasn't showing you how to destroy things, I was watching. That entire first weekend was excruciating."

Jerry threaded his fingers through Rex's. "Yeah? How so?"

"Because I wanted to talk to you… and touch you. Talking seemed like a better first step than running my hands over you."

"I wouldn't have minded."

Rex chuckled. "Well I didn't want to get punched in the face for hitting on a straight guy. Been there. Done that." He looked down at their clasped hands. "I didn't know if I'd ever get up the courage to speak to you."

"Why?"

"I was too damned nervous."

"You were nervous? *You?*" Jerry couldn't imagine Rex nervous in any situation.

Rex's breath hitched, and when he looked up, his eyes were glassy.

"Sweating bullets nervous. I got the words out and made a lame attempt at a joke. But then you laughed, and I knew I had to hear you laugh like that again. I *will* get us out of here." Rex's eyes turned hard, and his determination darkened the green. "I promise. No matter what it takes."

Understanding hit Jerry hard. "No matter what it takes." Jerry grabbed the front of Rex's shirt and opened his mouth to tell him not to do anything stupid, but the door opened.

The doctor stepped inside, pushing a cart and followed by Birdman without his mask. He held a gun at his side. He'd apparently ditched the Taser for something more permanent. Without her mask, Jerry could see fear etched deep into the face of the doctor. She looked to be in her thirties, but her blue eyes were weary. Everything had changed for her. She was a prisoner now. Jerry felt something for her, then reminded himself she'd been a large part of ruining their entire lives.

Rex stood, blocking her access to Jerry.

"Uh-uh." Birdman waved his gun. "I don't wanna have to shoot you. Geraldon wants you alive. But accidents do happen."

"What're you doing?" Rex asked the doctor.

She pursed her lips and glared at Birdman. "I have to get the IV going again."

Rex stared her down, and she looked away.

"Move." Birdman raised the gun.

Bile rose in Jerry's throat. "Rex, please."

Rex hesitated and then stepped to the side, but his stare didn't veer from Birdman.

The doctor grabbed her supplies. When she touched Jerry's hand, he noticed how she shook. Seriously, she was that scared? Wasn't she the doctor Geraldon had used to trick Tanyon into starting all of this, a willing participant? The way she fumbled items with her hands, she was past scared.

"Are you okay?" Jerry asked quietly. She didn't answer, continuing to prepare the IV site.

Jerry glanced at Rex. What if he tried something and got himself killed? If the former Jackos showed his face again, Rex wouldn't hesitate. The resolve covered Rex's face. The man who'd betrayed them would pay. It was unfathomable that a man who was a highly respected member of the king's guard was actually Geraldon's son. As Jackos, he would still have the king's trust, and access to Jerry's family. What if Geraldon's statement that the king wouldn't be ruling much longer meant his father was in danger?

He gritted his teeth and pushed back fear for those he loved. Rex had to get out. If given the chance, he had to leave Jerry behind and get help. Jerry couldn't get anywhere in his condition, even after he gave birth. It wasn't only their lives in danger. So many lives were at stake. If they could get that key fob from Derian, then Rex could get out.

"Where's Derian?" Jerry hazarded asking Birdman. The resulting scowl was deadly and expected, as was his lack of an answer.

"Hurry up." Birdman glared at the doctor. She finally got the needle into Jerry's vein. "Get that shot into him so you can get that baby out. They're prepping the room now. We have a deadline."

Jerry snorted at the remark. "I don't need a shot. I'm already in labor, and I hope you have time. First Anzuni births can take up to forty-eight hours."

The doctor shot him a sorrowful look and then picked up a syringe from the table. Before Jerry could protest, a sadistic chuckle came from Birdman. "Not if we cut the kid out."

A roaring noise filled Jerry's ears, and his vision dimmed. Would the nightmare never end? When he came back into his head, Rex had moved closer to Birdman, his body tight as a bowstring.

Birdman pointed his gun at Rex. "Try it. I'd like nothing more than to fill your chest full of bullets."

Rex growled. He looked crazed, ready to attack despite the consequences. He wouldn't help anyone with a bullet in his chest.

"Rex! Don't."

Rex clenched his fists but was otherwise motionless.

"You may get out of this room, but you won't get far."

"Seen Ty lately?" Rex asked.

"Tyranis, no doubt, made some large animal a nice snack. He was out of his fucking mind with what they were injecting him with. That was one failed experiment."

The doctor gasped, eyes comically wide, the needle trembling in her hand, face paling. Jerry feared she would pass out.

"Ty," she whispered. "He escaped?"

Jerry frowned as her expression turned hopeful. Her blue eyes looked right into Jerry's, and the intensity of the stare churned butterflies in his stomach.

"He escaped?" she asked again.

Jerry nodded, and the relief on her face was... unexpected. She knew Ty?

Birdman pointed his finger at the doctor. "Shut up and get him sedated!"

Rex lunged and knocked Birdman's hand. The gun dropped and skidded over the cement floor. Rex jumped on Birdman. The doctor's face twisted in rage. She leapt at Birdman and tried to stab the needle into his leg, but missed. Birdman wrestled with Rex, both fighting for the advantage, legs and arms flailing. The doctor tried again with the needle, but Birdman's booted foot connected with her face. There was a sickening crack, followed by gushing blood. She fell to the floor holding her face. Jerry got on his hands and knees and scrambled to reach the weapon that had been kicked under the cot. Fucking big stomach. He reached, pushing his shoulder painfully into the metal rail, his fingers barely touching the metal… almost.

"Fuck… come on." He swiped his fingers and the gun turned enough that he hooked his finger in the trigger.

He struggled to his feet and held the weapon up with shaking hands. Damn, he hated the things. He'd never held one. What was he supposed to do?

Birdman flipped Rex onto his back, straddled Rex's hips, and proceeded to punch him in the face repeatedly.

Fuck that! Jerry squeezed the trigger.

Nothing.

He tried again. Nothing.

"Shit!"

He lifted the gun and brought the heavy metal down on the back of Birdman's head as hard as he could.

Birdman howled and grabbed the back of his head as he turned a rage-filled glare on Jerry. That gave Rex the opening to tackle Birdman and swing his fist into Birdman's face.

"Fucking… asshole…. Fuck… you…. Fucking bastard." Rex's words gritted out between punches, until Birdman went limp, his eyes rolling back into his head.

Rex tried to climb off the unconscious man but fell on his ass. He wiped the blood dripping from his split lip. His knuckles were swollen, his face bright red. He'd be bruised in no time. He tried again to rise from the floor. His breath caught and he cradled his side.

Jerry fell to his knees beside Rex. "What's wrong?"

He grabbed Jerry's forearm. "We have to get out of here." He struggled to get up, twisting his torso. His breath caught again. "Fuck. May have bruised a rib or two. You need to go."

The door flew open and crashed against the wall. Derian entered, eyes afire. Jerry pointed the gun at him, adrenaline coursing through his veins. "Stop!"

The doctor, who'd managed to get to her knees, lunged at Derian, stabbing the needle into his meaty thigh and emptying the contents.

"What the fuck?" Derian stumbled.

The doctor scrambled back until her back was against the wall. Derian eyed the syringe sticking out of his leg. He yanked it out and flung it across the floor.

He swayed and his hand hit the wall as he caught himself. "You... you shhhhhould... shouldn't h-have done th—" His eyes fluttered, and he collapsed.

Jerry waited for him to jump up and kill them all, but he remained still.

"He'll be out for a while." The doctor held her bloody lab coat to her face. "There was an anesthetic in that syringe."

"Why did you do that?" Jerry asked, not that he wished she hadn't.

When she tried to sit up, she slumped back against the wall. She didn't look too good. "Ty. They said... if I didn't do—" She gagged and spit blood onto the floor. "If I didn't do what they told me to do... if I tried anything to mess it up, they'd kill him."

Jerry looked at Rex, who appeared as confused. He'd managed to stand but still cradled his side. "Why would you care?"

Blood ran from her mouth and trailed over her chin. Swiping at the blood with the back of her hand, she whispered, "He's my brother."

CHAPTER 31

JERRY GAPED at the doctor. Rex's groan pulled Jerry back to his task. He frisked Derian and came up with a set of car keys and the fob he'd seen earlier.

"He's your brother?" Jerry could see the resemblance now.

Her lip trembled. "Yes. He got out first and he'll keep them safe. That's all that matters now."

"Keep who safe?"

"My husband and son and the rest of them." She looked away and drew in a deep breath. "Get out of here. Go."

Rex headed to the door, but Jerry didn't follow.

"We can't leave you." Maybe she wasn't as culpable as they'd originally believed.

"I can't even see straight. Please find Ty. Remind him about what he promised me. Tell him to go to the house in the Adirondacks. He'll understand." Her eyes were glazed, no doubt from pain and shock.

Jerry shook his head. "I'm not going anywhere near him. He tried to kill me. I can't…."

Her pleading eyes were too much, and Jerry looked away.

"If you see him, can you at least tell him that I love him, please?"

Jerry cringed. He hated Ty, hated what he'd done, and she'd hurt people too, but had that been by choice?

"What's your name?" Jerry asked as Rex checked the hallway.

"Katy." Tears filled her eyes and her chin quivered. "I'm so sorry. I didn't want to do any of this. My uncle forced me. He didn't give me a choice." She huffed. "Seriously, who would've thought any of it would work. I wanted to call the police, but h-he wouldn't let me be alone. I tried to sabotage everything. I lied and tried to fail, but he knew. He threatened everyone I loved. He would have killed them all. I couldn't chance it." She sobbed harder.

"Jer, we have to go, now!"

Jerry regarded her with pity, but if she wouldn't go, he wasn't in any condition to make her. "I'll tell him if I see him." *If he's even sane.*

"Take two rights, then a left to get to the front door. Hurry. Go."

Jerry wasn't confident they'd make it anywhere. Rex was injured, though he tried not to let it show. And Jerry…. Well, he was as big as a cow and in the early stages of labor.

Katy closed her eyes. Jerry forced himself to follow Rex into the hallway, leaving Ty's sister to fend for herself. He felt like shit for doing so.

Rex looked around the corner, then faced Jerry and grasped his upper arms. "If anyone stops us, you run as fast as you can while I hold them off."

"Hell no, I ca—"

"Yes, you can." Rex laid a scorching kiss on his lips, stopping Jerry's argument. Jerry panted as Rex ended his attack. "For our baby," he whispered.

Jerry squeezed his eyes tight, then nodded. There was nothing else to say except "I love you."

"Love you too." Rex smiled briefly, then led Jerry around the corner. The building was quiet, as usual. Panic over leaving Keith again nearly stopped Jerry, but they had to get help or none of them would get out. If only his legs would stop shaking.

"One more turn. Let's go."

The large gray door came into view. Jerry's stomach lurched with the idea of freedom—until a sound to the left startled him. A guard exited through an open door. He halted upon seeing them and then tried to wrangle the gun from his belt.

Rex tackled him and they crashed to the ground. "Go, Jer! I'll catch up!"

Jerry waved the key fob in front of the scanner. There was a beep but nothing happened. "Work, you stupid thing!"

He frantically pushed buttons on the keypad, and then waved the fob over it repeatedly. He was about to punch the screen when the door unlocked. Rex grunted, still locked in battle with the guard. In the hall, voices shouted, coming closer.

"Hide. I'll… find… you!" Rex slammed the man against the wall.

Jerry fled through the open door. Hands seized his shoulders, yanking him back. Twisting around, he was face-to-face with the guard. The man wrapped his hands around Jerry's throat. He clawed frantically at the hands, which only tightened, cutting off all his air. Jerry dug his fingernails into the man's eyes and raked his hands downward. The man shrieked and covered his eyes. Rex jumped on the guard's back and wrapped his arm around the man's neck.

"*Run!*"

Jerry fled without hesitation, heading toward the garage. His heart beat painfully hard. The cool air seeped into his T-shirt and sweats, but he didn't stop. Running was nearly impossible, so he walked as fast as he could. He ducked around the building and tried the door, but it was locked. He had the car keys but had dropped the fob when attacked by the guard. He slammed his fist against the window of the door, but his hand merely bounced off the glass. Another punch and pain shot through his hand and arm.

The edge of the woods was about five hundred feet away. He had to hide and wait for Rex. If he went too far, Rex wouldn't be able to find him. He'd sit out of sight where he could still see the front door.

Looking around once more, he booked it for the woods in something that resembled a fast waddle-walk. He wrapped his arm under his stomach, supporting his screaming muscles. His thighs burned, and by the time he reached the first tree, he wanted to drop. He leaned his forehead against the bark of a pine tree and took deep breaths to calm his racing heart. He ignored the familiar twinges of pain in his stomach.

"Stay in there awhile longer, little one. We have to wait for Daddy to get here." He rubbed his belly.

Jerry listened for the sounds of anyone following him, but only heard the gentle rustle of leaves and the occasional bird.

"Come on, Rex." Jerry gripped the car keys and the sharp edges dug into his palm. If anything happened to Rex….

A shout from the direction of the building shattered the stillness of the forest.

"This way!"

Jerry had to hide and fought his way through the thick underbrush, sharp sticks digging into his body. He pushed his fear for Rex away and focused on sounding less like an elephant trampling through the trees. He'd give anything to be able to run, or at least climb a tree.

In the darkness beneath the thick trees, the ground was harder to see, a minefield of rocks, fallen branches, and tangled limbs. Even if he weren't pregnant, it would have been a nightmare. A cool breeze raised goose bumps on his skin, and he shivered. He could die of hypothermia on a spring night like this. He needed a place out of the wind and something to keep him warm. Fat chance of that in the middle of nowhere. He forced himself forward, spurred by the idea he was on a mission to save Rex and Keith and to see his parents again. His lungs burned, his belly tightened painfully, and his legs felt like Jell-O. He stumbled more than once and had to slow down. Prickly things stuck to his pants and scratched at his legs. He stubbed his toes and smacked his shins. The fading shouts of those searching for him meant he might be able to rest soon. A little farther and he'd sit.

He could see a gap in the trees and hoped to find a place to rest. He broke through the brush and stumbled when the ground shifted beneath him. The sensation of falling caught his breath. He held his hands out but still landed flat on his stomach, and the momentum rolled him down a hill. Rocks and sticks scratched his skin. He slammed into a rock, the back of his head connecting with the hard surface. Pain and blurred vision left him helpless on the ground.

THE THROBBING in Jerry's head couldn't compare to the pain ripping him apart from inside. He groaned and grabbed his stomach, nearly biting his tongue as his jaw muscles tightened.

"Fuck!"

He forced his breath in and out until the vise around his stomach loosened. He wasn't sure how long he'd lain there after tumbling down the hill. Maybe he'd blacked out? The cold from the ground chilled his legs, but his back and arms were warm. He lifted his head and looked down his upper body. He wore a brown fleece jacket. Was he hallucinating? He squeezed his eyes shut and opened them again. The jacket was still there. Maybe he was dreaming.

Pale blue light from the rising moon filled the clearing. The scent of pine and cedar filled the air. A low staccato beat pulsed in Jerry's head. His vision had cleared enough to see the sharp three-foot drop he'd stepped off. He'd rolled down a short slope where the boulder he laid next to kindly stopped him. Gods, he needed a painkiller.

A crack echoed through the clearing. A tall, dark figure emerged from between the trees, moving toward Jerry. A scream lodged in his throat as his muscles locked. The man came closer, and Jerry made out Tyranis's frowning face.

"Don't touch me." Jerry sobbed, exhausted, in labor, and trapped with the man who'd tried to kill him. "Please, don't."

Ty could enact his revenge, kill Jerry for denying him the crown, and Jerry couldn't do anything to defend himself.

"Don't hurt my baby. You can do anything to me, but please…." Ty couldn't possibly understand Jerry. He'd been beyond sanity in that cage and would rip Jerry to shreds.

When Ty hesitated, Jerry rolled onto his side and clawed at the ground, trying to move away. His self-preservation had kicked in, even if he wouldn't get anywhere. Fear tried to suffocate him as Ty came closer.

"Calm down."

The coherence of his words surprised Jerry.

"Calm down. I brought you some water."

Another contraction built to an intolerable level. Jerry rolled onto his back. He held his breath. The muscles in his throat bulged. The never-ending pressure and the hellfire-pain were too much.

"Breathe," Ty commanded. "You have to breathe through the contractions."

"Fuck… you!"

Ty chuckled, and it lacked the evil, vindictive quality Jerry had become familiar with.

Jerry released his breath. "Why don't you just get it over with? It should be easy."

"Get what over with?" Ty crouched, then touched Jerry's arm. He flinched, and Ty moved back.

Jerry had to get up and defend himself or even try to run, but moving seemed like a herculean effort.

"Just finish what you started at the mansion."

Yeah, Jerry, remind the unstable man that he hates you.

The silence that followed caused Jerry to look at Ty. He stood with his head lowered, his gaze fixed downward. "I'm sorry."

Not what Jerry had expected to hear. "Excuse me?"

Ty ignored Jerry's surprised reaction. "Where's your claxton, and how did you even get away?" Ty asked, ignoring Jerry.

Jerry rolled to his side and struggled to get onto his knees. Ty tried to grab his arm to help, but Jerry smacked his hand away. Maybe he could punch the asshole in the nuts if he tried anything. Ty squatted down to Jerry's level, rested his forearms on his knees, and waited. Jerry chanced glancing up at his former attacker. Gone was the wild and crazed look, the insanity, even his previous arrogance and superiority. Jerry swore Ty looked... remorseful.

Ty sighed. "Listen, I know what I did was unforgivable. And even if I told you there were reasons for what I did—"

"What fucking reason could you have for beating the crap out of me?" The surge of anger pushed Jerry to his feet. "You could have killed me and my baby, you motherfucker!"

Ty stood, and Jerry had to plant his feet to stop from moving away in fear. Ty could easily crush Jerry.

"That wasn't me. I'd never do anything to harm someone, especially to someone who's pregnant. I don't even like fighting."

Jerry snorted.

"But like I said, there's nothing I can say that will make what I did to you any different. This entire situation—Tanyon, my uncle...." Ty shook his head. "Right now, the best thing I can do is get you out of here, because you can't have that baby in the woods, and you definitely aren't having it here with me. I've got shit to do."

"Well, isn't that a great idea. Got a helicopter sitting around? Because I don't see anything but trees. Hundreds of acres of fucking trees and rocks and more trees. And in the middle of it is a fuckload of men with Tasers and prisoners in cages!" His stomach tightened again. "You're so smart, why don't you tell me exactly—" Jerry bent over, his breath held hostage in his chest once again.

Ty knelt before him. "Breathe. My sister had a baby, and I was there for some of it. If you don't breathe, it only makes it worse. It's like holding your breath while lifting weights. Let it out."

The pain magnified and doubled on itself. His stomach was going to rip open like the foil covering on Jiffy Pop. Ty made an annoying attempt to mimic how Jerry should breathe.

Jerry wanted to slug him, but he released the air. "I f-ff-uck-ck-ing… hate you."

"Noted. Take another deep breath. Don't pant, or you'll get light-headed."

Jerry drew in a breath, his body heating up, sweat coating his skin and causing him to shiver.

"Blow out."

For the love of the gods. Jerry's worst enemy tried to help Jerry while he envisioned kicking Ty in the nuts. Jerry blew out the air, nausea rising in his gut as his stomach muscles relaxed.

"Dammit, that's gotta be the worst pain ever." Jerry straightened slowly. His muscles protested, but he'd be damned if he was going to lie on the ground again. The position made him too vulnerable with Ty. "Did you say something about water?"

Ty grabbed a bottle off the ground behind him and handed it over. "I filled it with water from the stream."

Jerry stopped before the bottle reached his lips. "I'm not an outdoorsman or anything, but can't you get sick from drinking water from a stream?"

Ty smirked. "You could. I guess it depends on how thirsty you are."

Jerry's mouth was dry and gritty, as if he'd eaten sand. He couldn't resist. He gulped the cool water, then handed the bottle back. "You mentioned your sister."

Ty nodded, and pain crossed his face.

Jerry wasn't sure if he should mention Katy. What if she'd been lying? Didn't really matter if she did lie. "She's a doctor, right? And her name's Katy?"

Ty's eyes widened and his mouth opened, but he didn't say anything.

"You asked how I escaped. Katy helped us by stabbing Derian with a syringe filled with something to knock him out. Rex and I ran, but a guard jumped him before we could get out. Rex told me to go. They have him." Jerry took in a shaky breath. "Your sister got hurt helping us. I'm not sure how badly, but she knows you escaped. She said if I ever saw you, to remind you of your promise to take care of her husband and son. And something about the others? She wants you to go to the house in the Adirondacks." He couldn't believe he told this to someone who he hated. "Also, she loves you."

"Was she dying?"

"No, but she got kicked in the face by Birdman—"

"Birdman?" Ty looked at Jerry as if he were the crazy one.

"Guard who wore a mask with a beak. Ugly as fuck. That's what I call him."

Ty crossed his arms and frowned. "Nelson. He's one sadistic bastard. I'll fucking kill him."

"Stand in line. Anyway, your sister was bleeding pretty badly. And Geraldon is here claiming to be running the show and not Tanyon."

Ty sniffed. "Tanyon, that fucking bastard, Tanyon. I was so close, and then it all fell apart."

Gods knew why Jerry felt sorry for Ty, but something wasn't right. "You aren't acting like the same person I met or who attacked me."

Before Ty could answer, Jerry bent over again, forcing himself to breathe. The pain rose, a crescendo reaching unbearable heights. Just as a scream formed in his throat, the pain subsided. That C-section looked mighty good right about then.

"Was it worse than the others?"

Jerry shrugged and straightened. "Each time they get more intense, but they hurt like a bitch."

Ty, who'd kept his distance, glanced sideways, then chewed on his bottom lip. "Um… you know that first Anzuni births can last for days, right?"

Jerry burst out laughing. "Yeah, I've heard." He exhaled. "Sorry, I'm feeling a little punchy. Being in labor in the middle of the fucking woods is the icing on my welcome-to-hell cake."

"We have to get you somewhere out of the cold before you deliver this baby. There's an abandoned building not far from here. It's small and pretty run-down, but it's better than nothing."

"Wait. I have keys!" Jerry patted the pockets of his sweats. "I took the keys to a car from Derian!"

CHAPTER 32

THE KEYS glinted in the moonlight as Jerry held them up. "He said he parked a car down the road, but he lied about everything else so it must be parked in the garage, but it's locked. Maybe you can get it. We can get help. And then we can get Rex and Keith and the rest of those men back there, because they're going to move them soon!"

Ty's expression morphed into rage. Jerry booked it backward. Fuck. Why had he shown him the keys?

"Slow down. I said I wouldn't hurt you. I want to help."

"Excuse me if I don't trust someone who tried to kill me." Jerry's bravado fled fast, along with his energy. He was cold and tired, and any minute another contraction was going to try and turn his body inside out.

"What do you mean, move them?" Ty's expression was hard but no longer scary. What choice did Jerry have? He couldn't outrun him.

Jerry ran his hand through his hair. "Your uncle's moving the 'experiments' and going to destroy the building, with Tanyon in it. Your uncle's presumed dead so he can complete his plans, which aren't that clear to me." *Huge* understatement.

Another hearty contraction and Jerry's knees almost buckled. This time he allowed Ty to hold him up. Damn, that one had lasted longer than the last one. "What I wouldn't do for a nice soft bed and a dose of painkillers."

"The sooner we get out of here, the sooner your wish will come true. Now I could leave you here, and—"

"Fuck you! If you think you're leaving me here alone in the fucking woods, you really are crazy."

"Not very prince-like. As I was saying, I could leave you here and get the car, *or* you could come with me. It'll take longer if I have to wait for you, but I wasn't sure if you'd go, since you don't trust me."

"I don't have much choice, do I?"

"No, I suppose you don't."

Jerry made sure Ty walked in front of him. His former fiancé hadn't exaggerated when he said the walk back would take longer. What had seemed a short distance was now a thousand-mile journey with the contractions and navigating the dark woods.

They stopped again for a contraction, and so Jerry could throw up. When he was done, he took the water offered by Ty and swished it around his mouth. That was the second time he'd puked up nothing. Maybe he'd puke out the baby.

"So you didn't answer my question about trying to kill me and what fell apart."

Ty turned and started to walk again. "We have to keep moving. We've still got a way to go."

Jerry started after him and grabbed Ty's arm, feeling braver than he should. When Ty turned, that dark rage on his face was closer to the Ty Jerry had known. He braced himself for the beatdown, but Ty merely shook his head.

"Walk, and I'll tell you."

Jerry nodded, hoping the contractions would stay around the three-minute mark, where they'd been for an hour. He hadn't told Ty, but he'd dilated farther, meaning he was closer than suspected. He had to make it to that car.

Ty sighed heavily and rubbed his forehead. "I never wanted to marry you, and I never wanted to be king."

"Huh?"

Ty chuckled morosely. "I never wanted most of what my uncle expected of me. And when I say expected, I mean forced. My education, my career, my entire life has been orchestrated by my *uncle,* who told me over and over that I *had* to be king."

"Well, that's fucking wonderful. Not only would I have married an asshole but one who didn't even *want* to be with me?" Again, who hated him so much? "Wait, are you even gay?"

"I'm not an asshole! I acted that way so you wouldn't want to marry me! I had a life!" Ty pinched his lips. "And yes, I'm gay and…."

Jerry gasped as another contraction grabbed hold and tried to squeeze the life out of him. It hadn't been three minutes. He did the breathing, but that shit wasn't doing much good. He gripped his thighs, his fingertips digging into the flesh. The nausea hadn't appeared again. Was he losing it, or was this one lasting much longer?

"S-so... you—" *Gasp.* "—thought physical—" *Gasp.* "—abuse was a g-good—" *Gasp.* "—idea. Fuuuuuuuuck!"

He hated this and wanted to kill Rex for knocking him up.

"No! But my uncle knew I didn't want you." Ty paced, clasping his hands around the nape of his neck, muttering something.

The contraction let loose and Jerry straightened.

"I didn't want to hurt you," Ty said and started walking again. "Geraldon drugged me with something that was supposed to make me want you. I thought it was the medicine my doctor prescribed to prevent migraines. It backfired big-time!" He threw his hands up wildly. "Got me hornier than hell at first. Changed my personality. Threw me into fits of increasing rage and dissociation. By the time I attacked you, I couldn't control myself. I'd failed my uncle, and because of it he took.... He took everything that mattered to me. After that my uncle threw me in there with Tanyon. And then shit got weird."

"Tell me about it."

Who hadn't Geraldon fucked with? The man deserved to be thrown into a cage and pumped full of drugs and raped by a Braezelas, and even that wouldn't be enough.

"He's fucking crazy. I mean, my uncle is trying to create an army of Anzuni to combine with the US as some sort of dominant superpower."

Jerry barked out a laugh, believing Ty was messing with him.

Ty gave him an I'm-dead-serious look over his shoulder.

"You can't be serious. An army? That makes no sense."

"It makes perfect sense if you know how fucking crazy he is, and what he can do. When my sister was in her twenties, she worked on a research team that investigated the effects of growth hormones on Anzuni as a cure for some disease. My uncle forced her to modify her formula, and now he has the medical technology to speed the growth of an Anzuni, before and after it's born, like twice as fast."

"That's impossible," Jerry said, despite his prematurely burgeoning stomach as proof.

Ty pointed to Jerry's stomach. "You're full-term. That was kind of fast, wasn't it, since most human and Anzuni gestational periods are longer than normal. When are you due?"

Jerry laid his hand on his rock-hard stomach. "In two months."

Ty gave Jerry a snide grin. "And Derian. He was born in 2006."

Jerry choked on a snort. And had to ride out another contraction. After each one he'd managed to walk again, but it became harder each time.

"He's a pretty big ten-year-old." Maybe Ty was crazy and had just sobered up.

Ty cocked an eyebrow but stayed silent.

"A ten-year-old who looks twice his age." Even though he shook his head, Jerry couldn't accuse Ty of lying. Who'd make up this shit?

"Yeah, and he's not the only child of Geraldon's that he allowed to be experimented on. There were twelve of them in all."

Jerry frowned. "And you know this because…?"

"Listen, I'm going to tell you this because Geraldon needs to be stopped. Whether you believe me or not, I'm not on his side."

Jerry struggled to keep up with Ty. Fuck, he was tired, but he had to keep going. He'd decide whose side Ty was on if he helped him escape or not. "Okay."

"My uncle has been our guardian since Katy and I were little, but he didn't live with us. He hated kids. We had nannies and tutors. Katy's eight years older than me. He sent her away to medical school after college, even though she didn't want to go. So I was the only one living at home, except the woman hired to take care of me. When I was seventeen, things got strange. A bunch of women moved into our house. It was weird, but nice to have so many motherly types around. Katy also moved back. The weird thing was all those women were pregnant at the same time."

"Your sister too?"

He looked confused and then shook his head. "No, not her. She took care of the women, since she was a doctor by then."

"Really?" Jerry stopped for another fucking, asshole, motherfucking contraction. Ty waited patiently, and then they continued walking again.

"So the weirder thing was they all delivered after only a few months, and all at once. It was a couple of babies a day being born, and they didn't go to the hospital. They were born in the house. Derian was one of the babies. So many fucking babies. It was chaos, if you can imagine that."

Jerry didn't want to imagine twelve babies crying at once. Damn. "Did you ask why they were there? I mean, it sounds like a home for pregnant, wayward teens."

"Of course I asked!" Jerry ignored the reaction. "My uncle told me to mind my own fucking business, and the mothers ignored me after the births, for some reason…. And Katy, she said the less I knew the safer I'd be."

Jerry digested that info as they walked in silence. It seemed Jerry had pissed Ty off enough to shut him up.

Ty stepped over a fallen log and then helped Jerry over. At that point he didn't care that it was Ty helping him. He needed any help he could get.

"Thanks."

Ty nodded, exhaling noisily through his nose. "When the kids were around one, the mothers disappeared, and each kid had a nanny. They were in the house for another couple of years, but I'd learned to ignore them. I was taking college classes and trying to live a somewhat normal life." He chuckled, but it was a dead sound.

"What happened to the kids?"

"By the time they were three, they were all gone, but they'd been there long enough for me to notice that they were growing fast, *too fast*. They disappeared around then, along with Katy. My uncle said she was on another research project. When I asked where, he told me 'None of your fucking business.' By then, he'd started planning my future as king, and I had enough crap to deal with."

Ty stopped and took a deep breath, as if revealing so much of his crappy past was too much.

"Was that the last time you saw her?" Jerry wasn't sure how much farther he would make it. He'd slowed down considerably.

"No. She called me a couple of years ago. She was living in the Adirondacks, married and pregnant, and wanted me there for the birth of my nephew, Samsonus. So I went. She wouldn't tell me anything about her research, or what my uncle had forced her to do. She didn't want me to tell anyone—especially Geraldon—about her family or where she was or the 'others.'"

"Who are the 'others'?"

He shrugged. "I thought she was being overly dramatic, but my uncle *always* had something to do with anything that happened to us. Fucking bastard. He got Katy back into everything by threatening to hurt me.

"Her husband called me about six months ago, freaking out because she'd disappeared. Of course, it was my uncle, still controlling her life… *my* fucking life! I swear to the gods that once the people I love are safe, I'm going to kill him."

Those were the last words Ty spoke to Jerry. When Jerry lagged, Ty slowed again. Another contraction stole anything Jerry thought to say. He wanted Rex, and he couldn't block out thoughts of him any longer. Couldn't care about what Ty had said anymore. Fucking hell, they needed a miracle.

Ty half carried, half dragged Jerry as they reached the edge of the woods behind the compound. He was exhausted. Sweat poured off him, yet he was cold. The front of his shirt was soaked. The contractions were one on top of another, and the pressure… oh gods, the pressure and pain were splitting his guts open.

"I… can't." Jerry's legs buckled.

Ty laid him on the ground and lifted his T-shirt. Blood covered Jerry's taut skin, appearing black in the moonlight. Well, if that didn't signal something was wrong….

"Is it bad?" The pulsing pain between the contractions was truth enough, but Jerry needed to hear it was okay.

Ty didn't respond, except to heft Jerry from the ground and carry him. Jerry's head lolled on his shoulder.

"W-where're we going?"

Ty only grunted and shifted Jerry's weight. He groaned as he was jostled in Ty's arms. Was he running? In Jerry's narrowing vision, the lights around the building blazed brightly, and the gunmetal door appeared before them.

Ty had lied. He lied and was going to serve Jerry up to his uncle. Fucking asshole. Jerry was going to kill Ty when he could move again. Unless Ty killed him first.

Ty lifted his hand, holding a large hunting knife. Where the hell...? The sting of the blade against Jerry's throat reminded him that Ty couldn't care less for his life.

"I'm really sorry, Jerricho. But you need help now and my uncle has something that belongs to me."

"No." Jerry barely heard his own voice.

Banging filled his head, and then the door opened. Derian grinned wide.

"Get my uncle now. I have something that belongs to him."

Fucking traitor.

"Welcome back, cousin. We were sure you were kitty chow by now. And how nice of you to return the missing experiment like a good boy."

Where was Rex? Jerry needed him. He needed.... An inhuman scream rang through the hallway.

Derian chuckled and stepped back. "You're just in time for the fun."

Jerry cringed with each cry of agony. A loud *pop* filled the hallway, followed by deathly silence.

"Fucking A!" Derian raced down the corridor.

Jerry blacked out.

JERRY TRIED to roll onto his side, but was unable to move. The searing pain in his stomach cut through the hazy cloud in his brain. Floating, chasing one thought and then another, he couldn't string enough together to make sense of what was happening. He couldn't open his eyes despite fighting to do so. He'd been free, and then... he wasn't. How he'd been recaptured eluded him. What had gone wrong?

Another heated flash of pain lanced through Jerry, and he moaned. A hand stroked his forehead. The tender touch soothed, but that hand didn't belong to Rex. His hands were large and a bit rough. These were small and soft.

Why wasn't Rex with him? Something had to be keeping him away. If he could, he'd be there. Panic blossomed in Jerry's chest. Someone had been screaming, torturous high-pitched wails, and then the gunshot. Bile shot into Jerry's throat, and he gagged. The soft hands coaxed his head to the side, and what he threw up burned his throat.

He wanted to die.

"It'll be over soon. The head is crowning, and you're doing so well. Is there much pain?"

He was giving birth? He couldn't, not without Rex.

"Wh-why... can't... can't think straight?" He still couldn't open his eyes.

Another gentle rub of the hand. "We gave you something strong for the pain. You've lost a lot of blood, but you and the baby are okay. Not long now."

Jerry licked his dry lips and forced his eyelids to open. The bright light burned into his retinas, and he couldn't focus. He gasped as his stomach tightened painfully and the deep burning climbed up his spine.

"Head's out." Was that Katy?

A dizzying rush darkened Jerry's vision. He felt as if he'd been ruthlessly ripped open. He grabbed the arm of the person rubbing his forehead, moaning as sharp points of pain radiated across his torso and into his chest. Gasping, he clutched the arm tighter, terrified.

He was going to die.

"Breathe, Jerry. The shoulders are coming out. It's the worst—"

"Need Rex, please."

"Focus on getting the baby out. Worry about everything else later."

"Please."

She sighed heavily. "I can't. I'm sorry. He's gone."

Tears filled Jerry's eyes, spilling over his cheeks. They'd killed Rex and left Jerry alone to endure what was left of life without him.

A scream tore from Jerry's throat as the searing agony rushed like liquid fire through his gut.

"Baby's out," the disembodied voice announced. "It's a boy."

A boy.

Jerry felt vacant, the physical pain over, his belly empty, his heart dead. They'd sell his son to someone who only cared about owning a demon. Jerry couldn't stop them. Still he waited to hear his son cry, waited for that first wail of life that said he was okay. Nothing. Jerry lifted his head. The room tilted and the nausea roiled. He had to see his child—Rex's child. The only part of him Jerry had left.

"Come on, little one. Breathe for me."

His baby wasn't breathing. Instinctively, he tried to rise from the bed, but a hand held him down.

"You need to stay still. You've torn, and with the amount of blood you've lost, you might pass out if you stand."

"I have to see him." Jerry's vision focused, and he recognized Karen standing next to him.

"They're working on him now." Her brow was deep with worry.

"You helped Derian."

She winced. "I didn't know what he was doing. I knew him from the investigation into the disappearances, and he told me I'd be helping." She swallowed hard. "My brother's missing."

"Derian said he was investigating the disappearances?"

She nodded, then bit her lip. "That's what he told me. I believed him. I was desperate, and he used me."

In the suspended silence, his child's first wail filled the air.

CHAPTER 33

JERRY SOBBED with relief. Jerry thanked every Anzuni deity for his child's life. This child was his to protect, to love, even if Rex was gone. Jerry clenched his jaw and fists, rode through the panic suffocating him. He had to be present and not wallow in his grief. He had a child to worry about.

"I want to see my son." Jerry raised his head, determined to see him despite the swirling rush in his head. "Let me see him!"

He rolled onto his side and clutched the mattress, his muscles limp and weak. He'd walk through fire to get to his son. No one would stop him.

"I'm not supposed to let you see him," Karen said and tried to keep him on the gurney.

In the incubator across the room was the precious life he'd made with Rex. Katy was next to the baby, a fearful hesitancy on her face. Her nose had been taped, and her face was a mottled mess of bruises.

"He's mine." Jerry had to see for himself that he was okay, smell his scent, and kiss his soft skin. He already loved his son with everything he was.

"No. He's not yours." Geraldon stood in the doorway wearing his usual charcoal suit with an ugly maroon tie, his expression one of impassive interest. He went to Jerry's son and peered at the baby.

"Get away from him!"

Geraldon turned, an eyebrow raised, but he didn't speak as he approached the bed. Breathless, Jerry tried to maneuver into a defensive position, but who was he kidding. He was as weak as his newborn son. He lay back in exhausted resignation.

"You're in no position to tell me what to do. Your days as an overindulged prince are over." He glanced over his shoulder to the doctor. "Take the baby to the nursery."

"No! Please. At least let me see him. You can't sell him!"

Jerry clawed to get up while Karen held his shoulders firmly. Adrenaline rushed his system, dulling his pain and clearing his thoughts.

"Stop this right now!" Geraldon crossed his arms.

Jerry watched helplessly as Katy wheeled his son from the room. He hadn't touched him or given him a name.

"I'm not selling him. Once he's old enough, he'll go into the training program and be part of the greatest army in the world. And you—" Geraldon sneered. "—will produce more babies. Within a few weeks, you'll be ready to breed again, and you'll continue to provide Anzuni for my future endeavors until your body wears out. At least you'll be good for something. When I have no use for you anymore, you'll be disposed of."

Ty had told the truth. Geraldon planned to build an army of Anzuni, force their bodies to prematurely age, to defend his twisted vision of being a world leader. None of it was even plausible.

"You're a fucking psycho. The US has the largest military of any country in the world. What in the hell makes you think you could raise an army large enough to defeat them or their allies? They'll annihilate you."

Geraldon's gloating, self-assured grin hit hard. "I don't need to raise an army to defeat the US, because I have the backing of the most influential leaders in this country." He leaned closer, as if ready to divulge a secret. "Many of them fund my research because, you see, they share my vision. Increase the army to overthrow other powerful nations, then create a world government with us on top."

"Sounds more like a world war." Jerry couldn't comprehend Geraldon having that kind of influence and support, that ingenuity. He'd never been anything but a puffed-up blowhard to Jerry.

"More like restructuring the governments of the world into one. My first order of business is to become king of the Anzuni. Your poor father has lost interest in his people. He's coming apart, and without an heir, his reign will soon end. It will give me great pleasure to dethrone him."

Jerry wanted to scream at the injustice, but he wanted his son more. "I'll do anything you want. Please, just let me see my son. Even if he's part of this army, I could raise him. Please."

Geraldon scoffed. "The soldiers will be raised in the leanest of conditions from day one. Hardened and learning to obey without question. They won't get love and nurturing. It'll make them better killers. Rest up, Jerricho. You have to regain your strength to survive your next pregnancy."

Geraldon turned to leave, but paused. His cold eyes gazed upon Jerry, who shivered hard. "Resist or try to escape again, and I'll kill your demon spawn. Your child's safety depends on your obedience. At least with me, you'll know he's alive. Tanyon wanted me to sell him to some sadistic collector of demon children. You may even get to see him again… someday."

The doctor returned and slinked past Geraldon, shrinking back as he glared at her. "If you so much as sneeze wrong, Derian will put a bullet in your head."

Derian stepped into the room.

"How's the move going?" Geraldon asked.

"The second wave of experiments just shipped out. Four more are scheduled over the next two days. Any remaining experiments and equipment will be loaded Friday morning, and we should be out of here by 7:00 a.m."

"Make sure it goes off without a hitch. I have a group of important people coming to inspect our operations. I expect you to have everything up to my specifications."

Derian nodded. Geraldon slapped him across the face and his head snapped to the side.

Holy shit.

Derian turned his head back and faced his father. A fire burned in his eyes, which he quickly reined in. Bright red blood glistened at the corner of his mouth.

"You will *not* disrespect me. Now, answer me correctly."

Derian's face fell neutral. Vacant. "Yes, sir. Everything will be ready according to your specifications."

Geraldon scoffed and exited the room. Derian's face flushed with renewed anger. "Get the prince into a cage." He left the room.

Strangely, Derian had called Jerry "prince." Must have been the slap to the head.

Jerry was silent as the doctor stitched the tears in his stomach and helped him up to shower. Jerry went through the motions, his thoughts with his child, and his heart mourning for Rex.

JERRY GROANED as two guards dropped him onto a cot. Back in a cage. He couldn't see if Keith and Gunn, or any of the other captives were still there. Katy hung his IV bag on a pole by the bed and then messed with the flow rate.

"Are you in pain, Jerricho?" She sounded as if she'd plugged her nose when she spoke. The bruising around her nose and eyes had turned deep purple.

"I'm okay." He touched her hand. "Thank you for helping me to escape. They could have killed you."

"I wish you'd managed to get away."

"I saw Ty. He took care of me in the woods, then brought me back here."

Her brother's actions didn't seem to surprise her. "He had to bring you back, you know?"

He didn't and remained quiet.

She snorted. "He said you threatened to skin his balls if he brought you back."

Jerry had thrown out a few threats, but his memory was spotty about the entire ordeal. He did remember one thing. "I know Ty handed me over to get back something Geraldon had of his…. Wait. Why are you still here if he traded me to get you?"

Her expression grew heavy and worrisome, and then she smiled sadly. "It wasn't me he wanted, but I can't tell you what that was. I promised not to tell anyone."

Jerry's mind wouldn't rest until he found out what had been so important to Ty. But he dropped it.

"When I told him about his promise, he knew what I was talking about."

She nodded, a fond expression covering her face.

"He also told me about the growth hormone, and the babies that lived in your house. He told me everything—well, I think everything."

Her fondness faded and her eyes darkened. She ducked her head. "My uncle made me use the growth hormone I helped develop." Her hands shook, and she clasped them together. "The side effects were numerous and dangerous. Gods, it was a largely untested drug, and I used it on babies. They were all Geraldon's children that he sired at the same time to be used as test subjects for the drug." She swiped the back of her hand over her nose and sniffed. "I wanted to stop giving them the drug, but someone was always watching to make sure I followed protocol, until…." She smiled painfully, but her eyes lit up. "One of my uncle's men, Daniel—he's human and an ex-Marine—had no idea what my uncle was doing with the children. Geraldon told him I was developing a drug to help kids with growth issues." She shook her head. "Over time Daniel and I…. We became close. He was different than the others who worked for my uncle. Eventually I trusted him enough to tell him about the children and the growth hormone. Even then I couldn't stop doing what my uncle wanted because Daniel wasn't the only one of my uncle's guards there. He watched what was happening with disgust."

"But why did he put up with it? He could have turned Geraldon in." What was it with these people and their inability to stand up to the man?

"Daniel would have, but he'd fallen in love with me. He stayed to protect me. But we didn't just sit back and do nothing. We—"

A door slammed. Katy jumped to her feet and wiped her eyes. "I'll check on you later and"—her voice dropped to a whisper—"I'll let you know how your son is doing."

She left, and the cage door closed with a resoundingly cold click. Jerry's head spun with the events of the past few days. He had a son, one Geraldon vowed he'd never see again. A future soldier in some fucked-up army Geraldon had envisioned. They were all merely pieces of one messed-up plan. No one was off limits—not Geraldon's family, his friends or colleagues. Not even his own people, whom he'd vowed to lead selflessly and with integrity. Geraldon had always been a majorly selfish son of a bitch, but he hadn't outright done anything harmful to the Anzuni.

Jerry looked down the row of cages. Most were empty. Those who'd occupied them already moved, or worse, sold before Geraldon had taken over. He couldn't see into Keith's cage, and Gunn's cage was empty. Gunn had to have been moved and not sold, as Jerry feared. David and Tenyris were gone as well, but Paul and Henri were still in their cages along with several others Jerry didn't recognize.

Had the Braezelas Tanyon made before Geraldon took over been sold? Tanyon's sex-slave and drug operation had morphed into something more ridiculously fantastic and deadly. Tomorrow Tanyon would die in this place, if he hadn't already. Stupid man. Geraldon had played him for a fool, used them all, and would dispose of them all when no longer useful.

He slipped from the bed and pulled the IV pole with him to the door.

"Keith." His exaggerated whisper brought the attention of others. "Keith, are you there?"

A grumble came from that direction.

"Keith."

"Jerry?"

Jerry jumped and whirled around. Keith sat in the cage that had once held Ty.

"Fuck, Jerry. Where the hell have you been?" Keith surveyed the cages and frowned. "Where's Rex?"

That question dropped Jerry to his knees, sobbing.

"What's wrong? Was Rex sold?"

Jerry shook his head, unable to speak the words.

"He's not dead, is he?

Jerry managed to nod.

"Fuck!" Keith punched the bars of his cage.

"Stop. You're only going to hurt yourself, love." Gunn was in a different cage than earlier. It was like fucking musical cages. He was no longer in Braezelas form.

Jerry wiped his eyes. "I'm glad you still have Gunn." His throat threatened to close and the tears flowed again.

Keith's heartbreak and pity covered his face. Jerry didn't need pity. He was strong, and Rex would be proud of him for not falling apart. Jerry stood on shaky legs.

"Hey, you aren't pregnant anymore! Where's the baby?" Keith's hand went to his belly in a protective gesture.

"Geraldon took him."

Keith shook his head. "Geraldon's dead. Tanyon said so."

A weird half laugh, half guffaw came from Jerry. "Geraldon isn't dead. He's the real reason we're here, and why we're spawning his demon army and will continue until we can no longer reproduce, and then he'll kill us too." Jerry's breath caught. "Like he killed Rex."

"What about Tanyon?" Paul asked.

"If he isn't dead already, he will be." Jerry sat on the cot, pain flaring in his gut. "They've started moving everything somewhere else. In three days we will all be gone, and Geraldon is gonna torch the place with Tanyon inside. No one's going to rescue us. My father thinks we were all killed in the fire at Geraldon's summer house. Geraldon's cleaning up any traces of us and is going to get away with murder, and kidnapping, and a fuckload of other shit. He said he's being backed by the most powerful people in the US." Jerry no longer doubted that Geraldon had been telling the truth.

"In other words, we've been fucked dry." Gunn slammed his hand against the cage.

Henri curled up on his cot and sobbed. Paul tried to soothe him from his cage. Fucking unfair.

"What do you mean by 'demon army'?" Keith paled as he clutched the bars of his cage.

Jerry had to tell them everything and spare them from fruitless hope. Better they all harden now than to languish in a perpetual state of not knowing what would come next. He told them everything he knew and replaced their hope with reality, and he felt like shit for doing so.

When he got to the part of the adventure—as he called his trip through hell—where Ty had served him up to his uncle, Paul said, "Well, that makes more sense now."

"What makes sense?" Jerry asked.

"Ty came in here yesterday, no longer the fucking crazed animal he had been. The guards brought him to Stephanos's cage. I nearly fell over when Stephanos ran into Ty's arms, crying, like some huge sobby reunion."

"My uncle has something that belongs to me."

Ty had traded Jerry for that something. Ty didn't want to be with Jerry, didn't want to be king, because he already loved someone else. Stephanos was his. Even Ty had the person he loved with him. Jerry needed time to mourn the loss of Rex and his son. The best way to move forward was to get it all out now. And he did. He sobbed for hours, his face buried in the pillow. He ignored Keith's pleas to talk to him. When exhaustion pulled him under, he was grateful for the reprieve.

His cage opening woke Jerry. The doctor entered, and Jerry immediately raised his hand. "Don't tell me anything about him, please. I don't want to know."

Her confusion gave way to understanding, and she nodded. For his sanity, Jerry had to convince himself his child had died, and he needed her to play along.

A quick check of his belly, and she assured him he was doing well. He wished he weren't. Maybe an infection would set in and he'd die mercifully. He'd already imagined several methods of self-inflicted death to escape his prison. But each time, thoughts of his helpless son wouldn't allow him to plan further.

CHAPTER 34

JERRY ROSE tentatively, then relieved himself in his bucket. He'd lost all sense of modesty since being required to defecate in a bucket for all to see and smell. When he looked down, the ability to see his dick was another reminder he was no longer pregnant. Not that his stomach was back to his pre-pregnancy size. The skin still bulged and sagged, and he felt empty. He missed having a life rolling around and kicking inside of him. A lump rose in his throat. His child was no longer his, and only had been when safely inside of him. Two days ago, he'd given birth and it was the last time he'd cried.

He returned to his cot, and Keith stared at him. Jerry nodded to him.

"How're you doing?" Jerry pointed to Keith's stomach. With his T-shirt on, he looked like his normal self, but when Keith had changed earlier, Jerry saw the small bump under the healed incision and he'd only been pregnant for a couple of weeks. It should have been impossible.

Keith gazed down, then back to Jerry. His eyes were warm, yet he looked a bit overwhelmed. "Still can't believe I'm pregnant. It's...."

"Amazing, right?"

Keith nodded. "And fucking scary. They keep shooting me up with stuff." His expression showed his fear. "It's growing fast. It's too fast, isn't it?"

Jerry could only nod.

Keith swallowed hard. "I overheard the doctor telling someone they have to cut this kid out of me since my body can't give birth the way yours does. That'll be some scar. Guess I could brag about being in a knife fight." Keith laughed morosely. "Too fucking bad these assholes are going to take my kid once it's born." He spat the words as pain and anger flared in his eyes.

Jerry couldn't talk about their children without his eyes burning and his throat closing, so he changed the subject. "Not many of us are left here." Tomorrow morning, they'd be moved, and escape came to mind, but he quickly quashed that spark.

But he could tell Keith still held that hope. "If we get a chance, we're going to escape." He glanced at Gunn. "We all agreed last night."

"All" had to include Paul and Henri and the few others remaining in the cages.

"That'll only get you killed."

Keith nodded sharply. "Better than the future Geraldon has planned for us."

Jerry almost said, "What about your baby?" but there wasn't a future for their children. And didn't stinky hope whisper to Jerry that maybe escape was possible. Maybe.

But the next morning when the guards moved them from their cages, Jerry wasn't sure what he'd do if the others tried to escape. In the end he didn't have to worry. They'd been shackled like convicts, forcing them to shuffle to their transportation. Outside they were lifted into the back of a large cargo truck. There were four large cages inside and the men were divided among them. Keith and Gunn were in the farthest cage from Jerry, who didn't even look at the others with him.

Where was his son? Was he going to the same place as Jerry? Someone else feeding him, changing him, bathing him, hurt immensely. He couldn't stop images of Rex's body, left to rot somewhere where wild animals could take parts of him, or a charred skeleton in the burned-out building. He squeezed his eyes tight, warding off the macabre thoughts. He'd give anything to hear Rex whisper his name and hold him close one more time. Each memory brought pure pain, so he closed his eyes and eventually fell asleep.

Jerry jolted awake. The door opened, allowing him to see the landscape, or lack of it. Tall buildings surrounded the truck. The heavy air smelled of gasoline fumes and garbage. Gone were the trees and the mountains. The noise of traffic filled the truck. Why would Geraldon move them so close to other people?

Birdman grinned maniacally as he unlocked Jerry's cage. His face was a mass of bruising and swelling. Jerry silently cheered for Rex.

"Long time no see, princess."

Not long enough for Jerry.

Jerry hobbled out of the cage and followed the others down a metal ramp and into an empty parking lot. A tall fence blocked any view of them. Like sheep, they were herded into a large building that at one time had been a factory with its cinderblock walls and smokestacks. Inside the cavernous space reminded Jerry of an airplane hangar. Lo and behold, cages were lined up as neatly as at their previous location, as if magically placed there.

"Home sweet fucking home." Keith scowled as he looked around the room.

Gunn stuck as close to Keith as he could. Jerry noticed the cages held more Anzuni and Braezelas than he'd seen in their previous location. What surprised him even more...

"Eli."

Jerry tried to get Eli's attention, but he didn't move from where he lay on the cot in his cage. Had they decided not to sell him?

Jerry was led across the large room. There were several of the Braezelas that had disappeared at Tanyon's in the cages. Had any of the Braezelas been shipped out? If not, there had to be some pissed-off buyers out there.

"Get them ready. Our guests arrive in two days for inspection. And...." Geraldon smirked. "Some fun."

Jerry understood what Geraldon meant by "fun." He wasn't going to let his new sex slaves, or the drugs Tanyon had created, go to waste. Gods, Jerry should have been screaming and fighting the injustice of it all, but his self-preservation was practically nonexistent. Without a struggle, Jerry settled into his temporary home and waited.

"GET UP, maggots." Birdman banged his prod against cage bars as he walked down the line.

Jerry obediently rose. For the past two days, they'd been showered and shaved, fingernails and toenails clipped, hair cut and fucking coifed as if preparing to go to a fancy shindig. They'd be placed on display, or something equally humiliating, given the effort to clean them up. Being required to service someone had become his greatest fear. His stomach was still sore. Katy came a few times a day and shot him up with something to dull the pain. He was more than grateful for that.

When his cage was unlocked, Jerry joined the line of men being led out a door at the end of the room. To see them, it might have appeared they were being marched to the gas chamber for all their despairing and defeated expressions. Maybe being drugged against one's will wasn't a bad thing if being forced into sex. Anything to forget the fucking trauma.

Eli walked before Jerry, his head down and his shoulders hunched and shaking. Was he crying? No. His entire body trembled, including his hands. He looked strung-out and terrified. Jerry would be too, if being forced to do what Eli had done. He'd sucked another man's dick with gusto and desire. He probably wasn't even gay. What kind of shit that must do to a person's head was beyond Jerry.

He hoped he never had to find out.

Beyond the door was a small room. Three rows of folding chairs faced a large rectangular window with what looked like a posh living room on the other side. The window gave the illusion that they were peering into someone's house.

Even fancier than the digs at Tanyon's, the enormous and opulent room held wraparound leather sofas, upholstered high-back chairs, chandeliers, gilded tables, and a fucking bar, complete with a tuxedoed bartender and tables of food, more food than Jerry imagined could be consumed by the guests Geraldon expected. He wasn't messing around.

"Sit down," Birdman told them.

Jerry obeyed, although some refused and were assisted by the guards. In all, there were a little over twenty-five of them, a mixture of pregnant men, Braezelas, and men who didn't fit those categories. Keith sat next to Jerry, rubbing his belly in a nervous fashion with one hand while clutching Gunn's hand with the other. Gunn whispered something to Keith, but Jerry couldn't hear. His fear and anxiety and anger—yes, anger—morphed and grew within the room. They didn't know what would happen to them, but it wouldn't be good. Jerry searched for Eli and found him sitting near the front, his head still lowered, the shaking more pronounced. No one else appeared to be so fearful they were shaking.

In the other room, a door opened and men in expensive suits and women in fine dresses entered, many holding champagne flutes. Their laughter and conversation was social in manner, nothing close to the seriousness of kidnapping, rape, and slavery they would be privy to.

Keith patted Jerry's leg, and he forced a smile.

Geraldon entered last. "Ladies and gentlemen, if you would take a seat, we can get started with the part of the evening you've all been anxiously awaiting."

A round of clapping rose and Geraldon beamed. The piece of scum. Jerry noticed Derian standing off to the side, attired in a well-fitted black suit, his eyes trained on those in the room. Hatred for the man who'd betrayed Jerry and Rex, his king, and his people swelled in Jerry. Between him and Ty, it was a toss-up as to whom Jerry hated more for stealing his life and family. Maybe he shouldn't have given up so easily. Maybe he should be making a plan to get his child back.

Maybe he'd be shot trying.

"I want to thank you for joining me today. This is a great day for our cause. I've worked hard to bring my vision to fruition. Those of you here have embraced that vision. Our world can't continue as it has. Too many countries vie for positions of power; too many resources are wasted on supporting individual attempts to gain superiority. Current theories would have us believe that power and influence in the hands of many is necessary, and that one faction should never hold all the cards. We"—Geraldon waved his hand around the room—"disagree."

Fucking A, he sounded like a cult leader. Didn't they all crash and burn sooner or later—Hitler, Bin Laden, Stalin, Hussein? All greedy power mongers who, in the end, fell off their high horses in fantastic—and some not-so-fantastic—ways.

And who were those dumb enough to follow the deluded man? Surveying the guests, Jerry recognized a senator, and the woman with a graying blunt cut—wasn't she a congresswoman? Jerry wasn't into politics. Well, not American politics… or even Anzuni politics. Maybe he should have paid better attention to both.

Listening to Geraldon continue to rave about righting wrongs, bringing the nations of the world under one rule, being a visionary, a fucking messiah, a single word came to the forefront of Jerry's mind. *Revolt.*

Anyone who thought a dictatorship was ideal couldn't lead. Under Geraldon's rule, they'd surely die and these stupid people had flocked to his madness like flies to a pile of shit. They supported Geraldon's sick plan monetarily, and with their enthusiasm for change, that would bring them power.

Since arriving Jerry had counted no more than ten guards total for twenty-five prisoners. In the room with them were only four, although how many were needed when they had Tasers? He'd rarely seen them carry guns. Most likely afraid the experiments might get shot, or they might get hold of a gun and shoot themselves. You couldn't Taser twenty-five people at once. Separated by only a plate of glass were important people, people who could—*would*—do anything to avoid being implicated in such a major fuckup, and keep their cushy jobs and fat paychecks, and their limited power. Give them a choice, and this could all end here and now. A big idea that most likely would fail, but what did they have to lose? Their lives? They'd already lost those. He had to try, for his son.

From the corner of his eye, he saw Keith frown. Jerry glanced his way.

"What the fuck are you grinning about?" Keith whispered. "Are you okay?"

Jerry nodded. He had no plan on how to achieve his end goal: Take hostage a dozen or so of America's most important political and business leaders.

"Revolt."

Keith's frown deepened. Then his brow rose and his eyes widened. "How?"

Jerry grunted. "Hell if I know, but there are important people in that room. If any one of us gets a chance, we need to make a move. If we barricade the door out of this room, take down the guards in here, and smash the window, we can take over, right? And even with the number of people in that room, there are still more of us than them."

"You're fucking crazy."

Had the Braezelas of the past rebelled against their captors, the same people who'd created and enslaved them? If they had, that meant the Great War had been a revolutionary event, for a race of demons to escape slavery even knowing death was possible. Sometimes death was better than living a life of pain and suffering. Jerry didn't want to die, but he couldn't live the so-called life Geraldon had planned for him.

None of them could.

"Yeah, I am crazy."

CHAPTER 35

KEITH GRINNED. "I'm in."

"You're to stand back and only get involved if you're needed." Jerry had to protect Keith and his baby. "If... when we get out of this, our kids will get to grow up together. Protect your baby at all costs. Now, pass on the plan."

A slap to Jerry's head surprised him, and he jerked back. Birdman scowled down at him. "Shut the fuck up."

In his new take-no-more-shit attitude, Jerry refrained from provoking Birdman. He had bigger fish to fry. As Geraldon continued spewing his demented plan, Jerry let his mind wander to his son, and the brief glance he'd gotten of that tiny helpless half Anzuni, half human. A band tightened around his chest, bringing on a surge of panic. Jerry took the chance to speak to Keith again.

"If something happens to me, you and Gunn need to get my son to my parents. Promise me."

Keith gave him a hard stare. "We *all* get out of here. Today."

Jerry clutched Keith's thigh, stealing a glance at Birdman, who had his back to him. "Promise me you'll do it."

Keith nodded reluctantly. And Jerry breathed easier.

Covert conversations passed between the men. Jerry prayed it didn't end like those demonstrations where everyone passes one message, and when it reaches the last person, it's wrong. Even wrong, he had to trust that if one of them acted, the others would follow.

He'd lost track of what Geraldon said until the door to the right of the window opened, and a guard grabbed Eli. The Braezelas's body shook like crazy.

"What's wrong with him?" Keith asked.

Eli was dragged into the next room, front and center of Geraldon's audience.

"I don't know." But Jerry had an idea.

Geraldon beamed wide, as if Eli were his pride and joy. Expectant gazes were trained on Eli, who scowled deeply while nearly vibrating out of his skin.

"Ladies and gentlemen, this is Eli."

Ooohs and *ahhhs* were the only noises.

"He was Anzuni and is now a Braezelas."

"Are there any female Braezelas?" a rotund man in the back asked.

A flash of impatient anger crossed Geraldon's face, but he quickly smiled. "As per the information in the *packets* you received, the transformation only works on males despite what we've tried. In a delightful turn, however, for those not interested in the males, the drug PV35 can have aphrodisiac effects in females with a few added chemicals. Once the tests are complete, large-scale distribution can begin. I can assure you all will be the first to receive a shipment. Does that answer your question, Mr. Martin?"

He nodded with an expectant grin like that of a boy who'd just been told he's getting the latest game system.

"They're all fucking monsters," Keith whispered.

Jerry clenched his fists in his lap. "Evil. Pure evil."

Geraldon turned his attention back to Eli. "As I said before, the drug made with the blood of the Braezelas is a powerful aphrodisiac. Not only will this amazing drug induce a high that rivals heroin in humans without the addiction, but when given to a Braezelas, they become subservient with their only desire to serve whomever commands them. The aphrodisiac ensures their arousal and participation in all types of sexual fetishes."

"The drug becomes increasingly addictive in Braezelas, and they'll beg for it, do anything to get one more dose. Without the drug, *they* suffer withdrawal." Geraldon placed his hand beneath Eli's chin and raised his head. "Don't you, Eli? Last night you begged me to give you another shot, and then begged me to fuck. You served me well last night."

Eli glowered. Was the disgust clear on his face more for himself than anyone else? He shook harder, the withdrawal no doubt painful.

Gods, he fought something huge, something that eventually would break him.

"Fuck you, asshole."

Gunn gasped. "Shit."

Jerry waited for the painful retribution, but Geraldon merely chuckled. "I see that the withdrawal hasn't gotten to the point of desperation yet, but soon you would have been begging me for relief. Unfortunately, we don't have that kind of time."

Geraldon pulled a syringe from the pocket of his coat filled with the familiar red liquid.

Eli stepped back, fear marring his expression. "Get the f-fuck away from me!"

Birdman stopped Eli and held his arms behind his back. His struggles were useless. The prisoners around Jerry looked to him, waiting for the signal to act. But this wasn't the time.

"We have to do something," Paul whispered.

"Not yet," Gunn whispered back, and Jerry was grateful Gunn got that they needed to wait.

They'd have to watch the horror of what happened to Eli without intervening, and Jerry wanted to puke. He clutched the sides of his chair to keep himself from jumping up.

The needle plunged into Eli's arm, and he let out a bellow.

Geraldon capped the syringe. "Now watch as this resistant, uncooperative Braezelas loses his will, and desires only to pleasure."

Eli's shaking disappeared and his body visibly relaxed, his stern expression melting away. A hooded, pleasurable expression took its place. Sure enough, his cock tented his sweats. He fell to his knees and looked up at Geraldon with that sickening, expectant look.

Geraldon ran his hand over Eli's cheek, and Eli nuzzled into his palm. "You are so responsive, so eager. Gods, I'm of a mind to take you here and now."

"Please," Eli practically purred.

"Later. Now, I'm sure one of my guests would enjoy your ministrations." Geraldon raised a questioning eyebrow to the crowd. An older gentleman in a black suit with graying temples raised his hand. "Ahh, yes, Mr. Reynolds. Be my guest. You may use one of our several guest rooms. Derian, please show Mr. Reynolds and his wife out. And return quickly, please."

Derian waved his hand to the door beside him. The man and his wife stood as Eli was pulled to his feet and led from the room with a guard. Jerry watched them exit, as did the other guests. Were they crazy? Eli had been sent off to be raped. Jerry fought the urge to scream at each person watching and not intervening. Even knowing what would happen to Eli, acting at that point would be fruitless.

"That's all well and good, but he looks like a demon. Can he revert back to human?" The congresswoman ran her gold necklace through her fingers methodically. Jerry recognized the hunger in her eyes. Sick pervert.

"Unfortunately, I haven't been able to get that one to revert back." Geraldon frowned his displeasure.

"Where are those pregnant males you spoke of who can increase this supposed army in such short periods of time?" a younger man asked, shifting the thick black glasses on his face.

A handsome dark-haired man in the seat closest to Geraldon grunted loud enough to get the room's attention.

"Isn't he a senator or something?" Jerry asked.

"Senator Adams from California," Gunn whispered, and Keith frowned at him.

Gunn shrugged. "He's always on TV."

He seemed to be the most influential in the room, with many following his cue. He would be a good target. The senator stood. Damn, he was tall. Might take two of them to get him down.

"My main interest is not your pleasure slaves, Geraldon." He folded his arms, and his thick eyebrows bunched. "I'm most interested in hearing how your plans play into becoming a world power. Your claims so far have been compelling. However, we've waited long enough for proof." He sat, crossing his arms.

"Such the discerning man, Senator Adams. This is the beginning of our demonstration. We will get to that, if I can ask you to indulge me with your patience."

The senator narrowed his eyes and then reluctantly nodded.

"Good." Geraldon turned to the window. "Bring me the next pair, and let's also give them a look at some former royalty."

Jerry's heart slammed into his ribs. "Get ready."

Keith nodded as Jerry was snatched from his seat and led into the room. The carpet was plush and soft beneath Jerry's feet. He practically sighed from the comfort after walking barefooted on concrete for so long. He was surprised when Keith and Gunn followed.

Birdman positioned Jerry front and center, and the dozens of eyes on him felt like laser sights. Jerry met their stares. Some backed down, some challenged him. The door Eli went through opened, and Derian stepped into the room, meeting Jerry's glare without reaction.

"May I present the former prince of the Anzuni clan, who, might I add, gave birth to a baby boy a few days ago. We have his pregnancy to thank for making this entire venture possible." Geraldon stood next to Jerry's side.

Jerry gritted his teeth.

"Why don't you show my investors your true form?"

Jerry gave Geraldon a death glare. "I'm not a circus act, Geraldon."

Geraldon's fist struck Jerry's cheek, pain exploded across his cheek. Jerry went down on one knee and held his head. Fucking bastard. Jerry had to be strong. He rose without assistance and glared at his captor, despite the ringing in his ears and feeling off balance.

"Don't worry about the former prince. He's completely harmless. He couldn't hurt a fly right now." Geraldon passed Jerry. "This Anzuni male is currently pregnant."

"Hey!" Keith jumped back as Geraldon raised his shirt, exposing his slightly rounded belly.

Excited chatter rose in the room.

Maybe Geraldon would forget about commanding Jerry to transform.

Geraldon waved to a guard, who rammed his Taser against Keith's belly. Gunn shouted and no doubt would have throttled Geraldon if not for the fear of Keith being shocked again.

"Always the fucking bully?" Jerry closed his eyes and brought forth his demon form. He never felt comfortable with the horns and a tail.

Silence filled the room. Jerry opened his eyes. Most of the guests stared in disbelief, having never seen anything close to magic before. He imagined they feared what he'd do next.

"And who is this very large man next to the pregnant man?" the woman with gray hair asked, a lustful grin on her face.

"I'm glad you asked, Congresswoman Ross." Geraldon stepped closer to Gunn, who didn't attempt to hide his scorn. He could snap Geraldon in half, but the guard was sure that Gunn could view the Taser he had trained on Keith. "This is his mate, and he's a Braezelas."

"Shouldn't he have horns and tail as well?" the man with the glasses asked.

"Horns yes, but no tail. And he is in his human form. What my former colleague, Tanyon, found was that mated Anzuni could affect the transformation of their mates who have been changed into Braezelas. Let me demonstrate. When I inject the serum, not only will he become a compliant slave, he will turn into a Braezelas. Contact from his mate will facilitate his change back."

The skeptical looks on those in the room were almost comical. A guard approached Gunn warily with the syringe, but Gunn remained still to keep Keith and the baby safe as they administered the shot. He grunted, his brow drawn down from the pain of the transformation. Before their eyes, his face realigned and he grew the horns of a Braezelas.

Gunn's expression struggled between desire and disgust. He fought the drug, reminding Jerry of the first men transformed into Braezelas, most likely chosen for their submissive personalities, their nonconfrontational qualities. From what Keith had told Jerry, Gunn was far from submissive in his everyday life. He had a dominant personality that the drug had to suppress. If Jerry had to bet, he'd put his money on Gunn. Rex had failed to get hard and compliant on the drug. Jerry wanted to believe it had been because somewhere, deep down, he'd fought it. Gunn too had failed to get an erection or kneel, but no one seemed to notice.

When Jerry made eye contact with him, he saw Gunn was still there. If they believed he was harmless, they'd take their attention from him. Gunn could then make a move. How did Jerry convey that to Gunn?

"This one doesn't seem as submissive as the others." Senator Adams sat forward with great interest.

Keith stepped in front of Gunn to block the senator's gawking, but the guard pushed Keith aside.

"You're correct, Senator. The less submissive the personality, the more *fight* that remains. I assure you, though, he will obey and serve. Especially given that his mate will come to great harm if he doesn't. I believe that you desire someone who fights back a little, correct, Senator?"

The senator's eyes shifted for a moment with what appeared to be shame. Then his sights were set back on Gunn. He narrowed his eyes and nodded.

Fucking Geraldon played these people like finely tuned instruments he'd constructed himself. Why couldn't they see through his manipulation? Geraldon wasn't playing the same game he convinced them to join. Geraldon would be king of the mountain if he wasn't stopped.

"No, you can't have him!" Jerry lunged for Gunn, who caught Jerry in his arms. Jerry clung to Gunn, holding tight as the guard tried to pull him away, to make his attempt seem believable.

"Play along with the drug," he whispered to Gunn. "Look submissive. When you get a chance, get a Taser and grab Senator Adams."

Jerry was wrestled away from Gunn, and when their eyes met, Gunn nodded slightly. Keith tried to get to Gunn but was stopped short.

Geraldon tsked. "For someone who's just lost their mate, you surprise me, Jerricho. Although, someone with your questionable morals wouldn't be above trying to steal the mate of his best friend now that yours is gone."

Jerry didn't hide the scorn on his face. He was too busy suppressing his desire to throw up. Any minute they could die attempting to take over.

"Let's move on, shall we?" Geraldon approached Gunn. "Kneel, slave." A slight clench of his jaw but Gunn knelt obediently. He wasn't in a position to take anyone. No guard was nearby, no Taser. Would Gunn threatening to harm Senator Adams with only his hands be enough?

"Now, watch as the touch from his mate facilitates the transformation back to his human features." Geraldon waved his hand at Keith, who was pushed to kneel beside Gunn. Keith smiled tremulously and touched Gunn's arm.

"Kiss him." Geraldon's tone was sharp with impatience.

The tender kiss Gunn placed on Keith's lips was as much a show of Gunn's gentleness as their devotion to one another.

Jerry caught movement from the corner of his eye. He swore Derian had spoken to his hand. Had he lost his mind and started talking to his body parts? Maybe that was one of the side effects of the growth hormone Katy had spoken about. Crazy or not, Derian was a huge hurdle to overcome in their coup. Luckily, his allegiance to Geraldon was clear, and he'd do what he was ordered to do when they grabbed the senator.

"I would like some time with this Braezelas." A curvy woman on a sofa in the far corner stood. Her jade dress hugged her hips and exposed her cleavage. She practically salivated over Gunn.

"Of course, you will all have a chance to spend time with the Braezelas. Give me a few moments to speak of our next steps, and then we can retire for an evening of drinking… and pleasure for those of you so inclined. There are plenty of Braezelas for all to sample. First…." He waved to Derian, who opened the door and waited. For what?

"Will we be getting to the entirety of this plan anytime soon?" The senator huffed in annoyance.

Geraldon smiled, but his body was taut, and his jaw muscles pulsed. He'd Taser the politician right there if he could, no doubt.

"Yes, Senator. Please." Geraldon motioned to the open door. Katy entered, her eyes on Jerry as she wheeled a bassinet before her.

An icy cold slid over Jerry's skin, his heart skipped a beat, and his legs threatened to give out.

She positioned the bassinet before Geraldon, and for the first time, Jerry's eyes were on his son. His beautiful, perfect son created with Rex. Small button nose, bow-shaped lips, smooth pale skin, and a tuft of dark hair with a reddish tint in the middle of his head. He was all that remained of Jerry's lover. He barely breathed, yearning to cradle his child who he'd chosen to name Michael Rexford after his father. When Geraldon reached into the bassinet and placed his hands on Jerry's son, Jerry jumped at Geraldon.

CHAPTER 36

"GET YOUR fucking hands off my son!"

Jerry tried to push Geraldon away from the bassinet when a sharp blow to his back knocked him to his knees. He watched helplessly as Geraldon held his innocent baby. Smiling wide, Geraldon presented the once future heir to the Anzuni throne to his investors.

"Born after only three month's gestation. This child is only six days old, but is closer in size to that of a two-month-old. The new batch of growth hormones is more effective than expected. And to see the results I can yield in half the time, I give you my son, Derian. Come here, boy."

Jerry looked at Michael, but he couldn't tell if he'd grown or if he'd been that size at birth. He couldn't imagine Katy would use the hormone on his son. Not after the side effects she'd spoken of. Gods, would she have given it to him if threatened, even with dying? If she had given Michael the growth hormone, Geraldon was to blame and Jerry would make him pay.

Derian approached his father and stood facing the crowd, his lips stretched in a smile that didn't reach his eyes. Jerry half watched as Katy caught his attention. She glanced nervously around the room, appearing indecisive and scared, while at the same time determined, as if she were about to try something stupid. Jerry tried to catch her attention, but her gaze stayed on Geraldon and his guards. She slipped her hand into the pocket of her lab coat and came out with a fucking gun.

She pointed the weapon at Geraldon.

At Jerry's baby.

"Katy, don't!" Jerry could scarcely breathe.

Guards advanced on her, but she motioned them back, her face twisted with a sick hatred Jerry had rarely seen in another person.

"Oh, shit just got bad," Keith said as Gunn grabbed him and pulled him back.

A couple of women screamed and someone shouted, but Jerry focused on the burning hatred in Katy's eyes, which convinced him she would shoot. Her shaking hand could send the bullet anywhere.

"Katy, have you lost your mind? Put that gun down now." Geraldon looked to his guards. "Well, someone take it from her." Instead his guards stayed back from the crazy woman with the gun.

"Fuck you, Uncle. Someone has to stop you from taking any more lives and acting like you're a god, messing with creation and changing Anzuni. You're not a fucking god!"

Jerry had never seen a person pushed to the edge.

Geraldon chuckled in a mocking sort of tone, one that would've caused Jerry to pull the trigger.

"Shut up! Maybe I'm a better shot than you know. Daniel showed me a thing or two. I'm ending this now."

Before she could get a shot off, Derian appeared behind her and plucked the gun effortlessly from her hand. He wrapped his strong arm around her chest, causing her to kick her feet out.

"He deserves to die! You can't let him keep hurting people! He has to be stopped!" She struggled in vain against Derian's grip. "You have to stop him… please. I can't do this anymore." She sobbed, her fight dying along with her hope of taking her uncle's life.

For years Katy had done what her uncle forced on her, and this was the time she'd decided he should die. Something had to have happened to push her to that decision. Had something happened to Ty? Her husband or son?

The guests quieted and spoke among themselves. Derian continued to hold Katy to his chest, speaking softly into her ear. She shook with sobs, her eyes closed tight. She nodded slightly and collapsed against him. Whatever he'd said seemed to calm her.

"Get her out of here, Derian. I'll deal with her later." Geraldon's heated glare didn't come close to matching Katy's vehemence, but his point had been made. Derian shuffled her to the door and handed her off to another guard. Once she was out of the room, Geraldon quickly regained his composure.

"Please, ladies and gentlemen, forgive the interruptions. As you can see, the doctor isn't in her right mind. We will help her to calm down." Geraldon cleared his throat, still holding Jerry's son, who'd slept through the entire ordeal. Jerry had failed to take the opportunity to take over when the chaos erupted.

The room settled, and the entire incident was but an ugly memory. Derian returned and stood next to Geraldon. Jerry might have missed his opportunity, but he wouldn't make that mistake again. He crept backward on his knees, moving toward the door where the other prisoners were being held. If he could open that door and call them to action, they might have an advantage.

"As I was saying, Derian is my son, and he's a remarkable Anzuni, seeing as he was born only ten years ago." Murmurs came from the crowd, and the senator frowned.

"You want us to believe he's a grown man at ten?"

Geraldon's face lit up. "Yes, chronologically ten, but he's biologically and intellectually twice that age. With a recent reworking of the growth hormone, my hopes are this new formula will cut growth time in half."

The senator stood. "Impressive work, Geraldon. What are the next steps you propose? I mean, you can grow these soldiers, but then what? You have our support, but we're merely a small part of the government, some merely billionaires with too much money and time on their hands."

Geraldon grinned. "This entire plan does rest on the American government backing what we're striving to accomplish. What better way to do that than to place one of us into the role of president?"

Mocking amusement crossed the senator's face. "Being nominated by a party, much less winning, are odds too great for even you to control. You'll have to do better than that if you want my continued backing. Which I can tell you, without me, you won't get from anyone else in this room or the government."

"I agree wholeheartedly with you, Senator Adams. I'd like you to meet one of my oldest and dearest friends." The door opened, and Jerry had to be seeing things. He might not follow US politics, but he knew the goddamned Vice President of the United States when he saw him.

"Ted." Geraldon extended his hand without setting down Jerry's child.

"Geraldon. I'm glad be a part of this vision." The vice president turned to the senator. "Phil, it's nice to see you again. I'm sure we can count on your continued support, yes?"

Saying the senator was shocked, understatement. "Um… yes. I didn't know you were part of this cause."

"That was a fact I kept between Ted and myself, Senator Adams. He is the crux on which this entire plan rests."

Senator Adams nodded. "I take it you two have known one another for a while."

"Lifelong friends, in fact. We met as boys in our clan. I'm Anzuni."

"Fuck me!" Keith looked to Jerry, who couldn't believe his ears.

Jerry's father knew nothing of the Vice President of the United States being Anzuni. As determined as ever to stop Geraldon, he continued creeping toward the door. Everyone, even the guards, was too busy gawking at the vice president to pay attention. And being on his knees, he could move without being noticed by anyone, except for Gunn. He looked down on Jerry and raised a questioning eyebrow. Jerry gestured to the door behind him. Gunn frowned.

"The door," Jerry mouthed and gestured again.

Gunn nodded slightly and motioned toward the guard standing to the left and slightly behind him. Jerry hoped at that signal Gunn would take care of him. With a slight smile and a prayer, Jerry scooted back even farther.

"No, I didn't know that." Senator Adams's shock had disappeared, and he grinned, appearing giddy. Fucking power-hungry people fucking with everyone's lives. "And how do you work into this plan, Ted?"

Derian shifted to the right, not far, but closer to another door. Geraldon continued to hold the sleeping babe, and the self-satisfaction on his face was something Jerry would gladly wipe away—if his heart didn't burst open first. Cool sweat covered his skin, his weakness from losing so much blood while giving birth undeniable, but he wasn't stopping now.

"I'll become the president."

"Become the president? There's three more years until the election. And given President Richards's decline in popularity, highly unlikely."

Jerry snorted at the sarcasm in the senator's voice. Maybe Geraldon hadn't planned thoroughly. Jerry kept his eye on Derian and the guards. If they caught him, he'd be done. Reaching the door, he grabbed the knob, which turned easily. He'd be placing his son's life at risk with his plan, but Keith would grab Michael. He'd promised to take care of him.

"I'll be president within the month," Ted said smugly.

Stunned expressions covered the faces of investors as well as the guards.

Senator Adams's brow rose, and he squared off with the vice president and widened his stance. An odd movement. "How do you plan to accomplish that?"

Jerry didn't care how. It wouldn't happen if their revolt accomplished its goal. He closed his eyes and envisioned Rex, hair shimmering red and gold in the sun, bright smile, warm eyes, laughing heartily.

A tear slid over Jerry's cheek. "For you, Rex."

"When the president is assassinated."

Jerry's eyes popped open and his hand slid from the knob. What?

The senator looked over his shoulder to Derian. "Did they get that?"

"Every word."

Derian drew his gun on Geraldon, Vice President Hallman, and Michael.

"What are you doing, you stupid idiot?" Geraldon showed no fear until the gun appeared in Senator Adams's hand and pointed at him.

Jerry scrambled when the door behind him opened. Women and men dressed in black tactical uniforms, with FBI on the back, swarmed the room, guns drawn.

"You're both under arrest for conspiring to assassinate the President of the United States. On your knees!" Derian motioned to the floor with his weapon.

"No! Derian, what have you done?" Geraldon's eyes were wild, and he looked as if he would lose it with Jerry's entire world in his arms.

"The name's Jackos, and you don't get the right to call me *son*. Get on your fucking knees, or I'll shoot!"

Jerry sprang to his feet and ran to his son, desperate to stop what he feared most. He ignored the guns of the agents and Geraldon's guards.

"Jerricho, get down!" Jackos shouted.

But Jerry didn't care what happened to him. Geraldon's eyes widened, and he resisted as Jerry tried to get him to release his son.

"Give him to me! You're going to kill him!" His hands were on his son. He had to—

The vice president yanked Jerry from Michael and held a gun to his head. "Back off, or I'll blow his head off."

Jerry watched his son, who whimpered. He was beautiful.

"Threatening to kill a member of the Anzuni royal family is an automatic death sentence, Mr. Vice President, as you know. At least with the current charges, you'll only spend the rest of your life in jail."

Geraldon stepped back, and Jerry watched him scan the room frantically, his composure slipping and his desperation growing.

"Take me, please? Put my son down," Jerry pleaded. "Gunn, get him!"

Gunn, wide-eyed, his mouth open, shook his head.

"No, he'll kill you." The terror on Keith's face told Jerry they wouldn't help because of him.

Geraldon pulled something from his pocket. Another syringe. He held it close to Michael's chest. "I will *kill* the little bastard. Now everyone back off and give us a clear route out of here. The princes will assure our safe passage, or they will die."

No one moved a muscle in the room. Geraldon brought the syringe closer.

"Please... please do what he says." Jerry pleaded with his eyes, needing Derian—Jackos, whoever the fuck he was—to listen.

His jaw ticked, and his eyes narrowed.

"Please," Jerry whispered.

Jackos stepped back. "Everyone open a path. No one is to try and stop them." Jackos's eyes never wavered from them.

Ted pulled Jerry toward the nearest door. Keith looked prepared to bolt after them, but Jerry shook his head. Gunn pulled Keith back against his chest. Once they were in the hallway, Geraldon slammed the door. He opened the control panel and punched in numbers, and there was a *click* as the lock engaged.

"They're trapped in that room. This entire building is wired to lock down on my command. There are hidden access tunnels that lead to the subway line in the basement. A block from here is a building owned by one of my dummy corporation. My helicopter is fueled and ready, so let's get out of here."

Geraldon started down the hall, but the vice president grabbed his arm, his face a mask of rage. "I just became a fucking fugitive of not only the US government, but the Anzuni. Your son wasn't kidding when he said I'd be executed for kidnapping a member of the royal family, and we've got two."

"He's not my son. He's a traitor, and he's going to die for crossing me! And they have to catch you before they can do anything, so move it!"

Michael stirred in Geraldon's arms and released a sob, which steadily grew into a high-pitched cry. Jerry's instinct to comfort him kicked in.

"You'd better have a fucking amazing escape plan to some country without extradition, because this is your fuckup, Geraldon!"

Maybe they would kill each other. Jerry reached for his son, but Ted pushed the gun harder into his temple. "Don't move, Your Highness. I'd hate to have to blow your royal brains all over your kid."

Jerry dropped his arms as Michael continued to wail. Geraldon shook him, as if that would stop the crying.

"Stop it. Give him to me. I'll get him to stop."

Geraldon ignored Jerry's pleas and proceeded down the hall, the syringe still hovering over Michael's heart. Rounding the corner, there were more FBI agents with guns drawn. Jerry envisioned a hail of gunfire taking the four of them down in a bloody blaze of fucked-up glory.

"Don't shoot!" Jerry raised his hands.

Geraldon and Ted shuffled past the group of women and men, their guns following their movements. Michael wailed louder, and Jerry feared the noise would drive Geraldon over the edge.

"Make sure this corridor is cleared. If even one person is in the hallway, the prince here gets it first." Ted punctuated his sentence by stuffing the barrel under Jerry's chin.

Oh Gods, don't go off by accident.

"Clear the north corridor. No one is to interfere with their movement." Geraldon's head whipped around. Jackos appeared, gun trained on them. Geraldon's foolproof lockdown had been anything but.

"Anyone interferes, there'll be two dead princes on your conscience." Geraldon touched the needle to Michael's chest. Jerry was near hyperventilating and ready to throw up.

Jackos nodded in understanding. The evil spawn of Geraldon, or so Jerry had believed. Who the fuck was he? Jerry's thoughts were cut short as they moved on. The volume of Michael's wails increased as they echoed around the hallway. The agents had come to the entrance to the hall but had gone no farther. Around another corner, there were no agents.

"This way," a voice said from down the hall.

Ty stepped into the corridor, holding a gun next to his thigh. Fuck. He wanted to kill his uncle, and why would he care about Jerry's or his son's safety? Jerry swallowed hard, certain Geraldon and Ted would get to that helicopter.

"Where in the hell have you been?" Geraldon hastened to his nephew. Ted pushed Jerry along to keep up, the gun digging into the skin under Jerry's chin.

As they neared Ty, Jerry's eyes widened. Ty's face held no expression, an emotionless blank slate that reminded Jerry of a dead person.

His dark eyes appeared to look right through them. "Securing your escape. I was in the medical suite with Stephanos when I saw the warehouse being infiltrated on the monitor." Even his tone was flat.

Geraldon sneered. "I should have killed that little faggot when I had the chance. He nearly ruined everything, interfering with my plans for you. Your loyalties have never been with me, Tyranis, despite what I've given you."

Ty bowed his head, but not before Jerry saw his face contort into a combination of shame, hate, and sorrow. "I'm sorry, Uncle. I love him. I couldn't be without him. If you hadn't allowed Tanyon to have Stephanos after the marriage was called off, I wouldn't have lost it and attacked Jerricho. If you had allowed us to be together…."

"You nearly ruined *everything*!"

Ty nodded in resignation. When he looked up, his face was once again like the dead. "We have to go. The car's outside to take you to the helipad, and the pilot is ready to take off when you arrive. Your jet is on the runway. Within twenty minutes, you'll be in the air."

Geraldon had finally pulled the syringe away from Michael, most likely thinking he'd already won. Even with the gun shoved under Jerry's chin, he could break away before Ted could shoot. If he could get to Michael…. He *had* to get to Michael. Geraldon and Ted were going to a foreign country. And wouldn't want extra baggage. Once Jerry and Michael were no longer needed, Geraldon would kill them. If they got into that car, their lives would be over.

But when they reached the alley, there was no car to be seen.

Geraldon looked around frantically, his face twisting in rage.

"Where's the fucking car?" Ted dragged Jerry in a circle as he looked around.

Ty raised his gun at his uncle. He was calm, steady, not even a flinch. Jerry's breath caught. Ty didn't care if he died. That dead expression that had puzzled Jerry clicked as being that of someone with nothing left to lose.

"Put the gun down, Tyranis. Right now." Geraldon's fear had returned.

"You got your wish, *Uncle*. Did you know that? Stephanos is dead, along with the child he carried. The child you forced me to give him."

Mentioning Stephanos filled Ty's eyes with aching sorrow. His calm faded, his chest heaved, and he appeared to be on the verge of crying. Stephanos and his baby couldn't be dead.

"So what? He did nothing but interfere with my plans." Geraldon quirked his lip. Was he so insane he didn't realize what Ty planned to do?

"You don't talk about him that way!" Ty barked and moved toward them. "You fucking ruined my life. You took him from me. Your fucking drugs did it. My mate bled out giving birth because of what you did to him, and our baby girl died. You don't deserve to live!"

Oh, that had to be what had driven Katy to pull a gun on Geraldon. She might not have ended her uncle, but Ty looked as if he'd get that satisfaction. Jerry looked at Michael. If his child died, Jerry couldn't go on living. Not with Rex gone too.

Geraldon took a brave step closer to Ty. "You won't hurt me. *You* need me. You can't survive on your own. You never could."

"Only because you had to interfere with everything I did. I'm done with you."

"This baby *will* die if you touch me."

Ty shrugged. "He's better off dying now. You'll kill them sooner or later. You kill everything. Like you killed my parents." Geraldon balked, but Ty shook his head. "Don't fucking lie to me. Not now. Own up to your evils, you piece of shit."

"I'll shoot you before you can kill both of us."

Ty turned haunted, dead eyes on the vice president. "I welcome death, Ted. Do you?"

Ted stepped back, taking Jerry with him. The wail of the baby filled the alley as the standoff continued. Jerry cried out as he was shoved forward and slammed into the ground. The gun Ted held skittered across the pavement. There was a shout and a gunshot. Jerry tried to see what happened but was pinned. The weight lifted off Jerry, and he scrambled forward, flipping onto his back. He froze. He'd either hit his head hard or was dead.

"R-Rex?"

CHAPTER 37

JERRY WASN'T dreaming. Rex was alive and fighting with the Vice President of the United States. But…

Michael. Jerry shot to his feet in time to see Geraldon run into the building with his son. Ty lay on the ground, eyes wide. He coughed and spewed blood, which bloomed across his chest. Jerry couldn't help him. Geraldon could disappear within seconds through one of his escape routes. The man might be stark-raving crazy, but he wasn't stupid. And he had the vice president's gun. Jerry sprinted into the building. A hand grabbed his shoulder, and he swung his arm as he spun around.

"Rex!" Jerry jumped up, wrapping his arms around Rex's neck and his legs around Rex's waist.

Rex squeezed him hard.

"Oh my gods, you're alive. They said you were gone. They said you were dead." Jerry inhaled his scent deeply.

"Jer, gods, I couldn't find you. I tried, but I couldn't find you."

Jerry wanted to cling to Rex forever, but….

"Geraldon has Michael! He has our son! We have to get him!" He dropped to the floor and sprinted down the hall, panicked because they'd lost Geraldon. "No!" He yanked on door handles, but they were all locked.

Rex pushed against the doors as well, but none of them budged.

"We have to find him!"

"We will, Jer. Stay calm."

Jerry froze. "Shhh. Listen."

A barely audible cry. "I hear him." Jerry pressed his ear to a door. Rex joined him, and they checked door after door. Why the need for so many fucking doors?

"This one!" Rex pointed to the last door.

"Freeze!" Jackos peered around the corner, gun raised.

Jerry yelped and jumped back, his heartbeat speeding up.

Jackos lowered his weapon. "What the fuck are you doing here?"

"Getting my son!" Jerry shouted.

"Not you, him." Jackos pointed to Rex. When Rex shrugged, Jackos rolled his eyes. "Damn that fucking rookie Lopez. You didn't hurt him, did you?"

"He'll live. Kid needs more training in everything. Wouldn't have happened if you hadn't taken me into custody when you found me in the woods! I had to find Jerry!" Rex's tone was clipped, his expression threatening. They didn't have time for posturing here.

Rex had made it out?

"Couldn't have you messing up the entire operation."

Jerry rounded on Jackos and poked his finger into the supposed agent's chest. "If you can't open this fucking door, then get someone who can right now! Geraldon took Michael down there." They were running out of time.

Jackos stepped back in surprise "I have the code." He opened the panel on the wall, but the code he punched in did nothing. He frowned.

"Why didn't it open?" Jerry couldn't catch his breath. Fuck, he needed to calm down.

"Hold on." Jackos closed his eyes, his brow furrowing. He recited numbers under his breath. He opened his eyes and punched in more numbers. The lock clicked, and he opened the door. "I know where Geraldon's headed. Stay here. I'll get your son."

"Fuck you." Rex pushed past Jackos and headed down the stairs. Jerry did the same.

"This is an FBI matter now." Jackos followed close behind. "You need to let me handle it!"

"Fuck the FBI. I'm getting my son back. You can keep crying about it or help." Rex shouted over his shoulder.

"I need backup at grid thirteen." Jerry looked back and found Jackos talking to his hand again, which this time made sense. "Get your asses down to the basement. Door number 15 on the blueprints. Code is 35467. Main target has the baby and is attempting to flee through the subway tunnels. I also have a couple of civilians resisting orders to stand down. I need you to arrest their asses."

Jerry glared pointy daggers at Jackos, who glared back. "We don't have time for this." Jackos pushed roughly past them. "At least let me go first, since I have the gun and the expensive government training."

Rex reached for Jerry's hand and squeezed it tight. Jerry squeezed back. The touch helped to calm him. He had to keep it together for his son and now Rex.

At the bottom of the narrow stairway was a large, creepy basement area that looked like a scene from a Stephen King novel. All that was needed were the huge, blind, mutated albino rats. Jerry shuddered hard. In the distance, Michael cried, and the crushing guilt ached in Jerry's chest.

Jackos surveyed the room. Lifting his hand, he shouted into the mic, "Where's my backup?" Jackos was silent for a moment. "Shit, well get someone to crack the code to the door. I'm proceeding ahead. Get teams into the tunnels ASAP. Unsure what his intended exit route is." Jackos looked over his shoulder at Jerry and Rex. "The code on the door reset. Must be something Geraldon built in. We're alone until they get it open. You both need to listen to me."

Michael's crying echoed through the empty rooms, and it was hard to know which direction to head in. The lights were dim, with several rooms lacking any source of light. There was a loud click, and a beam of light filled the room. Where had Jackos pulled the flashlight from?

"Both of you stay put right here. I have no clue what's been rigged up down here. I didn't get to map out this level before Geraldon populated the place."

Rex snorted. "I'm getting my son. You're lucky I let you come along and didn't kick your ass for keeping me from my family."

"I've got a black belt in jujitsu and a gun."

"Well, at least the odds will be even, then."

Jackos chuckled softly. "I think I like you. Stay behind me. They'll have my ass if you get hurt."

The darkness around them was so thick, Jerry felt it would suffocate him. He focused on the concentrated circle of white light from the flashlight and the sound of his crying child. Abruptly the sound stopped. Jerry sucked in a breath and squeezed Rex's hand hard.

"Stay here," Jackos whispered. He rolled his eyes as Rex postured. "Let me scout ahead."

Rex pulled Jerry back against his chest. "You've got two minutes, and then we come after you."

"Roger that."

Rex wrapped Jerry in his arms. "It's okay. We'll get our son back. I promise you that I will get him back... if it kills me."

Jerry shook his head. "Don't say that. I thought I'd lost you once. I can't go through that again. They kept saying you were gone." His mate was alive. Geraldon had lied. Surprising.

"I made it into the woods, but I couldn't find you. I'm sorry I wasn't there when our son was born. I can't wait to meet him—"

"Michael.... I named him Michael after his dad."

"I like that." Rex leaned down, and their lips brushed briefly.

The damp coolness of the basement chilled Jerry and brought back memories of the woods and Ty. He'd lost everything. If he was dead, it would be a mercy.

An ear-piercing explosion rent through the stillness of the basement. Jerry jumped, and his heart froze. The thundering sound ricocheted off every surface. Jerry bolted, hearing his child's screams. He needed his fathers.

"Jerry, wait!"

But Jerry couldn't stop, couldn't focus on anything but finding his child. Panic clawed up his throat, requiring he scream, but he swallowed hard and pushed it down. He moved breathlessly, followed by Rex as he searched for a route to his crying infant. The dim light made traversing the rooms a nightmare. A perfect dwelling place for some subterranean creature.

Stay the fuck away.

"This way." Jerry followed Rex toward the increasing wails. Where in the hell was that backup Jackos had called for? Maybe they didn't need it. Maybe Jackos had shot Geraldon and, at that moment, held Michael, calming him.

Jerry turned the corner, and that fantasy fled. Jackos sat, propped up against a stone wall, bright red blood running from a hole in his thigh. He held his gun, finger on the trigger, but it rested on his thigh. He focused straight ahead.

"Stay back."

It took a moment to realize the words had been aimed at him and Rex. Jerry peered to the right. Geraldon held Michael and the gun. He balanced on a narrow piece of wood stretched over a large, black circular hole in the floor of the basement at least twenty feet in diameter. If he dropped Michael, he wouldn't survive.

"Don't move!" Jerry held up his hands and moved tentatively forward, but Rex grabbed his arm.

"Jer, stop. He could fall or drop Michael. Please, wait."

How was Jerry supposed to watch his son in danger and not rush to him?

"Geraldon, you're trapped down here. All the exits are blocked. Give up and return the baby." Pain gripped Jackos's voice, but he didn't waver.

Geraldon grinned that sardonic I-hold-all-the-aces look. Arrogant prick. "You're nothing but a traitor. My greatest joy, my own flesh and blood, and you turned on me! You're a piece of trash."

"Your greatest joy? Are you fucking kidding me? You took your children and used them for experiments in your fucked-up insane plans to lead the world. You turned them into mindless children in adult bodies. Well, those who survived, that is. You didn't care one shit that they were your own flesh and blood. You kidnapped your own people and turned them into baby-making sex slaves. You're psychotic and delusional and a fucking coward. Look at you, hiding behind a baby. And you call me trash?"

There were some messed-up family issues there, but Jerry didn't give a shit. As Geraldon teetered on that beam, Jerry's body shook, and the bright spots threatened his vision as his brain flooded with fear.

"Give me my son!" Rex apparently had reached the point of needing to act. This time Jerry stopped him from reacting. Geraldon could shoot him.

"You were my legacy," Geraldon stated.

Jackos shifted as if he wanted to rise, but he winced and sat hard. "Are you so stupid as to not see what was right in front of you? I'm not one of your fucked-up creations. Your children, the ones you experimented on, are damaged Anzuni. You grew their bodies and fucked up their minds. By the age of three, they were neurologically damaged, and many of them died. None were viable for your army. Your niece hid that from you, gave you the results you wanted to hear—for the life of me I have no clue why—when truthfully she was busy caring for a herd of your mentally disabled children. The real Derian has the mind of a toddler."

Geraldon narrowed his eyes. "Who are you?"

"My mother is Katarina Moscoff. I was born twenty-nine years ago and given up for adoption."

Geraldon surveyed Jackos, his expression one of confusion and offense. "You're lying. Katarina miscarried that baby. She told me so. And as for the others, my guards were with those children to assure that my niece followed protocol. Reports from my head of security, Daniel, told me that the experiments were a success! There were videos, pictures!" He'd paled and visibly twitched.

"She didn't lose her child. I'm living proof of that. And those are your fucking children, not some goddamned experiments!" Jackos stabbed his finger at his delusional parent. "Daniel, the man you praised for his loyalty to you, helped Katy to stop the experiments, helped fool you. Daniel didn't believe in what you were doing any more than your niece did. He fell in love with Katy. They were married and have a child, and together they've taken care of your damaged offspring, until you took her away from them again."

How did Jackos know all of that when Geraldon didn't?

"You're nothing but a fucking liar!" Geraldon's voice echoed off into the dark recesses of the basement and the hole beneath him.

"Am I? Daniel told me this himself, when I found him and your damaged children. My brothers and sisters. All of them are now under the protection of the US government. And you will pay for what you did to those innocent people."

Geraldon scoffed. The board teetered as he struggled to balance himself. As he shifted Michael in his arms, the gun he held fell into the blackness and, several seconds later, splashed into the water below.

"Jackos, stop it!" Jerry's heart couldn't take much more. Jackos only pushed Geraldon closer to dropping his son.

Geraldon's eyes looked far off, seeming to parse through the information, maybe even the direness of the situation. His voice was soft as he spoke. "You've ruined everything. I have nothing left to lose." He surveyed Jerry with cold eyes, causing his stomach to twist into tight knots. "What do you have to lose, *Prince Jerricho*?"

Jerry stepped toward the hole, peering into blackness.

"I assure you it's deep." Geraldon's gaze sharpened, but behind that clarity lurked something else…. Resignation? Acceptance? "It's a cistern that's been here for over a hundred years, collecting rainwater through pipes from the roof. I'd estimate this one is at least fifteen feet deep, and holds some of the nastiest water you've ever seen."

The rumblings of footsteps and voices sounded in the distance. If Jerry could stall, they might have a chance of being rescued by the other agents. Maybe Jerry could reason with Geraldon, show him there was a way to escape.

"Take me instead of Michael."

"No!" Rex tried to shove Jerry behind him, but Jerry resisted. "Jackos said you had ways to get out of here. Take me and I can help you get away, and then you can get rid of me."

"No!" Rex and Jackos both shouted simultaneously.

Jerry ignored them both. "Rex, when he gives me the baby, run with him and don't stop." That was, if his plan worked.

Geraldon appeared amused for a moment. "Certainly the life of your son is more valuable than yours."

Jerry couldn't argue with that, but he wouldn't let Geraldon flee with his son.

"You aren't walking out of here with my baby. He's innocent."

"*No one's* innocent." He looked to Rex. "I see your claxton has returned. I imagine you're thinking you've won. That you'll finally have everything you wanted."

Behind them was the faint *swish* of material and whispers of others moving toward them.

"No, I don't. You have all of the power here, which is why I want you to take me instead. I know that whoever you take, you'll get rid of. With me, you can have access to my bank account, and could even get more money from my family. You'll need money when you're on the run."

Geraldon snorted with disgust. "Do you think I don't have money hidden all over the world?"

"It's not doing you a bit of good right now, is it?" Jerry desperately needed this to work.

"Geraldon, hand over the baby." Jackos held his hand up, and Jerry hoped the action held back the agents from daredeviling into the room and forcing Geraldon into a corner. Would he drop Michael? Jump?

"Please, give me my son." Jerry raised his arms, stepping forward. Geraldon shifted on the wobbly board and Jerry gasped. "Please."

"I ask you again. What do you have left to lose, Prince Jerricho?"

"Everything!"

Geraldon stepped off the wood plank.

CHAPTER 38

"MICHAEL!" REX bolted toward the hole, then froze midstep. All noise ceased, except for Jackos's shouts to stay back. Geraldon splashed below. Fucking great, he'd frozen time, a power useless on Anzuni. Jerry flew past Rex.

"Jerricho! Stop!"

But Jerry *couldn't* stop. He couldn't breathe when his son was drowning. Reaching the hole, Jerry lost his footing on the crumbling edge. He stumbled and grabbed the plank, but it shifted and fell. Jerry plunged into a cold dark world.

Jerry flailed, fighting the cold tightening his muscles. The water was chilly, not icy, but way colder than his body temperature. He surfaced, gasping, searching frantically for signs of Geraldon and his child.

"Michael!"

The darkness didn't allow him to see far, so Jerry submerged, searching sightlessly, hoping to grab hold of something. The water was as deep as a swimming pool. The floor was a slimy mess of rocks and dirt. His lungs burned as he fought to search a little longer. The cold bit at his skin, the top layer already numb. His muscles contracted as the chill tried to reach his core. He surfaced, frantic to the point of hyperventilation.

A beam of light flashed over the edge "Over there! He just went under." Jackos shined the faint beam of light at the far side of cistern.

Jerry frantically swam to where the light illuminated the water, then submerged. His hand brushed fabric. An arm tried to push him away. Jerry managed to grab Geraldon's suit jacket. Geraldon fought back as Jerry struggled to haul him to the surface. His grip slipped, but he regained his hold. Geraldon ceased his fight, making it easier to swim up.

They both broke through the surface at the same time. Jerry didn't hesitate, smashed his palm into the asshole's nose, and took back his son.

Geraldon coughed and gagged on a yell, then sank back against the metal side of the cistern. Jerry swam away from him, pulling at the water with one hand, desperately holding his silent son with the other.

"Jackos, help!"

Jerry grabbed on to the plank sticking out of the water. It was partially submerged with one end shoved against the metal side below the water and the other disappearing into the darkness above. Jerry tried to pull himself up with one arm, but the board shifted. Instead, he attempted to lie Michael on the angled surface to get a good look at him.

"Hello! Anyone copy? I need paramedics down here, *stat.* Anyone copy? Fuck! *Someone* answer me!"

Jerry's jaw chattered as he propped his son up out of the water.

"Jerry, you need to unfreeze everyone! You froze everyone in the building!"

He'd frozen the cavalry too. But he could only concentrate on Michael.

He was limp and blue and there was no movement. "No, no! He isn't breathing! Michael? Breathe, baby!"

"Start CPR!"

"I don't fucking know how!" Jerry tired quickly from treading water. He managed to wedge his leg over the board without it shifting any farther.

"Babies have small lungs. Take in a breath, then cover his mouth and nose with your mouth. Fill your cheeks with air. Don't blow in any more than that. Then use two fingers to do chest compressions!"

"What if I hurt him?" Oh gods, Jerry couldn't do this. He couldn't....

"You have to get him breathing! Do it! Now!"

"Okay-okay-okay." Jerry shook off his fear and did as he was told. A breath, then compressions. He didn't count, his mind was too harried. "Come on, Michael... breathe for Daddy... please."

Hot tears filled his eyes, but he didn't stop. Another breath, then more compressions and, after what seemed to be an eternity, there was a spasm in Michael's chest. His little mouth opened and a rush of water came out, a gasp, and then more water was forced from his lungs. Jerry turned him onto his side. He whimpered, which turned into a weak cry. The fear and heartbreaking agony fled Jerry's body.

Noise filled the air above.

"Jerry! Did you get him?"

"Yes. He wasn't breathing, but I got him to start again. He's breathing." Jerry gasped and tried to stop from falling into retching sobs. "He's...."

"I hear him, Jer. You did good. Hold on. We're working on getting Michael out first and then we'll get you. I love you both."

"Don't worry about me. Michael needs help. He's so cold."

"Hang on, Jer." They had to fish Michael out of the cesspool before he died of hypothermia.

Remembering Geraldon, Jerry searched the area where he'd left him, but he couldn't see through the darkness. Jerry snapped his head around, searching, but found nothing. "I don't know where Geraldon is!"

"I can't see him. Maybe he drowned," Rex said.

That would be a fucking miracle.

"Jer, listen. They rigged up a sling for Michael. Put him in so we can get him out of there. Can you do that?" Rex's attempt at a calm voice came out weak.

Jerry didn't want to let go, but he agreed, rubbing Michael's limbs to warm his icy skin. "It's okay, sweetie. Your daddy is here, beautiful boy. Everything's going to be okay."

There was a noise in the darkness. Jerry slipped off the wooden beam, ready for Geraldon's attack. More light flooded the cistern, and men in black scrambled around the edge. Something was lowered over the side. When it reached him, Jerry fumbled to get the baby inside what amounted to a large jacket, wrapped in rope. Having him fall out on the way up terrified Jerry, but the sooner Michael was out, the better. His breaths were shallow and sharp, and he no longer was crying or even whimpering.

"Pull him up!"

"Okay, Jer. You're next. Okay?"

Jerry nodded as his teeth chattered. He felt groggy, as if his entire body had slowed down. Michael moved up painfully slowly. Jerry swore his body quit functioning as he watched his son rising higher.

"Rex…." Jerry struggled to tread water, failing several times to keep his head above the surface. His clothes felt like deadweight on his failing body. He coughed up stagnant water. Jerry continually failed to hold on to the board.

Rex raced around the opening, to the end of the plank. "You guys, help me! We have to pull him up!"

Men scrambled to assist Rex. "Grab higher, Jerry!" Rex and the group of men grabbed the board, ready to hoist Jerry up.

"I can't hold on." Jerry's ability to help himself faded.

Water splashed behind him.

"He's behind you!"

Jerry snapped his head around as Geraldon grabbed hold of him. "You're going down with me, *Prince*."

Jerry was going to die a watery death with Geraldon.

CHAPTER 39

JERRY CAUGHT a glimpse of the sling before the cold water overtook him. Geraldon had Jerry firmly in his grip. Jerry's mouth clamped shut, denying his body's instinct to suck in air. Twisting and turning, Jerry caught sight of Geraldon in a beam of light from above. Insanity colored his black eyes and his mouth twisted in a sneer. An involuntary spasm in Jerry's chest tried to force his mouth open, but he kept it shut.

His entire body screamed for oxygen. His muscles burned, and with his energy spent, his grip on Geraldon loosened. Visions of his son, his soul mate, his parents, Keith, all flashed before him. Rex and Michael would be okay with Geraldon gone. Jerry grabbed Geraldon in case he tried to surface. His last act of love for his family.

Letting go wasn't easy, despite knowing Michael and Rex were safe. His vision grayed, and he wasn't able to keep himself from opening his mouth for air. He didn't want to leave his son.

I'm sorry, Michael. Daddy loves you. Daddy loves....

Warmth spread through Jerry's chest. Different from the burn caused by a lack of oxygen. Heat rushed through him, and it felt like....

Michael. Was he in trouble?

Jerry had to twist around to release himself from Geraldon's grip. He stared ahead, not moving, appearing... frozen. Jerry forced his eyes to focus past the darkness invading his vision. He needed get to Michael. He struggled to surface with Geraldon in tow, failing to reach the surface. He was ready to release Geraldon when his hand hit the plank. He pulled himself up until he had their heads above the water.

Jerry coughed until he threw up a stomachful of water. Gasping, he tried to hold Geraldon, but the dead weight nearly dragged him back under. When he looked up, motionless faces peered over the edge of the cistern. No one moved, not Rex, not even Jackos. Geraldon remained frozen, his face contorted with a self-satisfied rage as he barely floated above the water. Cooing echoed against the metal wall, and the coat sling rocked. Jerry gasped, stunned. Anzuni were immune to his power of stopping time, so it had to be....

Michael.

"I'm okay, Michael! Daddy's okay."

Instantly, there was movement and noise filled the air. The sling started to rise again. Geraldon flailed, and Jerry braced himself against the plank. He punched Geraldon in the head as hard as his cramped muscles would allow. Over and over, he pummeled the man, until the asshole was too stunned to react. Rex shouted for him to stop before Jerry killed him. Death was too good for Geraldon. He had to pay for the rest of his life for what he'd done.

JERRY TWISTED his hands in his lap. He sat in a wheelchair outside of the NICU at some hospital in Los Angeles. The factory had been located at the outer boundaries of the city. Michael had been life-flighted as he continued struggling to breathe. His oxygen saturation, dangerously low, left worried faces on the EMTs the entire ride. Even after the fifteen-minute flight, Michael's skin had a bluish tint. They'd intubated his tiny son and hooked him to numerous machines. Such a rough beginning, and it could all end here.

Fuck.

Jerry leaned over and buried his face in his hands. He was alone, waiting to hear anything about his son. He'd left Rex behind in a panic because there had only been room for one more in the helicopter. When they took off, an FBI agent had led Rex to an SUV. Jerry prayed he arrived soon.

During the flight, Jerry'd held his son's hand. His skin had been too icy, reminding Jerry of death. He understood the fear, the terror of knowing your child might die. His parents had continually faced that fear since the day he was born. Constantly afraid someone would take Jerry and use him to get what they wanted. But they'd protected him, kept him safe, and what had he done? Fought them every step of the way. Until he'd created a life himself, he never understood how terrifying losing that life could be.

Tears moistened his cheeks and palms. He prayed to any Anzuni god he could remember to save his son. He would have gotten down on his knees if he was physically able, but his legs were too sore from being submerged in the cold water. Despite being hypothermic and swallowing enough stagnant water to seed a small colony of parasites, he'd adamantly refused to stay in the emergency room. He'd vetoed the X-rays, the blood work, and the multitude of other tests the doctor had suggested. What he agreed to was an IV cocktail of antibiotics that would, hopefully, kill any hangers-on, and a bag of warm saline. If he even appeared sick, they might not let him see Michael. So, Jerry ignored the current flush of hot and cold over his skin and the building pain in his head. Sooner or later someone would come and tell him whether Michael would live or die. He had to be there.

"Please let him be okay. Please... I'll do anything." He'd beg and plead until he was hoarse.

He barely registered the hand on his shoulder until his name was spoken. "Jer... is he okay?"

Jerry lifted his head. Rex knelt before him, eyes swollen, the whites a mass of red. If possible, his already pale face had gotten whiter. He was covered in dirt and mud. The black jacket he wore had been donated by one of their rescuers. He looked wrecked. Jerry pushed off the chair and fell into his arms. Rex caught him and wrapped him up tight.

"I don't know if he's okay. I'm so sorry."

"Shh." Rex rubbed his back. "When I saw you crying, I thought...."

Jerry shook his head and laid his cheek on Rex's shoulder. "He's in there... alone. They won't let me in."

"He's going to be okay. I know he will."

"But what if he—"

"No! We've come too far." Rex's adamant tone bounced through the hallway. "He's going to be okay, and we're going to take him home.

He's going to keep us up all night, and have lots of dirty diapers, and spit up on us, and... and just be okay." Rex shuddered and exhaled.

Jerry wanted to believe him, but he was tired and past rationalizing. A cold sweat broke out on the back of his neck, and his muscles screamed their displeasure.

Jerry's mother burst through the doors at the end of the hall and sprinted (Jerry had never even seen her even walk fast) toward them. "Jerry! Oh, my son!"

His father followed close behind with his guards, Lanzo and Fillian. Jerry released Rex in time to receive an armful of his mother. She squeezed him tight, then pushed him away at arm's length, surveying him.

"Oh, sweetie." She cried and kissed his forehead over and over. Strands of hair hung from the loose bun at her nape, and she was without makeup. Gods, she was a mess—a perfect motherly mess. "You feel warm. You should be in a bed."

"Mom. I'm okay." *Once I see my son.*

"My baby. I'm so grateful. I prayed so hard and here you are. How's my grandbaby?"

Jerry couldn't answer. Rex explained what Jerry had told him.

"I want to speak with someone. Now."

Fillian nodded to his king and headed down the hall.

Jerry peered up at his father—the haggard, lost expression was nothing Jerry had ever seen on his face. His father pursed his lips and knelt, carding his fingers through Jerry's hair. He hadn't done that since Jerry was a small child.

"It's so good to see you, son." His slight smile was belied by the glassiness in his eyes.

"You too, Dad," Jerry whispered and grasped his father's wrist. "I have a son. His name's Michael."

His father's chin trembled, and he nodded as he drew in a deep breath. "I know. I'm so proud of you."

Jerry's chin also trembled. Cupping the back of Jerry's head, his father pulled him forward until Jerry rested his forehead against his shoulder.

"He saved me, Dad. Michael…. He froze time. He even froze the Anzuni. I could feel him. He saved me."

His father's lips quivered as he nodded. "Like father, like son. He's connected to you, and he knew you needed help. Seems he has a bit of empath in him as well."

Jerry choked on a sob. "I don't… I don't know if he's going to be okay."

His father looked him straight in the eyes. "We'll get the best doctors to come here. We'll do *everything* we can to make sure he's okay."

Tears fell onto Jerry's thighs as he gave his father a shaky nod. His dad was there, and he'd make sure Michael had the best care. He wiped his cheeks. "Have you heard anything about Keith and Gunn? Are they okay?"

When his father's lips thinned, Jerry braced for the worst. "I was briefed in the car on the way here. I know that Keith and the other men found on the property were taken to a private wing at Cedars-Sinai. We have a couple of Anzuni doctors on staff there. Keith's fine, a bit feisty, and from what I've heard, most of the others are doing well. There are a few in critical condition."

Jerry heaved a sigh of relief. He could see Keith throwing a shit fit if he was forced to stay in the hospital. He hated them with a passion.

His father's expression turned to one of confusion, maybe disbelief. "They're still trying to figure out exactly what Tanyon and Geraldon did to everyone. I was briefed on the experimentations, the drugs, the operations on the Anzuni supposedly allowing them to get pregnant, growth hormones…. The Braezelas…." Jerry rarely saw fear on his father's face. "Jerricho, what exactly happened? Is it true? Were there Braezelas demons?"

Jerry twisted his hands as his stomach knotted, his nausea climbed, and his head buzzed with dizziness. "Yeah. Tanyon told us that all Anzuni history about the Braezelas has been falsified. They never enslaved our people, and the Anzuni never had to fight for their freedom. I think it was the other way around, since the Braezelas were created by the Anzuni."

His father nodded, as if processing the information all over again. Gods, how could Jerry tell him about Rex? Best to get it out there. He looked to Rex and raised a questioning eyebrow.

Rex's lips thinned, and he seemed to know what Jerry asked. "Go ahead, Jer."

"Tanyon turned a bunch of Anzuni and humans into Braezelas. And... Dad, Rex.... He-he's...." He feared his parents would hate his claxton, deny Jerry permission to marry him. Rex was still Rex, despite his ability to transform into a demon. "Rex was turned into a Braezelas too."

Jerry's mother gasped and clutched her necklace. Jerry's father looked to Rex, who didn't waver, despite the scrutiny.

"But you don't look any different." His mother studied Rex closely, as if there would be telltale signs.

"I can transform into my d-demon"—Rex tripped over the word, and his body appeared to tense—"my demon form, but only with the drug. Something about the bond between mates is the reason I can change back. I can't do it myself."

Jerry's mother's lip trembled, and she hugged Rex. His lips trembled as he hugged her back.

"Were the Braezelas really a creation of the Anzuni for...." His father looked as if he couldn't form the words.

"Sex slaves. And the pregnancy thing is true. They used something from my blood and the operation to make it so Anzuni men could get pregnant."

"It's so impossible." His mother released Rex. "Isn't it?"

Rex shook his head. "Keith's pregnant by his mate, Gunn. A man who was also turned into a Braezelas."

Jerry's father snorted, a highly unroyal sound. "Keith with a man *and* pregnant? The teen who used to practically chase anything with boobs? I'm not sure I can take much more." He wrapped his arm around Jerry's shoulders. "It'll take a while to sort it all out. I'm so happy to have you back. All of you. I can't wait to meet your son."

Jerry swayed but locked his knees and refused to give in to his exhaustion. He had to see Michael. "How did you get here so fast?"

"I told you. They were in the town closest to Tanyon's compound."

A determined Jackos wheeled down the hallway. Jerry's head cleared enough to remember that the lying FBI agent was the person he'd been waiting to confront.

CHAPTER 40

JACKOS'S LEG was wrapped from hip to calf and extended straight out before him. He wrestled to maneuver the wheelchair. Lanzo, who'd been waiting off to the side, smirked seeing Jackos and finally went to help.

"About fucking time," Jackos grumbled. His eyes had a hazy, unfocused quality, and his pupils were black pinpoints within the seas of his blue irises. "Fuck me, that was a long way." He groaned and closed his eyes for a moment.

"Shouldn't you be in a bed somewhere, hooked up to a morphine drip?" Lanzo mused.

Jackos shot Lanzo a deadly glare and momentarily his eyes cleared. Unfortunately, the former king's guard slash FBI agent wouldn't be forcing any retribution from Lanzo, not in his condition.

"It's only a flesh wound. And I got all the painkillers I need running into my arm." He pointed to the IV bags hanging on the pole attached to his chair.

Jackos had been entwined in the entire mess. From king's guard to Geraldon's son back to king's guard and around until he ended up as an FBI agent. He'd fucked enough with all of them already.

"You said you lied about my parents being nearby, and now you're saying you lied about lying?"

Jackos showed that annoyingly shitty grin of his. "Welcome to the world of the FBI."

"Fuck you!" Jerry had enough of everyone's lies and deception.

"Son. Calm down."

Jerry ignored his father. Rex rested his hand on Jerry's shoulder but remained quiet.

"How about the truth, like why you didn't stop Tanyon from taking us when you were outside of the Congressional Room at the mansion that day. Why, you knew what was happening long before Rex and I were kidnapped. You were working with Geraldon. You knew!"

"What?" Jerry's father glared as he towered over Jackos.

"Jackos, or should I say *Derian*... or is it Jackos? He was a member of your guard. Geraldon put him there. If you knew his plans an—"

"Whoa, whoa, wait a minute. Let me explain." Jackos pleaded with wide eyes as his king glowered at him.

"How could I not know he was a member of my guard?" Merano, then Tanyon, Geraldon, and then Jackos. So many men had pretended to be someone they weren't and had hurt so many by doing so.

"He looks way different than he did, Dad."

Jerry's father crossed his arms and hardened his expression. "Whatever you have to say, make it good, because if I'm not mistaken, you're Anzuni, and if you knowingly allowed a member of the royal family to be kidnapped, especially a pregnant prince, you will be held to the same level of culpability, FBI agent or not."

Jackos stared at his king, then looked away. "First off, I didn't know that Tanyon was planning to kidnap Prince Jerricho and his claxton, even if Geraldon did. Geraldon didn't trust me with much since he only met me last year. He never knew any of the children he fathered for his experiments. Hasn't even seen them in person. He received fake videos of a selected few to monitor their growth until they were eight or nine. Once he knew the formula worked, he moved on to other parts of his plan. He didn't even know what most of them looked like.

"I used that to my advantage to pose as one of his sons with help from Daniel, who was part of Geraldon's security for what Geraldon called 'the experiments.' I had to earn every bit of trust I have with Geraldon, and I have to tell you, he doesn't trust anyone one hundred percent. That day you went before the council"—he looked to Jerry and Rex—"Geraldon sent me off to look at the property here in Los Angeles. I was gone from the mansion before the council even decided your fate."

Rex opened his mouth to speak, but Jackos cut him off. "And when I tried to get you both out of Tanyon's building, I was trying to get you out. I didn't know Geraldon was going to be there, although I should have suspected it. The man constantly showed up where he wasn't expected to be. It was also true that Geraldon had me go in as a buyer to regain access to the building from Tanyon. I used that opportunity to get you out. If Geraldon had even suspected I was helping you escape, we would all be dead."

Jerry pursed his lips while he processed the convoluted information from Jackos. The room spinning around him might have also had something with his brain issues.

Rex grasped Jerry's arm and moved him back to sit in the wheelchair. He shook as his anger-fueled adrenaline wore off. He wiped his sweaty forehead. Had someone turned up the heat? It felt as if the water had been sucked from his body. Maybe he should get something to drink. Why wasn't the IV pumping him full of fluids working?

"How's the kid?" Jackos asked, bringing Jerry back to the room.

"We're waiting to find out." Jerry's father grimaced. "Exactly who you are, Jackos? So far, I know you're FBI. But other than that, how about you fill me in?"

Just like that, Jerry's father was back to business as he assessed Jackos with a wary eye.

Jackos nodded, then shifted tentatively. His gaunt paleness, the sweat beading on his upper lip and forehead, and how he grimaced said the agent had suffered more than a flesh wound.

"Special Agent Jackos Moscoff of the FBI. I was undercover, investigating allegations of corruption and treason in members of the US Senate and House, which led me to Geraldon. After further investigation, we learned of a possible plot to assassinate the president."

Jerry's father stiffened. "Damn. Add to that kidnapping a member of the Anzuni royal family. Well, three of them. Why wasn't I aware of an Anzuni in the FBI?"

"Because I grew up outside of the Anzuni community. My mother gave me up for adoption at birth. I was raised by a couple who knew I was Anzuni but had promised my mother to keep it a secret in case Geraldon tried to find me."

"So you were telling the truth. You're Geraldon's son." Rex seemed surprised.

A combination of scorn and shame crossed Jackos's face. "Yes, I am his biological son."

"And how did you end up investigating your own father? Did your adoptive parents tell you about him?" Jerry's father asked.

Jackos shifted again and uttered a pain-filled groan. Lanzo put his hand on the FBI agent's shoulder, as if checking to see if he was okay. Jackos waved him off. "No, they didn't. I learned about my *sperm donor* when I found my birth mother three years ago. After I'd been in the FBI for about two years, I decided to try and find her. When I did…. At first I thought she was crazy. She talked about Geraldon and his experimentation on his own kids, including my little brother, who's the real Derian. She hadn't seen Derian in over seven years, but she showed me pictures and videos and… well, I looked into Geraldon to locate Derian."

"Then you believed her?" The pity on Rex's face differed from Rex's usual reactions to Jackos.

"I did."

"The children, they're the ones Katy took away and lied to Geraldon about, right? Ty told me about them when we were in the woods." Jerry leaned into Rex's heat. Talking kept him from freaking out about Michael, and giving in to his body's need to collapse.

Before Jackos could answer, Jerry's father asked, "Katy?"

"Katy is Geraldon's niece and Tyranis's sister," Jackos said.

Jerry's mother appeared confused. "I didn't even know he had a niece. I only knew about Tyranis."

"He kept her pretty sequestered most of her life. Funded her through medical school and then her research on the growth hormone. He forced her to use that hormone she'd developed on those babies by threatening to hurt Ty. They have severe cognitive and physical impairments, with the mental age of a toddler. Before Katy realized the damage the drug had caused, it was too late."

"Those poor children. What kind of monster does that?" Jerry's mother scowled.

There was still the possibility Katy had used the hormone to speed up Michael's growth before he was born. After was still up in the air. Was that the same one used on those brain-damaged kids? Jerry's heart rate increased, his stomach churned, and his hands shook. What was wrong with him? And why were the doctors taking so long?

"You okay?" Rex whispered to him.

Jerry nodded, his lie making his head spin faster.

Jerry's father wiped his hand over his mouth and glanced around the hall, looking lost. "Geraldon perpetrated all of this? Tricked Tanyon?"

"Yeah. Geraldon has been developing this plan for over twenty years. Tanyon was a pawn in this entire scheme—a guilty pawn."

"So, you aren't ten years old then, like he thought?" Rex raised his brow.

Jackos laughed deeply, but the sound lacked any humor. "No. I'm not the result of some biological experiment. I'm twenty-nine and was born that many years ago."

"You sure? Because you act like a ten-year-old." Rex wore a satisfied smile.

"Better than a five-year-old."

Both men eyed each other, then laughed.

Jerry's father flopped into a chair.

Rex blew out a breath. "Shit, this entire thing is so messed up."

"And the connection to the vice president?" the king asked.

"Traitor Ted," Jackos mused.

Jerry giggled and then snapped his mouth shut, feeling a little loopy.

"He's known Geraldon since they were kids. There was nothing to indicate they even knew each other. Ted isn't even listed as an Anzuni." Jackos shook his head, a bitter expression on his face.

"Geraldon is one of the smartest and most persuasive men I've ever met. He's a master at manipulating people. He divided his operation to keep anyone working for him from knowing exactly what he was doing. His ideas and philosophies were attractive enough to snag the attention and money of powerful and rich people, including several politicians, but... I mean, attention isn't all you need. You have to convince people to take the risk, to believe in it, to want it, and to follow you, and Geraldon did that. He used friends, his clan, his *family*, to get what he wanted. No one was off limits." Jackos gave a disgusted snort.

"Just like he used Ty and Katy," Jerry muttered. "Ty told me how his uncle used Katy to develop drugs and threatened to hurt Ty if she didn't. He did the same with Ty to get him to go along. Ty didn't want to marry me. He was already in love, so Geraldon drugged him so he'd want me. It backfired because the drug made him crazy."

Rex's eyes widened. "Tyranis didn't want you?"

He remembered the image of the broken Ty, holding the gun on his uncle as he grieved for his mate and daughter. "No, he didn't. He loved Stephanos. He wanted to be with him, and now...."

Jackos sighed heavily. "Damn. We knew about Katy and Ty being coerced but not about his mate and child. It's going to take a shitload of time to sort all of this out."

"What else were you going to say, Jer?" Rex prodded gently.

Jerry drew in a stuttering breath as chills settled into his muscles. He'd give anything for a blanket and a nap, but needed to know if Michael would be okay. "Stephanos died giving birth, along with his daughter."

Jackos's eyes lightened, and he looked hopeful, which was odd given what Jerry had just said. "No. She didn't. From preliminary reports, a second baby was brought to this hospital, alive but in critical condition. You and Stephanos were the only ones who delivered. She's going to be okay."

"Oh fuck," Jerry whispered. "Ty thinks his daughter died. That's why he tried to shoot Geraldon. Is Ty dead?"

"Last I heard, he'll live. He's in ICU and under arrest, until we unravel this mess and find where the true culpability lies."

Everything was so jumbled in his head. Jerry never thought he'd be glad Tyranis was alive, but his child needed its father.

A sharp pain shot through Jerry's skull. He squeezed his eyes shut as the world whirled around him. Beads of sweat fell from his forehead. When someone nudged him, Jerry opened his eyes to see Fillian approaching with a woman in a white coat. Oh gods, what was she going to tell them? Was their son brain damaged? Or dead?

Jerry's anxiety spiked, racing his heart and kicking his breathing up a notch. It felt like someone had his head in a vise. "Jer, what's wrong?" Rex asked. He sounded as if he were speaking from far away.

As the doctor approached, the room tilted. His teeth chattered. The doctor knelt before him, and then her hands were on him, as if he was being examined. She had nice teeth.

"Mr. Trychovisca? Can you tell me what's wrong?"

Jerry wanted to know about Michael. When he tried to speak, his mouth wouldn't work. His entire body was numb and hot, so fucking hot, and he closed his eyes to keep the room from tilting further. Voices were muffled and far off, but Rex shouted his name. Maybe his mother as well, but he was too tired to answer. He'd never been so hot....

CHAPTER 41

JERRY CALLED out into the darkness for Rex, but he didn't answer, annoying Jerry. He was restless and wanted a damned drink of water. And his son. What had the doctor said about Michael? He tried to remember, and recalled information like *infection... fever... only time will tell... neurological damage... long-term care*. There were other voices and Jerry wanted answers to his questions, but he couldn't speak, which annoyed him even more. When he tried to get up, hands subdued his movements. Someone pleaded with him to stay still. Maybe his mom? He thrashed against the hands. Why wouldn't they let him see Michael?

He wanted him, despite his disabilities. He had to live. Michael would have a wonderful life. Jerry would make sure of it. He'd love him unconditionally.

But right then, he was tired, so frickin' tired.

A hand caressed Jerry's cheek, and he turned into the warmth.

"Jer, baby, come back to me, please."

"I'm right here," Jerry whispered to the dark. Fatigue overtook him, and he faded away.

SHARP PAINS ripped through his eye. He yanked away from the bright light, but his other eye received the same treatment. He protested with a groan. He batted his hand to push them away.

"Mr. Trychovisca, how're you feeling? Any pain?"

Jerry made some weird croaking sound when he tried to speak. His mouth was dry as sand.

"Open your mouth, Jer."

He complied and a small sponge soaked with cool water was placed into his mouth. He sucked it dry and managed to say, "More," with his clumsy tongue.

More cool goodness. He licked his dry lips.

Someone touched his stomach, which was tender, and he winced. "Does that hurt?" the woman asked.

Jerry nodded and opened his eyes. His vision was blurred.

"Anywhere else?"

Jerry assessed his body. His stomach throbbed, but nothing else hurt except his head. "My—" When he tried to raise his right arm to touch his head, his arm didn't respond correctly. He felt uncoordinated and partially numb on his right side. "My arm won't move right. And my leg…." He tried to move it, but his leg failed to obey his commands. "What's wrong with my arm and my leg?"

Jerry continually tried to lift his arm and leg. He'd pretty much lost control over half of his body. "They won't work right!"

"Jer!"

The sharp sound of his name stopped his thrashing. Rex leaned over him, those sure green eyes staring straight into his. Jerry focused on Rex, his panic subsiding.

"Hey, it's okay. Calm down."

Jerry lifted his left hand and touched Rex's cheek. Rex closed his eyes and rested his forehead against Jerry's, who soaked in the comfort of having his mate so close. Rex's warm breath puffed over Jerry's lips, and he ran his fingers through Jerry's hair.

"Everything's okay. You were sick. Really sick, and the doctors, they didn't know if…." His choked words hit Jerry hard. "They didn't know if you would be okay. You had an infection and a high fever, and a blood clot in your brain, and they weren't sure if…."

"The weakness on your right side is most likely something that will respond with therapy. The clot dissolved quickly, and I don't foresee any permanent damage, Your Highness." Jerry nodded. His lids were heavy.

"Thanks," Rex said and shook the doctor's hand. She nodded and left.

Rex visibly trembled. He looked like hell. Still pale, his eyes dull, and he had the dark circles of someone who hadn't slept in ages.

"You're tired. Lie down with me."

Rex chuckled, then bit his lip. "I don't think that's allowed, but now that I know you're going to be okay, I might be able to sleep."

"Love you," Jerry whispered, because Rex might need to hear it.

"You too, Jer. Gods, don't ever scare me like that again."

"Promise." Jerry yawned. He was weak and tired, but.... "Michael.... Is he okay?"

"He's right here. And he's beautiful." Rex moved out of Jerry's sight and returned with a bundle in his arms. "He's perfectly fine. They were afraid of pneumonia, and pumped him full of antibiotics, but he didn't get sick."

Jerry tried to raise his arms, but only one complied.

"Let me help." Jerry's mother appeared next to the bed. She placed pillows behind Jerry, and then kissed his forehead.

"Hi, Mom." She looked tired as well. He'd put all of them through hell.

"Thanks." Rex lowered their son into the crook of Jerry's arm.

Jerry stared in awe upon seeing his sleeping baby, who sniffled momentarily, then settled.

"He's beautiful," Jerry whispered. The smattering of hair on his head appeared even redder. Maybe he'd be a redhead like his father. Jerry ran his finger over his son's skin, never having felt anything so soft.

"He looks like you as a baby. Except for the red hair." His father settled on the side of the bed, beaming with pride as he kissed Jerry on the head. "And, as Rex said, he's perfectly healthy. I had one of the top Anzuni pediatricians flown in, and he gave Prince Michael a clean bill of health as far as the growth hormones were concerned. In fact, those hormones may have saved his life by maturing his lungs. Dr. Grykevsky said a newborn without that enhanced growth might not have survived nearly drowning."

Jerry shuddered. He'd come so close to losing both Michael and Rex. And he couldn't believe they were fathers. Their future held late-night feedings and diapers and crying. So normal, and Jerry couldn't wait to get started.

"You did good, *Dad*." Rex nudged Jerry's shoulder.

"You too, *Dad.*" Jerry grinned and then yawned again. They were going to have so much fun raising their son.

"You need to rest." His mother reached for Michael, but Jerry wasn't ready to let go.

"A few more minutes." He snuggled down, resting his head near Michael's. The baby was warm, and his rhythmic breathing lulled Jerry's eyes closed. Rex sat next to them on the bed, and with his family there, Jerry was content, and drifted off to sleep.

JERRY SHIFTED to get closer to Rex, who slept on a cot next to the hospital bed. Jerry's mind was hazy from sleep. Five days he'd been in the hospital. He was still weak from the infection, and his arm and leg still refused to cooperate much, but he could deal with that. What he had a harder time dealing with were those moments he got lost in his own head. Moments of true, unfettered panic, when he wasn't certain if they'd been rescued. Hallucinations of rescue were a real possibility, regardless of Rex's reassurance he wasn't stuck in a mind-made illusion. Jerry couldn't stop running over in his mind everything that had happened. The trauma would fade, but would they ever truly be free?

Jerry rubbed Rex's knee. He woke with a start, sleep clouding his eyes. "Is the baby okay?"

Jerry smiled. "He's fine. They took him to the nursery."

He'd gone after the nurse had pried him from Jerry's hands. Today they were being discharged. He couldn't wait to get him home and leave the hospital behind. Here, his physical therapist forced grueling bouts of walking to the bathroom and back.

"I'm sorry I woke you," Jerry said.

Rex's tense expression fell away. "It's okay." He gazed around the room. "Where're your parents?"

"They aren't here yet," Jerry said. "What about your parents? What did they say last night when you talked to them?"

Jerry knew very little about Rex's parents, other than he was born when they were in their forties, which put them close to seventy, and Rex was their only child.

Rex sat up. "They were relieved to hear from me and that I was safe. Before I called them, your father told me that he'd contacted them directly when he got the call from you. He told them we were missing while camping in the mountain and since we were highly experienced, we'd be okay until someone found us." Rex huffed. "Never even been camping. When we're ready to travel, we'll visit them. They can't handle the long plane ride. But they're glad I'm okay."

"So, they don't know you have a son?"

Rex looked away and shook his head. Jerry got it. How did you explain to your parents you had a biological half-demon child with another demon who was a male?

"Hey, I didn't think you would tell them about Michael. They would have had a million questions you couldn't answer. We can tell them we adopted Michael if that's easier. Most people wouldn't be okay with a demon grandson and a son-in-law who gave birth to him. And after what had happened at the factory, we know Michael is part royal demon."

Rex rested his forehead against Jerry's. "We're strong together, and we'll get through this. Geraldon's in custody. I *won't* let anyone hurt you ever again."

Jerry nodded, all words except "I love you" escaping him.

"You too, Jer."

Their lips met in a soft kiss, which increased in heat until they were interrupted when a throat cleared. Rex scowled. Jerry chuckled as Jackos wheeled himself into the room. His leg was no longer stuck out in front of him, but the outline of the bulky bandage around his thigh could be seen beneath his sweatpants He wore a blue T-shirt that said FBI in yellow across the front. Under that, in smaller letters, was "Fucking Brilliant Idiots."

Jerry laughed aloud.

Rex snorted and sat on the bed next to Jerry. "You've got that right."

Jackos grinned. He'd regained his color and lost some of the IV bags. "My boss hates it, which is, of course, exactly why I wear it." He looked to Jerry. "Glad to see you back in the land of the living."

"Yeah, I'm like the Energizer Bunny. I just keep going and going...."

"Let's keep your sex life out of this." Jackos gave him a look of disgust, but the smirk gave him away.

Gods, it seemed like years since he and Rex last had sex.

"Pervert." Rex appeared to be offended, but was thoroughly amused.

Maybe Jackos wasn't that big of a prick. His smile faded, and the serious FBI agent was back. "I thought you might want an update on what's happened since you decided to take your extended nap."

Jerry huffed his slight annoyance, then said, "Better that than a dirt nap."

"That it is." Jackos looked down at his leg, the gaze appearing mournful. He quickly put his professional mask back on. "I've been on the phone with my boss most of the day, and talking with several of the other agents working the case as well, trying to sift through the mess of information taken from Tanyon's and Geraldon's locations. That should take a few years to get through, but with what we already have, several politicians and influential leaders are on the hook with enough charges to send them each away for a long time, including the former vice president."

"Good." They deserved to know what forced captivity feels like. "What exactly happened to Tanyon?" Jerry asked.

Jackos's expression was unsettling. "The plan had been to blow up Tanyon's compound with Tanyon inside, along with others Geraldon felt weren't 'with the program.'" Said with air quotes. "Of course, I was the one to lay the explosives, which would only damage part of the building, far away from those left inside. Tanyon had the names of humans wanted by the FBI for trafficking. Everything was set, and then...." Jackos looked down, his jaw visibly clenching.

"Let me guess. Geraldon took care of Tanyon first. How'd I do?" Rex asked.

"Fucking Geraldon. Couldn't leave well enough alone when Tanyon started mouthing off. If he would have shut up.... But he had to poke the fucking snake and it struck. I've seen some things, but…. Geraldon went at him old-school and slit his throat from behind. The gurgling sounds… the blood…. Amazing how much blood there is in a body."

Jerry's stomach squirmed and pushed away visions of bright red blood. For all of ten seconds, he felt sorry for Tanyon until he recalled the venom-filled expression on Tanyon's face as he'd threatened Jerry's unborn child.

"Hopefully, we can get names and locations of the buyers from his computer files. They're encrypted, but we've got computer experts working on them now. Even if we don't get what we need, I hope we can find something to lead us to the location of the one Braezelas who's missing."

Jerry gasped. "Someone's missing?"

CHAPTER 42

JERRY'S MIND rushed through the faces of everyone he'd seen while in captivity. Rex gripped his hand, and Jerry held on tight.

"Eli Snow."

"Fuck," Rex whispered. "They used my blood to turn him."

"Hey, mine too. It wasn't our fault." Jerry ran his hand over Rex's chest.

"Reports coming from those who worked with Geraldon—those who are cooperating—say Eli left the property with the man and woman who I...." Jackos's face scrunched up into what looked to be guilt. "Who I escorted to another room after Geraldon shot Eli up. So I am the one responsible for him being missing."

Jerry was about to say he wasn't, but Jackos shook his head.

"During the chaos, they got out with him." He clenched his fists in his lap, and flushed red with anger. "I never should have let him leave the room. I thought...."

They'd all been freed, except poor Eli, still a prisoner, a piece of property to be used. "You couldn't know what would happen. It just did." But Jackos bore the full weight of his guilt and most likely would his entire life.

"It looks as if he's been taken out of the country. He may never be found."

There was a period of silence until Rex spoke. "Hey, you foiled a future drug cartel, a sex slave ring, crushed a future militant army, and uncovered a plan to assassinate the President of the United States, not to mention rescuing not one, but two princes and a claxton."

Jerry smiled at Rex's attempt to cheer up Jackos.

Jackos grunted. "Yeah, I'm a true superhero all right."

"Yes, you are." Lanzo entered the room. The tall guard seemed to fill the room to capacity. "At least that's what the president said when he called you last night."

Jackos eyed Lanzo with scorn, yet right before everyone in the room, that scorn turned into something resembling affection. The two men took each other in as if no one else existed. Jerry looked between them and knew they'd shared some kind of moment. What was that about?

"President Harrison called you?" Rex seemed impressed.

Jackos rolled his eyes. "Nice guy. Anyway, the case is far from closed, and I've got a shit-ton of work left to do. I'll be busy until—"

"Agent Moscoff! There you are." A haggard nurse in yellow scrubs rushed into the room.

Lanzo grinned wide. "Did I forget to mention someone was looking for you?"

"Bastard," Jackos muttered, then grinned sheepishly. "I may have been told not to leave my bed again. I was never good at following orders."

"You're recovering from a serious gunshot wound. Back to bed." She yanked his chair around to face the door.

"It's nothing."

"Nerve damage isn't nothing." Lanzo's expression bordered on pity.

"Fuck you." Jackos took off as the nurse huffed and followed.

Lanzo looked after them, then turned, the sorrow still in his eyes. "That bad?" Rex asked.

"The nerve damage is permanent. He'll walk again, but he'll limp."

His own father had done that to him. What a mind fuck. "Which means he won't be able to do his job anymore." Jerry sighed. *Shit.*

"Well, not field work, but the FBI has plenty of desk jobs. I don't know if that'll be enough." Lanzo waved to them and left the room.

Jerry wrapped his arms around Rex and snuggled into his chest. Their losses were great, but they had to focus on what they had and where they were going.

JERRY PACED—OR rather, stepped and slid with his uncooperative leg—around the confines of his hospital room. He was annoyed as hell that he couldn't stomp around with his restlessness.

Rex sat in the chair, watching quietly, since his last suggestion that Jerry relax hadn't gone over so well. Jerry hated being cranky, but damn, how long was he going to have to wait? A holdup in his final blood work delayed his discharge. Keith had called earlier, and since Jerry was supposed to be home soon, they'd decided to meet there. That was three hours ago, and Jerry was ready to get dressed, grab Michael, and leave.

"Jer—"

"Don't!"

Jerry flashed Rex a warning, but Rex wasn't deterred this time. He rose from the chair, his jaw clenched, his green eyes dark. Jerry didn't care. His irritation reached critical levels, and their first fight would go down right there. Jerry was ready.

"Gunn, stop touching me!"

Jerry grinned.

"I can walk without you practically carrying me. I'm pregnant, not disabled."

"You could fall. At least let me hold your arm." Gunn sounded exasperated.

"I swear to the gods, if you don't back off, I'm going to tie you to our bed until this kid is born!"

Jerry and Rex both snickered. Rex helped Jerry to the door. He had a full leg brace to assist his walking. They peered into the hallway. Damn, Keith's mate was large and dwarfed him. Despite his apparent annoyance, the hint of affection on Keith's face was heartwarming.

Gunn grinned maniacally. "With the leather straps?" He moved closer to Keith, who tried to push Gunn away, with little effect. Gunn bent down and rubbed their chests together. "And when I'm tied up and helpless, what will you do to me?" Gunn whispered something in Keith's ear. Keith groaned and wrapped his arms around Gunn.

"Oh, get a room," Rex said, and both their heads snapped around to look at them.

"Can we have yours for about an hour?" Keith smirked.

"Hell no. Now get inside. This is a hospital, not a motel that rents rooms by the hour." Jerry limped back into the room. When his leg cramped up, he stopped and rubbed his thigh.

"You okay?" Keith stepped up beside him, scrutinizing Jerry from head to toe.

"I'm good. Just a cramp."

Keith looked uncertain. "Damn, it's good to see you, Jerry."

He had to agree, as a lump pushed up into his throat. Keith appeared to have the same reaction. *Fuck it.* Jerry wrapped Keith up tight. Jerry had been so afraid of losing him. He wouldn't cry because Keith wouldn't hesitate to make fun of him, even if Keith also had the telltale glassiness in his eyes.

"I have to sit." Jerry couldn't wait until walking across a room didn't exhaust him.

He settled on the bed with Rex. Keith and Gunn sat on the cot.

Jerry had to ask. "How's the baby?"

"Great, from what they can tell. You should have seen the looks on the faces of those Anzuni doctors and nurses. Hearing that I was pregnant and not a royal, I might as well have been a mutant alien with two penises. They didn't know what to think."

"I bet." Rex rubbed Jerry's back. Gods, that felt so good.

Keith's eyes lit up. "Your kid is awesome. A little overbaked, but cute. Looks like Rex more than you, but we won't hold that against him."

Rex scowled, and Gunn elbowed Keith, who didn't bother to look repentant. Gunn wrapped his arm around Keith's shoulders, and he laid his head against Gunn's shoulder. How had they both gotten so lucky?

"So Gunn, how do you feel about being a father?"

Jerry cringed at Rex's question. Gunn had been forced into the situation as well. Maybe he wasn't as thrilled as Rex had been.

Gunn's face brightened. "I've always wanted kids, and I'd planned on adopting. Never thought I'd have one of my own, but I can't wait. I'm talking to a contractor now about putting a nursery next to the bedroom." Excitement practically oozed from him.

"Yup, I'm going to teach her to drive a nail, and Gunn here will teach her to decorate pastries," Keith said in a snarky tone.

"Decorate pastries?"

"You're having a girl?"

Keith and Gunn both busted out laughing.

"Yes, the doctor said we're having a girl. She's due at the beginning of October. And Daddy here is a pastry chef."

Jerry tried to imagine Gunn with his large hands decorating tiny pastries, but it wouldn't materialize. A phone rang, and Gunn pulled his cell from his pocket. Looking at the screen, he stood.

"It's the contractor. I have to take this, babe." He leaned down, kissed Keith, and then left the room.

Keith watched him go, smiling.

"He's great," Jerry said.

Keith beamed brighter. "He may be a little overprotective, but he's perfect. And a man. Go figure."

Jerry smiled, happy for Keith and Gunn. For all of them.

Rex touched Jerry's shoulder. "I'm going to check on your discharge. I'll be right back." Jerry squeezed Rex's leg in gratitude for knowing he needed some time alone with Keith.

For a few moments, they were both quiet.

"I'm sorry." Jerry's apology was weak. He didn't think he could apologize enough for the mess he'd caused.

"You should be." Keith appeared angry, and he had every right.

Jerry nodded, wishing he could go back and change what happened. "I know."

Hopefully, Keith—everyone involved—could forgive him.

"And you're going to pay for it."

Jerry's head snapped up, and the evil grin on Keith's face told Jerry he hadn't been following the gist of the conversation. Keith only got that look when he was going to....

"No!" Jerry scrambled back onto the bed, and then Keith straddled him, his finger digging into Jerry's sides. He burst out laughing as Keith tickled him relentlessly. Jerry wanted to kick him off, knee him in the stomach, but Keith was pregnant. And he'd known that Jerry wouldn't fight back because of it. "Ssss-tooooooooop. Keith... nonononono!"

Jerry could only suck in short breaths. Fuck, he hated being tickled. Especially by Keith, who could overpower him.

"Not until you say 'it's not my fault.'"

Confused, Jerry tried to speak, but his stomach muscles squeezed tight, and he couldn't breathe, so talking was out. He mouthed, "Don't know… what you're talking… about."

"Say it's not your fault, everything that happened. Say it now, or I start on your underarms."

Keith wouldn't back down. Jerry wasn't sure if he believed it enough to say it, but he couldn't handle the underarms. He'd puke from laughing so hard.

"Not… my fault."

Keith stopped and Jerry gasped for air. He might puke anyway.

Keith glared down on him, a fire in his eyes. He planted his hands on either side of Jerry's head and glared. "I can see it written all over your face, Jerry. You're taking the blame, because it was your blood. Well, knock that shit off right now, because the only ones to blame are Tanyon and Geraldon, and those fucking douche bags who gave them money, wanted to own demon slaves and get high. Do you hear me? It's not your fault."

Jerry swallowed hard. Keith climbed off him and pulled Jerry to a sitting position. Keith sat next to Jerry and wrapped his arm around his shoulders.

Keith ignored Jerry's sniffing. "It's fucked up, everything that happened. But it happened, and now it's over, even if…."

"Even if it won't ever be forgotten?" He looked up at Keith, not caring that tears filled his eyes.

Keith sighed heavily. "It's going to take time to get this shit right in our heads." He snorted. "I'm not sure if Gunn's going to be able to sleep with me constantly thrashing around. Nightmares."

"You're having nightmares?" Shit, Jerry needed to stop feeling sorry for himself. Everyone suffered in the aftermath.

"They aren't bad, and the psychologist they made me talk to said eventually they'd ease off. The leftover pregnancy hormones could be making it worse. I don't know."

Maybe they all needed to talk to a professional. "I'm sorry." He cut Keith off before he could protest. "I'm sorry you're having nightmares. And you're right. I have to deal with this guilt, because it wasn't my fault." Maybe someday he'd believe it too.

"Well, all righty, then." Keith lifted his arm from Jerry's shoulder and slapped Jerry on the thigh. "Gunn and I have a flight at noon. We have to get back and pack."

Jerry panicked a little. "Pack? Why?"

Keith smirked. "Didn't you hear? We're moving into the mansion until the baby's born. I can't be running around in public all pregnant and male, and your place is so much nicer than mine or Gunn's. A cook, maids, swimming pool, game room, home theater with surround sound—the list goes on and on."

Jerry chuckled, glad to hear that Keith would be close by, at least for the next four months. And then their children would grow up together. "Good, because I will get my *Halo* title back."

Keith grunted. "You can try."

Gunn and Rex returned, and then Keith and Gunn left for the airport. Jerry had to admit that Keith's unorthodox way of getting Jerry to admit his guilt was unfounded was sinking in. Now he had to get out of the hospital.

A half hour later, Jerry's father and mother entered the room, and, to Jerry's relief, with them was a harried nurse carrying a pile of papers. Jerry had a feeling she hadn't come willingly.

Jerry hugged his mother and then his father.

"We have a two o'clock flight home so we have to leave in fifteen minutes for the airport." Jerry's father smiled down on him.

"Home sounds great."

The nurse tried to review the discharge papers with Jerry as the baby was brought in, dressed to leave, and Jerry's mother fussed over him while Jerry's father tried to convince her to let him be. The doctor came in to bid Jerry and his parents good-bye. Rex fretted that Jerry wasn't paying attention to the nurse's instructions, and kept telling him to listen. Then Michael screamed and wouldn't stop until Jerry held him.

A collective sigh ran through the room.

"We'll take your bags and meet you out front in the limo." Jerry's father grabbed their bags.

"Wait. We will go with you."

"Hospital policy. You need to be taken down in a wheelchair. Someone will be up shortly." That could be hours.

Jerry's mother kissed the baby's cheek, Rex's, and then Jerry's. "Don't worry. The doctor left to light a fire under them. See you in the car."

"Thanks."

They left and the room was once again quiet. Jerry and Rex admired their son, who was too cute as he mouthed his fist.

"He does look like you. Do you think he'll have freckles?"

"Gods, I hope not."

"Why not? Your freckles are cute."

Rex growled. "They're *not* cute."

"Okay, macho man." Jerry placed Michael into his car seat and secured the straps. "Are too."

"I heard that."

Jerry chuckled and grabbed Michael's diaper bag and slung the strap over his shoulder.

Rex locked the handle of the car seat and picked it up. "Come on. Let's get our family home."

Jerry stopped Rex before he walked away and wrapped his arms around Rex's neck. He proceeded to kiss Rex hard and thoroughly. Rex groaned deep in his throat. Jerry sighed deeply and parted their lips.

Rex grinned. "What was that for?"

"For not giving up on us."

Rex wrapped his arm around Jerry's waist and pulled him close. "Never."

JAKE C. WALLACE started writing from a young age, but took a break for marriage, kids, and college (in that order). A few years ago, he rediscovered his passion for writing stories and ventured out into the brave new world of publishing. He has published several novels and short stories. Recently, his novel *Jerricho's Freedom* was a finalist in the Rainbow Book Awards.

At night and on the weekends, Jake writes about all things men, believing there is nothing hotter than two men finding and loving one another, whether for a night or forever. An avid reader of M/M romance, Jake loves a good twist of a plot, HEA, HFN, or tragic ending, and has over two thousand books in his library. He also writes what his best friend calls HUNKs (Happy Until the Next Kidnapping). In his daytime hours, Jake works with individuals with autism and behavior issues. He is owned by a beautiful partner, three kids, and two grandchildren. He lives in northern Vermont.

Website: www.jcwallacebooks.com
Facebook: www.facebook.com/jcwallacebooks
Twitter: @jcwallacebooks.com
E-mail: jcwallacebooks@gmail.com

Soul
Seekers

JAKE C. WALLACE

Nineteen-year-old college student Levi Reed has spent his life with hollow emotions and a darkness so deep that he's convinced he's losing his mind. He'd give anything to feel something, anything, real.

When a mysterious stranger appears, Levi is convinced the man is trying to kill him. When he's near, Levi experiences head-crushing pain and something surprising—real emotions for the first time. Jeb Monroe is arrogant, self-assured, closed-off, and handsome, but he isn't the harbinger of doom Levi assumed. Jeb's mission: help Levi find his missing soul.

Levi is pulled into the secret world of Seers and Keepers, those born with the innate ability to manipulate souls and tasked with balancing the negative energy they can produce. Levi learns he possesses a rare gift, and he's in danger. As Jeb and Levi grow closer, they discover a group of zealots who want to harness Levi's power to cleanse the world of damaged souls. Everyone Levi cares for is threatened unless he agrees to become their tool of death. But agreeing could spell the destruction of humankind. With no one to trust and nothing as it appears, it's up to Levi to save them all.

www.dreamspinnerpress.com

JAKE C. WALLACE

DARE
TO LOVE
FOREVER

New Vampire Justice: Book One

With pain and loss in their pasts and evil threatening their futures, two vampires will find a love that lasts forever… if they dare.

Carson Locke is dangerous, even by vampire standards. A rare Tabula Rasa vampire, he can wipe the mind of those he bites—human or vampire. Because of this, he's lived his entire life in isolation. When his family is murdered, Carson runs from those who want him dead. Injured, starving, and about to be executed, he meets Commander Lincoln Samuels, an officer in the New Vampire Justice police force.

Lincoln, a Sanatore vampire, possesses the gift of healing. The moment he encounters Carson, broken and terrified, trying to steal blood to survive, he is compelled to help the other man—despite the risk to himself. Their bond creates something the world has never seen, but others have plans for Carson and his destiny was written long before he was born. He'll either become a tool to control the vampire world or, with Lincoln by his side, find the courage to fight and become its savior.

www.dreamspinnerpress.com

A CHANCE FOR US

NVJ

NEW VAMPIRE JUSTICE: BOOK TWO

JAKE C. WALLACE

New Vampire Justice: Book Two

Love between a young man with a broken mind and the jaded New Vampire Justice officer who cares for him might be the last hope to stop a human-vampire war….

Justin Masters is stuck in a nightmare. Waking after seven years in a catatonic state, he falls desperately in love with the straight NVJ officer who saved him. Between that and dreams of being tortured and taking pleasure in the pain, which bleed into his waking hours, Justin's sure he's starting to crack.

The growing unrest in the vampire world should be Max Kincaid's focus, but Justin's struggle, along with Max's confusing feelings for his ward, have him reeling. When Justin's attacked, his resulting needs might be more than Max can fulfill, but he'll be damned if anyone else will touch Justin.

As the NVJ investigates humans missing from a high-end bite club, they uncover a deeper plot that traces back to Justin. If those who want him have their way, there will be bloodshed. Justin and Max are in a fight to save Justin not only from those who would use him, but from his own mind.

www.dreamspinnerpress.com